"A suspenseful tale of Nazis in Hollywood. *Code Name Edelweiss* is well-researched that sought to strike against the goodr. of fear and hatred. A story chilling yet brave against the struggles of adversity, readers will be challenged to ask themselves, 'If not me, then who?'"

J'NELL CIESIELSKI, bestselling author of *The Socialite*

"I love a good suspense novel, and *Code Name Edelweiss* kept me reading long after midnight. Knowing that it's based on true accounts of Nazi activity in prewar US made it even more chilling. Stephanie Landsem does a masterful job of showing how easily and insidiously hatred and prejudice can grow—and what our response to it must be. Well done!"

LYNN AUSTIN, bestselling and award-winning author of *Long Way Home*

"Taut and tense, Stephanie Landsem's superbly plotted thriller is a bold, chilling, and heart-racing look—through a young widow's eyes—at fascist hypocrisy and peril in America's 1933 Tinseltown. A page-turning tale, it's equal parts genuine danger, passionate bravery, and fearless truth. Offering life lessons we must never forget, it's a daring and inspiring triumph."

PATRICIA RAYBON, award-winning author of *All That Is Secret* and *I Told the Mountain to Move*

"Tense and thought-provoking in equal measure, *Code Name Edelweiss* brings to life the glamour of 1930s Hollywood—and the grit of the Depression. Stephanie Landsem presents a harrowing look at the real-life Nazi organizations in Los Angeles before World War II, the racism lurking behind the friendliest faces, and the honest temptation to give in to that racism when times are tough—all compassionately shown through compelling characters. An outstanding novel with a thriller of an ending!"

SARAH SUNDIN, bestselling and award-winning author of *The Sound of Light* and *Until Leaves Fall in Paris*

"Stephanie Landsem's newest—about Nazis in 1930s Los Angeles and the ragtag group of amateur spies who braved everything to stop them—is thrilling, vivid, expertly researched, and all too timely. Single mother and secret agent Liesl, aka Edelweiss, is a compelling character and readers will root for her."

SUSAN ELIA MacNEAL, author of *Mother Daughter Traitor Spy* and the *New York Times* bestselling Maggie Hope series

"Part John Steinbeck and part Mickey Spillane, this well-researched historical novel is a tale of inspiration and hope."

HISTORICAL NOVELS REVIEW on *In a Far-Off Land*

"Talented writer Stephanie Landsem brings to vivid life the glamour and grit of old Hollywood in this moving story of ambition and secrets, forgiveness and love."

JULIE KLASSEN, author of *A Castaway in Cornwall*, on *In a Far-Off Land*

"The stage is set perfectly with beautiful prose as Stephanie Landsem takes readers back behind the glamorous curtain of Hollywood, exposing the corruption on the other side. Like an enchanting, enduring motion picture, *In a Far-Off Land* will grip your heart with its timeless truth and captivate the theater of your mind."

MELANIE DOBSON, award-winning author of *The Winter Rose* and *Memories of Glass*

"This is a story I'll read again soon, knowing many more life lessons are there waiting to be discovered."

T. I. LOWE, bestselling author of *Lulu's Café* and *Under the Magnolias*, on *In a Far-Off Land*

"Both gritty and glamorous, Stephanie Landsem's *In a Far-Off Land* digs beneath the sparkle of gilded Hollywood to uncover the true gold of love, mercy, and forgiveness. Don't miss this unforgettable story."

REGINA JENNINGS, author of *Courting Misfortune*

"Depression-era Hollywood provides the perfect stage for the desperate and colorful cast of *In a Far-Off Land*. This tale is that of a journey from brokenness to healing, from emptiness to wholeness. Through the eyes of two characters who could not be more different, Stephanie Landsem gives us a timeless story of the prodigal traveling far from home and finding the way back again. Fans of Francine Rivers's *Bridge to Haven* will not want to miss this."

JOCELYN GREEN, Christy Award–winning author of *Shadows of the White City*

"From the first page, this remarkable story set in glittering Hollywood during the Great Depression captured my imagination. Aspiring actress Mina Sinclaire's amazing pilgrimage from the dark hollows of her despair into the light of unconditional love will offer hope to anyone who has ever believed themselves beyond redemption. Bravo!"

KATE BRESLIN, bestselling author of *Far Side of the Sea*, on *In a Far-Off Land*

"One of the best books I've read this year! *In a Far-Off Land* is a beautiful story echoing the power of mercy, forgiveness, and love as it peels back the multifaceted layers of those living in Hollywood during the Great Depression. Stephanie Landsem weaves a heroine with as much spunk and edge as heart and soul. Just a gorgeous, page-turning novel."

HEIDI CHIAVAROLI, Carol Award–winning author of *Freedom's Ring* and *The Orchard House*

"From beginning to end, I was riveted by this masterful retelling of the parable of the Prodigal Son and moved by the poignant exploration of the power of grace in the midst of shame. Superbly written and absolutely stunning!"

AMANDA BARRATT, author of *The White Rose Resists*, on *In a Far-Off Land*

"Fans of Susan Meissner and Kristina McMorris will be spellbound by Landsem's gorgeously researched historical. Told with heart-wrenching conviction, *In a Far-Off Land* is a lyrical and thematic treatise on redemption, loss, and love and wielded with such sur-prising grace the reader will have many breath-catching moments. Landsem is a treasure of inspirational historical fiction, and *In a Far-Off Land* is no less than a masterpiece."

RACHEL McMILLAN, author of *The London Restoration* and *The Mozart Code*

"Landsem's *In a Far-Off Land* immerses the reader in a world long forgotten yet achingly familiar. Old Hollywood meets *The Grapes of Wrath*, and the redemption, romance, and regret are all beautifully written and deliciously authentic. It's still dancing in my head and will be for a while."

AMY HARMON, *New York Times* bestselling author of *Where the Lost Wander*

"*In a Far-Off Land*—an engaging story set in a fresh era—deftly threads themes from the biblical story of the Lost Son through the burlap of the Great Depression and Hollywood's silk."

SANDRA BYRD, author of *Heirlooms*

CODE NAME EDELWEISS

A NOVEL

CODE NAME EDELWEISS

STEPHANIE LANDSEM

Tyndale House Publishers
Carol Stream, Illinois

Visit Tyndale online at tyndale.com.

Visit Stephanie Landsem's website at stephanielandsem.com.

Tyndale and Tyndale's quill logo are registered trademarks of Tyndale House Ministries.

Code Name Edelweiss

Designed by Eva M. Winters

Edited by Kathryn S. Olson

Published in association with DeFiore and Company Literary Management, Inc., 47 East 19th Street, 3rd Floor, New York, NY 10003.

Code Name Edelweiss is a work of fiction. Where real people, events, establishments, organizations, or locales appear, they are used fictitiously. All other elements of the novel are drawn from the author's imagination.

For information about special discounts for bulk purchases, please contact Tyndale House Publishers at csresponse@tyndale.com, or call 1-855-277-9400.

Library of Congress Cataloging-in-Publication Data

A catalog record for this book is available from the Library of Congress.

ISBN 978-1-4964-6066-0 (HC)
ISBN 978-1-4964-6067-7 (SC)

Printed in the United States of America

29	28	27	26	25	24	23
7	6	5	4	3	2	1

To Joanie Lang, Sue Davis, & Wendy Tarbox
sisters in faith
friends of my heart

Once there is confusion and after we have succeeded
in undermining the faith of the American people
in their own government, a new group will take
over; this will be the German American group,
and we will help them assume power.
ADOLF HITLER, 1933

It has been said that for evil men to accomplish
their purpose it is only necessary that
good men should do nothing.
CHARLES FREDERIC AKED, 1920

If I am not for myself, who will be for me?
But if I am only for myself, what am I?
If not now, when?
RABBI HILLEL (PIRKEI AVOT 1:14)

CHAPTER 1

LIESL

Los Angeles
1933

"A girl like you oughta be in pictures." Gary Perl turned away from his bird's-eye view of the MGM studio lot and appraised me from my Peter Pan collar to the toes of my sensible oxfords.

I tucked my feet further under my chair. What I "oughta" do was my job, not listen to Gary Perl's nonsense. I was in Mr. Perl's corner office to take a letter to the German film board, translate it, and post it before the end of the day. Was this too much to ask—to do my work and get home to my children by five o'clock?

Mr. Perl crossed the acre of Persian carpet like a lion on the prowl, his gaze pinned to my ankles. I sat ramrod straight and glanced at the desk clock. How long must I put up with this foolishness?

"You know, you're my favorite steno girl, Liesl." Mr. Perl stalked slowly around the green velvet settee and the rolling cart with sparkling decanters of gin and whiskey. He was close now, too close for comfort. He leaned casually against the polished edge of his mahogany desk. "You've got better legs than Crawford and a face made for the camera. And that accent . . ." He whistled a breath as if blowing out a match. "You sound like Garbo. I could get you a screen test."

I frowned at my pencil, poised over the blank steno pad. I did not have an accent, Greta Garbo was Swedish, not German, and I did not wish for a screen test. Furthermore, my skirt fell respectfully below my knees and, paired with the practical blouse, said secretary, not film star.

However, Gary Perl's expensive pin-striped suit with wide shoulders and silk tie said powerful. And so he was. Too powerful to displease.

"You know what they call you here, don't you, Liesl?" His smile failed to soften his sharp-featured face.

I did indeed know what they called me. The film stars all had nicknames—Mary Pickford was called America's Sweetheart, and everyone knew John Barrymore as the Great Profile—but the producers and executives at MGM thought it good sport to dub the secretaries and stenographers with monikers as well. As for the name they called me behind my back and sometimes to my face, it mattered little. I wished to do my job and nothing more.

I scooted back in my chair, away from his minty breath and sandalwood hair tonic. "The letter, Mr. Perl?"

He leaned over me and set one well-manicured hand on each arm of my chair. I was hemmed in, his obsidian-chip eyes only inches from my own. "Come now. All work and no play?" He raised his brows.

I quelled a sigh. I'd endured quite enough of Gary Perl's advances over the past several months. And yet the country was in a depression and MGM Studios wasn't immune to its effect. The girls in the typing pool reported memos about budget cuts, hiring freezes, films that wouldn't be made. Not to mention the new Dictaphones. Machines that would make stenographers like me—no matter how fast we took shorthand—obsolete. None of us was safe from the unemployment line.

Except for Mr. Perl, of course. He had a moniker of his own: Golden Boy. And while Mr. Thalberg was ill—nothing to be concerned about, Louis B. Mayer's memo assured us—the solvency of MGM was resting on Gary Perl's padded shoulders.

I met his gaze steadily and appealed to his better nature. "I'm sure you understand, Mr. Perl. My job is important to me, and Mrs. Adler—"

"You like me, don't you, Miss Weiss?"

"It's Mrs.," I corrected sharply. The nerve of this man. What I liked was my paycheck. Mrs. Adler didn't listen to excuses about amorous executives, and steno girls who didn't get their work done were soon replaced.

"Ah, yes, a widow." His mouth turned down in a mockery of sympathy and he eyed the ring on my left hand. "I'm sorry."

I wasn't a widow, and he wasn't sorry. Men like him thought nothing of a pinch or a pat, a casual brush-against, an accidental nudge—with photos of their wives and children smiling at them from their shiny desks.

"I do believe the film board is waiting for this, Mr. Perl." If I sounded peeved, it was because I was.

He straightened and walked around to the back of my chair, his hands landing on my shoulders, warm through my crepe blouse. "You're cute when you're angry, did you know that?"

I clamped my teeth together.

"How about this, sweetheart?" His hands massaged my shoulders and moved down my arms. "I'll dictate the letter . . . then I get a little kiss. Seem fair?"

Did men have nothing else to do but play these absurd games? I opened my notebook, put my pencil to the first line, and looked up at him with raised brows as if in acquiescence to his suggestion. Perhaps he would forget about the kiss.

He did not.

With the letter done, I stood abruptly and walked to the door. I did not anticipate his speed. He caught me halfway across the Persian carpet, chuckling as if this were a game. He grabbed my arm, spun me around, and pressed his lips hard against mine, his hands groping upward. The shock froze me in place—I had not been kissed since Tomas—and I twisted away, humiliation, anger, and something like grief hitting all at once.

He chuckled. "Come now, it wasn't that bad."

I lunged for the door, my heel catching on the fringe of the carpet as I stumbled quite ungracefully from his office.

"The Hun is on the run," he hooted as I rushed past his secretary, but not so fast I didn't see a smirk of laughter on her red lips.

Halfway down the third-floor hallway, I ducked into the women's lavatory and leaned against the door, my breath coming quick and my face burning. How dare that man? I looked into the mirror over the porcelain sink. The Heartbreak Hun. I detested the name and did not look the part at the moment. My finger-waved blonde hair was mussed, my fair skin flushed and my blue eyes dark with anger. Why had I not slapped the conceited smirk right off Gary Perl's face?

I took a deep breath and let it out. I needed my job—that was why. I had children and a mother depending on me, did I not?

I turned away from the mirror. *Tomas, what would you have me do?* Tomas did not answer. He never did.

I smoothed my hair, ran cold water over my wrists, and tucked my blouse neatly back into the waistband of my skirt. I marched back to the typing pool and deposited my steno pad on my desk with a slap. Stella, at the next desk, glanced at me without breaking the rhythm of her typing. Her perfectly plucked brows flickered.

I sank down in my chair. The clatter of keys striking paper sounded like artillery fire as I stared at my Remington typewriter. Someday, someone—perhaps a woman with less to lose—would put Gary Perl in his place.

CHAPTER 2

LIESL

Stella's carriage bell dinged like the close of a boxing match. She hit the return lever, snapped the paper release bar, and put the perfectly typed sheet in her completed work basket. "Come on, Liesl, let's go to lunch."

Heat like a kitchen on baking day hit us as we left the three-story steel-and-glass administrative building. The August sun shimmered the air over concrete roads, cinder block buildings, and barnlike soundstages. The hammer of ongoing construction ricocheted through the streets like scattered applause.

MGM was called the Tiffany of studios for good reason. One hundred and seventeen acres encompassed twenty-three soundstages and outdoor sets from Western towns to European villages and tropical lagoons. Louis B. Mayer provided a commissary, a doctor's office, even a barbershop to keep his five thousand employees churning out fifty box office sensations a year.

I knew the nooks and alleys of this corner of Culver City like it was my hometown—indeed, it had been since I was a child, when Mr. Ince had hired Vati as a camera operator and Mutti as a costume seamstress. It had changed hands over the years and expanded, burgeoning as quickly as the public's demand for entertainment.

A truck rumbled down Culver Avenue, its flatbed loaded with a scaled-down Egyptian pyramid, and left in its wake the scent of fresh paint and gasoline fumes. I skipped a step to keep up with Stella's long-legged stride.

"You should have slapped him," Stella said. "Good and hard in the kisser."

"And lose my job?" My anger had cooled in the telling of the tale but slapping Gary Perl's hawkish face would have been a great satisfaction.

"Might've been worth it," Stella continued. "Could you imagine, laying Gary Perl out on his office floor, like Jack Dempsey at Madison Square Garden." She gave me a hip bump, almost knocking me off the curb. "You could have done it, too, sent him straight to First Aid with a nosebleed."

I appreciated Stella's righteous anger, but we both knew what would happen—and what would not. There would be no consequences for Gary Perl, only for myself.

We passed the Lagoon set, where two elephants and a half-dozen scantily clad dwarfs made up as African Pygmies waited in the shade for their cue. One of the crew whistled. I ignored him but Stella responded with an unladylike gesture which set the Pygmies to laughing.

Stella wasn't like the other girls in the typing pool. She'd gone to the University of California in Berkley and studied philosophy. Her parents had insisted on Dickinson Secretarial as a backup. "Mother and Father are hoping I'll land a producer, get married, and give them some grand-children," she told me when Mrs. Adler hired her last year and she took the typing station next to mine. "I let them dream their dreams."

Not that Stella wasn't attractive. She had shiny dark hair, flawless skin, and a lovely figure. But she was tall—taller than most men—and most of it legs. Walking beside her made me feel like one of the Pygmies myself. What was more, Stella didn't follow the Dickinson Guide to Secretarial Dress. Today, in a georgette day dress printed in red and yellow poppies with a shockingly low neckline and red three-inch pumps, she looked less like a typist and more like one of the up-and-coming film stars.

"You should tell Mrs. Adler," Stella continued. "It's her job to look after us."

A cobweb of electrical wires snapped and crackled over our heads as we cut through an alley between the powerhouse and Wardrobe, a shortcut to the commissary I'd shown Stella when we had started taking our lunch together. "As she did for Norma?" I asked.

Stella frowned but didn't have a response. We found Norma one afternoon in the ladies' room, her makeup running and eyes red. Mr. Aronson in Accounting hadn't taken no for an answer and from what we could assess, he hadn't asked for just a kiss. Stella insisted on telling Mrs. Adler, who had assured us she would take care of it. The next day, Norma did not show up for work. When Stella asked Mrs. Adler about it, she was told to mind her own p's and q's.

A Model T truck, its box filled with mops and buckets, edged by us with a short honk. I waved at the woman driving it. Gina, one of Mutti's friends from the old days, waved back. As head of Housekeeping, she kept the studios and offices eat-off-the-floor clean with her crew of moppers and polishers.

"You should make a stink," Stella said with a nod toward Gina. "You have plenty of friends who would stand behind you."

My friends at MGM weren't anyone who would hold sway with the likes of Gary Perl. Gus in Security, Mutti's friends in Housekeeping and Makeup. "If I start putting up a fuss about every man who gets fresh, I'll be out of a job faster than you can say Dictaphone." I couldn't afford to make a stink, but I didn't expect Stella to understand. She liked her job, but nobody depended on her paycheck for food and a roof over their heads.

"A Dictaphone can't translate German. And Battle-Axe Adler knows you can type faster than any of us. Besides, you're like family here—what with your mother and all. They say that L. B. Mayer himself was afraid of her in the old days. You're the last one Adler would axe."

I didn't agree. MGM was not the same as when Vati worked the cameras and Mutti sewed costumes. What had been like a family was now a moneymaking machine in which I was just a small—and utterly replaceable—part.

I caught the scents of fresh-baked bread and Mrs. Mayer's famous chicken and matzo ball soup as we reached the commissary. Louis B. Mayer insisted upon good food for his employees, which made perfect sense—efficiency surged when employees didn't go off the lot for lunch. In front of the wide double doors, a trio of extras in black habits and white wimples passed around a cigarette. I smiled at them, recognizing two old-timers.

"Hey, sisters," Stella called out as we passed, "that's a dirty habit." They laughed like it was the first time they'd heard that joke.

I checked my wristwatch. Twenty-six minutes to eat lunch and get back to our desks. By that time, Mrs. Adler would be looking for the translation, and word would have traveled about Gary Perl's antics. There would be whistles and raised eyebrows from every man in Administration.

We joined the cafeteria line behind a cowboy in a Stetson jostling a bronze-skinned Indian chief for the last of the rhubarb pie. Stella filled her tray with an egg salad sandwich, a chicken leg, and a fruit cup with a mound of cottage cheese. I parted with a nickel for a cup of coffee and followed her to a table. The commissary was at capacity. MGM was filming on all four lots and half the studios, with production in full swing on eight pictures. It didn't look like money was tight, but looks—like the facades on the acres of MGM—were deceiving.

"These spots taken?" Stella asked two girls, both bustled and laced into brocade gowns, their faces powdered white. They scooted over to make room.

The commissary had a strict pecking order. Mr. Mayer, the producers, and directors sat in the executive dining room with white linen and waiters. Contracted stars—more than there are in heaven, like the posters said—claimed a long table along the windows. Today, John Barrymore and his brother, Lionel, split a sandwich while Myrna Loy looked cozy with Ramon Novarro.

I pulled my lunch—a hard-boiled egg and an apple—from my handbag while Stella tucked into her meal. I didn't have the sixty cents to spare that she did, and anyway my stomach twisted like a washing machine on agitate.

The ladies-in-waiting next to us continued their conversation in the nasal tones of recent transplants from the East Coast. "The director said they'd shut down the picture anyway. Because of that guy, the German somebody."

I peeled my egg and listened in.

"What does he care?" the other said, digging into a tapioca pudding.

"There's Jews in it—that's what I heard, at least."

I looked over at Stella. She was watching the girls and tearing into her chicken leg.

The second costumed extra frowned. "But isn't Mr. Mayer Jewish?"

Stella raised a perfectly shaped brow at the girls as they gathered their skirts and rustled away, leaving their dirty plates on the table. "There's Jews," Stella said to me, "and then there's Jews."

I gave her a look that said I didn't know what she meant.

"Listen, cupcake. There's Jews like my parents, who follow all the rules—" she waved at her plate of food like she was demonstrating a kosher meal—"and then there's Jews like Mr. Mayer, who only see the bottom line. Same with Thalberg, Laemmle over at Universal, all the rest. If the German vice-consul is threatening to stop distribution, you better believe Mr. Mayer is going to sit up and take notice."

"Why does the German market care if Jews are in films?"

"Don't you see the newsreels, Liesl?" she asked. "The new chancellor of Germany has a thing against Jews."

"I know that." I rolled my eyes. Of course I listened to the radio and read at least the headlines in the newspapers. "But the films?"

"Sure," she said. "The vice-consul kicks up a stink about any film that makes Germany look bad or Jews look good. He's spent more time closeted with Mayer than Ida Koverman herself. As if money wasn't tight, now they can't sell films to Germany unless he gives them the nod—not just MGM, mind you, but all the studios."

I took a last bite of my apple, my ill feeling growing. Not only did I have to worry about Dictaphones, but Mrs. Adler wouldn't need my translations if we didn't sell films to Germany. I checked my wristwatch. "Time to go." I brushed my eggshells and apple core into a paper napkin, folded it into a neat package, and took it to the trash can.

Stella finished the last of her fruit cup and followed me out. We stopped to say hello to Lottie, the head cook who kept Fritz and me fed in the old days. She was a sprite of a woman with a thick silver braid down her back, pale-blue eyes, and a talkative manner.

Lottie scooped a serving of mashed potatoes onto a swashbuckling pirate's tray as Stella complimented her on the chicken. "Come by tomorrow for the meat loaf." She winked at me. It had been my favorite as a child and now the one day a week I'd spend a quarter to have a hot lunch.

"I wouldn't miss it for the world, Lottie," I promised.

I did not know then, but Mrs. Adler was going to make a liar of me.

CHAPTER 3

AGENT THIRTEEN

Thirteen didn't like meeting in a house of worship, and sure not one that took up half a city block.

The Wilshire Boulevard Temple looked like something that belonged in one of those European cities. Except it wasn't hundreds of years old like the castles and cathedrals he'd seen over there. No, the fresh-cut stone was white as parchment and the stained-glass windows sparkled like the crown jewels. A six-pointed star sculpted in marble told him this was the place, all right.

He should turn around and forget all about Leon Lewis and his wild theories.

He parked the Cadillac, switched off the engine, and lit a cigarette. He watched the door for ten minutes. Nobody came or went.

When he was sure it was safe, he crushed out his cigarette and crossed the street to the wide concrete stairway. At the Goliath-sized triple doors of paneled oak, he hesitated. Could he even go into a Jewish temple? But this was where the man had told him to meet, and he was already late. Saying a prayer of apology to whoever might be listening, he pushed open the heavy door.

Inside, the sanctuary was cool and dim, but from what he could see, this place was made for men who knew what—who—they believed in. Black marble pillars loomed like sentries. Bronze chandeliers cast a sanctified light on gleaming walnut pews. At the pinnacle of the domed ceiling, a circular window of blue glass shone down like a great eye. Was it for God to watch over his people? Thirteen wasn't the religious type, so he couldn't say.

He considered the great space, the dim corners, the stairways that led to what he imagined must be a balcony. The whole shebang gave him an uncomfortable twinge.

A figure rose from a bench along the wall and came toward him.

Leon Lewis.

He looked like he belonged there, with the small hat on top of his head. Thirteen swiped his fedora from his own head, then felt like a fool. "Should I keep this on or not?"

"Off is acceptable," Lewis answered easily.

Thirteen shook hands with Lewis, then followed him to the bench and took a seat beside him. Thirteen had liked Lewis from the start. He'd seen him at the Disabled American Veterans post, taking on clients pro bono. When Lewis approached him with his proposal, Thirteen thought the man was off his rocker, but he decided to check up on him to be sure.

Thirteen still had friends in high places and they owed him some favors. What he found had confirmed his gut feeling. Nobody had a bad word to say against Lewis. The Jewish lawyer had served in the Great War, part of a secret intelligence operation. Came home to start a law practice in Chicago and moved to Los Angeles for his health with his wife and two daughters. He was legitimate and—as far as Thirteen could tell—not hiding anything.

Then he looked into what had Lewis worried.

He asked some questions. Made the rounds to a few places he knew from the old days. Listened to men who'd been treated badly by the government when they came back from the war. What he heard was disturbing. Men were angry, and there was a new group in town that gave them a target for that anger: the Jews.

Leon Lewis was right. The Nazis had come to Los Angeles.

Problem was, nobody seemed to care. Thirteen didn't blame the general public. Unemployment, rising rent, what the newspapers were calling the Depression—that's what had people worried. Sure, they read in the newspapers about the new German chancellor. They might tut over the book burnings, shake their heads about violence against Jewish shopkeepers. Terrible things happening in Germany, they'd say. Then they put on their hats and got on with their own problems.

Thirteen craved a cigarette but he didn't know if smoking was allowed. Instead, he considered the man beside him. Lewis was tall, maybe six feet—but not intimidating. He wore a gray single-breasted suit with a six-button vest and a subdued tie. No rings or diamond tie clips. Nothing flashy. His dark hair was trim, his light-brown eyes intelligent in an almost-boyish face. He didn't look like a spymaster, but what did Thirteen know?

Lewis waited patiently for him to speak. Thirteen started out with a report on the meeting at the Alt Heidelberg, where Lewis had sent him. "It was like you said, a lot of slogans and hogwash. Jews hate Gentiles and are cheating us in the market. The studios are run by Communists and kikes—pardon the language." He glanced quickly up at the blue ocular window looking down on them.

Lewis waved his hand to dismiss the slur. "What else?"

"Seems like they can't hand out membership applications fast enough," he said. "Four hundred new members signed up in the last month. They're printing leaflets, distributing them all over the city. Heard some whispers of land they've got out in the Hollywood Hills." He didn't know what that was about, but it didn't sound good.

"Who is supporting them?" Lewis asked.

That was the big question. Thirteen shook his head. "They keep pretty tight-lipped about that. The Christian Front, maybe the National Gentile League. The Klan for sure."

"Worrisome." Lewis rubbed a hand over his forehead.

Sure was. From what Thirteen saw, every man in Los Angeles—Jewish, Christian, and whatever else—should be worried. The newspapers said Adolf Hitler was a flash in the pan. But maybe they were wrong.

Things had been bad in Germany, that was a fact. Now, with Adolf Hitler and the National Socialists in power, the people there had food on the table and a roof over their heads. Their national pride restored. The new chancellor was a bona fide hero.

With his report made, he had questions that needed answers. "Why are you doing this?" Thirteen motioned to the sanctuary where they sat, but he meant the whole operation Lewis told him about. "Because you're Jewish?"

"Yes," Lewis said, "but also because I'm American. Adolf Hitler, the National Socialists—their rise to power did not happen by chance."

Nothing did, in Thirteen's experience.

Lewis explained. "Our own country paved the way for the National Socialists to gain power."

"How do you figure?" After the war was over and the treaty was signed, it seemed to him America wanted nothing more than to stay out of other countries' business.

"I was in Koblenz with the war relief."

Thirteen's respect for the lawyer went up a notch. War relief had been dirty work, cleaning up the sixteen million dead and twenty million wounded—all of them far from home. Not to mention the Spanish flu ravaging every country in the world. That took guts and grit.

"After the war, the economy of Germany was in shambles," Lewis went on. "American banks lent Germany the money they needed to rebuild. Finally there were jobs. Business was starting up again. People were starting to have hope. And then 1929."

The crash. Just after he'd walked away from his job at Pinkerton.

Lewis nodded as if he'd spoken the words. "The bankers in New York called in their loans they'd made to German banks. The German banks called in their loans to the folks in Germany, and the country collapsed." Lewis was as fervent as a revival tent preacher. "Tell me, who were those bankers?"

Thirteen didn't have to answer. Everybody knew who ran the banks.

Lewis answered for him. "Jewish bankers were to blame, or so said the National Socialist Party. The German people were angry. Hungry. And desperate. They started to listen to what Adolf Hitler said and believe it."

Thirteen could see the logic up to a point, but he couldn't blame bankers for doing what bankers did; it was like blaming the clouds for raining. "I heard it was the Communists who got the blame," he offered.

"True, Communist rabble-rousers played right into the National Socialists' narrative," Lewis agreed. "The Nazis made them one and the same—Communists and Jews." He got up from the bench and began to pace. "All those young men out of work? They signed up for Hitler's Brownshirts. Then—when Adolf Hitler got the chancellor appointment last January—he had a ready-made fighting force."

Thirteen watched the man he'd pegged as more collegiate than crusader. Lewis believed in what he was fighting for—and that was something. He looked around with a growing unease, making sure they were still alone. He didn't like how worked up the man was getting. He'd attract attention.

"So you see," Lewis kept on, "it is a conflagration—like storms advancing upon each other. And it has come to our shores." Lewis finally sat down and looked at him expectantly.

Thirteen hadn't heard an answer to his question. "Sure, it has to be stopped, let's say," he conceded. "But why you?" The man had a wife and kids and, from what he heard, wasn't in the best of health. "There's gotta be somebody else who could do this."

Lewis turned his gaze to where the light from the stained glass illuminated the raised altar and the ornate doors behind it. "If not me, who?"

Thirteen wasn't sure he subscribed to that kind of talk. But he had to admit, it would be good to believe in something again. "So how do we stop it?" He'd bet a ham sandwich Lewis already had a plan.

Lewis leaned forward and lowered his voice. "We bring them out in the open. Show the ugly truth behind the National Socialists. It won't be easy. We need proof before the authorities will listen to us."

Proof would be tough. "You have help?"

"You mean the police?"

Thirteen snorted. Most police were as trustworthy as a barrel of monkeys. A good lot of them were in the Klan or at least on the take.

"I have supporters," Lewis continued carefully. "Those who have pledged funds."

"The studios?" Of course it was the studios. They had money and were run by Jewish moguls. But money wasn't all they needed. They needed people. People who knew what they were doing. People they could trust. He said as much to Lewis.

Lewis acknowledged that truth. "You work on being my eyes and ears. Get in with the German-American Alliance and with the Friends of New Germany. Make them trust you. I'll look for more operatives." At Thirteen's look of concern, he added, "I'll be careful."

Thirteen hoped he would be. He'd seen the underbelly of this city, and a man with principles could end up floating facedown in the Pacific. He stood, ready to go.

Lewis shook his hand, then said suddenly, "I saw him once, you know."

"Who?" Thirteen said. "The chancellor?"

Lewis looked grim. "He wasn't anything then, just an agitator speaking in Munich in '20."

"What was he like?" Thirteen had seen pictures of the man in the newspaper and thought he looked more like a ferret than a statesman.

"Compelling. He is German, straight through. Ultranationalist. He said—" Lewis's voice dropped to almost a whisper, as if he couldn't speak the words in the place they stood—"he said he would see the contamination of the Jewish race wiped from the earth. Exterminated."

Thirteen didn't know what to say. It was a terrible way to talk and he was ashamed to admit he'd heard the words repeated at the Alt Heidelberg.

Lewis went on. "I remember thinking that night, if a man like this ever gains power, then God help us all. And now—" Leon Lewis's face was as serious as the grave—"that day has come. And no one can see it but me."

CHAPTER 4

LIESL

Stella was right. I should have slapped Gary Perl when I had the chance.

When we stepped into the artificial light of the administrative building at half past twelve, Mrs. Adler was waiting beside my desk. "My office please, Liesl."

My heart fell to my shoes. I glanced at Stella's surprised face and followed Mrs. Adler to her office, her square-toed lace-ups snapping in quick rhythm on the linoleum floor. Mrs. Adler did everything quickly—walk, type, even converse. In my seven years working in Administration, I hadn't spent more than a minute in conversation with her, standing at attention at the open door of her office. This was unusual and concerning.

She sat behind her desk—a tidy oak domain with a leather-bound ledger, crystal fountain pen, and a telephone set placed with regimental precision. "Shut the door please, Liesl, and take a seat."

The muffled clatter of the typing pool was the only sound as I sat down, my mouth as dry as day-old bread. I was a good employee. I took dictation and typed my letters with no errors. I dressed modestly, arrived five minutes early, and took my lunch for precisely thirty minutes. When I put the cover on my Remington typewriter and punched out, my desk was neat as a pin and my tasks completed.

"I'm sorry, Liesl," Mrs. Adler finally said, meeting my gaze. "I'm going to have to let you go."

I jerked back as if I had been slapped. Because of Gary Perl?

She spoke in her quick typewriter-like way. "There's nothing I can do. With the budget cuts and the box office. You see how it is."

I did not see how it was. Not at all. A surge of outrage momentarily shook me. But reacting in that way would not help my cause. I took a moment's pause, then spoke in a reasonable tone. "Mrs. Adler. I'm your fastest stenographer."

Mrs. Adler riffled through a stack of pink slips and did not look at me. "With the new Dictaphones coming in, we'll need less of that."

Panic rose in my chest but I tamped it down. She must reconsider. "Dictaphones can't translate into German." The only other German speaker was Eda Druker, and she'd only been at the studio for a month.

"We may not have a German market in the future," Mrs. Adler rattled out as if she'd practiced the line. She pushed a pink slip across the desk. "The board of directors demands it. As I said, I am sorry, Liesl."

My breath caught. I had a family to support. Children.

"You're not the only one, if it makes you feel better."

It certainly did not. "Who else is going?" As if it mattered.

She frowned and fanned the other slips over the polished wood. "Four from steno, two secretaries, three messengers." She took off her glasses and wiped them with her handkerchief. Without the wire frames, the lines of her face showed deeper.

I looked over the slips as if they could tell me how to change her mind. Her neat handwriting was easy to read. Maura Landgreen. Joan Lang. Debbie Mahoney. All good at their jobs. Maura and Joan still lived with their parents. Debbie supported her father, who'd lost a leg in the war. What would she do now? What would I do?

Mrs. Adler returned her glasses to her nose. "You'll get a week's extra pay—" she tapped the stack together to line up the edges—"and a glowing reference, of course."

A reference that wouldn't help when a new job was as likely as snow in the Mojave.

She picked up the pink slip, leaned over the desk, and shoved it in my hand. "I'm sure you'll land on your feet."

She was sure of no such thing. An angry retort flared but my throat was too tight to speak. Did Mrs. Adler know what it was like to sleep on a park bench? To beg for dimes so your little brother could have a hot meal? No. Mrs. Adler didn't know the terror of living without a home. But I did. When able-bodied men couldn't find a job—how was a woman to do so?

I found myself back at my desk, staring at my typewriter. The stack of letters. Gary Perl's dictation. The slip of paper in my hand.

Stella stopped typing. "What happened?" she whispered, glancing back at the office where Mrs. Adler was ushering Joan inside.

I could not answer. I shoved my hat on my head and pulled my cotton gloves over shaking hands. With a choked goodbye to Stella, I snatched up my handbag and walked out of the steno pool. I was almost to the door of Administration when I stopped suddenly. I might not have been able to get my job back, but there was one thing I could do. I turned on my heel and walked to the stairs, steeling my resolve with every step I took upward. At the landing of the second floor, I almost turned around. I remembered the kiss. The *wrongness* of it. And Norma. What she'd been through. I took off my gloves.

I marched up the last flight of stairs and into Gary Perl's outer office. His secretary—a bottle blonde with unnaturally dark lashes and brows—glanced up. "Mr. Perl is not to be disturbed," she intoned in a bored voice.

I didn't stop and headed straight for his office. Mr. Perl stood by the window, looking over the studio lot like a king surveying his castle keep. He jerked around as I marched across the Persian carpet. I stopped toe-to-toe with Mr. Gary Perl and looked him straight in the eye.

Then I slapped him across the face hard enough to make my hand sting.

I walked past the speechless secretary with her crimson lips parted in surprise. The Heartbreak Hun, indeed. Let them tell that story all over the lot if they wished, for I would not be here to care.

———————

The sun dimmed behind a bank of clouds as I passed through the gleaming marble columns of the Washington Boulevard entrance for the last time. A shiver ran over my bare arms.

Gus raised a hand from his post at the security gate. The aging guard was barrel-chested and cherub-faced and had known me since I was a little girl trying to keep my brother out of trouble. "You take care now, Miss Liesl."

I gave him a wave but didn't trust my voice to say goodbye as I walked from the make-believe of MGM to the real-life of Culver City, my legs still wobbly from my visit to Gary Perl's office. I didn't regret the slap. In fact, I wished I could have punched him in the nose.

The typical knot of onlookers, tourists, and film fans gathered outside the gate. "Is that somebody?" one of them asked.

Not somebody. Just me, saying goodbye to the place I'd spent most of my life. Goodbye to Gus, the old sets, the winding streets and soaring soundstages. Goodbye to where I had met Tomas and fallen in love. Goodbye to a regular paycheck and security for my family.

The trolley pulled up and I passed my punch card to the operator. A man in a sharp suit and fedora gave me his seat with a sour look. I watched the Metro-Goldwyn-Mayer sign grow smaller and then disappear as we turned the corner onto Overland. The trolley slowed for the next stop at the corner of Hooverville—a jumble of canvas tents and shacks made of discarded tin and packing boxes. The block teemed with the displaced and homeless, families who had come to California seeking relief and a better life. They'd found neither. A man stood outside a tent, stripped to the waist, shaving in a tiny mirror leaned up against an enamel bowl. Not five feet away, a woman tended a cooking fire while her children sat in the dust, eyes blank with hunger, faces smudged with dirt. The fancy-suited man standing beside me wrinkled his nose at the odor of outdoor latrines and garbage.

My insides curled in fear. Would that be us—Mutti and me and the children? Not again.

A man in a canvas jacket and shapeless hat got on with a boy of about eight years. They walked down the aisle, the boy holding out a tin cup to each passenger. The boy's face was thin, his lips chapped and raw. "Spare change?" the man prompted. "Anything helps."

I reached for my coin purse, then stopped. What if this dime was what I'd need to put milk on the table tomorrow? "I'm sorry," I said. Disappointment passed over the man's face and guilt pinched me. But I must take care of my own first. Was that not proper and right?

The streetcar jerked to a halt. It wasn't my stop yet, but I stood and made my way down the aisle. I'd walk the rest of the way and ready myself to tell Mutti the bad news. I passed the boy and his father standing in the center aisle and turned my face away.

I hurried along Vermont Avenue into Germantown—not really a town, but the neighborhood had been called by the name for as long as I could remember. It was a tidy place—not as falling-down as little Mexico nor as seedy as Chinatown. The houses were painted; the grass trimmed; calla lilies and tuberoses bloomed in window boxes. Neat backyards held clotheslines with scrubbed shirts and bright-white aprons billowing in the rising wind. Grundbacher's grocery displayed prices for wurst and speck in the window, and the corner tobacconist carried hand-carved pipes and German-language newspapers.

Not long ago, Germantown was a place of fear. When war broke out with the kaiser, every German was watched as if we were spies. It angered me how we were treated. Vati was the most patriotic American I knew.

When the call came for volunteers to fight the kaiser, he was one of the first to enlist. "It is my duty to serve my new country," my brave father said. I was thirteen and Fritz was just six years old when we brought Vati to the harbor to board his ship. "Take care of them," he'd whispered in my ear. I promised him I would.

America won the war, but we lost Vati.

The clouds had darkened into a gray bank and the wind was damp. A storm was coming, gathering over the ocean, moving toward us. As I turned on Pico, the first drops of rain began to fall.

Not long after we got the telegram, Mutti became ill with the influenza that swept every corner of the country. It was months before she was recovered and by then, we'd fallen behind on the rent and the rest of the bills. At first, we stayed with friends, sleeping on floors at different houses. For a while, we stayed in a church basement with other women and children. The worst times were when we slept outside—on park benches or in well-lit squares. Some days, I went to school; mostly I looked after Fritz while Mutti looked for work. I tried to do as Vati had asked—take care of Mutti and Fritz—but I was terribly afraid. Even now the memories of those days gave my stomach a twist.

I walked past the Stahrs' home, right next to ours. Miriam and Yitzak's lawn was neatly trimmed, the hedge in front perfectly shaped. A jump rope and a rubber ball lay discarded on the sidewalk. I could see Miriam's bright headscarf in the garden behind the house, as she gathered ripe tomatoes before the storm hit.

Miriam. How I wished to tell her of my despair. She would understand. My steps slowed. She'd know my worries of Mutti and Fritz. How I feared losing our home. My concern for my children. Miriam stood, rubbing her back, and her gaze fell on me. She looked away quickly and went back to her work. I continued on my way. I could not turn to the comfort of Miriam's friendship. Not anymore.

I went slowly up the walk to my own house—a clean white bungalow with neat green trim and a small square of yard. The grass was in need of cutting—Fritz's chore when he could be bothered to do it—but the walk was swept, the porch tidy, and the geranium on the stoop bright and cheerful. Behind the house, the vegetable garden had not a weed nor was a vine out of place. The home I'd first entered with Tomas when the world was full of promise. *We'll be together until we're old and gray,* he had promised me.

A lie, for I was only twenty-eight years old and he was gone.

The rain began in earnest, the wind tugging at my hat. I straightened my shoulders and lifted my chin, stowed my worry and my anger. It would not do to indulge in either when I had a family who depended on me.

Tomas, how could you leave me so alone?

CHAPTER 5

LIESL

I walked in the door to find Mutti starting the Thursday night pork schnitzel. The children played crazy eights at the kitchen table with Fritz. I said hello to Tess and welcomed Steffen's exuberant embrace, then told my news immediately and without drama. I did not mention Gary Perl.

As it was, Mutti made enough of a ruckus.

"I'll march over there and give Mrs. High-and-Mighty Adler a talking-to." She slammed the frying pan down on the stovetop. At the clatter, Steffen put his hands over his ears and Tess watched with wide eyes. "I knew that woman when she was using the only typewriter at Goldwyn Studios." Mutti scooped a spoonful of bacon grease into the hot pan, where it sputtered and sizzled. "You were never sick one day. Always on time. Not like some of the girls there. I could tell you about the trouble they got up to."

"Mutti, please." I picked up the dishcloth and wiped the spatters of grease. I knew plenty about the trouble girls had gotten up to at the studio and didn't want to hear about it. "It's not the same as it was in your day."

I hung up the dishcloth and went upstairs to the room I shared with Tess and Steffen. I slipped off my skirt and blouse and hung them in the chifforobe, then put on a flowered wraparound housedress. I pulled open the top drawer and took out the silver-framed photograph I had told myself not to look at again.

Tomas and me on our wedding day.

A year after the war ended, Mutti was hired back at the studio. We found rooms in an affordable boardinghouse in Germantown. Mutti worked long hours and we spent our days on the lot where Mutti could keep an eye on us.

When I turned eighteen, I signed up for a course at Dickinson Secretarial School and graduated at the top of my class, then marched into Administration with my certificate. Mrs. Adler hired me on the spot. I found satisfaction in the orderly work of typing and filing, the systematic logic of Gregg shorthand and the regular hours. With me bringing in twelve dollars a week, Mutti didn't need to work so hard nor worry so much. She did both, nonetheless.

And then I met Tomas.

I was twenty-one and had perfected the cool reserve that was a shield among the pinching and patting executives of Metro-Goldwyn-Mayer. Tomas was tall and handsome in his security uniform, with an easy smile and quick wit. He'd known from the minute he saw me that it was meant to be. That's what he said, at least.

I ran a finger over the smooth glass, remembering the scratch of his cheek, the hint of laughter on his lips.

Tomas had a knack of turning up wherever I was at MGM, always with a joke and a piece of Juicy Fruit chewing gum. At the commissary, behind me in line. "Why don't melons get married, Miss Bittner?" he said, slipping a wrapped piece of gum onto my tray. "Because they cantaloupe!" He was there when I brought Fritz for a haircut at the studio barber. "Fritz, are you getting a haircut?" He slipped two sticks of Juicy Fruit to my brother with a straight face. "You should get 'em all cut."

He found me at the MGM mail room one day. "What's the secret to a good mailman joke?"

I shook my head and considered ignoring him again.

"The delivery." He handed me the chewing gum like a prize for sticking around. Then he asked me on a date and I said yes. "You're so serious, Miss Bittner," he told me. "I can't help but want to make you smile."

Was the very quality that drew him to me also what drove us apart?

Tomas kissed me for the first time in the Property building on a rainy afternoon. "Will you be my girl?" he asked, his blue eyes holding mine while thunder rumbled all around. I said yes and kissed him back, the sweetness of Juicy Fruit on his lips. "I'll make you happy, Liesl," Tomas said when he asked me to marry him just months later. I said yes again. Tomas was spontaneous while I was scheduled. Whimsical when I was practical. He was everything I needed.

I looked at the photograph of the man I loved. The discordant whisper of doubt murmured in my heart as it had these last two years. Had he loved me but stopped? Or had he never loved me at all?

I shoved the frame back in the drawer. I must see to matters at hand. The children needed dinner and there was work to be done. I shut the drawer and locked away my memories.

Back downstairs, Mutti had the potatoes boiling. "I don't understand why you of all the girls," she muttered, jabbing a fork at one of the potatoes as if it were Mrs. Adler herself.

I did not know the answer.

"It's the Jews, Mutti," Fritz decreed over his hand of cards, "like I've been telling you."

"Don't be ridiculous," I told him. "And take off your hat in the house."

"It's true." He swiped off his police cap and tossed it toward the hat hook in the front room. It landed on the floor. "Captain Hynes told us. They're weeding out the Gentiles from the studios—and everywhere else. Before you know it, they'll take over the whole country."

"What a load of baloney," Mutti said, flipping the schnitzel. "Battle-Axe Adler is a pain in the backside, but she doesn't hate Gentiles."

"What's a Gentile?" Tess asked, taking a card from the pile in the center of the table. Her delicate face and mop of blonde curls were that of a porcelain angel, except she was no angel these days, with temper tantrums that could try a saint.

I hung Fritz's hat on the proper hook, then sorted through the jars in the pantry shelves for pickles. "Mrs. Adler didn't fire me because she's Jewish and I'm not." The very idea.

"Think about it, Liesl," Fritz said. "Who else got ousted?"

I straightened the canned goods on the pantry shelf. Beans, carrots, evaporated milk. I moved a can of corn to the right of the carrots and considered Fritz's words. Maura, Joan, Debbie. None of them Jewish.

"And who still has a job?" Fritz asked. He leaned over and looked at Steffen's cards. His blond hair matched Steffen's, as did his cornflower-blue eyes. Fritz pointed to a card and whispered a suggestion. Steffen nodded with understanding.

"No helping!" Tess complained.

"He's only four. He needs help," Fritz said. He put down an eight and declared, "Hearts."

Stella, Lilian Zucker, and Eda Druker were still employed. All Jewish, just like Mrs. Adler, but it didn't prove his point. "It was budget cuts. And the new Dictaphones."

Tess laid her card and so did Steffen.

Fritz put down a card with a snap. "It's the kikes."

"What's a kike?" Tess piped up.

"Stop it, Fritz." My tone was hard now. Vati had many friends who were Jewish. Other camera operators, men from Property and Building. "Vati wouldn't have let you talk like that."

"And he's not here to stop me," Fritz said with a bitter edge.

"Your Vati was a hero." Mutti turned, wielding the spatula. She rarely chastised Fritz, but speaking ill of Vati was *verboten*.

Fritz ignored her and tipped his head to Tess and Steffen. "When I was their age, I got called a dirty hun. Don't you remember?"

I remembered well. Germans were looked at with distrust—some even accused of treason. Vati had proved his patriotism with his life. "It was the war," I said. "People were afraid."

Steffen slapped down his last card.

"No fair!" Tess groaned. "Mutti, he cheated!"

"I'm afraid," Fritz said, gathering the cards into a pile. "I'm afraid the dirty Jews are going to take over the country Vati died to protect."

I felt my temper rising. Fritz's talk was not welcome tonight. I grabbed the garbage and slammed out the back door. I deposited the scraps in the trash bin and looked over the fence at Miriam's kitchen window, the lowering sun glinting off the glass. What had gotten into my brother? The way he talked and with Miriam and Yitzak right next door. How could he speak like that about our friends? At least they had been.

When Tomas and I had moved into this house, I found my neighbor, Miriam, to be quiet, even shy. In time I realized her quiet way hid a deep reserve of thoughtfulness. Unlike my other neighborhood acquaintances, Miriam eschewed small talk and gossip. Instead, she dove deeply into topics that were close to her heart: marriage, children, and even her faith. She spoke of her feelings openly and asked me to do the same. I had not been raised to speak so directly about personal subjects and was taken aback. But soon I found I was drawn to her and also began to share my feelings in a way I never had before known with a friend.

Of course we had our differences. I was orderly and organized. Her home was cluttered in a way that my fingers itched to straighten and tidy. She dressed haphazardly, as if she threw on the first garment that came to hand, while I took care with my appearance. And yes, she was Jewish and I, Christian. I knew some of the people in Germantown disliked Jews, but our differences in religion mattered little, or so I thought.

Frieda was born and soon after, Tess. Our children grew, and so did our friendship. In Miriam, I found a friend unlike myself, yet so much of what I needed.

Mutti called out that supper was ready and I turned away from the house next door. What was done was done and could not be undone. But I missed Miriam, and on days like today, when I was so alone, I felt her absence like a great hole in my heart.

CHAPTER 6

The telephone rang through the silent house, jerking me awake. The bedside clock said 6:43. I had overslept.

The piercing ring came again.

"What nitwit is calling at this hour of the morning?" Mutti's voice, peevish and strident.

Tomas. The foolish hope swelled within me.

In the night, I had woken in the dark as I often did since Tomas. I had slipped from the warm bed I shared with Tess and Steffen and silently walked the dark house, checking all was well. Mutti had been snoring softly in her bedroom. The kitchen was scrubbed clean from dinner, the table set in readiness for breakfast. The sitting room, tidy and quiet.

I'd been a faithful child. I'd learned my Bible and sang along with the hymns in church. When Vati had died, I'd gone to his grave and imagined him in heaven. When Tess was born, I'd thanked God for the blessings of our family—everything I'd ever wished for. And with Steffen, proof that God was good, indeed. But after Tomas, my prayers changed from those of faith to cries of doubt. *Are you there, God? Do you really care for me? If so, why did you give me so much, just to take it away?* My questions, as always, remained unanswered. Back in my bedroom,

I had consoled myself with a touch to Steffen's smooth cheek, a feather-light brush of Tess's hair—soft as dandelion fluff—and had gone back to sleep.

Now Tess flopped over and mumbled. Steffen buried deeper under the quilts. I scrambled out of bed as the telephone shrilled a third time. "I'm getting it, Mutti." I stumbled down the steps and reached for the receiver. "Hello?"

"Good morning, sunshine." It was Stella. My ridiculous hope deflated. "Can you meet me for lunch?" she said, not a word about why she was calling so early. I didn't ask. I looked at the hall clock. She had seventeen minutes to get to work or risk Mrs. Adler's ire.

"Yes."

"At the Lagoon," she said.

I put the receiver back in its cradle, my knees wobbly. Not Tomas. Not after almost two years. Still, every telephone ring, every knock on the door roused a preposterous hope, then a bitter disappointment that left me weak and shaking. In the kitchen, I filled the percolator and lit the burner on the stove. I locked away thoughts of Tomas. I had worries far more pressing.

Three weeks without a paycheck.

I'd looked for work until my feet ached. Stenographer, typist, secretary. *Sorry, miss, not hiring.* I'd lined up wherever an opening was posted. Shop assistant, hotel clerk, cook. *Leave the jobs to the men. They have families to support.* I, too, had a family to support. Two children, a mother. A brother who did not pull his weight in the household.

Fritz. A thread of steam rose as the water came to a boil. I was still furious at him.

I'd cornered him a week after I lost my job at MGM and showed him the threatening letters from the utility and telephone companies. What was he doing with his weekly pay? I asked. Could he not help with the family bills? He slammed out of the house and then . . . and then!

The water came to a boil and I turned off the flame.

And then he came home with an auto, of all the idiotic things.

He was like a child with a new toy when he drove it up to the house. "I've been making payments, but Neville—that's the guy I bought it from—he said I could take it home and pay him every week."

I couldn't speak with the anger that choked me. Here I was, struggling to put food on the table and he appears in a Ford Model T that looked to be on its last breath of life. Had he no sense at all in that head of his?

"Mutti, tell him to take it back," I said through gritted teeth.

"He's a grown man," she said as if she had no authority over him, which indeed she had not since he turned twelve. Only Tomas had been able to talk sense into Fritz, and when he left, my brother had become more impossible.

A grown man took care of his family. Was that not so?

I went upstairs and dressed quietly, letting the children sleep. A button-up day dress of light-blue cotton and a pair of canvas loafers would do. I'd get the Tuesday laundry started, then change before I left for Culver City to meet Stella. What did she have to tell me? Word of a job, I hoped. *Please, let it be that.* I laid out the children's clothing and straightened my side of the bed.

Mutti was starting the oatmeal when I came back to the kitchen. She was dressed impeccably in a pressed cotton shirtwaist. Her silver-threaded hair was braided and coiled on top of her head like a crown.

"We're out of eggs and butter and bacon," Mutti grumbled.

"*Guten Morgen* to you, too, Mutti." I needed no reminding of the contents of the icebox.

Fritz clattered down the stairs and flopped into a chair. Tomas's chair. In his police uniform of navy jacket, black pants, and pressed white shirt, he had a passing resemblance to my husband. But Tomas had sat tall, his broad shoulders always straight, a smile on his face. Fritz slouched over the coffee Mutti set before him and sniffed. "Oatmeal again?"

I bit my tongue before I let it loose on my brother as he deserved.

The buses and trolleys had always been adequate for Mutti and me. Why must he have an auto?

Tess appeared in her pink cotton pajamas and slippers, toting the chenille stuffed dog Tomas had given her when she was three. "*Guten Morgen*, my sweet." I kissed the top of her curly head and turned her around back toward the stairs. "Go up and get dressed. Then help Steffen."

She crossed her arms and got that mulish look on her face. "No, he can dress himself."

"Tess—" I did not have the patience for this.

Mutti stepped in. "I'll get him."

"No, Mutti." How many times did we have to go over this? "It is Tess's responsibility to help her brother dress in the morning before coming downstairs."

Tess turned to her grandmother, always her ally against my rules. "But—"

"No buts." It looked like it was going to be another test of wills. One I might not win.

"Hold on there, Tess." Fritz hooked an arm around her and pulled her closer. "How did Mr. Dog sleep last night?"

She was immediately distracted. "He didn't sleep at all," she told Fritz. "Didn't you hear him howling?"

"I'll arrest him and put him in doggy jail." Fritz held the little dog's front paws as if he were putting him in handcuffs. "You go get Steffen dressed."

Tess scampered up the stairs.

I should thank Fritz for preventing a battle. But with the thought of the ridiculous auto, I determined I would remain silent. I must talk to Tess about obedience . . . again. The girl spent more time in the corner than she did out of it these days.

Fritz watched her go, then stood on his chair and tucked Mr. Dog above the icebox. "That should take her some time to find," he said.

She and Steffen would try to find Mr. Dog while Fritz was at work. It was their daily game and Mr. Dog found his way into spots all over the house.

Fritz had loved Tess from the moment he'd seen her—and the same when Steffen had been born. And yet . . . *I did sums in my head for the hundredth time.* The rent, the gas meter, the grocery account. Our cupboards were as bare as the icebox. Why couldn't he help with the household if he cared so much for the children?

I dished up the oatmeal, adding a spoonful of molasses, and poured the milk.

Tess and Steffen thundered down the stairs like a pair of baby elephants. Steffen's shirt was buttoned crookedly but Tess had managed to get his shoes on the right feet. Steffen went to the back door, opening it to find Chester waiting for his morning cream.

"Can I go to Hildy's after breakfast?" Tess asked.

"Not today." I scraped the last of the oatmeal into my bowl. "I have to go out and you have chores." On Tuesdays the children washed the windows and wiped each windowsill with a damp cloth, then emptied the wastepaper baskets.

Tess let out a loud, put-upon sigh.

Tomas had resented my strict adherence to the daily schedule. *Alles ist in Ordnung, Liesl,* he teased when we were first married. *Everything in perfect order, it's hard to live with,* he said later, in frustration.

Was it so wrong to wish for order? To teach it to our children?

Fritz left for his shift at the precinct, the engine of the abominable Ford clattering like a bucket of bolts. I sorted the laundry into piles, then applied a paste of borax and water to the grass stains and jelly spots.

I let the clothes soak and inspected the chores when Tess announced them done—clean and mostly streak-free windows, the garbage deposited in the trash can outside. "Has Chester been fed?" Steffen nodded. He rarely forgot his responsibility to the cat.

"Can we play now, Mommy?" Tess whined.

Children should have fun, Liesl, Tomas's voice in my head admonished.

"Yes, go outside. But keep an eye on your brother."

I filled my largest pot with water and turned on the flame.

When I'd worked at MGM, we sometimes sent the dirty clothes out to Ming's Chinese Laundry on Vermont. Mrs. Ming worked wonders with stains and delivered the clothing fresh and pressed. Such luxuries were no longer possible.

"Not too much soap," Mutti reminded me as she dabbed kerosene on an oil spot on Fritz's old dungarees.

"Yes, Mutti." I'd been doing the washing since I was twelve and still she reminded me not to overdo the soap flakes. I could see the worry in the lines of her face, hear it in her snappish tone. The remembrance of fearful times when hunger gnawed at us. "Don't worry. Johan will let me get by another week."

She snorted disapprovingly. Mutti didn't go to Johan Grundbacher's grocery store anymore. She had had words with him about a cut of pork he sold her. "All gristle," she'd told him. "You call yourself a butcher?" Better for me to do the marketing, especially with our shamefully over-due account.

I put the children's clothing and kitchen towels through the wringer and hung them on the clothesline, then dressed to meet Stella. I'd tele-phoned her the night after I'd been fired. "I'm sorry," she'd said sincerely, then filled me in on the office gossip. "Every girl in the typing pool thinks you're an honest-to-goodness hero, Liesl, for what you did to Perl."

I didn't feel one bit like a hero. I felt like a failure.

My tweed pencil skirt and pressed white blouse fit more loosely than three weeks ago, but it couldn't be helped. I smoothed my hair with a dab of setting lotion and applied a coating of rose lipstick. "Do not do the bed linens without me," I told Mutti sternly as I picked up my handbag and gloves.

Steffen threw his arms around my legs, clinging to me like a starfish.

"I'll be back after your nap," I said, my heart breaking at the desperation he'd begun to show each time I left the house. I peeled his hands from my legs and crouched down beside him.

"Remember what I said?" I asked.

He whispered, "You always come back."

I traced a small heart on his forehead, then kissed it. "Always."

He watched me from the door as if I were deserting him. Tess ignored my goodbye, still sulking over not going to Hildy's, and I left with a heavy feeling of failure. What was I doing wrong? Were their behaviors because of Tomas—or because of me? Or were they a normal part of childhood?

With a pang of guilt, I caught the trolley and turned my mind to finding work instead of the unrelenting questions of motherhood.

CHAPTER 7

LIESL

At 11:20, I arrived at the Culver Boulevard entrance to MGM. The guard nodded me through without checking his clipboard.

Lot One, the acreage between Culver and Washington Boulevards, called to mind a jumbled storage attic, but one of immense proportions. A covered wagon parked next to a striped circus tent. A drawbridge tucked behind the deck of a pirate ship. On Western Street a blacksmith shop and old-time mercantile stood beside a New York skyscraper and art deco theater. The scent of newly cut wood drifted from the lumberyard as I took a detour around a traffic jam of boom trucks loaded with cameras and sound equipment.

Stella was waiting for me at the Tarzan Lagoon, which was nothing more than a narrow wedge of water fringed with wilted foliage. She looked like a magazine model in a pale-pink linen sundress with a cape-style jacket that must have cost more than she made in a week.

I sat down next to her on a plaster rock in the shade of a palm tree. "Is there anything? An opening?"

"Not even a 'Hello, Stella, how's your love life?'" she said in mock dismay.

"I'm sorry." I felt terrible. She'd telephoned me twice in the past three weeks, but I hadn't been much for conversation.

"Don't get all sad-sack about it." She smiled. "I know you're in a tough spot." Her brows flickered down and her smile faded. "MGM is firing, hon, not hiring. Same goes for the rest of the studios."

I tried to hide my disappointment. I took out sandwiches—cheese and pickles on the bread Mutti had made yesterday—and handed her one along with a napkin.

"Things are real bad, Liesl. I heard Louie B. is going to ask everyone to take a pay cut of 50 percent." She bit into her sandwich, looking heavenward in delight. "Your mother's pickles are to die for."

"Everyone?" Fifty percent was outrageous.

She took another bite and spoke around a mouthful. "Box office is in the pits. Thalberg still isn't well enough to work, which makes the big man nervous. But you know they've been twisting their hands since Warner and RKO filed bankruptcy last year." Stella chewed and looked sympathetic. She might not have money troubles, but she'd always been understanding of my responsibilities. "There's one thing, though. Might be worth a shot."

My hope flickered. "I'll take anything, Stella."

"I heard Mrs. Porter is working over at an agency, Stevenson's on Flower Street."

An agency. It wasn't much, but it was something. I thanked her as I gathered the waxed paper and crusts of bread. "I'll go see her today." I handed her the untouched half of my sandwich. I was too worried to eat and it was the least I could do after ignoring her.

"Good luck, Liesl," she said, her eyes meeting mine sincerely and with a hint of something else. Perhaps guilt that I'd been fired and she still had her job.

I paused. "Thanks, Stella," I said, my throat tightening. "You're a good friend."

"Oh, don't start with that." She gave me a shove. "Go see Porter and don't take no for an answer."

———————————

Stella was right. I couldn't take no for an answer.

On the bus, an older woman in a Hooverette housedress and kerchief sat with a child on her lap. He was thin and his cheeks pale. He blinked at me with disinterest. When had the child last had a good meal? A workingwoman sat across the aisle, her modest brown serge and low-heeled T-straps straight out of the Dickinson Secretarial Handbook. I hoped she wasn't going to Stevenson's Agency.

The trolley stopped and I got off. That's when I saw the line of men stretching along the sidewalk for an entire block. Some were in suits and ties and shined shoes. Others were shabby, in trousers and shirtsleeves. A few held signs. *Need Work* and *Will Work for a Dollar a Day.* One man had two children in tow, both of whom held signs that said *My Children Are Starving.*

My knees weakened and my hands went damp.

"Hey, lady," a man said as I moved past him, "leave the jobs to the men. We've got children to feed."

So do I. I put my shoulders back, lifted my chin, and picked up my pace. I couldn't blame them. Desperation was as catching as the influenza. Would I be this desperate soon?

A man with a clipboard stood in the doorway to the agency. His jacket was off and his white shirtsleeves rolled up. He looked as harried as a hotel maître d' during the lunch rush. "Liesl Weiss to see Mrs. Porter," I said and held my breath.

He checked his clipboard and frowned.

I met the man's polite scrutiny with a steady gaze. *Stand up straight, Liesl,* Mutti told me countless times when I was a gawky adolescent. *Don't cower like a ninny.* Mutti had never cowered a day in her life and had the respect—indeed, the fear—of everyone in the studio, including the actors and the executives. "She'll know who I am," I said, hoping it was true and saying a small prayer for a miracle.

"One moment." He turned on his heel and disappeared. He was back in a moment. "Second door on the left." I let out my breath slowly and went through the door. The next task would be harder.

Mrs. Porter sat at a tiny desk in the back room of the agency, little bigger than a closet. "Liesl," she said politely, "I wasn't expecting you."

Mrs. Porter was in her fifties, with intelligent gray eyes and a sharp-featured face. Her short ebony hair clung like a shining cap to her head with a bright threading of silver at the temples. She'd been a teacher at Dickinson School and had told me more than once I was the best stenographer she'd ever taught.

"I heard you worked here and was in the area." I smiled and sat down on the chair across from her without an invitation. Her brows flickered. Her desk held a tidy stack of folders, a telephone set, and a notepad filled with her neat shorthand. I set my handbag in my lap and took a breath. "I was hoping, perhaps, you could help me find work." I tried not to look desperate. "Anything, even temporary."

She frowned. "You're not at MGM anymore?"

I shook my head. "I have a reference from—"

"I'm sure you do," she interrupted me. "You were an excellent student." She gestured toward the busy office and the crowd outside. "But we have thousands come here every day. And less than fifty jobs." She rested her hand on a stack of forms.

"I'll take anything," I repeated and heard the note of desperation in my voice. Mrs. Porter knew I wasn't one of those flibbertigibbet girls looking for a paycheck to buy dancing shoes and dresses. Neither was I working to snare a rich husband. I had a family to feed just like those men out there.

"I can have you fill out a form, put it on file." She looked genuinely sorry. "If something comes up, I'll call you, Liesl. I promise."

Tears prickled behind my eyes. I dipped my head silently.

"Just a moment then." She left the office and I sat looking at her desk. Anxiety clutched at my chest as I thought of the bills waiting for me at home. Of Mutti revisiting those terrible days after Vati died. Hooverville just down the street. *Don't take no for an answer.*

I could see Mrs. Porter out the half-open door. She'd been waylaid by the man with the clipboard. I glanced at the stack of work orders on her desk. Perhaps if I just looked . . . if there was something she'd missed. I leaned across the desk and angled the papers to read. Construction foreman. I pushed it aside and read the next, a pianist for a one-night engagement.

I glanced out the door, my pulse speeding. Mrs. Porter had finished with the interruption and was at the front desk, collecting a stack of papers. I flipped to the next order and the next. Mechanic, dockworker, and then . . . secretary. I scanned the requirements. Typing, stenography, German. The office was close to downtown. I glanced up. Mrs. Porter's back was still turned. Why had she not told me? Did she have someone else who could do this? Someone better than me?

Before I could consider further, I slipped the work order out of the stack and tucked it in my handbag. I heard the clip of purposeful heels and straightened the files into perfect alignment, then sat back in my chair and tried to settle my breath.

Mrs. Porter's gaze remained on the form in her hand as she stepped into her office. "Fill it out completely, with references. Then bring it back and I'll call you if anything comes up that suits."

I felt the weight of guilt and a weakness in my legs. She was a good woman and I had just betrayed her trust. "I'm—I will, thank you." I left the building, passed by the desperate men again, and walked toward downtown. What had I done? I should go back, confess my moment of desperation.

I did not do so.

When I was out of sight of the agency, I took out the work order and read it over again. A secretary position with a lawyer by the name of Leon Lewis at an office on Seventh Street. I tucked the work order into my handbag and turned toward downtown.

Guilt prickled at me, but I dismissed it. My family must come first.

CHAPTER 8

LIESL

I considered the nondescript four-story building with dismay as I realized the truth. I hadn't thought this through.

Mrs. Porter would find the work order missing. And she would call this lawyer—Leon Lewis—and my deception would be discovered. But if I convinced him to give me the job first . . . then perhaps I could deal with Mrs. Porter.

The door opened into a small foyer and I climbed the scuffed linoleum stairs to the third floor. Down a short hallway I stopped at number 312, as indicated on the work order in my handbag. The nameplate read *Leon Lewis, Attorney-at-Law*. I pulled back my shoulders and lifted my chin, pinned a smile on my lips, and turned the knob.

It was locked.

I stepped back. It was after lunch on a Tuesday. Surely someone should be here?

I knocked. After a moment, a light footstep and the door opened just wide enough to see the face of a man. Middle-aged, with bright eyes and a longish nose. He looked at me carefully, then glanced behind me down the hallway. "May I help you?"

"Mr. Lewis?" I put out my gloved hand. "My name is Liesl Weiss. I understand you are in need of a secretary?" This was not a lie.

He shook my hand, then opened the door to take in my appearance from my hat to my sensible shoes. I did the same. Tall, trim, his suit a light-gray pinstripe, moderately cut and single-breasted. His tie was slightly askew, his shirt crisply pressed. "I am, Miss Weiss."

"Mrs.," I corrected.

His brows went up. "Pardon me. Please, come in." He ushered me through the door. "I take it Mrs. Porter has sent you?"

I stepped into the office and immediately ascertained that the man was in dire need of a secretary. The room smelled nicely of pencil shavings and ink but the desk was cluttered with stacks of newspaper clippings, the floor littered with handwritten notes and strewn with file folders. I was drawn to make order from the chaos—to straighten the piles at least—but he awaited my answer. "I saw her at the agency just now." Again, not a lie.

"Wonderful," he said and motioned me to a chair—a cushioned and tufted affair better suited to an elderly aunt's sitting room than the office of an attorney. He sat down behind the desk, leaned forward, and clasped his hands. "Tell me about yourself, Mrs. Weiss."

My neck began to heat, the flush traveling upward to my face as I contemplated what to say. I should tell him the truth, of course. But he would send me away.

"Mrs. Weiss?" he prompted, not unkindly.

I tilted toward him. "I was trained at Dickinson Secretarial in typing and shorthand. I've worked for a total of six years at MGM Studios and—"

Mr. Lewis's gaze sharpened. "MGM? Is that so?" He cocked his head. "Please, go on."

I took a breath. "Yes. I did stenography and also typing and translating for the international bureau." I stopped for a breath and to gauge his reaction.

"You speak German as well as read it?" he asked. "Fluently?"

"Yes. I can read and write it almost as well as English. My shorthand speed is—"

"What style?" he interrupted again.

"Gregg."

"Good," he said, nodding sharply.

I went on, listing my typing speed, my filing skills, and everything else I'd been taught at Dickinson and learned at MGM. Mr. Lewis listened intently and his attention did not waver from my face, which was a refreshing change from men like Gary Perl.

When I'd reached the end of my list of skills, I waited for him to respond.

He did not speak. Instead, he stood and walked to the window, looking out of it as if considering the Los Angeles skyline, then turned to me abruptly. "Forgive me, Mrs. Weiss, but I must ask. What is your situation—at home, I mean?"

It wasn't an unusual question—most employers wondered why a married woman would need to work—but something about the way he looked at me with kindness, so much like Papa, made my mouth dry. I did not wish to lie to him again but I did. "I'm a widow, Mr. Lewis."

His gaze softened. "I'm sorry." His sincerity was genuine.

I went on quickly. "I have two young children and a mother to support." I did not mention Fritz, although I supported him as well.

He rubbed his chin. "Of course. I see it is difficult for you." His sympathy was touching and the weight of my guilt increased.

He turned back to the window. Three floors up gave a good view of the Hall of Justice, the enormous edifice that was said to resemble the Acropolis in Greece. Mr. Lewis turned his back on the great monument and returned to his desk, perching on an uncluttered corner. "Mrs. Weiss," he said, "is there something else you'd like to tell me?"

He waited. The clock on the wall ticked loudly in the silence. A knot tightened in my chest. He seemed a good man. He didn't look anything like my father, who had been a robust, stout German man with wheat-blond hair and a bushy mustache. It was the kindness of his gaze that reminded me of Vati.

Vati would be ashamed of me, of my dishonesty—even to support my family. He would tell me to tell the truth. But how could I?

And yet how could I not? He would know eventually from Mrs. Porter, perhaps within the next few minutes. I let out a breath. Better to tell him myself. "The truth is—" I looked at my hands, clasped tight around the strap of my handbag—"Mrs. Porter did not send me."

Mr. Lewis did not look surprised. I stood to leave, humiliation burning through me.

He raised a hand to stop me. "Mrs. Weiss, please sit," he said gently.

I sank into the chair again. He went around to the other side of the desk and sat. "Angela—Mrs. Porter—she was given some very specific instructions about what I needed in a secretary. You do not meet those criteria."

Shame flooded through me and my face burned as hot as an iron. What qualifications did I not possess?

"But—" he laid his palms on the smooth wood and leaned forward—"I may have need of you nonetheless."

A flicker of unease went through me at those words. The way he said them. *Have need of you.* What did that mean?

Mr. Lewis regarded me with utmost seriousness. "Let me ask you a question—a very important question. And please, it is imperative that you answer honestly."

I agreed to that request. It was the least I could do after lying about Mrs. Porter.

He lowered his chin and his dark eyes met mine. "How do you feel," he said slowly and carefully, "about Adolf Hitler?"

CHAPTER 9

AGENT THIRTEEN

Thirteen parked the Cadillac in front of the Biltmore, a hotel of red brick and white marble that couldn't decide if it was a Spanish hacienda or an art deco fortress. He tossed the keys to the valet. "Give her a wash if you can find the time, Tony."

Tony caught them high above his head with a grin. "Sure thing, sir."

The lobby, billed as "luxury heaped upon luxury," was a triple-story cathedral of carved arches, crystal chandeliers, and twenty-four-karat trim. Men in tennis whites escorted smartly dressed women down the double staircase. He recognized a fellow he knew from Warner Brothers and a woman with top billing at MGM—but he didn't stop to gab. He'd missed breakfast and it was well past lunch. He was hungry and he was angry.

"I'll find my way, Adrien," he told the maître d' who guarded the door of the Emerald Room. Adrien—who looked the part of a fancy Frenchman but was really a barkeeper's son from Brooklyn—ushered him through.

He made his way to his regular booth under a mahogany-beamed ceiling and murals of hunting dogs. Out of habit, he noted each diner he passed—some regulars, some strangers. No one who looked suspicious, but that didn't mean much. He'd get a meal under his belt; then he'd tell Leon Lewis what had him hot under the collar.

He didn't regret agreeing to work with Lewis, even if they didn't have much in common. Thirteen wasn't Jewish and he wasn't a family man. Not against families, just not cut out for one himself. Still, he figured he and Lewis agreed on something: they didn't like bullies. The new chancellor of Germany and his ilk were bullies, straight through.

When Lewis had told him about his precautions, Thirteen was impressed with the man's forethought. They decided on the unlucky number as his code name and to communicate carefully, using Thirteen's answering service and the mail. After today, he was glad they took care.

Lita brought him a glass of water and one of tomato juice. "The usual?" she asked, her cheeks turning pink like they did when she took his order. "Or something else? The manicotti is terrific."

"Just a steak," he answered. She was a cute girl but he wasn't interested. He watched the other customers while he waited. Watched and thought about the Hitlerites.

It had taken him three weeks to gain the trust of the leaders of the German Alliance. Thirteen went first to the Aryan Bookstore at the Alt Heidelberg, where he struck up a conversation about the latest German pamphlets, all shouting about the great strides Herr Hitler was making in the fight against Communists and radicals. The next week, he went back for *The Protocols of the Elders of Zion*, a book praised by Henry Ford of automobile fame. It said some pretty terrible things about the Jewish people and made him glad he owned a Cadillac. But he got the attention of the owner of the place, so it was worth the two bits.

Paul Themlitz was easy to figure, a weak-kneed toady whose job was to bring likely Nazi candidates to the men who made the decisions. After Thirteen said all the right things—including a direct quote from *Mein Kampf*, which he'd held his nose and read in one night—Themlitz invited him to dinner with his chums.

They met up at the Lorelei Inn, a restaurant straight out of Bavaria with forest-green walls and bucolic paintings of alpine meadows. He knew right off that these were the men he needed to get in with. Hans Winterhalder was close to forty, athletic, with close-clipped hair and a brush mustache along the order of the German führer. "I do recruitment, among other things," he said when he was introduced. Seemed to Thirteen that he spent most of his time eyeballing every woman in the room.

The fellow sitting next to Winterhalder was a different animal altogether. Hermann Schwinn dressed like he'd just stepped out of a Fine and Dandy men's store, but his cold blue eyes had the look of a soldier for hire. "We can't be too careful, you understand?" he said with a slight German accent. "There are plenty of Jew lovers in this town."

When Thirteen asked Schwinn about his job with the Friends, the answer made his blood run cold. "My position is like a priest. It is my job to teach the Nazi system."

Schwinn asked for his papers and he'd produced his military documents and medals. It helped that his father was a general in the Bavarian army before he emigrated. Funny, the only good his father's name had done was get him in with this bunch of lowlifes. They asked about his mother, but he sidestepped that question. She didn't deserve to be dragged into this muck.

"Ever married?" Hans Winterhalder asked as he ogled a waitress with blonde braids and a buxom figure setting a platter of sausages and sauerkraut on the table.

"Came close once," Thirteen lied. "Dodged that bullet."

The men laughed like he figured they would.

And then there was the wife. Thekla Schwinn stopped by the table as they finished the sausages. She was just as well-dressed as her husband, middle thirties, with shiny gold hair and a flirtatious manner that would put most men at ease. Thirteen wasn't fooled. She kept a sharp eye on her husband and everyone else in the room.

After that scrutiny, he put in his application to join. He was just what they were looking for—a veteran of the Great War, angry about the shabby treatment he and his fellow soldiers got at the hands of the US government. And no friend of the Jews, as far as they knew. A week later, his application was approved and he'd taken the oath. His new friends invited him to today's noon meeting at the Alt Heidelberg.

That tied a bow on it.

It started with music, a Wagner march played on a phonograph. Then speakers, including Winterhalder in English and Schwinn in German. Thirteen got the gist of it—Jews conspiring to take over, the "bastardization of the homeland."

"It will not take long to turn the tide of America in our favor, but we must be vigilant," Hermann Schwinn said in his Bavarian-accented German. "There are race traitors who wish to hinder our progress—some even working with Jews. We know who you are, where you work, where your children go to school, your wives and their families." His voice was cold as steel. "Traitors will be shown no mercy. The mission. That is of utmost importance. The mission."

Thirteen felt like he had a rock in his gut.

The Nazis had it all worked out. Anybody working against them would suffer—their jobs. Their wives. Their children.

Made him glad he didn't have family.

The meeting finished up with a recorded speech by none other than Herr Hitler himself. Then everyone threw their arms in the air and barked out *Sieg heils*.

He drove away from the Alt Heidelberg wondering what the world was coming to. He passed by a church, the stained-glass windows reflecting the harsh sunlight. Not for the first time he wondered about God. If he was as good as they said he was, why didn't he stop this evil? Why didn't he rain down fire and brimstone on people like Winterhalder and Schwinn—smite them like he did the Egyptians in the Bible stories he'd read as a kid? It's not like they didn't deserve it. Maybe God had given up on the men he'd created. Maybe he figured they were too far gone to save.

Lita returned to his table with his lunch—a sizzling New York strip, a baked potato, and whatever vegetable was in season in the San Fernando Valley. Today it was a mound of green beans topped with a pat of butter. "Thanks, Lita," he said as she hovered. It wasn't his intent to make her think he was interested, but Frankie knew how to cook a steak and the Emerald Room was close to home.

The steak was tender, the potato fluffy and hot. He ate all the beans, half the steak, and a few bites of the potato. Lita put what was left in a paper bag and he gave her two dollars. Her smile made him wonder if he'd been wrong—maybe it was the two-bit tip and not his good looks that made her glad to see him. Women were hard to figure and he'd stopped trying years ago.

Besides, he didn't need to get caught up with a woman. He needed to tell Lewis what they were up against and Lewis needed to find them another operative. Because the Nazis were gaining strength and had to be stopped.

CHAPTER 10

LIESL

How did I feel about Adolf Hitler?

One of Tess's favorite books was called *Alice's Adventures in Wonderland*, about a girl who fell down a rabbit hole into a nonsensical world. I didn't like it myself. The world Alice explored had no order at all—what with grinning cats and mad hatters and potions. If Alice had any sense at all, she would do all she could to return to the sensible world of her sister and family.

I felt like Alice now, in that upside-down world.

The truth was, I didn't have much of an opinion on the new chancellor of Germany other than what I'd heard from Stella and some of the talk from Fritz. What could Leon Lewis be after? I looked away from his sharp scrutiny to his disorderly office, as if it could give me the answer I sought.

Books jammed on shelves. Piles of the *Los Angeles Times* and the *California Staats-Zeitung*. On a credenza behind the desk, a teetering column of notepads and a framed family photo of the man before me and an equally serious-looking woman, two girls with dark curling hair, one about Tess's age, the other a few years older, standing in front of a stone building with a six-pointed star above the door. A sudden understanding snapped into place.

I glanced back at him quickly. Leon Lewis was Jewish.

The chancellor of Germany didn't like Jews—I knew that—but the newspaper reports didn't agree about Adolf Hitler. Some newspaper headlines told of a man with progressive ideas about rebuilding Germany. They denied the stories about his hatred of Jews—claims fabricated by the Jewish media. *Lügenpresse*, they called it. Lying news. Other reports said Adolf Hitler was truly an anti-Semite, but members of his cabinet would temper his policies. Almost all said the new chancellor was bringing Germany back from the brink of collapse.

I considered my words carefully. "I'm not prejudiced, if that is what concerns you." I had Jewish friends. Stella and the other girls at MGM. Miriam. A jolt of guilt—Miriam had been my friend not long ago.

"I'm glad to know that," Mr. Lewis answered. He waited, his hands steepled in front of his chin.

I decided the truth must do. "To be honest, Mr. Lewis, I have enough to worry about in my own home—my children, my family. I don't pay much attention to what is happening on the other side of the world." He could think what he wanted of me, but I didn't lose sleep over the leadership in Germany. I lost sleep over Steffen's fears, Tess's tantrums. Mutti and Fritz.

"Mrs. Weiss. Let me ask you another question." He went on without my assent. "Are you a woman of faith?"

I felt a jab of discomfort. A woman of faith? I said grace before meals and made sure the children said their prayers each night. But my solitary prayers in the dark of night were not those of faith. They were of confusion and doubt. Did that mean I had no faith?

"I believe in God," I said, and that was the truth. I did not doubt his existence. "I'm a Christian."

He nodded as if he had expected the answer. "I am in need of a woman with courage. And one who has integrity. I believe you have both."

I was not courageous and as for integrity, I had just lied to him. I would describe myself as nothing more than desperate—and uncertain of where he was heading with this strange talk. I took matters in hand. "Mr. Lewis. What job, precisely, do you need me to do?"

He smiled and leaned over his desk toward me. "If you promise to allow me to explain fully—before you give me your answer—I will tell you."

I was suddenly reminded of the Cheshire Cat in Alice's story. I did not want to promise this man anything. Yet I could not let go of the hope of a job—any job. I dipped my head in assent but with reservation.

What he said then was utterly unexpected.

"What I am looking for—what I desperately need, Mrs. Weiss—is a spy."

For the next ten minutes, Leon Lewis proceeded to tell me what he wished for me to do for him, and I realized that I had, indeed, tumbled down a rabbit hole. Only my promise to hear him out kept me from standing, bidding him good day, and walking out the door.

"You are about to say it is a preposterous notion," he said finally. "And perhaps it is."

Preposterous, yes. And ridiculous. Absurd. Unbelievable. Yet he looked so reasonable. So earnest.

"Mr. Lewis, forgive me," I said. Perhaps I had misunderstood. "You think . . ." I tried again. "You believe that these National Socialists—"

"Nazis, they call themselves."

I started over. "You believe Nazis are coming from Germany to Los Angeles? That they will try to . . . take over our country? Do to Jews here what they might be doing there?"

If what was happening in Germany was true—and I wasn't certain it was—of course I felt terrible for those people. The Jews. But that the German government was sending their people to Los Angeles to set up— what did he call them? Hitler cells? In Germantown? My own neighborhood? Despite what Fritz had sometimes said, no one wanted to actually hurt Jewish people, even if they didn't like them. Not in this country.

Mr. Lewis could see my disbelief but was undeterred. "Believe me,

Mrs. Weiss, this hatred has come into Los Angeles. And Adolf Hitler will not stop there."

I felt a rising alarm and not toward this Adolf Hitler. Wasn't there a word for people who believed someone was out to destroy them? Paranoia, I thought they called it.

Leon Lewis leaned forward and continued. "It's not just the Jews they are against—it's Catholics and Negroes, anyone who is not like them."

A chill of unease ran through me at the fervent light in his eyes. "And you have spies—"

"Operatives, I call them. Not many."

"—who pretend to be these . . . Hitlerites. Is that correct?"

He nodded. "German-speaking and Christian, such as yourself."

"If they—the Nazis—are the threat you imagine," I interjected, "why not tell the police?"

He shook his head as if I were a slow student. "At least some of the police in this city are supporters of Hitler. The others won't believe me until I can give them proof of illegal activity. To that end, I need information. Evidence to present to the authorities, proof of these illegal—treasonous—activities."

Treason. Was this another case of good Germans being called traitors, just like during the Great War?

I had heard enough. I stood. It was time to leave Leon Lewis and this upside-down world. I needed a steady paycheck, not a preposterous crusade. I should not have come here; perhaps Mrs. Porter had known that all along. No help would be coming from her agency when she found out I had deceived her. Despair was like a lead weight under my ribs. "Mr. Lewis, I wish you well. I'm sorry for taking up your time."

"Mrs. Weiss, please." He jumped to his feet and I had a sudden jolt of fear. Would he try to stop me? But he did not come any closer. "Just one more thing, if it might prompt you to reconsider."

I looked at his earnest face and again, a remembrance of Vati.

"I can promise you thirty dollars a week."

CHAPTER 11

AGENT THIRTEEN

Thirteen spent the rest of the day and part of the night keeping an eye on the Schwinns. He didn't learn much, except that Hermann and Thekla Schwinn had a late dinner and Hermann's driving after they left the Lorelei suggested he'd had too much schnapps.

Back at the Biltmore, he stopped in at the front desk for his key. "How was she?" he asked Jimmy, a clerk he'd come to know pretty well since he moved back to California.

"Good as gold." Jimmy gave him his room key and two squares of Biltmore stationery. With a soft click of nails on travertine and a low woof, a silver-muzzled greyhound rounded the desk. Thirteen stroked her smooth head and silky ears before passing a dollar bill to Jimmy. They climbed the five flights of stairs and the dog waited patiently while he unlocked the door to his room.

After he relocked the door and turned the dead bolt, he emptied the brown bag of steak and potato onto a plate and set it on the floor. "Have at it."

The dog set to work on the lunch scraps and Thirteen poured himself two fingers of Scotch. Prohibition was as good as over and liquor was easy to get, not that he'd had any trouble when it was illegal. He toed off his wing tips, sank down on the sleek leather divan, and pulled the telephone messages from his pocket. The first was from Eva—*Call me, urgent.* He crumpled the paper and tossed it in the trash can. The second was from L1—Lewis's code name—with just a telephone number. He finished his drink and picked up the telephone receiver from the side table. He gave the number to the switchboard operator.

"Thirteen here," he said in greeting.

"Thank you for calling," Lewis said. "What do you have?"

Plenty, but he'd start with the good news. "I'm in. Just like you said. A card-carrying Nazi."

"Congratulations," Lewis said dryly and Thirteen almost smiled. It wasn't funny, but you had to take your humor where you could get it. He'd learned that in the war.

"They said they usually spend more time investigating a new recruit, but considering my history, they made it quick."

"You told them about Monterey?" Lewis asked.

"Some of it." Thirteen shifted, suddenly uncomfortable on the leather cushion. Lewis listened to his report on the Alt Heidelberg building, where his new friends had given him a tour after he took the Nazi oath. It was nothing much on the outside, a squat brick building set on a corner next to a barbershop. A mediocre restaurant, meeting rooms, a hall for bigger gatherings. The Aryan Bookstore. "The second floor is where the offices are," Thirteen went on. The headquarters of the Friends of New Germany was a nice setup. Fancy furniture, a big office for Hermann Schwinn with a set of file drawers Thirteen would give his big toe to get a look at.

"So," Lewis said thoughtfully, "they are set up for more than dances."

"That's not the half of it," Thirteen said. He was getting to the bad news. "They brought me to the basement." He told Lewis what he'd seen. A clean, well-lit space. Rows of beds and a mess hall. Nicer than anything he'd seen in the army. And the men—defeated men glad to have a place to rest their heads. "They're taking in veterans."

Sure, it sounded charitable and Winterhalder had played it up. "Isn't it wonderful?" he'd said, showing Thirteen stores of clean shirts and trousers, even shoes in various sizes. "You veterans are getting a raw deal from Roosevelt," Winterhalder said like a broken phonograph while the grateful men thanked him for the bed and chow.

Winterhalder wasn't wrong about that. The plight of veterans was what had brought Thirteen back to Los Angeles. These men had gone to war for their country, done their duty. Those who were lucky came home like he had. But plenty of them were broken. Physically, mentally, and—if you believed in that sort of thing—spiritually. The country they'd served had turned its back on them. Benefits cut, no place to live, and the lines at soup kitchens stretched for blocks. Men were desperate and hungry and most of all, they were angry.

And here was the Friends of New Germany, giving them charity and someone to blame.

"What you're saying," Lewis spoke carefully, "is that the Friends of New Germany are raising an army." The line crackled between them. "Where are they getting the money?"

Thirteen wondered the same. The barracks in the basement, the food and clothes. None of it was free. He'd been as casual as he could when he'd asked Winterhalder how he was funding the operation. "We have a plan," he'd said.

"I heard some about the Stadtverband, the alliance that oversees all the German American groups in Southern California. The alliance has money—a lot of money—and land. If the Friends can take over the executive board, they can get their hands on both."

"Can they do it?" Lewis asked. Thirteen could almost hear his mind turning over the implications. With funds, the Hitlerites could go from a rumble to a roar just like they did in the fatherland.

"The board election is coming up. They need to get one of their men in the top spot. Get access to the coffers."

Thirteen had learned from listening in that Schwinn had some kind of deal going with Max Socha, a man whose prospects for election were iffy against the more popular John Vieth, whom the old-guard Germans supported. Unless he missed his guess, Schwinn and his thugs were planning on rigging the election.

Lewis changed the subject abruptly. "I'm close to getting an operative inside the Alt Heidelberg. And we need to keep you situated." Thirteen wondered at the acrobatics that went on in the man's head. He always seemed to be one step ahead of Thirteen's reports, as if Thirteen was confirming something he already knew. Thirteen reminded himself never to play chess with Lewis.

"I'm putting in time in the basement, helping out with the chow and such," he said. The work made him look good to Schwinn and he didn't mind talking to the veterans. "And I'm supposed to pick up Schwinn and Winterhalder tomorrow, early," he said. "They have something going on out in the hills." A Sunday drive, Schwinn had told him with a wink. He didn't think they'd be going to church.

"Let's meet Monday," Lewis said. "You can tell me about it."

Lewis told him the place and Thirteen hung up the telephone. He pushed himself from the divan and went to the bedroom, not bothering with the light but opening the window. Gasoline fumes mixed with the scent of the eucalyptus trees lining the brick-paved walks of Pershing Square across from the Biltmore. The hum of autos and laughter of women floated up from the sidewalk. People going about their daily lives.

He looked to the horizon, the twinkling expanse of Los Angeles. Out there in the dark, the likes of Hermann Schwinn and the National Socialists were growing in number—all the more dangerous because nobody thought them a threat. Nobody but Leon Lewis. He hoped Lewis was right about getting someone inside at the Alt Heidelberg. Whoever it was, he better take care.

Thirteen shrugged out of his jacket, stripped off his silk tie—never got used to something around his neck—and threw his shirt on the floor. The dog stood beside the bed, waiting.

"Okay, girl," he said. She jumped up on one side of the huge bed, turned in a circle, and lay down.

He stretched out, turned on his side, then his back. Tried to get comfortable.

"Pray we can get more people on our side," Lewis had said just before he hung up.

The thing was, Thirteen didn't believe in prayer—Jewish, Christian, or otherwise. He believed in being able to sleep at night. Which meant standing against the bullies of the world, not standing beside them.

He'd tried things the other way and it had just about killed him.

CHAPTER 12

LIESL

I dressed carefully for my first day of work as a spy. The whole business seemed even more absurd in the bright light of a Monday morning.

I slipped into a claret-red rayon blouse with a shawl collar and pulled on a fitted skirt in russet wool. I had agreed to Leon Lewis's offer not because I believed his wild theories against my neighbors, but because I needed the money. I pulled on my best stockings and straightened the seams. Tess would start first grade today and had been up before dawn in excitement. I would just have time to walk her to Los Angeles Consolidated #14 before catching the trolley to my new job. My apprehension grew as I smoothed the finger waves I'd set in my hair last night.

Why had I agreed to this?

Mr. Lewis had seen my disbelief when he mentioned the pay. "You wonder how I can afford such a salary. Am I right?"

I agreed that he was and sat down on the tufted chair in front of his desk. For thirty dollars a week, I could hear him out.

He took his seat and leaned forward. "Who do you think pays me for this work?"

Someone with money. Someone who believed his claim that the German people were a threat. "A Jewish organization?"

"Yes," he said with approval. "Local Jewish interests have raised money for this operation."

Local Jewish interests was just another name for the studios. Mr. Mayer and Irving Thalberg. Adolph Zukor and the Warner brothers. The same people who fired me due to budget constraints but could afford to spy on my German neighbors. And yet, why should I not take their money? Did not they, of all people, owe me something?

"Why me?" I asked. Surely he could find some of his own people—someone who actually believed his preposterous notion?

"I believe I am a good judge of character," Mr. Lewis answered. "And the work itself cannot be carried out by Jews."

Of course it could not, I realized. Germans who followed the new chancellor—if, indeed, Mr. Lewis's fears were to be believed—would never trust someone who looked like Miriam or Stella. True Germans were tall, blond, and blue-eyed. True Germans looked like me.

"Mrs. Weiss, let me assure you that this is hardly a secret," he said. "Last month, you may recall, no less than three thousand people came to a rally to decry the Nazi influences both at home and abroad."

I remembered something about a Jewish gathering, a short article in the newspaper, but hadn't taken much notice. Jewish concerns were hardly my own when I was barely making ends meet.

I had not yet agreed to work for him, but Leon Lewis began his instruction nonetheless. "You must not speak of this work to your family and friends, do you understand?" That would not be difficult. Mutti would think me as crazy as a cuckoo. "You may very well be reporting on people you know, even your own neighbors."

I did not fear that I would be required to turn in my neighbors. The German families I knew—the ones I'd known for years—perhaps weren't friendly with their Jewish neighbors, but they weren't traitors to America. My fear was that this man could not really pay me thirty dollars a week. And to do what?

As if he followed my thoughts, he switched topics. "You will work in a volunteer position at the Friends of New Germany."

The Friends of New Germany. I'd never heard of such a group. "But how will I—?"

"I will arrange it," he said quickly. "A woman named Thekla Schwinn will contact you. Her husband is the new head of the Los Angeles branch and they are in need of a secretary."

"Does Thekla Schwinn work for you also?" I asked.

"She does not." His voice was firm. "You are to take great care to not let them know of me."

This was sounding ever more doubtful. "And the other . . . operatives?" I had trouble using the word. "Who are they?"

He shook his head. "I keep no written records of my people. Only in here—" he pointed to his temple—"and none know of each other, for extra safety."

I dismissed a shiver of worry at precautions that seemed outlandish. "I'm just a secretary. I don't know how to spy."

"Exactly," he answered. "And why you are ideal for this position. No connection to me whatsoever and every reason to work for a German social club."

Ideal? I did not agree. And yet he seemed so sure.

"We will speak by telephone and correspond by mail or telegram when necessary. You shall receive your pay in this post office box each Friday." He gave me a key with a tag attached to it. "Check it every day and mail your reports to this box number," he said, passing me a paper with a number written upon it. "One other matter," he continued. "All my operatives go by code names. We'll need one for you."

Had I agreed to his scheme? I supposed I had. But a code name? "Surely that is not needed."

"A precaution I feel is justified, Mrs. Weiss," he said. "In case we are overheard or our correspondence is intercepted." He gazed at me, tapping his lower lip in thought. "How does Edelweiss suit?"

Edelweiss. The flower of Austria? It was ridiculous. But at MGM I'd been called "kitten" and "sweetheart"—not to mention the Heartbreak Hun—for far less than thirty dollars a week. I still did not understand. "What am I to do—at the Friends of New Germany?" I asked him. Not the secretary part, I knew how to do that. But how did one go about being a spy?

"It is quite simple," Lewis said in his earnest way. "Gain their trust. You are a good Aryan woman, an efficient secretary. Fired from MGM by Jews because you are a Gentile." He stood and paced to the window and then back. "You are angry at what you see happening in the studios. The immorality of the films, the loss of the American way. You worry for your children." He raised his brows.

"So I am to lie?" Lying was wrong, was it not?

He looked at me with sympathy. "There is every reason to believe these people are plotting treason against our country."

Treason was what they accused us of in the Great War, even as Vati signed on to fight for his country. "And if they aren't?" What if Leon Lewis was concocting this threat from nothing? If this was another attempt to turn against German Americans?

He did not take offense at my doubt. "If there is nothing to report, then we shall all be glad. Me, most of all." He scribbled on a scrap of paper. "If you must, call me at this number. My code name is L1. Take great care, Edelweiss."

I found myself on the trolley with a job and the distinct sense of waking from a disturbing dream. Yes, I loved my country, but also I loved my German heritage. Would I be forced to choose between the two?

That evening, Mrs. Thekla Schwinn telephoned me just as Mr. Lewis had said. "We're in such dire need, Mrs. Weiss." Her voice was pleasant, with a lilting Bavarian accent. "We'd be so grateful."

I agreed to meet her at the Alt Heidelberg—just two trolley stops from home—on Monday morning. Mutti was so relieved when I told her I found a job, she didn't ask questions. A knot of worry lodged in my chest as I went to bed that night. When I woke in the dark, walked through my home, and touched my sleeping children for reassurance, my questions to God multiplied, as did my doubts. Was I doing right by them, by Mutti? Was working for someone like Leon Lewis a mistake?

Now, with the thin light of morning streaming into my bedroom window, I positioned a crimson wool beret over my blonde curls and wondered if I was a fool or perhaps only desperate. I applied a subdued rose lipstick and a few pats of powder to my nose and took a last look in the mirror of the chifforobe. The woman looking back at me with her blue eyes and fair hair looked perfectly Aryan. "Why in heaven's name am I doing this?" I asked myself.

"For thirty dollars a week," the woman in the mirror replied.

I pulled open the drawer of the chifforobe. The silver frame of our wedding photograph glinted in the morning sunlight. If Tomas were here, what would he tell me to do? The knot in my chest tightened. If Tomas were here, I would not be in this predicament.

I shut the drawer and left both Tomas and my reflection behind.

Downstairs, all was chaos and disorder.

Mutti cut slices of our last loaf of bread, her back to Steffen, who teetered on a kitchen chair, stretching for the jam jar on top of the icebox. Tess rummaged through the hall table, tossing papers and pencils to the floor willy-nilly. The cat was on the table licking the butter, while Fritz sat reading a newspaper, oblivious to the tumult around him.

"Steffen, sit!" I said sharply, scooping up Chester and tossing him out the back door. Tess pulled a packet of colored crayons from the back of the drawer with a yelp of victory and stowed them in her schoolbag. "Get your sweater, Tess. We must go."

Tess raced up the stairs to her room. I gathered the strewn pencils and paper and stowed them back in the drawer, then leveled a gaze at Mutti. "You must rest today," I said with little hope that she would comply. "And soak your hands this afternoon." We'd be able to get her injections by next week, if all went to plan.

"Fiddlesticks. I'm not some invalid," she said and pushed two paper bags in my hand. My lunch and one for Tess. "Go now. You'll be late."

Tess clattered back down the stairs with Mr. Dog. "You almost forgot," she accused Fritz.

Fritz took Mr. Dog on his lap and pretended to feed him a spoonful of oatmeal, complete with slurping noises. "I have a hiding place you'll never find."

Steffen suddenly realized what my hat and handbag meant and scrambled from his chair. He threw his arms around my legs and blinked eyes bright with tears.

I stooped down and sketched the heart on his forehead, my own heart hurting for my little boy. But I must work. "I'll always come back," I reminded him.

He nodded silently.

"Look after Oma and Chester," I said with a cheerfulness I did not feel. "And only one cookie with lunch."

Mutti winked at Steffen and he gave her a watery smile. Mutti was a pushover when it came to handing out extra cookies. If it made him happy, I didn't blame her.

I walked out the door with Tess and less than ten minutes to catch the trolley. The morning air was cool on my bare arms but with the promise of September heat in the cloudless blue sky. I quickened my steps. Tess didn't start in with her usual chatter. In fact, her little face was drawn as she glanced at the Stahrs' house.

"What is it, sweetheart?" I asked, but I knew. Last year on this day, we had walked to school with Miriam and Frieda.

She slipped a hand into mine, unusual enough to increase my concern.

Tess had always been different from other girls. Defiant and headstrong—much like her Oma—but also as fragile as spun sugar. She did not look for affection, not even as a baby. When other girls played with dolls, she spent her playtimes turning the sitting room into a castle or the backyard into a jungle kingdom, dictating her imaginative games to Steffen and Frieda, who were glad to do her will. In the past year, she had turned inward. She sulked easily and talked back to me and to Mutti. And there was the problem with Frieda. What was I to do with my bewildering daughter?

Don't fret so much, Tomas had often said. But how could I not? Both of my children were unhappy—Tess showed it in moodiness and tantrums, Steffen by clinging and tears. How was I failing them?

Now, as we approached Consolidated #14, a group of first-grade girls sat on the concrete steps—all blonde braids and pink cheeks, pastel dresses with matching sweaters. Except for Frieda Stahr, who was alone beside the tetherball pole in a navy pinafore and white blouse, dark hair, skin bordering on olive.

"Tess!" Hildy Grundbacher called out. "Come sit with us." Margot Scholz scooted over to make room for her. "We've been waiting for you."

Tess's steps slowed and her hand dropped from mine.

The girls looked pleased to see her and welcoming. Was that not good? Tess glanced toward Frieda. Frieda turned away. Tess's face pinched in distress. My chest squeezed in response. Had I done wrong by my little girl? I leaned down to kiss Tess goodbye. She pulled away before my lips met her cheek and walked toward the group of girls—without a word and without a backward glance.

CHAPTER 13

I checked my wristwatch and quickened my steps to the trolley stop. If I missed it, I would be late. My worry for Tess kept pace with my quick strides.

Tomas, if you were here, our little girl would not be suffering so.

It was almost two years ago that Friday evening when Tomas did not come home from work. At first, I was unconcerned. I telephoned the Germantown station where he was a patrol officer. He was not there. Then I was angry. Had he gone to a beer hall with Mickey? Without even the courtesy of letting me know he would not be home for dinner? He had promised not to do such a thing again.

When the children were in bed and the clock struck midnight, I began to worry. We had quarreled that very morning. "Let's get out of California, Liesl," he'd said. "Oregon is the place, or further north to Seattle. An adventure." But I did not want adventure. I wanted order and security for our children. Mutti and Fritz close by. Was he still angry I had opposed such a ridiculous idea?

When he was not home the next morning, I panicked.

He was hurt somewhere—injured or even kidnapped. The officers at the Germantown station looked at me with sympathy and filled out forms. I went to every friend and neighbor, telephoned all our acquaintances. Miriam watched the children while I searched for Tomas and desperation welled within me. *Tomas, where are you?*

Two days after Tomas disappeared, Mickey O'Neil and Captain Hynes knocked on my door. Mickey was second-generation Irish, with red hair and a brogue. He'd been Tomas's partner since he got on with the force. A nice enough man, but not a family man.

"Can we come in, Mrs. Weiss?" Captain Hynes asked when I opened the door. He was in his fifties, a sturdy man with thinning hair and a ruddy hatchet-sharp face. My stomach sank to my knees. Had they come with bad news? Was my husband dead?

They sat down on the divan and told me the truth.

I refused to believe it. Not at first.

Mickey twisted his cap in his hands and didn't meet my eyes. "It's happening a lot, Mrs. Weiss. What with the way things are."

No. Tomas wasn't like those men who lost hope and walked out on their families. "The poor man's divorce," they called it in the newspapers. He wouldn't. He loved us. Didn't he?

"I don't want to tell tales." Mickey pulled at his collar. "He said a few things. Talked about starting over somewhere else. Florida, maybe Oregon."

My disbelief turned to a piercing pain. I couldn't breathe. Not the father of my children. He would not do such a thing.

"Mrs. Weiss," Captain Hynes said sadly. "I'm sorry. I didn't want to believe it either, but from what Mickey says . . ."

"Some men . . ." Mickey looked at his hands. "Family life isn't for them, you know?"

Still I didn't believe it. Until the next day, when I got the money in the mail. It was in a plain envelope with my name on it and our post office box, neatly printed. I counted it. The exact amount of his usual weekly pay. A crumpled piece of paper with two words—*I'm sorry.* Tomas had left us, and this was his goodbye.

I went to Miriam. She didn't believe it either. "He loved you and the children, Liesl," she said. "He wouldn't leave." I told her about the money. She held me in her arms as I wept out my heartbreak.

Tess asked after her father with increasing anxiety as the days turned into weeks. Perhaps that was why, when Tess found a tiny gray kitten abandoned in the park, I relented—from grief or exhaustion I knew not which. For a while, the excitement of the kitten—which Tess named Cheshire Cat but shortened to Chester—was a happy distraction. Tess and Frieda quickly decided the pet would be shared between our two households. I forbade a cat indoors, but Mutti—as I should have known—did not enforce my rule. Soon Chester was more often inside than out and I gave up the battle.

But the kitten did not assuage Tess's questions for long. I finally told her a half-truth. "Your father went on a long journey."

"Like in Cinderella?" Tess asked.

"Not exactly, but yes."

Did I do right to let her keep hoping? Yet I still hoped. I hoped with each ring of the telephone, each knock on the door. Every blond, broad-shouldered man I caught sight of from the trolley. Weeks turned into months and my hope was in vain. First Mutti, then our neighbors realized that Tomas was not going to return. It was not spoken of. But it was there in every look, every whisper behind my back.

It was then that I began to wake in the night, check each room of my home as if Tomas would somehow be there in the dark where he was not in the light. My prayers became cries of distress to God. Questions begging for answers. If I had been wrong about Tomas—whose love I'd believed to be bedrock until it crumbled out from under me—what else had I misjudged?

In the light of day, I locked away the aching questions of my soul and addressed more practical concerns. I needed to provide for my children. Mrs. Adler rehired me as a stenographer for fifteen dollars a week. Mutti moved in with us, and Fritz also. With her war widow pension and precious little help from Fritz, we managed.

When autumn came that year, we had our heads above water and Tess began school.

I expected Tess to thrive in kindergarten. On the first day, she and Frieda walked hand in hand—Tess bouncing with expectation, Frieda more subdued. Miriam and I watched them push through the heavy doors of Consolidated #14 with apprehension and pride. We'd turned to each other and Miriam had pulled me into her embrace. I was not one to show affection in that way, but I let her do so. "They'll do fine," Miriam said. "They have each other."

But Tess was not fine. Two weeks into the year, Mrs. Eberheart telephoned me for a meeting. I arrived at the school and settled into a child-size chair across from Mrs. Eberheart's desk. The kindergarten teacher was thin and angular, with thick auburn hair pinned in a traditional German braid. Her sharp green eyes regarded me as if she were administering a test and expected me to fail. She folded her hands on the desk. "Tess doesn't play well with the other girls."

That, I had not expected and did not believe.

"She tends toward flights of fancy and a certain . . . bossiness," Mrs. Eberheart said primly. "The other girls shy away from her."

I bristled but remained polite. It would not help Tess if I antagonized her teacher. "What about Frieda Stahr?" They'd been friends all their lives. Surely they played together at school?

"Of course," Mrs. Eberheart said, her lips flickering down. "She and the Stahr girl are like two peas. But you must admit it's not healthy, having only Frieda Stahr as her friend. Socialization is very important at this age, as you know," Mrs. Eberheart said in a meaningful way.

I did not know. My schooling had been a haphazard affair. I'd gone to this very school in Germantown, but after Vati died, after we lost our home, I did not return to Consolidated #14. I earned my high school diploma between helping Mutti and chasing Fritz around the ever-expanding MGM lot. Fritz—when we could make him do so—took his lessons with the child actors in the makeshift schoolroom behind the commissary.

I had no experience with girls who jumped rope at recess or met at the soda fountain after school. Instead, I helped Mutti fit dresses for Mabel Normand—who was always kind, despite her many scandals—and sew costumes for Will Rogers, who taught me how to ride a horse and shoot a gun between takes. Lottie kept us fed and Gus kept Fritz out of trouble, but I longed for a true friend of the heart. I did not find one until I met Miriam.

Mrs. Eberheart looked pointedly at the black-and-white clock ticking loudly over the door. "It is your duty to help your daughter make friends like herself, Mrs. Weiss. I'm sure you'll find a way."

I arrived at the Alt Heidelberg at precisely 8:00. I tucked my worries over Tess's sullenness and Steffen's distress away and replaced them with qualms about my task for Leon Lewis.

The Alt Heidelberg was as familiar to me as Grundbacher's grocery and Helm's wurst shop. As a child, I'd come here for *Volkstanz* and German grammar lessons. Then came the war, and our heritage was something to hide. The Alt Heidelberg was closed up, a testament to the distrust aimed at the German customs I cherished.

"Liesl Weiss?" A woman of about thirty stepped from under the shade of the awning. She had marcelled platinum waves and a narrow face. Her wool suit of marigold yellow with a matching cloche hat edged in velvet fit her trim frame with tailored perfection. She did not look like someone with a nefarious plan against America. "Pleased to meet you. I'm Thekla Schwinn." I shook her hand. She raised brows markedly darker than her hair toward the doorway. "Shall we?"

As we stepped into the building, memories of childhood—when all was good and Vati was with us—gave me an unexpected lift of cheer. A small vestibule with worn damask chairs, dark-green wallpaper. The restaurant that smelled of sausage and caraway seeds.

Thekla Schwinn's fashionable two-toned pumps snapped against the linoleum floor as she set a quick pace through the first-floor hallway. "Mrs. Porter spoke highly of you," she said over her shoulder. "And we are in such need of someone to help here. With my own housework and my committee duties, I just can't keep up."

Mrs. Porter had recommended me? I filed that away to consider later.

At the foot of the stairway, we passed a bookstore. It had been called the Deutsches Buchmarkt when last I was here, but a new sign, brightly painted in red and black, proclaimed it the *Aryan Bookstore*. I glanced inside to see a selection of German newspapers—*Der Stürmer* and the local *California Staats-Zeitung*—a few serious-looking books, and displays of pamphlets.

"The bookstore is recently under new ownership," she said, following my gaze. "Paul Themlitz. A wonderful man, very active with the Friends."

I climbed the stairs behind Mrs. Schwinn. The black, red, and yellow flag of the Weimar Republic hung from the second-floor balcony. Next to it, a red-and-white flag with a black swastika, the emblem of the new National Socialist leadership in Germany.

Mrs. Schwinn stopped beneath the flags and tipped her head to the side as if considering her words. "Mrs. Porter told you this is an unpaid position, did she not, Mrs. Weiss?"

"She did mention it," I said.

She put a gentle hand on my arm and went on brightly. "You are a widow with children, is that correct?"

I glanced down at my wedding ring. "My husband has been gone for almost two years." Not quite a lie, but close enough to pinch my conscience.

Her eyes softened. "I'm so sorry, my dear. I can understand how you must be looking for a way to fill your days."

Fill my days? I had more than enough tasks to fill my days, but I just smiled. She clearly imagined my husband had left me well-off. How long before the gossip of Germantown reached the ears of Thekla Schwinn and enlightened her of my overdue bills and late rent?

"Hermann and I were not blessed with children." She looked away and I felt a stab of pity for the lovely woman. "But you'll find us very much a family here, Mrs. Weiss." She set her immaculate white-gloved hand on my arm and looked at me sincerely. It occurred to me that anyone looking at us together might guess we were sisters. "I can tell you are a credit to your country." I assumed that she meant America, but with the flags hanging above us, perhaps she meant Germany.

"Please, call me Liesl."

My untruthfulness weighed upon me as we reached the top of the stairs. She seemed a kind woman and I was lying to her. Suddenly the thought of Leon Lewis was distasteful. He had said terrible things about this woman and did not even know her. I would give this woman the benefit of the doubt, even if he would not.

Thekla opened a door and motioned me to precede her. "Here we are," she sang out.

I stepped into a room that smelled of fresh paint and lemon wood polish. Tall windows, sky-blue walls, and white wainscot. A large desk with a telephone set and a new-model typewriter. Beyond the desk, a comfortable waiting area with two armchairs of pale-green satin, a matching divan, and a low, polished walnut table strewn with magazines and newspapers.

Two men stood politely as we entered. The one nearest me stepped forward eagerly. He was solidly built with a smooth-shaven, classically handsome face. His hair was streaked honey gold and combed severely off his high forehead, showing his straight Roman nose and sharp cheekbones to best advantage. A narrow blond mustache outlined full lips most women would envy.

Thekla motioned to him. "Liesl, this is my husband, Hermann Schwinn. He is general secretary of the Friends here in Los Angeles."

Mr. Schwinn made a small, formal bow and reached for my hand. *"Sehr erfreut,* Frau Weiss."* He bestowed a kiss on my glove. He was as charming as his wife and they made an attractive couple.

Thekla turned to the second man. "And here is Mr. Paul Themlitz, the bookstore owner I told you about."

Paul Themlitz was six inches shorter than Hermann Schwinn, with a broad face and protruding eyes. He was close to fifty, with wisps of salt-and-pepper hair and a sliver of a mustache over a wide mouth. He clasped my outstretched hand firmly. "Good to meet you, my dear. The Lord has brought us the help we prayed for."

I smiled at Mr. Themlitz with another crimp of guilt for deceiving a devoted Christian. I was not doing the Lord's work, but Leon Lewis's.

"Before we talk about your duties here, Liesl . . ." Hermann sat down in one satin armchair and motioned to the other. I perched upon it. "I have a few questions." Thekla settled herself in the desk chair and Paul Themlitz lowered himself to the divan with an expression of polite interest.

A knot of alarm tightened in my chest. "Of course." This was the moment I would have to relate the fabricated story from Mr. Lewis I'd been rehearsing in my head.

"You came highly recommended, Mrs. Weiss," Hermann Schwinn said. "We were told—in confidence of course—about how unfairly you were treated at MGM." He frowned and shook his head. "We needn't talk about that terrible business. But if you don't mind, please do tell us a little about your family."

This was not unusual for an employer to ask of a woman my age who would normally be home with her children. I swallowed and began, "I have two children, a boy and a girl. My husband—"

"Yes, of course," Hermann interrupted. "Your mother and father, I mean, were they both German?"

"Oh!" I was taken aback but told them Mutti and Vati had come from Germany over thirty years ago. Both from near Berlin. "They met on the boat and were married in New York, then made their way to California by train. Vati was trained in camerawork, Mutti a seamstress."

"Wonderful," Mr. Schwinn said, glancing at Paul Themlitz. "And your grandparents? Were they natives of Germany?"

An unusual question but reasonable—we were in a German social club, after all. I answered easily that my ancestors had been in the same small town for generations.

Mr. Schwinn gave a brisk nod to his wife. "I believe you'll do very well here, Liesl."

Was the interview over? Thekla looked pleased, as did the jovial Mr. Themlitz. "Thank you, Mr. Schwinn."

"And please do call me Hermann," he said with a smile that crinkled the corners of his ice-blue eyes. "We're all good friends here."

CHAPTER 14

LIESL

I settled into my work at the Friends of New Germany, immediately at ease with the familiar tasks and polite company. Thekla asked after the children each morning and often complimented me on my attire. Friendly, but not a friend. Not like Stella . . . or Miriam.

I had only myself to blame for the loss of Miriam's friendship.

Two weeks after my talk with Mrs. Eberheart about Tess, Gertrud Grundbacher had telephoned. "I'm starting a mother's group for the kindergarten class," she enthused. "Everyone's invited."

Everyone, of course, did not include Miriam.

I should have refused the invitation, but Mrs. Eberheart's pointed notes about Tess's behavior at school continued. Tess was acting up at home, throwing tantrums and defying Mutti. I was worried for her and increasingly uncertain that I was doing right for my children. Was it not my duty to help her make friends?

I went the next Saturday to the three-story brick house next to the grocery store. Gertrud, an imposing woman with a confident air, greeted me effusively. She wore a linen suit of lemon yellow, her brimmed straw hat weighed down with silk daffodils. Thickly applied coral lipstick did nothing for her pinkish skin.

"Hildy," Gertrud said to her daughter in a voice like sugar syrup, "take Tess back to the tea party." Hildy complied obediently. I gave Tess an encouraging smile as she followed Hildy outside.

Silka Scholz, whose husband owned Scholz's Soda Shop and Pharmacy, passed a plate of pfeffernuss and continued a conversation with half a dozen other women from Germantown. "Of course," she said, "we need to take care that the neighborhood remains the family-friendly gem that it is now." She was a fluttery woman of about thirty with mouse-brown hair styled in fluffy curls. Her ruffled day dress perfectly matched her pale-blue eyes.

"Surely Karl is trying to keep the undesirables out of the area—" Gertrud took up the discussion with a pointed look at Neele Weber—"but we know how hard it can be."

Neele sipped her coffee and remained silent. I didn't know her well, even though she'd lived in Germantown for several years. She was perhaps twenty-nine, with a freckled complexion and three rowdy young boys who were chasing each other in a game of tag outside. Her husband, Karl, was almost twenty years older and a veteran of the Great War. He owned several houses in the neighborhood—including my own and the Stahrs'—but unlike Gertrud and Silka, Neele didn't wear her wealth like a fancy hat for all to admire.

Gertrud passed me a delicate cup and saucer. "Part of our job as parents is to protect our children." She gave me a knowing look. "I don't know how you manage it, Liesl. I'd be so concerned about the germs."

I did not react, but I knew precisely what she meant. The Spanish flu had left in its wake a fear of germs that dominated women's magazine articles and compelled housewives to vigilance. However, the germs Gertrud and Silka referred to were not those of influenza but of Miriam Stahr and her family.

Silka put down her cup with a delicate shudder. "It keeps me up at night, worrying about those people."

I sipped the bitter coffee. Miriam's home might be cluttered, but it was clean. And Yitzak took better care of his lawn and hedges than

Fritz did of ours. Still, as a guest, it would not be proper to argue with my hostess.

Conversation turned to discussion of Mrs. Eberheart—*isn't she a dear?*—and her methods, the most advanced in child development. I kept one ear attuned to the discussion and one eye on Tess in the backyard. She seemed to be getting along well with Hildy and Margot, which was a great relief. To that end, I found myself assuring Gertrud that I would return the following month.

When we left, Margot and Hildy waved and called out goodbyes and see-you-at-schools. Tess was quiet but seemed to have enjoyed the other girls' company.

That night, I listened to Tess and Steffen say their prayers, then tucked Tess into bed. She regarded me with a wrinkle of worry between her pale-blonde brows. "Mutti, does Jesus have germs?"

I had heard many surprising things from Tess, but this went to the top of the list. "Why do you ask that, sweetheart?"

She toyed with Mr. Dog's ears. "Jesus was Jewish, wasn't he? It says it in the Bible and we learned that at Sunday school."

I frowned. What was this about? "Yes, he was."

"And Hildy says that Jews are dirty and have germs."

I pulled the covers up to her chin and kissed her brow, wondering how to talk to a child about people like the Grundbachers. Was she not coping with enough, with her father disappeared and her mother at work all day? Talk like that could wait until she was older. I tucked Mr. Dog into bed beside her. "Jesus did not have germs. Go to sleep now."

Steffen burrowed into my pillow and pulled the blanket over his head. I tickled him until he came out from under the quilt, breathless and giggling. He wrapped his arms tight around my neck and pulled me down to lie beside him. He kissed me somewhere near my left eye. Steffen might be stingy with his words, but his affection was generous.

In that moment, I forgot about the bills, the Grundbachers and the Scholzes, and germs. I had the two people I loved the most in the world beside me, these children who held my heart. That was enough. Surely all the other matters would work themselves out.

Two days later, Tess told me she was part of a special club at school. I had endured a long day at MGM and Mutti had greeted me with complaints. I sent her to soak her hands in cold water, put on my apron, and began to cook a dinner of macaroni and frankfurters.

"Hildy and Margot started it," Tess went on. "We meet in the corner of the playground and tell secrets and play pretend."

"That sounds like fun." I sliced a frankfurter and wondered if Fritz would be with us for dinner.

"It is." Tess snuck a piece of macaroni into her mouth. "But boys can't be in the club, and neither can Frieda."

I looked up then, but she did not meet my eyes. "Why not Frieda?"

Tess shrugged. "They just said she can't. Frieda said she didn't mind."

I should not have remained silent. I should have spoken with Miriam. But I did not. It was not long after that I betrayed Miriam myself, and then it was too late to make amends.

CHAPTER 15

AGENT THIRTEEN

Monday afternoon, Thirteen parked the Cadillac at the meeting place. The morning chill had burned off to a hard, bright heat. He stepped out of the sweltering auto and stood in the shade of a palm tree to take a good look around.

Westlake Park was hardly a secure meeting spot. A wide-open slope led down to a duck pond. A hedge of rhododendron bushes dripping magenta blossoms provided no cover. It wasn't a busy time of day—there was that at least. An occasional pedestrian walked briskly along the concrete strolling path that rimmed the shore—smartly dressed shopgirls and suited businessmen. Nobody suspicious.

After ten minutes of observation, he was satisfied that only the ducks were watching him. He chose a bench next to the water's edge and sat, unfolding the newspaper he'd picked up at the Biltmore lobby, where he'd left the dog. He could have taken her along, but people noticed dogs. He stared at the black-and-white print but didn't read a word. Instead, he considered what to tell Leon Lewis about his Sunday drive with the Nazis.

"Aren't I lucky to have a pal like you?" Schwinn had said when Thirteen picked him up at his address on Broadway. It was a newly built town house, probably expensive. Schwinn met him outside, dressed in casual tan trousers and a crewneck sweater as if he were going to a tennis match. Thirteen was nobody's pal, least of all this kraut's. But it went with the job, so he let it lie. Hermann Schwinn liked to have him drive. Maybe it made him feel like some kind of general for the kaiser, having a driver and a nice-looking automobile at his beck and call. It worked fine for Thirteen. A driver heard things—he'd learned that when he worked for the studios.

They picked up Winterhalder next, who looked worse for wear in a wrinkled suit, his eyes pouchy and red-veined. Winterhalder directed him up Canyon Road, toward the Hollywoodland sign and past the big spreads and estates owned by the film stars and oilmen. Before long, they were kicking up dust in the mountain scrub. "Take this turn," Winterhalder said, bringing them into a wide spot in the road crammed with half a dozen autos—a couple old Fords, a shiny Pontiac coupe in pale blue, and a dusty Chevrolet sedan that could hold a dozen men.

Winterhalder led them down a trail heavy with the scent of dust and mountain sage. The sky was a blameless blue with wisps of serene clouds, the Pacific an uncertain mirage on the horizon. It would have been a nice walk, except for the company he was keeping.

Winterhalder stopped at the top of a rise. "Here they are," he said with a prideful look at Schwinn. "The Silver Shirt Legion."

Thirteen looked over a valley where a couple dozen men kitted out in uniforms and jackboots lined up in haphazard formation. Even from a distance, he could see the red armbands and black swastikas. And he saw something else that made his blood heat and a pounding begin in his chest. These soldiers were nothing but kids. Kids who were barely shaving, with thin necks and Adam's apples and scrawny shoulders.

Schwinn didn't look impressed.

"They're just starting out, of course," Winterhalder said quickly, "but they have right thinking and that's what we need."

Thirteen schooled his face to a passive expression and made himself breathe evenly. Right thinking. He knew what that meant. He'd read the copies of the *Silver Ranger* magazine Themlitz passed out like candy at the Aryan Bookstore.

Schwinn still hadn't said a word.

"We'll have a hundred more by the end of next month." Winterhalder was babbling now.

"A good start," Schwinn finally said. "And they all have family here in town, you have said. That is good."

Thirteen's dread grew to alarm. Reprisals. That's what Schwinn was talking about. If these boys got cold feet—or talked out of turn—he knew where they lived and with whom.

A man shouted an order at the front of the ragtag group. Even from a distance, he was an impressive figure. He had to be six and a half feet tall, fitted out in shiny-new denim trousers, polished boots, and a leather bomber jacket like he was going to star in a war movie. Thirteen would bet his last dime that he was the owner of the fancy coupe back on the road.

Winterhalder started down the path. "Come on, you'll like what else I have to show you."

Thirteen highly doubted that.

Winterhalder led them past the kids doing drills to a small outbuilding. Inside was a setup much like one of the army command centers Thirteen had seen in France, smelling of freshly cut wood and dirty socks. A desk and a few chairs. A roster of names on a clipboard. Maps pinned to the walls.

"Look here." Winterhalder showed them what looked like a blueprint laid out on a table. "The San Diego National Guard Armory." He stuck out his chest like he'd swallowed a balloon. "I've got the location of ammunition, lockers, rifles, and lists of the officers who would be sympathetic to our cause."

Schwinn bent over the blueprint and Thirteen was glad he had a moment to hide his shock. Connections to the armory. Arms and ammo. This was bad.

The big man who had been outside with the recruits came in the door, ducking his head so as not to hit it on the frame. He took up more than his share of the room.

Winterhalder straightened to attention. "Gentlemen, meet Travis Monroe."

"Welcome to the circus," Monroe said, sticking out his hand. Thirteen shook it, not wincing when the man squeezed hard enough to crack his knuckles. It was like that, then. A big man who made sure everybody knew it. Informative.

Monroe did the same number on Schwinn, and a muscle ticked in the German's square jaw. Schwinn didn't like not being the heavyweight in the room. Interesting.

"How are your troops?" Thirteen asked, jerking his head toward the window where he could see the recruits finding spots to sit in the shade, drinking water from jars.

"Mostly useless grunts," Monroe said with disdain. "Some might have potential if I work with them." Monroe punched him in the arm. "You're welcome to come out anytime and help me show these idiots how to fight. Might learn something yourself." He had a faint Southern accent but that wasn't what made Thirteen's hackles rise. It was the way he talked about those kids out there. Like they weren't real people.

Monroe turned to Winterhalder. "We need more recruits."

"I'm working on it," Winterhalder answered peevishly. "But we need funds to equip them."

"That will be taken care of," Schwinn answered without glancing up from his study of the armory blueprint.

Thirteen walked casually to the small window and looked out at the kids in uniform. He wanted to ask questions, but these men weren't dolts. Too many questions and they'd get suspicious. But he knew now that they had connections in the National Guard. They had money coming from somewhere—maybe out of the country—and they had a long-term plan. This was a bigger operation than either he or Lewis had imagined.

After a few more minutes listening to Monroe's bluster, Thirteen had his measure. He wasn't the brains behind the operation; he was the brawn. And he was the kind of chump who acted like the hero of his own film.

He drove Schwinn and Winterhalder back to the city, gritting his teeth while the two men complained about the state of the country and agreed it was up to them to set things right. They'd start by taking the power-hungry Jews out of their positions in Los Angeles. "We're good Christian folk," Winterhalder declared from the back seat. "It's our duty."

He was hard put not to show his disgust. Good Christian folk. From what he figured, the Nazis liked to toss the C-word around for the public, but their idea of God was the fatherland and they worshiped at the altar of Adolf Hitler.

Thirteen checked his watch. Lewis was late.

He watched the ducks glide from one end of the pond to the other. His father had considered himself good Christian folk. He'd used the excuse of his godly duty every time he administered a beating to his son or wife. Thirteen didn't buy it then and he sure as heck didn't buy it now. Sure, there were good Christians. And good Jews. Probably good people of every religion. But the ones who called themselves good anything and then spouted garbage like the Nazis—that really got his goat.

And those kids in uniform. He'd been there himself—a boy looking to be a hero. Somebody needed to tell those kids the real enemies weren't the Jews or the Catholics or Negroes, like the Klan and the National Socialists wanted them to believe. The real enemies were poverty and injustice and ignorance—and hate. It wasn't too late to set them straight. Give them a second chance. Didn't everybody deserve that? He hoped so, for their sake and his own.

Lewis sat down on the other side of the bench, startling Thirteen out of his thoughts. What was wrong with him? He couldn't afford to let his guard down. One wrong move and he'd be found out. And the Nazis didn't give second chances.

Lewis opened a paper bag and scooped up a handful of bread crumbs, scattering them on the grass. With a chorus of approval, the ducks waddled out of the shallows.

"Anything to report?" Lewis asked as the squadron of ducks advanced across the grass.

"Plenty."

Between handfuls of bread crumbs and feathered shenanigans, he told Lewis what he'd witnessed in the shadow of the Hollywoodland sign. Lewis showed little reaction but for the concerned furrow between his brows. He spread the last of the crumbs and crumpled the bag in his hands. The ducks turned and slid into the water, gliding out with hardly a ripple into the center of the pond. "We have a new operative," Lewis said without commenting on the Silver Shirts. "Someone to give us reports on the Friends of New Germany. Perhaps find the money trail."

"Good," he said. "Whatever is going on, there's gotta be proof in that office." A new operative worried him, though. "Tell him to watch his back," he said. He'd been with Schwinn and Winterhalder long enough to know a few things. "The people there, they might seem like the salt of the earth, but they're a dangerous bunch."

Lewis nodded but didn't give anything away.

Thirteen had said his piece. He just wished he knew how his pieces fit in with what Lewis knew. It occurred to him as he looked out at the rippling pond that Leon Lewis was much like those ducks out there—gliding calmly on top of the smooth water but paddling like crazy underneath.

"Next time, boss," he said, standing up and stepping carefully around the duck droppings, "choose a meeting place where I won't mess up my shoes."

CHAPTER 16

LIESL

By Wednesday, I was quite sure Leon Lewis's dire notions about the Friends of New Germany were utterly unfounded.

My first task had been to set up systems that ensured the office ran with utmost efficiency. All was properly ordered and organized. Letters to be typed were deposited in my basket, outgoing mail placed in a separate basket near the door. A log sheet on a clipboard recorded all incoming telephone calls for later reference. Membership applications were attended to each morning, as was the bank deposit. The Friends had the newest model of Corona typewriter—a pleasure to use after my Remington at MGM in which the *W* key was forever sticking—and an up-to-the-minute addition machine that could total a stack of membership dues as quick as a wink and with no possibility of error.

"What would we do without you?" Thekla exclaimed with a sincerity that warmed me.

At eleven o'clock, Mr. Schwinn took coffee in his office and I took dictation. I set the percolator to heating in the small back room that contained office supplies and a hot plate, and considered my agreement with Mr. Lewis. I had done as he asked—listened and kept notes in shorthand—with a twinge of guilt and an unpleasant sense of wasted effort. What possible use to him were letters regarding sauerkraut dinners and children's summer camps?

The percolator came to a boil and I allowed the coffee to bubble for exactly three minutes, the scent filling the small room. Was it not my duty to tell Mr. Lewis of his wrongheaded ideas? But if I did, would he pay me the money he promised? It was a common opinion that Jews tried to cheat Gentiles. I did not believe that, and Mr. Lewis had seemed trustworthy, but perhaps on Friday I would not receive the thirty dollars in my secret post office box.

If that were so, I didn't know what I would do.

Our accounts at home were precarious. The electric bill was overdue, as was the rent. The icebox contained a half bottle of milk, three eggs, and a smidge of butter. It would be cabbage and bread until Friday unless I begged Gertrud Grundbacher's forbearance on our account once more.

I turned off the hot plate and poured a cup of coffee into a bone china cup. Balancing the cup and saucer in one hand, with my steno pad tucked under my arm, I pushed open the office door. "Mr. Schwinn?"

"Call me Hermann, Liesl." He looked up from his desk with a mock frown.

His office was as pleasant as the rest of the newly decorated second floor of the Alt Heidelberg. Spacious and welcoming with a bank of tall windows that let in the breeze and the sounds of autos and birds. A set of file drawers dominated one wall and several chairs offered comfortable seating.

I set the cup and saucer on the corner of his desk beside a photograph of a young Hermann Schwinn in a dark uniform. Hermann noticed my interest and looked pleased. "I was such a young man then," he preened, surely aware he was still as handsome as in the photograph. "A member of the old Sturmabteilung. And my dog, Lump." He looked with a fond smile upon the dog, a German shepherd showing his teeth to the camera. "He could take down a grown man in thirty seconds. How I miss him."

I was glad he no longer had such a dog, and sat down to take the morning's dictation—Hermann advocating for German heritage classes in our schools. "Just for the real Germans," he dictated. Not an unreasonable request and certainly welcome. Mutti and I spoke enough German at home that Tess and Steffen had an elementary understanding, but writing the language and learning grammar would be a wonderful way to teach them their heritage, just as Vati had taught me. Miriam took Frieda to Boyle Heights every Wednesday for Hebrew school; wasn't that much the same thing?

"I'll have this typed and in the post before I leave," I promised Hermann and returned to my desk and the shiny typewriter. I rolled a fresh white sheet of paper and a carbon into the carriage. Yes, Hermann and Thekla were kindness itself after what I'd been through at MGM. I wished only that the Friends could pay me a salary and I could put an end to my association with Leon Lewis.

My next task was the letter from Paul Themlitz to Schlegel's Department Store on Broadway, warning the manager of a potential boycott of German businesses by opponents of the New Germany. The telephone rang as I typed *Faithfully yours, Mr. Paul Themlitz.*

"Friends of New Germany," I answered.

I pressed the button for Hermann's extension, announced the call, then proofread the letter. Not a single error. The contents might be considered pejorative against Jews if you were looking for that kind of thing, but I could not fault Mr. Themlitz for trying to help German businesses. These were difficult times. Was it fair to punish German Americans for what might—or might not—be happening on the other side of the world?

I took my lunch in the small courtyard behind the building and returned to find Hermann with Hans Winterhalder, whom I'd met on my first day at the Friends. He was in his forties, with bristling sandy hair, a thin mustache, and a roving eye. Not one to be caught alone with in an elevator or deserted stairwell. Now they were in a jovial after-lunch mood, Hermann's cheeks a bit flushed and Mr. Winterhalder smelling faintly of schnapps.

"Come, Liesl," Hermann said. "You must see what we are working on downstairs."

I followed Hermann and Mr. Winterhalder down the stairs and through a door to the basement. I expected to see a musty storage space from years past but was ushered into a large, brightly lit hall that smelled of soap and baking bread.

"Isn't it wonderful?" Hermann said. The room was filled with men— perhaps two dozen, between the ages of thirty and fifty. Most sat at a long table eating. A group played cards in the corner and a few men slept on cots that lined the back wall.

"Veterans," Mr. Winterhalder explained at my questioning glance. "We're doing what we can."

Hermann directed me toward the small kitchen in the back. "Liesl Weiss, meet Travis Monroe," he said with a flourish. "He's lending a hand with the veterans operation. Travis, this is Mrs. Liesl Weiss."

A man ladling soup gave me a dazzling smile. "A pleasure, Mrs. Weiss."

Travis Monroe was well over six feet tall, with impossibly broad shoulders. He had a shock of curly auburn hair and vivid green eyes, and his jaw was as square as a brick. Goodness, he looked like a film star. I realized the three men were awaiting my reply. "Oh, of course." I flushed. "Very good to meet you, Mr. Monroe."

"Call me Travis," he said with a grin and I realized his words held a trace of Southern charm.

"Come, Liesl," Hans Winterhalder said abruptly. "Let me show you what we do here." I tolerated the overly familiar touch of his hand on my waist as he guided me through the room. "We give them a hot meal to start," he said. "Then clean clothes, a place to sleep."

"It's the least we can do to help our German neighbors and others who think as we do," Hermann added.

"The government has betrayed them," Mr. Winterhalder said. "But we won't. We'll make them proud to be German again."

I looked at the veterans around me—German men who had served America well, just as Vati had done—and my admiration for the Friends increased. It was a good thing they were doing for our German community. A very good thing.

I took my leave of Hermann and Mr. Winterhalder, said goodbye to the handsome Travis Monroe, and climbed the stairs back to the Friends office to resume my duties. I did not glance up at the crooked cross of the National Socialist flag hanging above me.

I found Thekla removing her hat in front of the small wall mirror, just returned from her meeting with the Christian Women's Brigade, of which she was the chairperson. "Liesl, I'm so glad to get you all to myself for a moment," she said.

I sat down in my chair and she perched on the corner of the desk. She wore a stylish linen day dress with narrow sleeves and wide shoulders. I tucked my legs with their many-times-mended stockings out of sight.

She smiled kindly, a crinkle around her eyes. "I'm speaking for all of us here at the Friends when I say we are so very pleased with your work. I do hope you are happy with us?"

A rush of pleasure warmed me. Never, in the years that I'd worked for Mrs. Adler, had the woman expressed the slightest appreciation toward me. Not for my skills nor my dedication. I'd been at the Friends for only three days and was valued more than all my years at MGM.

"I do so wish we could pay you." Thekla's voice dropped to a whisper. "I understand now how difficult things have been for you."

My smile froze. What, pray tell, did she understand? That I was not a widow after all?

"Don't worry," she went on. "It really is no one's business but your own." She patted my arm. "But, Liesl, I want you to take this home with you." She pointed out a box stowed between my desk and the wall. "We received so many donations today, far more than we can use."

I glanced at the contents. A bag of potatoes, a dozen eggs, a jar of sauerkraut, and several packages wrapped in butcher's paper. Enough to feed us for days. "I couldn't."

"Don't be silly." She stood and smoothed her skirt. "It is decided. It's the least we can do with you donating your time here. I'm going to make some coffee for Paul and Hermann. Would you like some?"

She went to the back room. I looked at the box of food and wondered. Someone had made it their business to tell her I was in financial distress. It had been kind of her to offer me sympathy and not judgment, and the groceries would be a great help. My eye fell on my handbag, with my shorthand notes stowed inside to send to Leon Lewis. He was wrongheaded about the Friends and I was helping him—betraying these good people for thirty dollars a week. It might as well be thirty pieces of silver.

At three o'clock, I put on my hat and picked up the box of groceries. Thekla looked up from where she sat in the armchair reading an issue of *Photoplay*. "We shall see you tonight, of course?"

"Tonight?" Tonight I would be helping with the children's homework and doing the Wednesday mending that I had forbidden Mutti to touch.

"Yes, at Turnverein Hall?"

The German Alliance meeting. I'd been answering calls about it for the past three days. The vote for the new president of the alliance was of great importance, according to Hermann's letters and telephone calls.

"There will be such a crowd, and I could use more hands with the ballots." She looked at me hopefully.

I thought of her kindness and the men downstairs. Of the good that the Friends were doing and how I was deceiving them. "Of course I'll be there," I answered.

"*Wunderbar!*" she exclaimed. "Come at half past six to help me set up. You're such a darling."

"I'm glad to do so." It was not completely untrue.

At the foot of the stairs, Paul Themlitz was standing in the doorway to the bookstore. "Liesl!" he said loudly, his bulbous eyes wide. "You must come in for a moment."

I had not yet been inside the bookstore and I did not wish to today. The trolley would pick me up in five minutes and with the box to carry—

"I insist, my dear."

To refuse would be impolite. I put down the box and followed him inside. The space was smaller than I remembered, cramped with tall shelves, and dimly lit. The smell was pleasantly familiar—leather bindings, ink, and a slight mustiness—and brought back a sudden recollection of Vati bringing me in to purchase the *California Staats-Zeitung*. At home, he would read aloud the successes of German immigrants in America. "This country has been good to us," he often said.

As my sight adjusted to the murky light, I became aware we were not alone. A tall unsmiling man stood in the shadow of a bookcase.

"Allow me to introduce you to one of our members," Paul Themlitz effused. "Liesl Weiss, this is Wilhelm Otto."

"Pleased to meet you, Mr. Otto."

The man gave me a curt nod and no smile. "Miss Weiss."

"It's Mrs.," I said quickly.

Wilhelm Otto's expression did not flicker. In the shadows, I could make out cold gray eyes, hard lines of cheek and jaw, sleek brown hair. A short mustache that called to mind a caterpillar crawled across the center of his upper lip. A chill went over the back of my neck.

I turned abruptly to Paul Themlitz, forgoing manners. "I really must catch the trolley—"

"Before you go, please—" he trotted to a table near the front—"take one of these." He plucked a book from a stack. *Mein Kampf* by Adolf Hitler. "Have you read it?"

I held up a hand in denial. "No, I couldn't." I had neither the time nor the funds for books.

"You must," he insisted once more. "We give them away for free here. It is part of the service we provide for the Friends. Do tell me you'll read it."

I cast about for any reason to refuse. I did not wish to read of Adolf Hitler's struggle, yet neither did I want to prolong this encounter nor look ungrateful. "Thank you," I said, putting the book in my handbag. "I really must go."

After saying goodbye to both men, I hefted the grocery box in my arms and hurried out of the building. The fresh air and sunlight were a relief, yet even in the heat of the sun, I shivered at the remembrance of Wilhelm Otto's watchful gaze.

CHAPTER 17

LIESL

I was late to the meeting, and I detested being late.

I had missed the 3:05 trolley and walked home, toting the box of groceries. I did the Wednesday mending while Mutti made dinner, then fed the children cabbage soup with wurst, fresh bread, and an egg custard for dessert. After I helped Tess with her spelling words, I had only enough time to dash upstairs, change into a fresh blouse, and reapply my lipstick.

"Where on earth are you going?" Mutti demanded.

I raided the tea tin for two nickels for the trolley. "Make sure they are in bed by eight o'clock," I reminded her without explaining my plans. "No excuses from Tess." I gave Tess a look that meant business. "Mind Oma Nell, young lady, or I will have something to say about it." As Steffen clung, I performed our ritual goodbye with my usual feelings of guilt.

Turnverein Hall—the full name was Turnverein Germania but no one called it that anymore—was a great gabled building taking up most of a block on West Washington Boulevard. I'd never been inside, but Vati came here for help with his citizen papers when war broke out with the kaiser.

Thekla was waiting at the arched entrance. She'd changed into a businesslike suit of black and burgundy, but her perfectly made-up face held a pinched look of annoyance as she glanced at her wristwatch. Her sour expression shifted abruptly to a bright smile when she saw me approach. "I knew you wouldn't let me down, Liesl. We must hurry now," she said briskly, turning on her alligator heels to march through the door.

The reception hall was spacious, with a domed ceiling and three sets of doors leading to an auditorium. Thekla stopped at a table holding a stack of papers and pencils. Ballots with two names and instructions written in both English and German. "Pass these out," she ordered. "Just to the men, of course."

The auditorium was filled to capacity, men and women already seated in rows of folding chairs. Two flags hung limply on either side of a podium in the front of the room—the American Stars and Stripes and the red, white, and black flag of the National Socialists. A low hum of conversation buzzed through the room.

"It's wonderful, is it not?" Thekla asked. "You start on that side, *ja*?"

I picked out a few familiar faces in the crowd as I passed the ballots down the rows. Gertrud Grundbacher with Johan beside her. Neele and Karl Weber sitting beside Silka Scholz and her husband, Peter.

"Entschuldigen, bitte." A man and woman waited at my elbow to make their way to two empty seats. The man's right leg was amputated below the knee and I moved aside for his crutches. A war veteran, one of many in the room. I gave him a ballot.

At a commotion in the back of the room, heads turned. A line of uniformed men marched through the door, Hans Winterhalder in the lead. Each man wore black trousers and a light-gray shirt, armbands displaying the black swastika. I watched the men march in formation, noting the clipped hair and regular features, then the jolt of a familiar face.

Fritz. What was he doing here?

"Liesl, take these." Thekla pushed the remaining ballots into my hands and hurried to the podium, raising her hands for quiet with an authority that I had not expected. The room settled almost immediately as she smiled warmly and thanked everyone for coming. "I've been given the honor of introducing our speaker for this evening. And then we will take the vote for the alliance, *ja*?"

The waiting crowd applauded. I looked at the ballot in my hand. Two candidates—John Vieth and Max Socha. Both had been visitors to the Alt Heidelberg over the past three days. Both had been treated cordially by Hermann Schwinn and Thekla.

"Our speaker tonight," Thekla continued, "is our liaison with the Disabled American Veterans, of whom many of you are members." She turned her girlish smile toward the right side of the raised stage. "The Friends of New Germany look forward to working closely with the very charming and handsome—" she looked at the crowd with a little wink and received scattered laughter—"Captain Wilhelm Otto."

I looked up quickly, as a man stepped out of the shadows of the National Socialist flag. In the bright lights of the auditorium, Wilhelm Otto looked no less intimidating than he had in the Aryan Bookstore. I noted his hair was a shade lighter than I'd first thought. Chestnut, rather than dark brown. The hard face and the unattractive mustache were just as I remembered. He didn't look old enough to have been in the war and yet had a military bearing that was unmistakable as he waited for the complete attention of the audience.

I moved closer to the front of the room and took an empty seat next to the veteran who had arrived late. All eyes were on the man at the podium. "America," he finally said in a deep voice that carried well, "needs waking up and shaking up." Applause erupted from the uniformed men along the windows. "Our veterans have been given a shabby treatment." He looked around the room. "What we need to see is the threat that is growing all around us."

The man on my left—the one with the missing leg—spoke to his wife in loud whisper. "He means the Jews."

I looked at him sharply, then back at Mr. Otto. Did he?

"We must rid America—our America—of these dangerous elements that are poised to take over both our politics and our culture. We must," he said firmly, "be a strong force against the threat of economic ruin by unscrupulous neighbors. As German Americans it is our duty to stand together. To once again be a proud people."

The man next to me nodded and whistled in agreement. The uniformed men—Fritz included—clapped in accord. Wilhelm Otto continued confidently, saying the German community must take care of each other, strengthen our families, beware of Communist sympathizers who wished to subvert our culture. That we must stop the attack on our values, the indecency and immorality running rampant in our country.

I felt a ripple of unease. What he said was not incorrect. Of course we must care for our families. Was that not what I woke each day to accomplish? And we must stop the Communists. Everyone knew that. But it was the way in which he spoke . . . as if there was another meaning, a dangerous meaning underneath his words, as a river hides currents under the smooth surface.

"What about Adolf Hitler?" a voice from the audience demanded. All heads turned toward a youngish man standing near the back with dark hair and a baggy suit. "Is he part of what the alliance stands for?"

A murmuring went through the crowd.

Wilhelm Otto didn't respond, but the men along the wall did. At a command from Hans Winterhalder, Fritz and another uniformed man approached the heckler. Lightning-quick, they took him by the arms and disappeared through the auditorium doors. It was over in a moment and I was left wondering what had happened.

Wilhelm Otto resumed speaking. "The alliance of German Americans stands for good Christians and the American way."

Applause and shouts of approval followed as he left the podium. Handsome—as Thekla had claimed—I did not think so. And charming, he was not.

The two candidates for the alliance president—Max Socha and John Vieth—spoke next. They concluded to weak applause and Thekla was at my side. "Help me collect the ballots, Liesl." She motioned to the auditorium doors.

For the next half hour, I received ballots and stacked them in a lock-box. As I did, I searched the faces in the crowd for Fritz. "Are we to count them tonight?" I asked Thekla. I glanced at the clock above the auditorium doors—9:25. I had not spotted Fritz and wanted nothing more than to catch the 9:30 trolley home, away from the unease that was pricking down my spine.

"Tomorrow will be soon enough," Thekla answered, turning the key and tucking the lockbox under her arm.

Thankfully, I gathered my handbag and gloves and was about to make my goodbyes, when Thekla grasped my elbow. "Liesl, you must say hello to the Friends."

I hid a pinprick of irritation. I could not be rude. I was beginning to understand that Thekla enjoyed nothing more than male admiration and so was not surprised when we joined Travis Monroe, Max Socha, and Wilhelm Otto, along with Hermann.

"Max, Wilhelm." Thekla smiled at the men, her dimples coming out in full view. "This is Liesl Weiss, the new secretary at the Friends."

Travis Monroe was just as dazzling in a navy sports jacket over cream-colored trousers as he had been in work clothes this morning. He greeted me with a smile and an appreciative glance that I did not miss. Max Socha said hello and thanked me for my help with the vote.

"Mrs. Weiss," Wilhelm Otto said, his glance like an electric shock. He did not smile. I saw, upon closer view, the hint of a scar on his upper lip, just outside the edge of the mustache, that pulled his mouth into a slight sneer. I looked away quickly, a shiver of apprehension running across the back of my arms.

Max Socha regarded the lockbox under Thekla's arm. "All is in order?"

She smiled and patted the box. "You are assured of the win. I can feel it and I am never wrong about these things."

"Of course you aren't," he said with a wink.

I suddenly felt the weight of the day, the unease and questions, upon me. My worry for Fritz and whatever he was involved in. I turned to Thekla. "If you are not in need of me, I really must get back to the children." If I hurried, I might yet make the trolley.

"Liesl," Hermann Schwinn said smoothly. "You must allow me to drive you. It is far too late for a pretty girl to be taking the trolley. Is that not so, Thekla?"

Thekla opened her mouth—to voice her objection, I was certain—but I forestalled with my own. "That is kind, but—"

"It is decided," Hermann declared. "It won't take but a moment."

I was too tired to argue and bade Thekla and the other men goodbye. I felt the silent flintlike gaze of Wilhelm Otto remain on me as I walked away.

Outside, Hermann opened the door of his beetle-green Ford Roadster and I slid into the seat with a sigh. The ride on the trolley had taken twenty minutes; in his auto it was less than ten to return. I gave him directions to my home, and Hermann kept up an easy conversation. I thought I might ask him about the man who had been removed from the meeting but the cautionary voice of Leon Lewis stopped me. *Take great care, Edelweiss.* I would ask Fritz. Surely there was an explanation.

When we turned onto Pico, Hermann Schwinn's hand dropped from the steering wheel to rest lightly on my knee. I jerked and made a small sound of surprise.

"Pardon me, my dear," he said. "That was unintended."

I murmured something, an acknowledgment of sorts, but my body reacted with an urge to flee. When we arrived at my home, I did not wait for him to come around to my door but opened it myself and stepped out. "Thank you again, Mr. Schwinn."

"The pleasure was all mine, Liesl," he answered with an easy smile.

"Auf Wiedersehen!" He did not drive away until I had gone inside and shut the door firmly behind me, letting out a long breath. Of course it had been an innocent mistake. Hermann was a devoted husband and a good man.

Mutti waited for me in the sitting room—with Tess and Steffen asleep beside her on the divan. "It's about time you're home. Where on earth—?"

"Why are they not in bed?" I interrupted.

She shrugged and did not look contrite. "Tess wanted to listen to the radio. I didn't see any harm."

Irritation made me turn my back on her. No teeth brushing and they weren't even in their pajamas. Tess's doing, of course. Mutti continued her excuses as I scooped Steffen into my arms and prodded Tess awake. Mutti—a woman her age—could she not stand up to a six-year-old's will? She might have raised us in a haphazard kind of way, but I would not do the same with my children.

I put them to bed and shut the bedroom door on Mutti's excuses. I should be grateful for her help but I was not. I undressed and considered the evening. What was it causing me such unease? Fritz in the gray-shirted uniform with the swastika armband? I brushed my hair and patted my face with cold cream. Wilhelm Otto's military demeanor, his talk of a threat growing around us? *He means the Jews.* I wiped the cold cream from my face. Was it my own imagination—an overreaction caused by Leon Lewis's talk of conspiracies—or had a malevolent current run underneath the patriotic tone of the German alliance election?

I slid into bed next to Steffen but did not turn out the bedside lamp. I lay back on the pillow and looked at the plaster ceiling. Perhaps—yes, probably—there had been some anti-Semites among the crowd tonight. But most of them were just like me—like Thekla and Hermann—those who wanted jobs, security, to raise their children as German Americans. That was hardly a conspiracy worthy of Mr. Lewis's suspicion.

Steffen's even breathing and Tess's soft snore marked the time with the tick of the bedside clock. The bed was warm and I had no desire to wander the house tonight. Neither did I want to continue my litany of questions to God. Perhaps if I wrote out my report for Mr. Lewis, my mind would rest. I slipped out of bed and went to my handbag for my steno pad and pencil. Instead, I found the book that Paul Themlitz had pushed into my hands. *Mein Kampf.*

We give them away for free here.

I had heard, of course, of Adolf Hitler's book. It was said to be quite sensational. A treatise of his plan for the fatherland, written while he was in prison for some kind of political rabble-rousing. This book might answer my questions, maybe show that Leon Lewis was exaggerating and my fears were unfounded. Even at that moment, perhaps I knew I was clutching at straws. I scrambled back under the covers—close to Steffen's warmth—opened the book, and began to read.

CHAPTER 18

I was late to work the next morning but Thekla's displeasure was not my greatest concern.

I had opened Adolf Hitler's book last night, expecting—what?— I did not know. The first chapters had been wandering, tedious reading but unease rose within me as I turned the pages. Adolf Hitler blamed the Jewish people for all that had gone wrong in Germany. In itself, not unusual in Germany or even America. But the intensity of Adolf Hitler's hatred was unlike any I'd heard of in our own newspapers and radio programs.

Inhuman, he called the Jews. *Sub*human. A race that was polluting and destroying the Aryan people. I saw Miriam's face, her broad smile and kindness. Stella, with her sharp wit, and Leon Lewis's understanding gaze. According to Adolf Hitler, these people were the source of all evil and in need of eradication. *Extermination.* I checked to make sure I had read it right. I had.

No. This cannot be. Vati had taught me that being German was something to be proud of—a culture that valued work and orderliness, love for family and duty to country. But Adolf Hitler's treatise spoke of Aryan dominance. He wished to gain control of the schools, the newspapers, and businesses. To drive the Jews out of his country.

What I read on these pages was a twisted mockery of all Vati held dear, of the Germany I had been taught to respect. Pride in our culture was not the same as dominating—eradicating—another race. Surely the Friends of New Germany did not espouse these same ideas?

The tick of my bedside clock was the only sound other than the turning of the pages as I read the solution for "the Jewish menace." They must be defeated, Adolf Hitler said, "by wiping the parasitic race from the face of the earth."

I closed the book with a slam that made Tess flinch in her sleep.

I considered once more the Friends of New Germany and what I had seen in the past three days. Paul Themlitz, jovial bookstore owner. The charitable works for veterans with nowhere to turn. Hermann and Thekla, a stylish couple promoting the heritage and customs of the German people. Only Wilhelm Otto seemed to be truly frightening. And what of Fritz and the men in uniform? He had been the one to remove the young man from the auditorium. His talk of Jews over the past few months was suddenly far more insidious. Could my own brother believe what I had just read? I shoved the book under the bed and still felt its menacing presence as if it were a living thing. As dawn lightened the sky, I fell into a fitful slumber and woke late. But before I could rush to work, I needed to talk to Fritz.

I cornered him in the kitchen when he returned from his night shift. "Does Mutti know what you're involved in?"

"Don't tell her," he said, taking off his hat and sitting down at the table. "She'll just worry and you know how she is."

I stared him down with my big sister look.

"Please, Liesl," he said, "don't tell Mutti." It sounded so much like my little brother, when he'd gotten into trouble on the MGM lot and I'd promised not to tell. He was right; Mutti would worry. And when she worried, we were all miserable. I wanted to ask him about last night, about what I'd read and what he believed, but I could not. Perhaps I was afraid to hear his answer. "For now," I said. "But you tell her before I have to."

I walked Tess to school and ran for the later trolley. As I stood in the swaying crowd, I wondered if I was overreacting. Yet Leon Lewis's intelligent manner came back to me. I had agreed to help him, even as I had not believed him. And now did I believe him?

I did not know.

Inside the Alt Heidelberg, I found high spirits. Max Socha had won the election and this pleased Thekla and Hermann immensely. I thought briefly about the locked ballot box. Who had counted the votes? And when? But it was hardly my place to question the validity of the alliance vote.

"What a wonderful turnout we had last night," Thekla said. "So very gratifying to see so many who think as we do."

"It was all we could have hoped," Hermann agreed. "And to unify our people under one banner will help our cause."

Were they good-hearted ambassadors or was there an undercurrent of menace in their words? I did not know. But I would find out.

When I had completed my morning work, I went downstairs to the Aryan Bookstore. Paul Themlitz welcomed me eagerly. No Wilhelm Otto lurking in the shadows was a relief. "It was enlightening," I told him when he asked if I had read Adolf Hitler's book.

"Wonderful!" he enthused. "Take this next." He pushed a thick pamphlet into my hands. "Henry Ford paid to print over twenty thousand copies."

I read *The Protocols of the Elders of Zion* at my desk during my lunch hour and wished I had not. It took very little time to get the main premise, that the Jews were conspiring to turn non-Jews into slaves and control the economies of the world. It went on to show how Jews were responsible for all past disasters, from the French Revolution to our current financial crisis. That they needed to be stopped.

"Liesl?" Thekla, who had been sitting on the divan reading *Ladies' Home Journal*, said suddenly. "Are you ill?"

I started at her concerned voice. The hard-boiled egg I had eaten sat like a rock in my stomach. Hermann came out of his office with Wilhelm Otto on his heels. He stopped midsentence at Thekla's question and approached my desk with a concerned look.

"Oh, my dear." Thekla came to me, put her hand over mine, and acknowledged the volume in my hand. "It is quite upsetting, is it not?"

I glanced down. "It is indeed." There was no untruth there. "It is . . . unbelievable."

Thekla squeezed my hand. "We must do our best to make a better world for your children, Liesl. I know you believe that."

Hermann murmured agreement. Wilhelm Otto was silent.

I wished to snatch my hand from Thekla's cold grasp. Did they truly believe the claims stated in this treatise? I realized with a sickening awareness of my own cowardice that, as with Fritz, I did not want to know the answer.

"I—It's just . . ." I strove for an honest response. "I don't know what to think."

Thekla's sympathy was sincere. "I understand completely, my dear."

I glanced up to find Wilhelm Otto's watchful gaze on me.

Hermann's voice was filled with compassion. "Liesl, you needn't worry your pretty head. The Friends are here now and we'll do what must be done." He glanced at his wife. "You see, my dear," he said, "I told you she was one of us."

Hermann Schwinn's words, intended to comfort, gave me a shudder of dread.

CHAPTER 19

LIESL

Friday afternoon, Hermann Schwinn cornered me in the supply room.

I had spent twenty-four hours trying not to think of Leon Lewis or Adolf Hitler. I typed letters, addressed envelopes, and took dictation. I responded appropriately to Thekla's pleasant comments and smiled at Hermann and Paul Themlitz. Wilhelm Otto came and went. I avoided his gaze with determination. I kept my mind on the tasks at hand.

My final duty of the week was to make an account of the office supplies according to Thekla's orders. She kept meticulous records of every item—each sheet of paper and staple—that we used. I was also counting the seconds until I could flee the Alt Heidelberg and push my questions about *Mein Kampf*, the *Elders of Zion*, and the Friends of New Germany into a file in my mind marked "Do not consider."

I turned to find Hermann Schwinn very close behind me. I jumped in surprise. At the familiar look in his eyes, a realization came to me. Hermann Schwinn's touch in his auto had been not as innocent as he claimed.

The supply room was small, hardly more than a closet, lined with shelves and a small table on which the percolator and a hot plate stood. Hermann Schwinn stood between me and the door, with only a few inches on either side of his body. I calmed my racing heart. I'd dealt with this behavior on a daily basis at MGM. Be firm but polite. "Excuse me, Mr. Schwinn." I looked pointedly at the door behind him.

Hermann stepped closer still. "Call me Hermann, Liesl." His gaze was not on my face but considerably lower.

My irritation rose and I considered my options. Thekla was not in the office. I wielded only a clipboard and a pencil for defense. "Mr. Schwinn, I have work to do."

"Of course, Liesl, don't let me deter you." He turned sideways, allowing me just enough room to squeeze past him. I let out a breath and inched past him. He leaned forward, trapping me against the shelving, his body in full contact with mine. He winked as if we were playing a game. Perhaps he was, but I was not. A shudder of revulsion went over me and I considered giving him a good shove, but I needed to stay in his good graces and making a fuss would not do.

That was when I saw Wilhelm Otto watching from the doorway.

The scene looked, of course, as if Hermann and I were having a dalliance in the storage room while Thekla was out. I scraped past Hermann, the clipboard tight against my chest, my cheeks flaring hot. Wilhelm stepped aside so I did not brush against him in the slightest as I passed.

Hermann chuckled as if nothing untoward had taken place. "Wilhelm, let's go over that list of veterans, shall we?"

My pulse settled as the door to Hermann's office clicked shut. Had Wilhelm Otto thought I was welcoming Hermann's attentions? Thekla was a jealous woman. She not only wanted all of her husband's attention; she wished for every man to see her as the only woman in the room.

But Wilhelm Otto rarely even spoke. Surely he would not tell tales to Thekla.

At three o'clock Hermann came out of his office as if nothing had happened. "Liesl, I'll drive you home," he said with the authority of a man who was used to being obeyed.

"No." My reaction was immediate, the remembrance of his hand on my knee, the incident just half an hour earlier in the storage room. I took a breath. "I mean, thank you, Hermann. But there's no need."

Hermann was undeterred and reached for his hat. "Of course I must—"

"I'll drive her."

I'd forgotten Wilhelm Otto's commanding tone. It seemed to stop Hermann for a moment, but he recovered quickly. "It's no trouble—"

"Mrs. Weiss?" Wilhelm Otto opened the door as if Hermann had not uttered a word.

I did not wish to be alone in an auto with Hermann Schwinn, but was Wilhelm Otto any better?

He raised his brows at me with a look of slight impatience. I did not have a choice. I smiled and preceded Wilhelm Otto through the office door and down the stairs in complete silence. He opened the passenger door for me to slide into the thickly cushioned leather seat of his waiting sedan. I settled into the seat as he walked to the driver's side. Was I—as Mutti would say—jumping from the frying pan into the fire?

Wilhelm Otto pushed an electric ignition and the engine started with a subdued roar. He rolled down his window, lit a cigarette, and pulled out onto the street. Unsurprisingly, silence prevailed.

I thought of what I knew of the man beside me. Little, except for Thekla's mention of his rank. He exuded a military-type control in his every movement. Other men—even Hermann—listened when he spoke, which made him even more menacing.

We came to a stop at the streetlight on Olympic and I could stand the silence no more. "Were you really in the war?"

"Yes," he said simply, then threw his half-smoked cigarette out the window.

"You don't seem old enough."

"I wasn't," he answered with little feeling. "I was big for my age."

He was still big, and I wondered exactly what his age was.

"I'm thirty-one," he said without taking his eyes from the road, "if that's what you're wondering."

I did the mathematics. "You were fifteen?" He'd practically been a child.

"Sixteen by the time I saw action." He shrugged his wide shoulders. "Forged my father's signature. Not that he would have cared, just easier that way." He glanced sideways at me and I had the distinct impression that he hadn't meant to disclose that personal detail.

The silence stretched. I glanced at his profile, noting the aquiline nose and sharp jaw. He looked perfectly at ease with not speaking, and so I determined I would be also.

My relief was acute when we pulled to the curb outside my home. I gathered my handbag and readied myself to leave the auto, then looked up to see Wilhelm eyeing the thin gold band on my left hand.

"What happened to your husband?" His question was a jolt of lightning out of a blue sky.

I was momentarily speechless. Then the lie came to my lips. "He died."

His expression remained blank. "That's not what I heard, Mrs. Weiss."

My mouth went dry and my pulse pounded in my ears. "What do you mean?"

He shrugged eloquently.

Anger welled within me. At whoever was whispering my secrets. At Tomas, for leaving me. And at this man, for questioning me about my personal life. I looked out the window at the geranium on my stoop, dripping red petals. "One day he went to work and never came home." The stark words somehow didn't seem fair to Tomas, as true as they were. He had been a good husband and a good father. Not the kind who would leave his family, but I was not about to explain this to Wilhelm Otto of all people.

Wilhelm was still watching me. "Have you ever looked for him?"

I caught my breath at the sudden pain the question caused. "Of course the police did." Until Mickey told me about what Tomas had said. Then they stopped looking. But I never stopped. I looked for him every day. Everywhere.

Wilhelm raised one brow as if to say what he thought of the police. "A private detective is what I mean."

Of course I'd thought of it. But even if we could afford such a thing, I couldn't do it. What if I found out that he had left me for another woman? Or was living in Texas or just across town? Then I would no longer have hope when the telephone rang or the doorbell chimed. I would no longer be able to dream of him walking through the door, telling me he loved me and he had a good reason—he'd lost his memory, he'd been kidnapped. I'd considered it all. Better to cling to the ridiculous hope that he might someday come back than to give up and face a life without him.

He met my eyes. "Knowing is better than not knowing, Mrs. Weiss."

He was wrong. Not knowing was infinitely better than knowing that your husband had been miserable when you thought he was happy. That the life you thought was good was unbearable to him. That the man you loved beyond all reason never really loved you.

I realized just then that I had not told Wilhelm Otto where I lived. He knew my address and he knew about Tomas. A shiver of fear raised goose bumps on my skin. Was there more he knew? About Mr. Lewis and why I was at the Friends?

I wanted nothing more than to leave the presence of this horrible man.

I pushed open the door and fumbled out of the auto and then took a breath. I would not run like a frightened child. Before I shut the door, I bent and looked at Wilhelm Otto's inscrutable face. "I'll thank you to mind your own business."

He let me have the last word and silently pulled away.

I did not walk up the sidewalk to my door. Instead, I watched the sleek auto disappear down the street and around the corner. My hope that Wilhelm Otto would mind his own business was a vain one, indeed.

How easily I had doubted Leon Lewis. And I had been wrong to do so.

After Wilhelm Otto's automobile disappeared, I took Steffen and Tess for a walk to the Germantown post office and found the thirty dollars in an envelope addressed to Edelweiss. I paid down the bill at Grundbacher's, had Johan wrap up a beef roast, and let the children pick out penny candy. I should have felt relieved but instead I felt . . . guilty.

Guilt and a shame that grew sharper with every step toward home.

Did I feel remorse for spying on the Friends of New Germany? No. I was realizing they were not as they seemed. Was it because I was lying to Mutti and Fritz? I should feel some shame there, but I did not. As we passed the Stahrs' house, I knew.

My guilt and remorse were because I had betrayed Miriam. I was no better than Gertrud Grundbacher. I should have defended Miriam. I should have stood up against the judgment she faced every day.

I should not have remained silent.

After Tomas disappeared, my world had shrunk to a small orbit of necessary concerns: the children, Mutti, Fritz. Putting in my hours at MGM, getting my paycheck every Friday. Steffen's winter ear infections and the cost of Mutti's arthritis injections. The rent and our account at Grundbacher's.

I told myself that was the reason for my silence.

One day last spring, I stopped at Grundbacher's for a cheap piece of pork and a can of beans. Gertrud leaned on the counter in a serviceable dress covered in a pristine white apron. Tess had been accepted among the other German girls in her class and Mrs. Eberheart had ceased her complaints of misbehavior, but my uneasiness with Gertrud Grundbacher remained. Behind Gertrud, the refrigerator case brimmed with pink sausages, yellow cheeses, and vats of pickled vegetables. Johan Grundbacher stood on a ladder, stocking the shelves with canned peaches.

Gertrud's coral lips stretched into the likeness of a smile. "Liesl, how good to see you." Was there a word for people who acted as friends but in truth were not? There should be. As she paged through the account book to the *W*s, Gertrud recited her usual litany of Hildy's perfect scores on her spelling and geography tests. She did not mention my overdue account, but it was there between us. The bell over the door chimed and Gertrud glanced up.

Her mouth pursed like she'd bitten into a bad pickle.

I turned to see Miriam and Frieda. I was momentarily out of sorts. Miriam had never to my knowledge shopped at Grundbacher's, I'd always assumed because of their dietary restrictions.

Gertrud spoke up loud and strident. "We don't have kosher meat, Mrs. Stahr. If that's what you're looking for, you'll have to go to Rhein's."

"Just a small jar of yeast, please, Mrs. Grundbacher," Miriam said with a glance at me. "I was making bread and hadn't realized . . ." She trailed off as Gertrud turned her back on her without a word.

I ignored Gertrud's rudeness.

Frieda crept closer to the enticing display of candy. Her small hands hovered at the glass, her face hopeful, her voice a whisper. "Mommy, can I please—?"

"Don't touch the glass, little girl." Johan's voice was a bark from above that made Frieda jump. "I just washed it."

Frieda seemed to shrink inside herself, moving back to stand behind her mother. Miriam's cheeks were pink and her eyes snapped with anger. My own sensibilities responded in sympathy for the soft-spoken girl who spent as much time in my kitchen as her mother's. Whose sweetness was the perfect balance to Tess's difficult nature.

Yet I did not speak out.

What should I have done? Something. Anything but stand silently as Gertrud returned with a jar of yeast and a testy sigh. Miriam fished a quarter from her pocketbook, then took Frieda's hand and turned away.

"Really," Gertrud said before Miriam was halfway to the door. "They should go to their own stores. I don't know how you stand it, Liesl, living so close."

Miriam stopped then and looked back. I should have said something in her defense. But I did not. My mind was paralyzed, my mouth unable to form words. Miriam pushed through the door, the jingle of the bell sounding of reproach.

I had replayed the encounter many times. Why did I not speak up for my friend? Had it been my overdue account with Gertrud? Fear that Tess would be ostracized from the girls who had finally accepted her? Or was I simply a coward?

I was afraid I knew the answer.

When I told Mutti, she sputtered, "You march yourself right over and apologize, young lady," as if I were twelve years old. But I didn't. I couldn't. I was ashamed of what I'd done. And afraid Miriam would not forgive me. I avoided the backyard when Miriam was in her garden. I did not step over to say hello on Sunday afternoons. Spring turned to summer. Weeks stretched to months, and the gulf between Miriam and me widened so far it became uncrossable.

I had lost the friend of my heart through my silence. And nothing would bring her back to me.

CHAPTER 20

I woke Saturday morning with bone-deep loneliness.

My midnight survey of my house and family had yielded me no peace. I walked the floor, checking each room. All was in order but myself. I doubted my every decision. My children. My work with Leon Lewis. God.

As a weak morning sun lit the room, I slid my feet into my bedroom slippers, pulled on the pink chenille robe Tomas had given me on our first Christmas, and went down the stairs. Two days of reprieve from duplicity was a welcome thought in my dark musings.

In the kitchen, Mutti was cracking eggs, a plate of crisp bacon ready, thanks to Mr. Lewis.

Mutti handed me a cup of coffee lightened with a splash of cream. *"Guten Morgen,"* she said with a smile. *"Hast Du gut geschlafen?"*

"Ganz gut," I lied. I had not slept well but Mutti was in fine spirits at least.

An hour later, the children were fed and in their Saturday work clothes—a stained seersucker playsuit for Steffen, Tess in yellow cotton overalls that she'd almost outgrown. I dressed in my own cleaning clothes—a worn cotton blouse and a pair of Tomas's old trousers, rolled at the cuff and belted with a scarf.

I gave Tess and Steffen their Saturday tasks: dust under the beds, shake and beat the hall carpet, and wipe the baseboards of each room. "After the breakfast dishes," I reminded them.

"First we have to find Mr. Dog," Tess pushed back. Fritz had come home from work, then gone to sleep in his tiny attic room after hiding the toy for the children.

"First the dishes."

Tess whined as she washed a dish and passed it to Steffen, who stood on a stool to dry. "Hildy has a *Putzfrau* who does all the work. She uses a vacuum cleaning machine right in the house."

I shook my head in disbelief. "Why would I need a maid when I have you?"

She did not smile. "After chores can I go to Hildy's house?"

"We'll see," I said with a flash of regret. I wished for the days when Tess, Steffen, and Frieda would run about the yard with the carpet beater, pretending to be knights on horses. Miriam had welcomed Steffen into her home as well as Tess. Gertrud Grundbacher, unsurprisingly, did not invite Steffen to play.

Steffen's crestfallen face showed that he missed those days also.

"You and I will look for lizards," I told Steffen, and he brightened. I did not relish the thought of searching for creatures in the sidewalks and ditches, but his affection for the crawly things of nature—including, to my horror, spiders—bordered on obsession. He captured whatever he could in a jar and observed it carefully, before gently returning it to the exact spot in which he'd found it.

"She's getting spoiled rotten," Mutti said of Tess's mulish behavior, "with all the time she spends at that fancy house."

Mutti had no room to criticize about spoiling, but I didn't remind her how many times she'd given way to Tess's demands and done the same for Fritz.

She started the upstairs cleaning, washing the walls of every room with water and a drop of kerosene. I began with the bathroom. The house might be cramped and the linoleum worn thin, but it would be as clean as a hospital ward or my name was not Liesl Weiss.

I was sprinkling scouring powder in the bathtub when the doorbell rang. The familiar hope flashed before I pressed it down. *Not Tomas.* Of course not. I glanced in the hall mirror as I went to the door. With my hair escaping wildly from the headscarf and my face bare of makeup, I looked terrible enough to frighten away any brush salesman.

I opened the door to find Gertrud Grundbacher, Neele Weber, and Silka Scholz on my stoop.

"Liesl!" Gertrud sang. "It looks like we've caught you at a busy moment."

Gertrud wore an emerald day dress and a white straw hat. Silka and Neele were similarly dressed in heels and hats that declared they did not do their own cleaning on Saturday. But it was the small lapel pin on Gertrud's bosom that caught my attention. A black circle with the red swastika of the National Socialist Party.

My reprieve from deception had not lasted half the morning.

I found my voice and my manners. "Of course not, please come in." I ushered them into the sitting room while I slipped the scarf from my head and smoothed my hair.

Mutti came out of the kitchen with the bucket and scrub brush. "What are they doing here?" Mutti had never liked Gertrud and Silka and wasn't shy about making that known, although she said good things about Neele on occasion. Her sharp eye took in the details of each woman's appearance, landing with a frown on Gertrud's lapel pin. She opened her mouth.

"Mutti," I cut her off before she could blurt out more rudeness, "could you bring us coffee, *bitte*?"

She harrumphed and stomped to the kitchen.

"Please, have a seat," I said, motioning to the divan and chair while I silently turned over the same question. Why were they here?

Gertrud took her time settling on the divan, which I hoped was free of Chester's gray hair. "I was so pleased to see you at the alliance meeting the other night," Gertrud began. "I said to Silka and Neele it has been too long since we've visited Liesl."

Silka nodded.

Neele smiled apologetically. "You are working for the Friends of New Germany, is that right, Liesl?"

"I am," I answered her carefully.

"*Wunderbar!*" Gertrud sang out. "Thekla is such a dear."

Of course it had been Gertrud gossiping to Thekla. She couldn't help herself.

Gertrud set her gloved hand on my arm. "The girls and I—" here she looked over at Silka and Neele—"at our meeting for the Christian Women's Brigade—Liesl, you really must join—had a perfectly wonderful idea." She lowered her voice and looked pleased with herself. "Wilhelm Otto."

My hand wobbled and my cup clattered against the saucer. What could she mean?

"Wilhelm is handsome," Silka explained as if that answered my shocked look. "And quite well-off. That auto, his suits." She raised her artificially arched brows.

"I think you'd get along wonderfully," Gertrud said. "And he's great friends with Johan. We could go to the Lorelei together. Do say you'll think about it, Liesl."

Think about it? It was absurd. He was terrifying. And there was that mustache. But more to the point, I was still married. "I couldn't," I sputtered.

"You're still so young, Liesl," Gertrud said, leaning close to me with an expression of sympathy as she guessed my reasoning. "You could petition for a . . . divorce," she whispered the word. "None of your friends would blame you. We certainly would understand."

Heat rose in my face. I looked to Silka, who was smiling like a nincompoop, then to Neele, who shifted uncomfortably and examined her coffee.

I did not want a divorce and I certainly wanted nothing to do with Wilhelm Otto. Gertrud Grundbacher had no right—with her *Putzfrau* and her in-house vacuum machine and ridiculous orange lipstick—to talk so freely about my personal life. She was not my friend and never would be. I stood abruptly. "Don't let me keep you. I'm sure you all have busy days planned." The words came out snappish, but I didn't care.

The three women exchanged glances, then finished their coffee in a hurry. Gertrud was not deterred. "Well, perhaps we'll see you at Deutscher Tag tomorrow."

I had no intention of attending the German celebrations at Hindenburg Park the next day. I opened the door. "Perhaps." I wished them out of my house at once.

As we stepped onto the front stoop, all three ladies stopped suddenly.

"What are they doing?" Silka said in a ridiculously loud whisper.

Yitzak and Miriam Stahr were in the side yard not fifteen feet away, their kitchen table set under the shade of a small oak. A luncheon was set upon it as they often did on Saturdays. Miriam carried a pitcher of lemonade to the table, where Yitzak sat with Frieda and his father—a black-hatted gentleman who lived in Boyle Heights and visited each week. All were dressed in their best clothing and smiling . . . until they spied Gertrud and her friends staring at them.

"My goodness," Gertrud said with a hand on her heart as if she were startled. The black-and-red lapel pin glinted in the sun. "I had no idea they were so uncouth. How do you stand it right next door, Liesl?"

Silka shook her head as if it were a crime to picnic in your own yard.

"Liesl, do join us at the Christian Women's Brigade." Gertrud's voice was louder than need be and clearly she meant it to carry. "Our motto is simple and yet so true. To do our *Christian* duty." Her meaning was as clear as the Nazi lapel pin on her bosom.

Miriam's gaze met mine across the short expanse of green lawn.

Unlike the day at the grocery, this time I knew exactly what to say to Gertrud. I would tell her that she was a wrongheaded bigot. That Miriam Stahr had every right to have lunch with her family on her Sabbath. That Miriam was a better woman on her worst day than Gertrud was on her best. And that I wouldn't darken the doorstep of Grundbacher's grocery again if I had to walk ten miles for potatoes. But I couldn't say anything. For the sake of Leon Lewis's operation, I must remain silent.

Miriam turned her head away and I thought I saw the glint of tears in her eyes.

CHAPTER 21

AGENT THIRTEEN

Thirteen's mouth tasted like the bottom of an ashtray. This week, he was going to stop smoking. The sun slanted through the curtains and across the bed where the dog was curled in a ball. Thirteen sat up, cracked his back, and rubbed a hand over his hair. He was getting too old for this kind of work.

Another early morning drive to Hollywood Hills. At least this time he knew what to expect.

What's more, he had backup.

He'd recruited a new operative, somebody he trusted. He'd met the veteran at the Turnverein on Wednesday night. That travesty of a vote burned him, but nothing he could do about it. Max Socha was a puppet of the Friends of New Germany and now they had access to the alliance's bank account and the land in the hills.

The new agent was a perfect fit, a kraut who deplored what Adolf Hitler was doing to Germany. When Thirteen danced around the idea of getting information by posing as a Nazi, the man agreed to jump in the ring. Lewis checked him out. A day later he gave Thirteen the go-ahead and Seventeen his code name. Then came the tough part. Thirteen had to get the Nazis to trust a new man.

It helped that Hermann Schwinn and Winterhalder liked their booze.

He told Seventeen to show up at the Alt Heidelberg last night, where he'd been invited for drinks with the two men. "Make it seem like we're old friends, running into each other," Thirteen said. Seventeen had played his part well, buying a round of beer and quoting right out of *Mein Kampf.* By the early hours of Saturday morning, Leon Lewis's newest agent passed muster with the Nazis.

Thirteen took a shower and dropped the dog at the front desk; then he picked up Seventeen at a nice bungalow in Germantown. Next stop was for Schwinn at his fancy town house. Lastly, Hans Winterhalder dragged his sorry-looking self into the back seat along with a foul odor. Didn't the chump own a toothbrush?

"Are we sure we can trust this guy?" Winterhalder groused, jerking a thumb at Seventeen. Maybe he didn't remember much of the night before.

Schwinn looked over his shoulder at the new agent. "If we can't, we'll have to shoot him."

Schwinn and Winterhalder laughed, and so did Seventeen, but Thirteen felt the cold touch of fear on the back of his neck. A joke like that didn't strike him as funny.

They turned up Canyon Road as the morning fog blew out, exposing the blue and gold of the sky and lighting up the scrubby chaparral and silver-needled pines that thrived in the arid hills. Thirteen rolled down his window to let the tang of sage wash away Winterhalder's sour breath.

"What do you think of our new secretary?" Schwinn asked nobody in particular as the Cadillac nosed up the mountain road. "I haven't seen legs like those since the Berlin dance halls." Winterhalder said something foul. Thirteen had no opinion. "Of course I'm a happily married man," Schwinn amended quickly, "but no harm is coming from looking, *nicht so?*"

Thirteen took the next turn fast and Hermann Schwinn knocked into the door. "Sorry," he said. He wasn't. If he didn't have a job to do, he'd teach Schwinn a thing or two about respecting women.

"Themlitz is quite smitten with her," Schwinn said.

"Themlitz has his eye on more than a secretary," Thirteen said.

Schwinn looked at him sharply. "What do you mean?"

Thirteen shrugged. Time to put a bug in Schwinn's ear about Themlitz. "He asked me some questions about the alliance money, the bank, that kind of thing. Not my business." He'd leave that there for Schwinn to stew on. A little suspicion between friends.

Winterhalder had gone quiet in the rear seat of the Cadillac. That was interesting for a man who rarely shut up. Thirteen wondered if he had his eye on the alliance bank account as well. He put that information in his pocket to think on later.

They pulled onto the dirt road and his concern kicked into high gear.

The place had changed. A gate stretched across the road. The gate had a guard, and the guard had a gun. Not an old hunting rifle or antique service weapon, but a brand-spanking-new Colt revolver. Did the pimply-faced kid even know how to use that weapon? Thirteen was afraid he might.

They were waved through and parked on the grassy spot above the training ground. Instead of a half-dozen autos, there were three times that number, including the sky-blue Pontiac. What's more, the valley below looked like an army camp. The grass was mowed short, with a parade area on one side, a shooting range, and the outbuilding he'd been in last time painted a dull gray with a German swastika on the side like a target. Thirteen didn't look at Seventeen, afraid he'd see his own alarm reflected back. These men weren't just playing soldier.

This was an operation.

Winterhalder and Schwinn were out of the Cadillac and greeting the man who came out of the shack. Monroe. Not Thirteen's favorite Nazi.

At least he knew more about him. Came from hanging around in the basement of the Alt Heidelberg jawing with the veterans. That, and he'd managed to eavesdrop on a long-distance telephone call Monroe made to his brother in Atlanta, asking for a cash wire. It was clear from the shouting that the answer was no. Yet, from what he'd heard from Schwinn, the big Southerner threw his money around like it was feathers and he had a bed made out of it. Something more to think about.

He introduced Seventeen, and soon Monroe was busy dropping a who's who of Hollywood names. A dozen silver-shirted recruits were sitting at a makeshift table under the shadow of a lone white fir. Thirteen saw his chance.

Seventeen followed the plan they'd set up. "What's in here?" he asked about the outbuilding. Monroe was glad to give him the two-bit tour. While Seventeen kept Monroe and the others busy, Thirteen opened the trunk of his auto. Early that morning, he'd stopped by the Butterfield Bakery on Sixth Street and bought them clean out of doughnuts. He had bags of them—fresh and warm and dusted with sugar.

He carried the bags to the parade ground and gave the recruits a once-over. They were young. That's why he was here instead of sleeping in at the Biltmore. They still had a chance. He had to find a way to reach them before they did something terrible that changed the way they saw themselves. It was hard to turn back after something like that— downright impossible, maybe.

He knew a little about these young men. Most had been kids when their fathers went to war. Some of those fathers came home; most ended up as telegrams on the mantel. These boys had grown up wanting to be heroes, just like their fathers had been—to make a difference for their country. Then men like Winterhalder had come in and given them something to fight for—trouble was, it was something evil.

It was these kids who kept him awake at night.

As he figured, the doughnuts made him pretty popular. He sat down and asked the kids their names. Where they were from. Some of them didn't answer—those were the smart ones. Others told him everything he wanted to know and then some. He didn't blame 'em. They were just kids. And the more he knew, the more he'd be able to help them.

"How often do you come up here?" Thirteen asked a sunburned

redhead called Lenny with shoulders like coat hangers. The kid had wolfed down two doughnuts in thirty seconds.

"Every weekend, sometimes during the week. There'll be more men here by afternoon," he said, spitting crumbs. "But we've been here from the start."

Not good news. "That guy—" Thirteen jerked his head toward the shed where the other men had gone. "Monroe. You like him?"

"Sure," said a kid called Kurt. He and the younger boy beside him had the same white-blond hair and Aryan features. Had to be brothers. "A real tough guy."

"Talks funny," Lenny added.

A yellow-headed blackbird made its presence known, one bright eye on the doughnuts. Thirteen pushed the bag closer to the younger blond brother and shooed off the bird.

Kurt spoke up. "He says he was supposed to be Tarzan, but they hired Weissmuller instead."

"Wilshire Boulevard Jews stick together," Lenny said. The others nodded, mouths full. "Said he'll be glad when he sees 'em all dead."

Thirteen wanted to slap the kid and ask him what his mother would think of that kind of talk. Instead, he worked over the new information. It figured. Monroe had missed his chance in film and blamed Irving Thalberg and Mayer and the other big shots of the studio systems.

"He's what they call a marsh-all arts expert," Lenny said in a slow way that made it clear he didn't know what that meant.

Thirteen wouldn't want to get in a hand-to-hand with Monroe, that was for sure. The man outweighed him by at least fifty pounds. "They don't really expect you to fight, do they? You're just playing around, like the Boy Scouts?"

The kid frowned and took the bait. "No sir. We're going to be fighting. Communists and Jews and all that."

He put a disbelieving look on his face. "Says who?"

Kurt chimed in, "Monroe. And the other guy—what's his name?"

"Winterhalder," said a kid who had been quiet up to then, eating a doughnut with care, keeping the sugar from falling on his uniform shirt. He had glasses and carefully combed mouse-brown hair. Looked like he should be doing math problems, not learning to fight. "They're just waiting for the right timing—"

"Eldrich!" An older recruit approached the table. He had blond hair, filled-out shoulders, better skin. His uniform was clean and pressed; even his shoes were shined. "Don't go jawing about it."

But Thirteen needed to hear more, and so he pushed it with the bookish kid. "Come on, pal." He put disbelief in his voice. "They're jerking your chain."

Eldrich shook his head and insisted, "No, I heard 'em. They call it *der Angriff*—"

"Shut it, Eldrich," the clean-cut blond growled.

Eldrich did, but Thirteen had heard some of what he needed. *Der Angriff.* The attack. That didn't sound good. Thirteen made a mental note to watch the clean-cut kid the others seemed to listen to.

He saw the door to headquarters open and Schwinn sauntered out, his hand shielding his eyes from the sun. Looking for him. He was out of time.

Thirteen shook hands all around and told them to finish the doughnuts, but inside, he was churning. It was coming, whatever it was, and he needed to stop it—stop these dumb kids from doing something they'd regret the rest of their lives. These boys were too young to die, and no matter what they thought to the contrary, they sure as shooting didn't want to kill.

CHAPTER 22

AGENT THIRTEEN

Thirteen stood in a doorway across from the meeting place, lit a cigarette, and watched the rain shine the dirty street.

As a rule, he stayed out of Chinatown.

The alleyways were too narrow for an auto and poorly lit. The ramshackle buildings were cockeyed in a way that made him nervous, like he might get trapped in their labyrinth of side streets and dead ends. What's more, he didn't speak the language, and that was hard to get past. Not that he wanted to eat what was on offer in the restaurant windows—dried fish, shriveled roots, ducks plucked naked and hanging from their paddle-like feet.

No thank you.

Still, it was a shame the whole place would be gone soon, what with the construction of the Union Passenger Terminal. All of it—the shops, herbalists, opium dens, and fishmongers—torn down by this time next year. Kind of felt sorry for the people here, losing everything they knew. He took one last puff of the cigarette. Progress. It was rarely the rich men who bore the brunt of its cost, but they sure did reap the rewards.

Thirteen had called Lewis and set up a meeting as soon as he got back from the excursion to the hills. He'd fixed it so he drove Winterhalder and Schwinn home, then compared notes with Seventeen. They'd decided

Thirteen would meet Lewis alone. Safer that way. Thirteen couldn't help feeling responsible for the new agent. He was sticking his neck out and with what Schwinn said about reprisals . . . he had too much to lose, what with a family and all.

Chinatown was within walking distance of the Biltmore and it was a cool night, so he couldn't complain about the venue. The thing was, he needed to talk to Lewis. If he didn't get this new trouble off his chest, he'd never be able to sleep. He dropped the rest of the cigarette, the sparks flaring, then drowning, on the wet sidewalk. Might as well get it over with.

He opened the gilt door of Man Jen Low's Chinese restaurant. He didn't appreciate the chime of bells when he entered. Every face turned to look at him, then kept looking as he walked past booths lit by hanging lanterns. The sound of a foreign language in his ears, the smell of exotic spices. No, he didn't like this spot at all, but he was hungry. And the smell of food—even unfamiliar food—was making him hungrier.

"Boss." Thirteen lowered himself on the other side of the table in a private booth. Once he was seated, nobody could see him. Problem was, he couldn't see the door and that made him jumpy. Lewis had a teapot on the table in front of him. He figured it wasn't Scotch Lewis poured into two cups missing their handles. "Thanks for coming out." He raised one eyebrow at the surroundings.

"Not your kind of place?" Lewis asked with a hint of a smile. He passed one of the cups across the table.

Thirteen shrugged. "It's not the duck pond." Even if it did have ducks.

Lewis looked around meaningfully. "I imagine it isn't somewhere your Nazi friends would frequent."

So it wasn't the chop suey that brought Leon Lewis to Chinatown. He was always smarter than Thirteen gave him credit for. He should have remembered that.

The waitress, a tiny lady as dried up as an old mushroom, came to the table and said something Thirteen didn't catch but he figured she wanted their order. He looked at Lewis and shook his head.

Lewis asked for fried chicken—Thirteen liked the sound of that—and egg foo yong. That didn't sound so appealing. Thirteen waited for the old woman to move away. She might not speak English, or then again she might. What he had to say was for Lewis alone.

He took a drink of tea and grimaced. It tasted like dirt. Then he told Lewis about the trip to the Hollywood Hills. The Silver Shirts. That kid with the red hair, he couldn't get him out of his mind. Something about the way he'd gone after those doughnuts, like he'd been hungry his whole life.

"They're planning something, calling it *der Angriff*."

Lewis rubbed his chin, the only indication of his concern at this development. Thirteen liked that about him. No drama. He took the news and immediately filed it away for reflection instead of getting riled up. It was the sign of a good leader, like the men he'd known in the war. "No idea of what they will do or when?" Lewis asked.

"Nope," he answered. "Seventeen got another look at the control room, out on the training grounds. There's a map. He couldn't see much, but it looked like all of Los Angeles, some of Culver City."

After Thirteen finished his report, he drank more of the dirt-flavored tea, let the silence stretch while Lewis did some thinking. Thirteen wasn't dumb enough to think Lewis told him every angle he was working, but he trusted the man. Leon Lewis was intelligent, honest, and worthy of respect.

At one of the Nazi meetings he'd endured, he'd heard that the Jewish race was guided by the forces of evil—a tool of Satan, they said. Lewis was more like a dry-witted angel if Thirteen wanted to be fanciful about it.

The mushroom-lady brought out two platters of food that threatened to tip her over. The chicken was coated in a sticky sauce but it smelled darn good. The egg foo yong looked like a cross between a pancake and scrambled eggs, but he dug in.

"Good?" Lewis asked, nodding at the chicken.

Thirteen believed in giving credit where it was due. "Delicious." It was gonna be hard to save some for the dog.

After they finished eating, Lewis asked for the check. "How are they set for funds?"

"Not sure." He forked the egg pancakes into the paper bag the little waitress brought him. "They have guns, but not many. The kids buy their own uniforms, and they don't get fed."

"So they're low on money, at least for now," Lewis finished. "We have that in common."

Thirteen lit up a cigarette, took a puff, and let out a cloud of smoke. "Your other agent, anything there?"

Lewis shook his head. "Nothing we didn't already suspect or know."

He didn't elaborate on the other agent. It was the kind of thing that Thirteen didn't like about the spymaster.

Lewis leaned forward. "How are you doing at getting them fighting among themselves?"

Thirteen snuffed out the half-smoked cigarette. "Setting it up for Schwinn and Themlitz." Neither of them trusted the snaky Winterhalder, so stirring that pot wasn't hard.

"Good," Lewis said. "That should slow them down. And what about Mr. and Mrs. Schwinn? Marital discord would help our cause." He took a sip of his tea. "As you know, we are best served not by foiling a plot but by impeding its development."

"Sure thing, boss," Thirteen said. It would be easy enough, the way Hermann Schwinn was already moving in on the new secretary. She was pretty. Beautiful, not that it mattered. Friendly with Thekla—didn't take offense at their talk of Jews and spouted the same herself. She was a real kraut, what with her Aryan looks. A shame, really.

Yet there was the story about her husband. It wouldn't take much to run that lead down, but he'd keep it to himself. He didn't want Lewis thinking he was taking too much notice of a pretty woman. If he found something of interest, then he'd bring it to Lewis.

Lewis took out a few bills and put them down on the table. "Keep in touch, Thirteen." He stood, put on his hat. "We're on the right side of this, have faith in that." Then he was gone.

On the right side. Since when did that matter? He'd been on the right side of the Great War, and good men had died. He'd been on the wrong side of what happened in Monterey. *Have faith.* Thirteen didn't buy that either. No matter how much faith you had, bad things still happened to good people. His mother had been a faithful woman. His sister had said her prayers every night. Faith hadn't saved either of them.

It seemed like whatever they did—whatever progress they made— the Nazis progressed further. They had no idea when or what *der Angriff* was, and everywhere they turned, the threat was growing. How were they supposed to fight what was becoming an army with just himself, a Jewish lawyer, and a couple of amateur detectives?

Thirteen waited a good ten minutes, drinking the rest of the tea and wondering if what he was doing—what Leon Lewis was doing—would make any difference. Then he walked into the dark city, the bitter taste of the tea still in his mouth.

CHAPTER 23

AGENT THIRTEEN

Thirteen knocked on Winterhalder's door at seven thirty on Sunday morning.

The man answered in his boxer shorts and a ribbed cotton undershirt, smelling like a distillery. "Come on in." He swept his arm out like some kind of king in his castle.

Thirteen didn't go in. From the door, he could see enough. A dirty place, clothing on the floor and smelling like an ashtray and gin. "I'm just here for the keys."

He'd balked when Winterhalder telephoned last night, begging to borrow his auto. The Cadillac was temperamental and he didn't like anyone else driving her. Winterhalder wanted to take some floozy out for a night on the town, and much as the thought disgusted him, he had to keep in the man's good graces. This morning, he took the red line trolley to the place Winterhalder kept on Green Street. A place his wife didn't know about.

If the Cadillac looked anything like this apartment, he'd have something to say to the man.

"Sure, got the keys here somewhere." Winterhalder rubbed his hair, sticking up on one side like a badly trimmed hedge. "What you doing up so early on a Sunday, anyway?"

Thirteen spotted the keys on the floor beside the hall table. He ducked in and retrieved them.

A woman appeared in the doorway, blonde and dressed in little more than a scrap of fabric and some lace. Thirteen looked away before he saw more than he wanted to.

Winterhalder turned on her, his voice hard. "Beat it, Ida."

The dame disappeared into the back room, then came out in a ratty coat, carrying a paper bag. "Thanks for nothing, Hans," she muttered, passing him by and scurrying out the door.

Thirteen left right behind her, wishing he could wash his hands. He drove directly to a service station, cursing Winterhalder all the way. The gas tank was empty and cigarette butts with crimson lipstick smears littered the floor. He cleaned the auto, filled the tank, and was at the Hall of Justice by eight. He had some digging to do.

He parked on the street in front of the marble fortress—nobody around but the street cleaners and the bums. Inside, he went directly to the police archives. He'd once known a woman who worked there nights and weekends. He figured she might have the same shift and he was right.

"Donna, you're looking good," he said.

Donna was a brunette with a pretty face and a quick wit. She raised one brow. "Haven't seen you in an age." She went back to a slow pecking at the typewriter with bloodred fingernails.

Thirteen leaned against the desk. "Been outta town a couple years."

The carriage dinged and she pulled the paper out. "Still hanging out on street corners and taking pictures?"

"I'm doing some different work now, but I could use your help." He didn't try to charm her; she was too smart for that. Told her what he wanted straight out.

She frowned, rolled another paper onto the spool, and shook her head. "You trying to get me fired?"

"I think you owe me one, at least," he said mildly. He'd done a few favors for her over the years. One had been to get proof that her boyfriend—a real bum—was cheating on her with her own cousin. Hadn't even charged her a fee.

"Everybody in this town owes you at least one. That's how you operate," Donna grumbled. She sashayed off to the file storage room, where she was gone for a good long time. Finally she brought him what he needed, sliding the paper across the desk after making sure nobody was looking.

"Thanks, Donna." He glanced down at the report and the signature at the bottom.

She resumed typing. "Just don't show your ugly mug here again." By the way she said it, he knew she didn't mean it.

He was turning to go when he saw a familiar face—the clean-cut kid from the Silver Shirts. Instead of the light-gray shirt and Nazi armband, he wore the blue-and-black police uniform and a police cap with the City of Los Angeles emblem.

"It's Fritz, right?" he asked, although he knew it was. He carefully folded the report from Donna and tucked it in his jacket pocket. "Didn't know you were on the force." He should have guessed, though. The kid had training—he'd seen that right off.

Fritz stuck out his hand and greeted him with a firm handshake. "Just a cadet," he said. "Hoping to make officer by Christmas."

Thirteen made himself smile. Fritz was no doubt a good recruit. Polite, smart, probably from a decent family. Thirteen looked at his wristwatch. "You getting off soon?"

"Just punched out," Fritz answered.

"I was about to get some breakfast." He hadn't been but he could. "You hungry?"

Thirteen and Fritz settled into a booth at Lucy's Café, a place most of the force liked to frequent because they had good coffee. "Eggs and bacon?" he asked Fritz and ordered for them both. A waitress with iron-gray hair and downy cheeks poured their coffee. He had plenty he wanted to ask the kid. Figuring out how to go about it was the trick.

He started easy. "You always work nights?"

As much as the kid was closemouthed at the training ground in the hills, he seemed to open up this morning. Fritz was one of Hynes's men and joined the Silver Shirts after the police chief encouraged it. The waitress delivered the eggs and bacon with thick slabs of toast and a bottle of ketchup.

"What does your father think of you being on the force?" He'd bet his last cigarette the kid didn't have a father, and he was right.

"The war," Fritz said and shoveled the eggs in his mouth. That said it all.

"I'm sorry about that," he said. "You got a mother?"

Fritz spoke around the food in his mouth. "A mother, sister, her kids."

Thirteen frowned. "Must be tough, being the only man of the house."

Fritz rubbed the back of his neck and looked down at his clean-as-a-whistle plate. "Maybe I haven't done so hot with that."

Thirteen considered the man in front of him. Probably twenty, twenty-one. Old enough to step up, take responsibility. He was lucky if he had a family. But he didn't need a stranger giving him a lecture on it. "Well, you can always try harder" was all he said. "Good families are tough to come by these days."

Fritz didn't meet his eyes. "You're probably right about that."

Then it was the tricky part. "So . . . *der Angriff.* Monroe told me about it. What do you think?"

Fritz looked up quick, then away. He shrugged.

Thirteen's heart sped up a touch. He reached into his pocket for his packet of cigarettes and offered one to Fritz.

Fritz shook his head at the smoke. "I'm not sure what it is, to tell you the truth," he said finally. "And I don't know . . ." He trailed off and looked away.

Thirteen took a breath. He knew from experience he could be intimidating. Didn't mean to be. He concentrated on lighting his cigarette.

Looking casual. "Don't know what?" The kid looked like he wanted to get something off his chest.

Fritz leaned forward and lowered his voice. "It's just—"

"More coffee?" the gray-haired waitress interrupted and, without waiting for an answer, filled their cups. Thirteen held back a groan at her timing.

Fritz pulled back and seemed to reconsider.

"What?" Thirteen prompted. He was losing the kid.

"Nothing," Fritz said quickly. He looked at the clock above the door. "Listen, I gotta go. Monroe told us to show up at Hindenburg Park today. You going?"

Thirteen tried not to look as frustrated as he felt. He'd been so close. "Can't," he answered. It was the truth. He'd rather go to the festivities at Hindenburg Park—polka band and all—than what he had to do this afternoon. But he'd been working on this lead for a while and it couldn't be put off any longer. Besides, he figured the Deutscher Tag wasn't going to get him any new information. Buncha krauts drinking beer and slapping each other on the back. "Got somewhere to be."

Fritz stood and put out his hand. "Thanks for breakfast."

Thirteen watched Fritz walk out the door. What had the kid wanted to say? He drank the rest of the coffee and pulled out some change for the waitress. Had it been about *der Angriff* or something else? He seemed like a good kid; maybe he was having second thoughts.

When he couldn't put off the inevitable any longer, he drove the Cadillac to the one-story building on Figueroa Street. The September sun was starting a slow burn and he wiped the sweat from under his hatband while he watched the front door. Nobody going in or out. He walked around the block. It was like he'd figured—a back door. Three men standing watch. He approached them, slow and careful.

One of them, a guy with stooped shoulders and the expression of an undertaker, spoke up. "Password?"

Thirteen sized up the men and took his time answering. When Lewis asked him to infiltrate this group, he'd gone to a chump he used to know. Terrance Brown had worked on and off in unsavory doings for the studios in the twenties. Thirteen never liked him, but the weak-chinned fixer bragged more than once about his membership in a secret club that wasn't all that secret. Last week, he'd tracked Brown to a flophouse that smelled of urine and boiled turnips. For five dollars, the chump gave over the password.

Thirteen asked Brown what the word meant and the old man smirked. "When you meet somebody you think is one of us," he said, "you say 'ayak,' which means 'Are you a Klansman?' and they say 'akia' back. Means 'A Klansman I am.'" Brown laughed then, falling into a fit of coughing.

"If this doesn't work," Thirteen had told Brown with a level stare, "I'll be back for that five dollars."

In the dry heat of the back alley being sized up by three men, Thirteen tried to look like he knew what he was doing. "Ayak," he said, feeling ridiculous, and waited.

The undertaker raised an eyebrow. He looked at his two sidekicks. "Come on in, friend."

He followed the man inside, cursing Leon Lewis for having to do this.

When he'd been a Pinkerton detective hired to find wayward sons and cheating husbands, he'd been good at his job. He could pass himself off as just about anything—a bum, the police, a newspaper reporter. He was a good actor. A Klansman, though. That was a level of moron even he would have a rough time pulling off.

He did it, though, not that he was proud of the fact. An hour later he had a pounding headache, fifty new friends, and a membership in the Ku Klux Klan.

CHAPTER 24

Sunday morning, the sanctuary where Tomas and I had married and our children were christened was oppressively hot. Steffen squirmed and Tess fidgeted through the thankfully short sermon. With an announcement about Deutscher Tag from the pulpit, including the information that there would be cotton candy and pony rides, Tess looked at me with pleading eyes.

"No," I mouthed. Goodness no. She sulked, and I instantly felt the familiar weight of guilt. Tomas would have said yes. He would have reveled in a day at Hindenburg Park listening to a polka band, eating bratwurst, and trying his luck at *Nagelbalken*. *Have some fun, Liesl. You're too serious all the time.*

Mutti made it out of church after insulting only one person—the lead soprano in the choir whom she told to find another way to serve Jesus. "Mutti!" I apologized to the teary-eyed woman.

"Just being honest," Mutti huffed.

Honesty was why I could never tell Mutti of my work with Leon Lewis. Danielle Bittner was incapable of lies, no matter the consequences.

"Where is Fritz?" Tess asked with a whine when we got home from church. Mr. Dog lay on the divan just where she had left him.

"Go up and get changed out of your church dress," I told her. I had little idea where Fritz was from one moment to the next except that he hadn't gone to church with us for the third week in a row. I would change clothes and prepare for supper, then take the children to the park to make up for saying no to Deutscher Tag. Sunday was supposed to be a day of rest, was it not? I needed rest from the Friends of New Germany.

Fritz was still not home when the afternoon sun slanted through the sitting room window. Tess and Steffen were tired from our visit to the park, where I'd forgotten my worries for an hour as I pushed the swings and spun them in dizzying circles on the wooden roundabout. Steffen observed a blue-bellied lizard while Tess climbed the twenty-foot ladder and slid down the scalding-hot slide with shrieks of delight that made me laugh even as my heart was in my throat.

Now I stood at the kitchen sink, looking at the Stahrs' house—the neat hedge, the cut lawn. Miriam's garden and the scattered toys. I missed her with a deep ache. It was on Sundays like this that I would take lemonade and sit in the shade with her, sharing our week.

Sometimes we'd speak of faith. I'd tell her about the sermon I'd heard. She would tell me what her rabbi had said the day before. I'd never talked to anyone like that. Mutti taught Fritz and me our night-time prayers and brought us to church, but she didn't speak of her own faith. "It's between me and God and nobody's business," Mutti said. That was what I believed until I'd met Miriam.

When I'd shared my doubts with her after Tomas left—my fear that God didn't hear my prayers—she did not have a ready answer. "I don't think I pray correctly," I had confided.

"There is no wrong way to pray, Liesl," she said. "I don't think so anyway. And if you have questions and hurt, is that not your prayer? Doesn't he know your heart already?"

Of course it made sense, even if she was Jewish and I was Christian.

The rumble of an engine turned my gaze to the street. A police car. Was it Fritz?

No, it was Captain Hynes who stepped out of the auto and slammed the door. Mickey O'Neil came from the driver's side. My stomach dropped. Tomas?

But they did not come to my front door. They moved with determined strides to the Stahrs'.

I hurried out on the stoop. What was happening? Was someone hurt?

Miriam opened at their knock, a look of confusion on her face. And then everything happened quickly. "Is this the residence of Yitzak Stahr?" Captain Hynes said in an official tone. Mickey moved in, pushing past Miriam. He came out with Yitzak—handcuffed and struggling.

What was happening?

Miriam found her voice. "Yitzak—"

"Ma'am, stay where you are." They both took hold of Yitzak and yanked him toward the street.

Miriam ignored the order, rushing after Yitzak. "Wait—you can't—"

Mickey barked, "Don't make this harder, ma'am."

Frieda appeared on the front porch, watching her father get shoved into the police auto. Mutti, Tess, and Steffen stood behind me in the doorway. Across the street, Frau Mueller watched from her front lawn.

"Yitzak!" Miriam wailed.

The tires let out a sharp screech as Mickey pulled onto the street. What was this about? Yitzak was hotheaded, yes. He had a temper. But he was law-abiding. He didn't drink or gamble. Miriam needed to follow him, to be with him and find out the charges. I hurried across the grass to her. "Go," I said. "Get to the station. I'll keep Frieda."

She'd gone without so much as a word, not even changing her clothing. I settled a silent Frieda on the divan. Steffen brought Chester and put him in her lap. Tess offered to let her hold Mr. Dog. Frieda remained pale and silent.

I had a sick feeling as I paced through the early afternoon. Was this something to do with me? With the Friends of New Germany or Leon Lewis? But how could it be? And yet I could not dismiss the twist under my ribs as I looked at the Stahrs' empty house.

When Fritz drove up in his rattletrap Ford after the sun went down, Mutti told him about Yitzak. He looked unsurprised and shoveled left-over sauerbraten like he hadn't seen food all day.

My unease deepened to alarm. "Fritz, what do you know about Yitzak?"

He shrugged and spoke with his mouth full. "He deserves whatever he gets."

"What on earth are you talking about?" Mutti snapped. She'd always liked Yitzak, in her own way.

"Didn't you hear about Deutscher Tag?" Fritz asked. "A bunch of thugs showed up, shouting about Adolf Hitler and throwing bricks. One of them shot a gun. A woman and her daughter had to go to the hospital—a *child*, Liesl. They tracked it to the Jewish Brotherhood."

"Shh!" I looked at Frieda, asleep on the divan next to Chester. "But Yitzak couldn't have—"

"It was him," Fritz said quickly. "They covered their faces. Good thing we were there—we ran them off."

"Who do you mean, *we*?" Mutti demanded.

I looked at Fritz and he swallowed. "Nothing, Mutti. Just me and some guys."

She narrowed her eyes at him.

"It wasn't Yitzak." My voice didn't hold as much conviction as it should. "He wouldn't be involved in that."

Fritz pushed his plate away. "I saw him—the guy was tall—and anyway, he's always going on about how Jews are treated. You've heard him. I told Hynes about it and it turns out he's on their list of possible members of the Brotherhood. Hynes was glad for my help." He looked at me in triumph. "Don't go all bleeding heart for Yitzak. You know what Jews are like."

He'd turned Yitzak in himself? Our neighbor and friend? *You know what Jews are like.* When had our friend and neighbor turned into a nameless enemy in my brother's mind? Where had my brother gone and how was I to get him back?

A knock sounded on the door. Miriam. I looked at Fritz—his expression defiant, mine accusing. How could I face her, knowing that Yitzak had been arrested because of my own brother?

I opened the door. Miriam stood on the stoop looking weary.

"Is Yitzak . . . ?" I looked behind Miriam, hoping that her husband had been released, that it was all a terrible mistake.

"He's in jail," she stated. "Thank you for keeping Frieda." Polite but cold as ice.

"She can sleep here tonight if you . . ." We'd done it many times—let the girls sleep and sent them home in the morning—when we were friends.

"No." She jerked her head. "You've done enough." She looked over my shoulder at Fritz with an accusatory glare. "He was home all day," she said suddenly. "But they won't believe me. They have a witness."

I wilted in shame as I realized she knew Fritz's part in her sorrow. "Miriam, I—"

"Don't, Liesl." She pushed past me. "I can't stand it from you, too. Not today." She went to Frieda on the divan, looking down on her sleeping face. "I can't afford a lawyer." Her voice broke. "And now—" That's when I saw what I should have noticed months ago. She was expecting.

"Oh, Miriam." She'd waited so long and finally a brother or sister for Frieda. And she was alone, Yitzak in jail—looking at prison if he didn't find a way to prove his innocence.

She leveled a look at me that stopped any more words—a mixture of betrayal, anger, and sadness that pierced me like a knife. She picked up Frieda and carried her out the door without another word.

I shut the door behind her. This was my fault. Mine and Fritz's. I didn't know how to reach my brother but I could help Miriam. I waited and paced the house until Fritz and Mutti were in bed and all was quiet. I took a slip of paper from my coin purse and quietly picked up the telephone. "Boyle Heights 4404," I said to the operator in a low voice.

"It's Edelweiss," I whispered when the call was answered on the first ring. "I need your help."

CHAPTER 25

LIESL

I would be late to work, but I must meet with Leon Lewis. For Miriam's sake and for Yitzak's. And somehow for Fritz.

I had slept not at all. Tossing and turning with my regrets. Walking the dark rooms of my home and holding conversations in my head—accusatory ones with Fritz, remorseful ones with Miriam. Questioning ones with God. My eyes were gritty and my limbs heavy as I stepped off the trolley on Broadway, the sky a lowering gray mass. The streets of downtown were crowded with suited men walking to work, mothers holding children's hands as they crossed the street.

I found Mr. Lewis in the back booth at the Blue Owl, a tiny establishment tucked around the corner from the grand structures of city hall and the Hall of Justice. The smell of grease and burned coffee hung like a fog under the low ceiling.

"Edelweiss," he said as I sat down. His voice held the weariness of a sleepless night such as my own. A folded newspaper and an ashtray with two half-smoked cigarettes lay on the table. A waitress poured me a cup of coffee, refilled Mr. Lewis's cup, and whisked away the ashtray.

The thick white mug before me had a smear of crimson lipstick on the rim. "What happened with Yitzak?" I had not the time for pleasantries.

"He's being released." Lewis took a sip of his coffee and grimaced. "He'll be home by noon."

I let out a relieved breath, but my companion didn't look pleased.

"Why did they arrest him?" I asked. I didn't want to pry—but Fritz. I needed to know if he was involved.

Lewis pinched at the corners of his eyes. "Yitzak is a member of a group, the Jewish Brotherhood. They are a—" he tipped his head to the side as if considering his words—"somewhat-radical bunch. The police had a membership list. His name was on it."

So it hadn't been just Fritz's word. Yitzak was in the Brotherhood. "Why did he do it? Attack the people at the Deutscher Tag?"

Lewis shook his head. "He didn't—and neither did the Brotherhood." At my questioning expression, he tapped the newspaper in front of him. "I have reason to believe it was the Nazis themselves."

I jerked back at the preposterous notion. "Why?" For what reason would Germans attack their own?

"It's an effective tactic, used extensively in Germany and elsewhere— plan an event, plant your own people to stage an attack, blame it on your enemies. Garner sympathy for your cause."

I picked up the mug, my cold hands warming on its sides. I raised the mug almost to my lips, remembered the lipstick smear, and put it down again. "How can they do that? The woman and a child?"

"All the better. The newspapers grab on to the narrative and the victims have instant support. For the Nazi Party, the ends always justify the means."

The words chilled me. "Did you tell the police?" They needed to know this, do something about it.

Leon Lewis shook his head dolefully. "I'm afraid that's exactly what I did." He sat back and let out a breath. "I told Captain Hynes my theory. It was the wrong move, a very wrong move."

"What do you mean?" Captain Hynes. I pushed the remembrance of him in my sitting room away.

"He denied the theory utterly. Called me a 'Jew looking out for his own.' Quite what I've been trying to avoid." Lewis's voice went hard. "He had the gall to defend Adolf Hitler and his ideas. Right to my face. He said Germans were taking action to save their country from Communists. And by Communists, he of course meant Jews."

My insides knotted. I didn't know what to say. Where to look. I was ashamed of the captain, of Fritz. Of myself for thinking Yitzak was guilty.

"We can safely say that Captain Hynes is not on our side. In fact, I believe he is involved with the Silver Shirts, possibly even recruiting for them." He looked at me intently. "Mr. Stahr suggested that your brother—Fritz, is it?—is a part of the Nazi organization as well."

"I'm sorry," I said. My lack of truthfulness sent a flush of heat from my collar to my cheeks. "I should have told you."

"Yes, well." Lewis let out his breath. "You weren't aware of the dangers."

Indeed I had not been, but that was changing now. How was I to get through to Fritz? To change his heart and mind? To save him from himself? "Why do these people—" my brother, I meant but could not say it—"get involved in something like the Silver Shirts?" He hadn't been raised that way, not by Mutti and not by me.

"I don't know." Lewis looked sympathetic. "Perhaps because so many boys don't have fathers after the war. Or because they lack faith in a higher power."

Fritz grew up without a father, but he had Mutti and me. And we had faith in God. Surely Fritz did as well.

Lewis went on. "Perhaps it is simply a response to fear. Fear for themselves, of something that is not like them. Fear for their families. At least, that is my hope, because fear can be faced. And if it is confronted, people can change."

"How?" I asked. The answer was suddenly of utmost importance. How could Fritz change? How could he come back?

Leon Lewis looked at me sadly. "I don't have that answer, Edelweiss. But I do know we must not meet that fear with anger, no matter how angry we are, for that only fuels the fire. Perhaps only love can change their minds." He shrugged. "Or perhaps that is a sentimental notion."

Love? Fritz was loved. By Mutti and me and the children. And yet, when was the last time I'd shown him anything other than anger?

"What about everyone else?" I asked. "There have to be good people, good Christians, who could do something. Why don't they speak up?" Even as I said it, guilt pierced me. Why had I not spoken up?

"There are many who sympathize. And who would not actively oppress those who are Jewish—or Negro or Mexican. They do not keep Jewish people from their stores nor forbid them from the clubs." Lewis's voice took on a hard edge. "But they shop at those stores, are members of those clubs. They may even have friends who are Jewish, but they remain silent in the face of the oppression."

My guilt swelled into shame. He was describing me.

He continued with growing passion. "There are those who say, 'Of course I don't agree, but who am I to tell others?' These people are, in effect, taking the side of the oppressor. Silence is oppression in itself, although not perhaps as egregious." He took a long breath as if to calm himself.

Silence. Through my silence I'd given Gertrud Grundbacher permission to continue her attitude toward Miriam and those like her. I'd let Tess do the same to Frieda. I'd stayed silent in the face of Fritz's growing anger toward those not like himself.

"Then there are those who are not passive but active in their opposition. Whether it be by using the law or by standing up and voicing what must be said. They are in much fewer supply."

Suddenly I wanted to be one of those. I'd forsaken Miriam when she needed me. In thinking I was doing right for Tess, I'd let her turn her back on her best friend. Let Fritz speak his poisonous words in my home and not challenged him. And now the Nazis—perhaps even the pleasant people I worked for—wished to eradicate people they deemed not even human.

Leon Lewis. Miriam and Yitzak and Frieda. Stella.

I could no longer remain on the sidelines, wringing my hands and wishing for things to be different. I must join a side. Because this fight was no longer Leon Lewis's alone.

It was mine as well.

I arrived at the Alt Heidelberg twenty-seven minutes late and prepared to face Thekla's displeasure. She was at my desk, newspapers strewn in disarray, but waved away my excuse. "Have you heard?"

"About Deutscher Tag?" I did not have to feign my distress. I thought of Miriam and Yitzak. The woman and her child. Frieda waiting for her father to return.

Thekla frowned in her pretty way. "A terrible thing, Liesl. And just what we've been worried about."

Hermann came out of his office. "Didn't we tell them? Wasn't it exactly as we predicted?" he demanded with an undercurrent of energy I found disturbing. "Those people."

I wet my suddenly dry mouth. "How are they?"

Thekla glanced up at me. "Who?"

"The woman who was hurt and her child."

"Minor injuries," she said dismissively. "It could have been so much worse. They've arrested a Jew, did you hear?"

I nodded, my throat too tight to speak.

"You must take over the telephone, Liesl. We have much to do."

Through the morning, I answered dozens of telephone calls from Germantown residents. Some were outraged, some frightened. I told them how to become members of the Friends of New Germany and recited the address where they should send their dues. A steady stream of men went in and out of Hermann Schwinn's office. Paul Themlitz, Hans Winterhalder, Max Socha. A general buzz of excitement—like a holiday or a special event—permeated the office.

"Isn't it wonderful?" Thekla said as I logged another new membership. She had ceased to pretend outrage and was positively buoyant.

"*Ja,*" I answered. So wonderful my stomach was turning over.

Hermann dictated letters to the editors of the *Daily*, the *Times*, and the *Examiner*. "Do not let the attack on our German neighbors go unheeded. Protect your families from the growing menace in our city and our country." Hermann repeated the same words in every letter. "We must strike with the hot iron," he'd said when I brought them into his office for his signature. I typed the letters with carbons to file and slipped the shorthand pages under my blotter.

Thekla—all smiles and graciousness—treated me to a lunch of egg salad sandwiches from the corner delicatessen. "We have much to celebrate today."

When we returned, Hermann was waiting for us. "Liesl, come into my office."

I followed him, Thekla on my heels. Hermann sat down behind his desk. Wilhelm Otto leaned against the file drawers in his shirtsleeves. My heart jumped in alarm. A leather holster was buckled across his shoulders, and under his right arm I saw the unmistakable butt of a gun. He was as dangerous as I'd imagined. I settled uneasily in a chair across from Hermann.

"We were planning on waiting, but with all you've done for us today . . ." Hermann pushed a sheet of paper across the desk toward me with a smile. "We'd like to make it official."

I read the paper in front of me.

I pledge my allegiance to the Friends of New Germany. I acknowledge the leadership principle upon which the FNG is formed. I belong to no Semitic organization. I am of Aryan stock and have neither Jewish nor colored blood in me. I acknowledge and support the work of the National Socialist German Workers' Party both at home and in the fatherland.

A prickle of fear went up my spine. I glanced quickly at Wilhelm Otto. He was watching me with his stone-gray eyes. Could he see my hesitation?

"It's a great honor, my dear." Thekla nudged me. "And don't worry, we'll cover the dues."

"I don't know what to say." And yet this was a chance to do exactly as Leon Lewis had asked. Gain their trust.

Hermann held out his own fountain pen and I took it with what I hoped was a steady hand. I signed my name, wondering if I could cross my fingers like Tess did when she made a promise she didn't intend to keep. Support the work of the National Socialists? I would do the opposite.

Hermann blew on my signature to dry the ink, then pulled open the bottom drawer of the oak cabinet behind his desk and tucked the signed paper into a file.

"One thing more." Thekla took a small item from her pocket and leaned forward. She pinned it to my blouse and patted it in place. "Keep this over your heart, Liesl, where it belongs."

I looked down. It was the same pin Wilhelm and Hermann and Thekla wore. The same that Gertrud Grundbacher proudly displayed on her emerald dress. A red-and-white background with the black swastika. Thekla leaned back as if she was waiting for me to speak.

The words came from somewhere. "I can't tell you what this means to me." Indeed, I could not express my revulsion.

Hermann reached across his desk and put his heavy hand on mine. "Welcome to the Nazi Party, Liesl."

My duties that afternoon for the Friends of New Germany were much the same as the previous week: I typed letters, addressed envelopes, and answered the telephone. But my eyes had been opened.

What seemed a wholesome endeavor for German American goodwill was a lie.

Every letter and dictation was punctuated with the thinly disguised code of the National Socialists and Adolf Hitler. "Expose the

Communists" meant rid the country of Jewish Americans. "Restore Christian values" meant institute hatred. "Take back our country" meant indoctrinate prejudice.

I had deciphered the language of the Nazi Party and it was despicable. This was not a way to honor the country of our forefathers. This was a twisting of what it meant to be a German American.

"We need evidence of treason," Lewis had said before I left him at the diner that morning. "Membership lists, supplies bought with foreign currency, funding from outside sources. The proof must be in that office."

He was right. Thekla and Hermann were Germans to the core and therefore kept meticulous records. I reasoned that these records must be in the locked file drawers in Hermann Schwinn's office. If I was going to do my job for Leon Lewis—and I intended to do so—I must see those files. And yet Lewis's final instruction had been given with utmost seriousness and must also be heeded. "Take care to keep their trust, Edelweiss. Do not let them doubt you."

At three o'clock, I gathered my hat and gloves and prepared to catch the trolley. My shorthand dictation and jotted notes were safely stowed in my handbag. Thekla had stepped out to do some shopping and Hermann was on the telephone in his office. I let myself sigh with relief that the day was over. I wished only to get home and make sure Yitzak was back with his family.

I was not that fortunate.

When I left the building, I found Wilhelm Otto leaning against his car, waiting for me. The breeze held the hint of coming rain, but I'd rather get wet than get in that sleek auto. He ignored my polite protest and opened the door. I had no choice but to comply. I was thankful for his silence as we pulled onto the street but as it stretched too long for propriety, irritation flashed through me. If he refused to speak, I could certainly do so as well. I clamped my teeth together and counted the cars that passed us. As we turned down Pico, I let myself turn my perusal to him.

He was perfectly relaxed, one elbow leaning crookedly out his open window, the other hand resting lightly on the steering wheel. He caught me watching him and one eyebrow flickered. I turned my head to look out the window at the passing houses. Finally we reached my own.

"Thank you, Mr. Otto," I said and did not wait for him to get out and open my door but pushed it open myself and stepped onto the curb. I watched the auto disappear around the next corner.

I must find a way to avoid this daily torture.

But for now I gathered my courage and turned toward Miriam's front door as rain began to fall on Miriam's roses. I knocked at the door, unsure of how I'd be received. Not with gratitude, since neither Miriam nor Yitzak knew that Leon Lewis had come to his aid through my efforts.

I did not expect hostility.

Yitzak jerked open the door and I gasped. His face was a mass of bruises, one eye swollen shut. He held his right arm close to his body, slightly hunched over it. "Yitzak," I said, "what happened?"

His good eye pinned me with a furious stare. "Ask your brother and his friends on the force."

Shock jolted through me. Fritz could not have done this. "I didn't— he didn't . . ." Did he?

Yitzak stared bullets at me. Miriam appeared behind him and for a moment regarded me with anxiety. Her gaze dropped to my lapel and her expression hardened. I had forgotten about the lapel pin. I reacted with pure instinct, raising my hand to cover the black swastika, but it was too late.

My cheeks burned with shame. What would she think? The symbol over my heart was no less than a slap in the face to her. I had betrayed her at Grundbacher's and now I wore a sign of hatred to her people. I had no way to explain.

Yitzak looked at me with disgust. "Do not," he bit out, "ever speak to my family again." He shut the door firmly in my face.

CHAPTER 26

AGENT THIRTEEN

Thirteen walked down the back stairs to the basement of the Hall of Justice. The detective he was looking for must have really ticked somebody off to get shoved into the bowels of the building. But from all accounts, this was the man to see if you had questions and wanted to keep them quiet.

Thirteen was still burned up about the Deutscher Tag yesterday. There he'd been, yukking it up with the Klan while the attack took place at Hindenburg Park. How could he have missed what they were planning? And why hadn't Hermann Schwinn let on about it? He must not be as trusted as he needed to be.

He had a good idea of who the real brick thrower was and not whatever Jewish man they picked up and pinned the blame on. He tried to get the story at the Germantown precinct last night but none of his pals were working on a Sunday. Then he got a call from Lewis and dragged himself to a run-down diner at dawn this morning for the details.

The Germans themselves set up the attack and it worked just as they'd planned. They got a good write-up in the newspapers and of course people believed it. Winterhalder was pulling in new recruits, the Friends of New Germany signed on a hundred new members, and Thirteen's job was ten times harder.

"Do you think this was *der Angriff*?" he had asked Lewis at the diner.

Lewis gave it some thought, then shook his head. "I believe this was a precursor to something much bigger."

Thirteen rubbed a hand over his tired eyes. It was enough to make him lose faith in humanity.

When he showed up at the Alt Heidelberg, Schwinn had sent him to the hills to check on the recruits. Thirteen had brought sandwiches this time and done more listening than talking when Lenny and the farm brothers—Kurt and Kyle—wolfed them down between training exercises. He was right about the kid, Eldrich. He'd spent his lunch break reading a book about math. Since when did they write books about math? Eldrich let on that it was his father who forced him to sign on with the Silver Shirts and he wasn't all that keen.

"Monroe calls us the elite force," Lenny told him proudly, dismissing Eldrich's complaints.

Thirteen almost choked. These kids, an elite force?

They weren't bad kids. People—most people anyway—weren't born bad; they were made that way. By bad fathers, maybe, like his and possibly Eldrich's. Circumstances. For some of them, he figured it was plain old fear. Fear that got turned on its head and came out sideways as hatred for somebody. Whatever it was, it could be stopped. He believed that. He just had to figure out a way.

Then why was he at the Hall of Justice this late in the day, running down a lead that probably didn't mean anything?

Because something about the story he'd heard smelled rotten. A Nazi secretary with a missing husband. It didn't sit right with him. And he'd learned to follow his gut.

He found the office he was looking for and stood in the doorway. The man sitting at the desk seemed absorbed in the newspaper in front of him. He was older, barrel-chested and wide-shouldered in a neat tweed suit. Thinning brown hair combed over a freckled scalp and a thick walrus mustache. Looked more like a farmer than a police detective.

"Detective Brody?"

The man looked up and Thirteen had the distinct feeling the detective knew the whole time he was being sized up. "Yep. What can I do for you?"

Thirteen introduced himself and stuck out his hand. "Looking for some information, is all. Heard you were the man to see."

Brody's bushy brows rose a fraction; then he stood and shook Thirteen's hand with a firm grip. He motioned to a rickety chair and they both sat. "Let me guess. Old case? Unsolved?"

Thirteen raised one eyebrow. "How'd you know?"

"I'm two months from retirement and not a team player, if you get my meaning. Most of what gets sent my way is just to keep my nose out of their business."

Thirteen frowned and wondered exactly what business Brody was referring to. Graft? Money laundering? Corruption was rampant in the force—everybody knew that. He'd have to be careful around this man if he was as sharp as his first impression seemed to imply. "Missing person."

"'Course it is." Brody looked unimpressed. "Tell me what you know."

After he'd given Brody the details and was assured he'd look into the matter, Thirteen thanked the man. "And, Detective," he said before he left, "no need to get anyone else involved."

Outside, the drizzle had turned into a downpour and he didn't have an umbrella or an overcoat with him. When he slid back into the Cadillac, his hat was dripping wet and the shoulders of his suit coat were dark with water. He started the auto, but he didn't go anywhere. He watched the rain slide down the windshield and considered his position.

Most of what he had to do came easy. Watching, listening. He'd suggested to Schwinn that Winterhalder was gunning for his job at the Friends. That had paid off. Schwinn kept the Silver Shirt leader on a short leash now and questioned him about every move he made with the recruits. It was wearing on Winterhalder, as it was meant to.

Today he'd done the same kind of job with Thekla Schwinn. He'd had a chance when he drove her to the meeting of the National Gentile League. Made a reference to the secretary and implied she had a thing for the boss. He felt a little bad about that. Mrs. Weiss didn't seem a bad sort, but he didn't have much sympathy for Nazis, no matter how pretty.

So why was he checking up on Tomas Weiss?

Eva once called him a white knight. She'd meant he couldn't help himself when it came to rescuing damsels in distress, even if he didn't like them much. But this visit to Detective Brody wasn't him trying to help Liesl Weiss. This was him making sure he followed all the leads at the Friends of New Germany. He didn't like surprises. Surprises could get you killed.

He pulled away from the curb and put Liesl Weiss out of his mind. He had work to do.

CHAPTER 27

LIESL

On Tuesday, there was a new sign on the front door of the Alt Heidelberg written in both English and German: *No Admittance to Jews*. If I had any doubts left, the sign would have been the end of them. As it was, I no longer doubted Leon Lewis.

I'd dressed carefully in a pink crepe blouse with a high collar and a soft gabardine skirt of navy blue that fell within ten inches of my low-heeled lace-ups. "You look positively dowdy," Mutti remarked.

"*Danke,* Mutti." Precisely what I was hoping to achieve. Hermann's interest was an unwelcome hindrance to my mission.

Hermann barely glanced at me as I entered. *Gut.* "If only we could be as advanced as they are in the fatherland," he was saying to Paul Themlitz as I removed my hat. "With the chancellor's power, they are removing opponents from the political and academic realms. I have heard they have a special holding camp outside München for all those who oppose our leader."

"And the book burning! Did you see the pictures?" Thekla said from her seat on the divan. The men agreed that the removal of non-Aryan books from libraries and schools was a great good for the country and one to be realized in America.

Book burnings and camps for those opposed to the Nazis—that

could never happen here, could it? I vowed it would not, if I could help Leon Lewis accomplish his goal. To that end, I was determined to get a look at the files in Hermann Schwinn's office.

"*Guten Morgen,* Liesl." Paul jumped up with enthusiasm as he saw me and motioned to a box on my desk. "I wanted you to be the first to see the new flyer. Tell me what you think of it."

I did not fail to notice Thekla's quick frown. She did not like to share the attentions of any man, even frog-like Paul Themlitz. Hermann came across the room to stand behind me as I sat down at my desk—so close I could feel his breath on the back of my neck. I opened the box to the sharp scent of fresh ink.

The headline shouted in black capital letters: "AMERICANS UNITE AGAINST THE JEWISH CONSPIRACY."

Below the words, a drawing of a hook-nosed man with deep-set eyes pointing a rifle at the American flag. I held my breath and read the smaller black print declaring Jewish radicals had amassed machine guns at their headquarters in Boyle Heights and were planning an attack. It concluded at the bottom: "WE WILL NOT BE SAFE UNTIL THE JEWISH VERMIN ARE OUT OF AMERICA." Then the address of the Friends of New Germany and an appeal for membership and funds.

No words came to me in response to the vile missive.

"Paul," Hermann said, reaching over me to slide the top flyer off the stack, "the caricature is most effective. You've outdone yourself."

"Do you think it's a little too . . . overstated?" Paul Themlitz asked, considering the flyer.

"If anything, it is not alarming enough." Hermann was adamant and his accent became more pronounced. "We must say the truth clearly, simply. People want slogans, not explanations. Words that make them feel—" he thumped his chest—"not think." He passed the flyer to Thekla, who studied it with a critical eye.

"Goebbels's strategy is working wonderfully in the fatherland," Thekla said. "Sow confusion, then give the people the answers they seek in a way that is simple and easy to understand. The Jews have proven throughout history to be our enemy. We must make that clear, *nicht so?*"

"Quite right," Hermann said, tapping the repugnant face on the flyer and giving Themlitz a meaningful look. "These people killed our Lord and Savior, Paul."

His pious statement sent goose bumps over my bare arms.

"Liesl," Thekla said, picking up her copy of *Sunset* magazine and settling back on the divan. "Make sure those get out to all the members in today's mail."

"Of course, Thekla," I said. But I had another task to complete. One of utmost importance.

Later in the morning, Hermann and Thekla went together to a meeting for the German Alliance at Turnverein Hall and Paul Themlitz returned to his duties at the Aryan Bookstore. I took my chance and entered Hermann's office. My pulse pounded in my ears and my steps sounded loud in the empty room. I had been there many times, taking dictation and getting his signature. But never alone. It smelled faintly of his hair tonic and stale coffee. I dismissed the ripple of fear along my spine. They would be gone for at least an hour. I needn't be worried.

I slid open the top drawer of the file cabinet. Heavy objects clinked and thudded. An almost-full bottle of gin and almost-empty one of whiskey. Another object slid heavily in the back. I pulled the drawer fully open.

A gun.

I picked it up. Not a revolver as I'd seen in the cowboy films. A pistol, like the one Tomas had carried on the force. I checked the chamber. Loaded. I replaced it as I'd found it and shut the drawer with a shudder of apprehension. Wilhelm Otto and now Hermann. A social club in which the members carried guns was hardly social.

The second drawer held files, each neatly labeled in Thekla's decisive printing and alphabetically arranged. I couldn't take a chance in removing them. I opened my steno pad and began to jot notes.

America First and the American Nationalist Party. Both files held little that looked important. The California Homesteaders had a few weeks' worth of typed agendas and meeting minutes. The German American Alliance file was bank statements and letters from Max Socha. Next, the Ku Klux Klan. I gave the contents a quick glance. The secret organization was hardly a secret, complaining about Negroes and Mexicans, holding rallies, and getting their pictures in the newspapers. The file held a list of names, some of whom I recognized from the Germantown police force. The National Legion of Mothers of America held newspaper clippings about school districts and Thekla's handwritten notes.

Would any of this be helpful to Lewis? I didn't know, so I wrote down as much as I could in quick shorthand.

The last file and the thickest was labeled Silver Shirts. I took a moment and thumbed through it. Membership applications, stamped with a red swastika. I flicked through the alphabetical stack to *Bittner, Fritz.* His handwriting hit me like a slap in the face. What was he thinking? And something else. In the upper corner scrawled in sloppy cursive—my address. *Danielle Bittner, mother.* Then my name and . . . Tess and Steffen. Their ages. Tess's school. My legs wobbled and I almost lost my grip on the folder. What need did they have for this information?

I made a note of it. Looked at the clock. My time was running out.

I shut the drawer and tugged on the third and bottom drawer. It was locked.

Why? Because it was something important. Where would Hermann keep a key? I went to the desk. The shallow top drawer held pencils, paper clips, a stapler. I checked the wall behind the file cabinet for a hook, then patted through Hermann's overcoat. Nothing.

I heard a step and froze. The murmur of voices—Thekla and Hermann. My heart leapt into my throat. I looked quickly around the office. Had I left any evidence of my visit? My steno pad was on Hermann's desk. I swiped it up and scurried to the door.

Too late. The outer office door opened and Thekla entered just as I cleared Hermann's doorway. I was afraid my face showed my guilt, and I was right. Thekla pinned me with a suspicious gaze. "Liesl, what have we caught you at?"

I thought like lightning. "Just getting my steno pad. I left it in Hermann's office." I tapped the pad with my fingernail, willing my knees to stop shaking. The steno pad in question—if Thekla could decipher Gregg shorthand—was damning evidence of what she had caught me at.

"Did you?" Hermann said, coming in behind his wife. "I hadn't noticed it there."

I walked smartly to my desk and sat down before my gelatin-like legs gave way. "No matter, I have it and I can get at those letters."

I proceeded to roll a fresh paper and carbon into my typewriter as if nothing were amiss. Thekla went immediately to Hermann's office. I prayed nothing was out of place.

Thekla was unusually silent for the rest of the morning but she kept me in her sight. No chance to look at the remaining drawer and no idea where to find the key. Thekla had no reason to look at my steno pad, nor did I think she knew how to read shorthand, but the presence of the notes right out on my desk kept me on edge. I needed to get them to Leon Lewis. The thought of my children's names on Fritz's application worried at me as I did my tasks. Why?

When my lunch break came, I walked to the park on First Street to eat my apple and sandwich. I had managed to secrete the shorthand notes and an envelope into my handbag. At the park, I addressed the envelope to L1 at his post office box, licked a stamp, and slipped the envelope in the postal receptacle on the corner with relief.

As I turned back toward the Alt Heidelberg, my relief shifted abruptly to alarm.

A figure stood across the street, back turned as if perusing the display of men's oxfords in the Clark's Shoe Store window. I recognized the platinum bob and perfect posture, not to mention the cherry-red wool suit with ermine trim that she'd been wearing at the office this morning.

Thekla Schwinn was following me.

I quickly boarded a trolley and returned to the Alt Heidelberg, wondering if she'd seen me deposit the envelope in the mailbox. She did not voice a word about it when she returned twenty minutes after I had settled at my desk.

"Liesl," she said breezily, "Paul has another box of the flyers ready. Please go downstairs to collect them."

"Of course," I said crisply.

It was a relief to leave her suspicious gaze and I took my time walking downstairs to the Aryan Bookstore. Paul Themlitz kept me for a few moments, showing me a new display of propaganda just arrived in the international mail. I admired the latest issues of the state-run German newspaper and a new pamphlet with the title "America for Americans" in red, white, and blue print.

When I was able to politely say goodbye, the box of flyers in my grasp, I left the bookstore to see Karl Weber in the hall. "Mrs. Weiss." He greeted me with a tip of his hat. "What are you doing here?" Karl had the soft, doughy look of a German Santa Claus but he was a sharp businessman. He had always been a fair landlord, even when I'd struggled to pay on time each week.

"I work here, Mr. Weber," I answered.

He looked a bit taken aback. "At the Friends of New Germany?"

"Yes, are you going there now?" I hadn't thought him one to be involved with the National Socialists. But Neele was friendly with Gertrud Grundbacher, so perhaps I was wrong.

He hesitated, then said quickly, "I'm meeting Travis Monroe downstairs. He's going to introduce me to some of the veterans."

I wished him a good day and went on my way while he took the stairs to the basement. In the office of the Friends, I found Travis Monroe and Hermann lounging on the green silk chairs, Thekla on the divan. Wilhelm Otto was leaning on the window frame, dressed in his usual somber suit and a pristine white dress shirt and tie. I wondered if the man owned anything less formal. Travis was regaling Wilhelm Otto and Thekla about a screen test he'd had at Warner Studios years earlier. "I'd have had the part but the director thought I was too handsome. Can you believe it?"

"I certainly can," Thekla twittered. It seemed the actual employees at the Friends of New Germany could find time to chitchat, while the unpaid volunteer did all the work.

They continued flirting as I went to the storage room, looking for more carbons. They were on the top shelf and I didn't wish to get out the ladder. "Mr. Monroe," I called, "could I have your assistance for a moment?"

He appeared immediately and was tall enough to reach the box without even stretching and gave me a dazzling smile as if he'd accomplished something heroic. I remembered about Karl Weber. "Oh," I said, "Mr. Weber just went downstairs looking for you, in case you were waiting for him here."

"Weber?" Travis frowned. "Thanks for letting me know, Mrs. Weiss."

Back in the front office with my carbons, I saw Wilhelm Otto send a dark look after Travis as he went out the door.

I wasn't the only one who noticed Wilhelm Otto's ire. "What do you have against our friend Monroe?" Hermann asked.

I folded a flyer and slipped it into an envelope I'd typed earlier in the day, trying to look as if I was not listening.

Wilhelm Otto answered, "Something smells wrong with him."

I licked the envelope and glanced at the men. Hermann leaned forward, his brow creased in concern. Wilhelm shrugged casually. "The amount of cash he carries. Expensive auto. Where is it coming from?"

The back of my neck tingled. Fold, stuff, seal. Wilhelm Otto was implying something—perhaps, like me, Travis Monroe was receiving pay from Leon Lewis to spy on the Friends of New Germany. Perhaps he was the other agent.

"You might be right," Hermann told Wilhelm. "Keep an eye on him."

A shiver of apprehension went down my spine. Wilhelm kept an eye on everyone connected to the Friends of New Germany. That included me, as he demonstrated with his questions about Tomas. If Travis Monroe was an agent, he would need to take great care indeed.

I finished the envelopes just as the clock ticked to three thirty. "I'll bring these to the post on my way home," I told Thekla.

"Wilhelm will drive you," she answered abruptly, not even glancing up from the copy of *Sunset* magazine in her hands.

Wilhelm Otto stood like a dog at her command.

Did she not trust me? "Of course," I answered smoothly. "That's very kind."

I put on my hat, turning to the mirror to adjust it. In the reflection, I could see Wilhelm Otto and Thekla exchange a glance that confirmed my suspicion. Wilhelm Otto had been told to watch me, just as he was watching Travis Monroe.

Wilhelm politely carried the box of envelopes and the stack of outgoing mail and helped me into his auto. After a silent ride to the Germantown post office, he parked. "I'll take them in."

I watched him bound up the steps, his long legs taking two at a time. It had crossed my mind to dump the offensive flyers in one of the trash barrels on the corner. Was that what Thekla had suspected? I would have to be very careful—far more than I had been—around Thekla. She was not easily fooled. What would she do if she discovered I was working for a Jewish lawyer? I didn't want to consider the thought.

The journey between the post office and my home was predictably silent and though I wasn't comfortable with Otto's silences, I found them preferable to his questions.

Wilhelm Otto was helping me out of the auto outside my home when I heard Tess's voice. "Mommy!" She ran from the backyard, with Steffen and Mutti following. Steffen barreled toward me and I caught him as he tackled my legs. Tess showed me her spelling test. "The only word I missed was *truncate*, but I think that's wrong. If a tree has a trunk, then it should be spelled with a *k*, not a—"

Mutti reached us, puffing a bit. "Who are you?" she demanded of Wilhelm Otto in her abrupt way.

I wished only to leave the watchful presence of Hermann Schwinn's guard dog, but with a knot of fear in my chest, I made the introductions. Wilhelm removed his hat and gave Mutti a polite nod.

"Hmm." Mutti eyed him from his polished shoes to his toothbrush mustache, landing on the swastika pin on his lapel. She scowled.

I continued. "This is Tess and Steffen." I gave them a look that told them to be polite. "Children, this is Mr. Otto."

Tess stepped forward, putting her small hand out. "A pleasure to meet you, Mr. Otto. I'm Theresa Violet Weiss. Is Otto your first name or your last name?"

After looking at Tess's small hand for a moment, he shook it. "Wilhelm Otto," he clarified. He pronounced his name in the American way, unlike Hermann, who said it as the Germans did.

He offered his hand next to Steffen, who was holding a small glass jar. Instead of shaking his hand, Steffen silently gave the jar to Wilhelm Otto. The towering man held the jam jar up to the weak sunshine. Inside was a large black spider. He examined the spider just as he did people—with an intense gaze and silence. I shuddered as he returned it to Steffen with an appreciative look and Steffen, to my surprise, rewarded him with a smile.

"Mr. Otto," Tess said, "did you know that you shouldn't pet a porcupine? They have long quills with hooks that grab you." She curled her fingers into hooks, but before he could answer, she went on. "Are you going to drive Mutti home every day, Mr. Otto? So that she doesn't have to take the trolley? Do you ever take the trolley or do you only take your auto? Can girls drive autos? Do you like graham crackers?"

I'd never seen Wilhelm Otto look anything but completely assured, so his hesitation when confronted by a child was an interesting sight. He opened his mouth, then closed it, as if unsure which question to answer first.

I saved him from choosing. "Tess, take Steffen inside. You may have graham crackers and jam."

"Two each?" she asked, distracted from her interrogation and back to her attempts to bend the rules.

"One," I answered in a tone that told her to behave herself. Tess dragged her feet as she went to the house, Steffen following. I turned to the silent man beside the auto. "Thank you for the ride. I won't keep you—"

"Otto, did you say?" Mutti barked out, her eyes narrowed. "Didn't you work at MGM?"

Wilhelm glanced away, watching Tess and Steffen clamber up the stairs and into the house. "No, ma'am. Never worked there."

"Hmm," Mutti said again.

Wilhelm replaced his hat. "Good to meet you, Mrs. Bittner. Goodbye, Mrs. Weiss."

He shut the door of his auto with a decisive slam and was gone. I let go of my breath and realized I'd been clutching my handbag hard enough to leave an indent in the leather.

Mutti watched the auto disappear around the corner. She turned to me, her gaze going deliberately to the red, white, and black pin over my heart. Then she looked away and walked to the house.

She did not say another word about Wilhelm Otto or the Nazis. But I should have known it wouldn't be the last I heard from her on the subject.

CHAPTER 28

AGENT THIRTEEN

The early evening drive to San Pedro Harbor might have been pleasant, what with the sun hanging low in the washed blue sky over the sparkling water of the Pacific. Too bad the nice drive was spoiled by the Nazis sitting in his auto.

Schwinn, riding shotgun, raised his voice to be heard over the wind rushing in the open windows. "Prettier than Pittsburgh, wouldn't you say?" Schwinn had spent some time in the East, he said. It was where he met that piece-of-work wife of his. Thirteen hadn't been back East since his father died and even then just for the time it took to sell off the old place and tie up loose ends. Hadn't shed a tear for the old man and doubted he ever would. But he knew there were pretty places in Pittsburgh, not that he'd bother to tell Schwinn about them.

He was worried about this trip to the harbor—too worried to make small talk even if he was good at it, which he wasn't. When Schwinn had asked him along on the trip, he'd said not to bring Seventeen. "I like your pal," Schwinn said. "But we have some concerns."

"Who has concerns?" Thirteen tried to sound casual but alarm prickled his neck.

Schwinn shrugged and glanced back at Winterhalder.

"Monroe," Winterhalder answered. "Don't get all bent out of shape.

Just taking care, you know. Some people want to get us in hot water. If Monroe smells trouble, he won't do the training we need him for."

Thirteen let that go as if it weren't his concern, but having Monroe suspicious wasn't good for anybody's health. He'd tell Seventeen to be more careful.

They got to Long Beach in about an hour, then took the winding road that crisscrossed between the railroad station and the canneries. "Look at this place," Schwinn sneered. "Open to attack at any time. You would think Americans would put up more of a defense in a harbor with such strategic value."

Interesting remark, considering the US wasn't at war. But maybe they were. Just a war that nobody knew about except for Leon Lewis and his agents. And the Nazis. What he needed to know was where the first attack—*der Angriff*—would be.

He parked along a line of warehouses. A breeze carrying the stench of fish and smoke hit them as they walked out on the pier. The breakwater stretched into the ocean like a long sea snake. Within the calm water of the harbor, a fleet of mismatched vessels—sloops and steamers with thick white smoke surging from their stacks—bobbed on the waves. Tugboats chugged between the ships like fat gray ducks.

"Look." Schwinn pointed to a refit battleship from the Great War with the Nazi swastika flag flying high. "The *Estes*. Isn't she a beauty?"

If by beauty, Schwinn meant a dangerous sign of Germany getting ready for another war, then sure, she was a beauty.

They were welcomed aboard with *Heil Hitler*s and Nazi salutes. A tall man with the cold gray eyes of a pit bull stepped forward. He wore a black uniform with an insignia on his lapel Thirteen hadn't seen before.

Schwinn made the introductions in German. When he got to Thirteen, he switched to English. "*Obergruppenführer* Waldman is a member of the new *Stosstrupp*—shock troops would be the English," Schwinn told him. "The SS is an elite group that report directly to

Reichsführer Himmler, who is of course within the personal circle of our great leader himself."

He switched back to German and spoke in an apologetic tone to Waldman. "My friend does not speak the language of the fatherland."

Thirteen was glad he'd never mentioned that he grew up speaking German.

Winterhalder smirked and leaned toward Thirteen. "These SS men think pretty highly of themselves."

Thirteen figured from the tightening of the SS man's jaw that he spoke English and Winterhalder had just made a tactical error. But he didn't mention that.

The *Obergruppenführer* pivoted on his black-booted heel and proceeded to give the three men a tour of the *Estes*. They spent about an hour looking over the ship, with Schwinn and Winterhalder occasionally translating for Thirteen. Waldman was all business, responding to Schwinn's jocularity with cold impatience.

He got the gist of what was happening. Schwinn was making a report, telling Waldman about the recruitment of new members and some talk about the San Diego armory. He heard the word *Juden* plenty, and he didn't have to know German to understand what they thought of them. When they reached the deck again, an alarming discussion got his heart firing like a Gatling gun. At first, he thought maybe he wasn't following the German. But he was. A cold sweat broke out on his back. His hands itched to check his weapon, just to make sure it was still there. But he didn't let himself reach for the security of his gun.

What he'd heard—what these men were planning—he needed to get this to Leon Lewis. And quick. Things were worse, *much* worse, than they'd realized, and the naval officer with the personality of a prison warden was delivering instructions from Adolf Hitler himself.

The clincher came when they were about to disembark. The *Obergruppenführer* passed a fat sealed envelope to Schwinn and the two men commenced with a heated argument about the German vice-consul, Georg Gyssling.

By the time they were back on American soil, Thirteen was fighting a rising panic.

This was moving fast. Too fast.

This was war. Not with guns and tanks—not yet at least—but with words and ideas, with ideology. And wasn't that how war always started?

———————

It was full dark by the time Thirteen dropped Schwinn at his place downtown, and all he wanted was to go home and think.

Except there was Winterhalder, insisting they stop for a drink at the Lorelei. Thirteen wanted nothing more than to punch the Nazi in the face, not buy him a whiskey and hear him talk about how he could run things better than Schwinn. But if it meant getting more information, he figured it was worth it.

Winterhalder, it turned out, didn't have the fatherland on his mind. He downed three double shots and started making moves on a barmaid with blonde braids and pink cheeks. She gave him the cold shoulder. Winterhalder called her a foul name under his breath and Thirteen excused himself to use the bathroom and cool his temper. He came out to find Winterhalder pushing the barmaid into a corner of the hallway and taking what she wasn't offering. The barmaid screamed and dug her nails into the side of his face. Thirteen pulled him off her and didn't think twice about giving Winterhalder a punch that knocked him out cold. In fact, it felt good.

The girl—Greta was her name—was shaken but not hurt. He put her in the care of the bartender, who promised to call her mother. Then he drove Winterhalder home and dumped him on his front lawn. He probably wouldn't even remember what happened when he woke up in the morning, but he'd have a scratch to explain to his wife and a sore jaw for a week and that was something.

Sometimes Lewis didn't pay him enough to do this job.

He got to the Biltmore close to eleven and picked up the dog. "Sorry I'm so late, Jimmy," he told the night clerk and rubbed a hand over his tired eyes.

"No problem, sir," the kid said. "The chef gave her some scraps and we took a stroll in the park." He took the extra dollar Thirteen passed him. "Good night, sir. Get some rest."

Turned out, a good night wasn't in the cards.

He took the dog on the elevator. Not something he normally did but he was too tired for five flights of stairs. A few years back, the Biltmore manager had needed some help with his brother-in-law, a guy handy with his fists when it came to his wife and kids. Thirteen hadn't done much, just gave him a talking-to that included some veiled threats. The chump cleared out fast enough. Now the sister was getting along fine and the kids were safe. In return, Thirteen had a room on the sixth floor whenever he needed it. It was nice enough for a bachelor with no ties. But it wasn't what he wanted.

Problem was, he didn't know what he wanted.

When he got up to his room, he made a telephone call to Leon Lewis, sorry he was getting the man out of bed. They set up a time and place to meet in the morning. He hung up, took off his coat, and lay down on his bed, too tired to even take off his shoes. The telephone rang. Did Lewis forget something?

He picked it up. "Yeah?"

"Sir, this is Jimmy at the front desk." The voice was strained and he could hear a ruckus in the background—a crash, a woman's angry words. "We have a . . . situation here that needs your attention."

It was Eva. He'd know that angry voice even after four years. She always did have the worst timing.

He took the elevator down and as the doors opened, he saw her. She was propped against the front desk in a deep-purple evening dress that hugged every curve and showed plenty of skin. A fur wrap hung from one limp hand. A shattered vase, a scattering of roses, and a pool of water were at her feet.

She turned as he approached, swayed, and slurred, "Don't you answer your messages?" She was clearly sozzled.

He walked across the lobby and put his arm around her waist, leaning her unsteady weight against his side. "Sorry about that, Jimmy." He jerked his chin at the mess on the floor. "Put it on my bill."

He brought her to his room. There was nothing else for it and she looked about to topple.

Eva kicked off her satin heels and flopped on his divan. The dog jumped down and slunk into the bedroom. Thirteen wished he could do the same. He poured her a glass of water and found some crackers, gave her both. "Drink this, eat that." He knew she hadn't eaten; she never did when she drank. "Where's the kid?"

As soon as he asked, he regretted it. She looked up at him. "What, you think I'm a terrible mother? I'm not. I'm a good mother." She threw the crackers at him as if they had insulted her. They scattered on the carpet. She looked away. "I'm a good mother," she said again, blinking her baby blues.

"Where is she?"

She laid her head back on the divan. "She's still with my ma if you have to know."

Thirteen relaxed a little with that. Eva's mother was a nice woman, lived in Santa Monica in a cute little bungalow. "What's this about, Eva? You need more money?"

She glared at him. "I don't want your money, buster."

She'd never said no to it. He'd been sending her part of his pay for the last five years. He figured it had bought her that fancy dress and that fur, but as long as she took care of the kid, he wouldn't complain.

"Then what?" He was tired. Bone weary. And he had an early morning tomorrow.

Eva struggled to sit up straight, then collapsed back on the divan.

"Just wanted to visit an old friend," she said, her eyes half-closed. "Is that so wrong?" she whispered. Her eyes closed all the way and she was out.

Thirteen sighed. He took the water glass, still propped in her hand, and put it on the side table. He slid one arm under her knees and the other under her shoulders and carried her to the bedroom, settled her on the bed next to the dog. He looked at her for a moment. He should have gone to her place, talked to her. Not avoided her and the kid. He thought sending them the check each month would be enough.

He grabbed a pillow and an extra blanket, kicked off his shoes in the living room. It had been a day.

He lay down on the divan and went to sleep.

CHAPTER 29

AGENT THIRTEEN

Thirteen left Eva three dollars for breakfast and a taxi. He snapped a leash on the dog and took the stairs to the lobby.

The dog followed on his heels as he walked the dozen or so blocks to the plaza. He needed to get her a real home. A place with a yard and maybe a kid to play with. He'd found her when he moved back to Los Angeles, nosing around a garbage can in an alley. Probably had been a racing dog that lost too many times and wasn't earning her keep. He gave her half his sandwich and she followed him home.

The thing was, a hotel was no place for a dog. A dog needed a family and a family wasn't in the cards for him. Sure, it would be nice to come home to a wife who loved you and a few kids. But after Lily and Ma . . . he just couldn't risk it. Heck, he hadn't even seen Josie since she was a baby. Eva asked him to come around; he'd even sat outside her mother's place a couple times, trying to get up the courage. But he couldn't.

He was afraid if he was completely honest.

Afraid he'd fall in love with her. Not with Eva—that train had left the station—but with Josie. He knew himself well enough to know he'd want to take care of her, protect her, make sure she was raised right. But what if something happened to her, like it had to Lily? He couldn't go through that again, that feeling like his heart was ripped from his body and nailed inside a small coffin. It just about killed him.

He wasn't a family man and that was that.

As he approached the plaza, he turned his attention to what he needed to tell Lewis. It was a safe enough place at this time of the morning. Not likely any of his Nazi associates would be palling around with the Mexicans lined up for daywork or sitting beside the bums sleeping off benders. The dog stopped to sniff at a man dressed in what looked like a tailcoat from the previous decade and striped pants mended at the knees.

"Come on," he said softly, "let him sleep." Poor mac, he probably was a real Dapper Dan before the crash.

He found Lewis sitting on a bench under a stand of bamboo. He held two paper cups and was dressed in his typical suit and tie, looking every inch the bland businessman. Looks could sure be deceiving.

Thirteen wished just once he'd have some good news for Lewis. He sat down and Lewis passed him a cup. He took a gulp—coffee, hot and strong enough to strip paint—and instantly felt better. The dog set about sniffing each corner of the bench, then settled at his feet.

"Tell me what you've got," Lewis said.

He liked that about Lewis, too. No chitchat. Thirteen started with what he'd seen on the *Estes*—what Schwinn and Winterhalder had translated unnecessarily for him. "They've got Silver Shirts training in Seattle, Portland, and San Fran," he said. "At first, I thought Winterhalder was a crank, but now . . ." He shook his head. "I'm worried. Real worried." That was an understatement. Winterhalder was a man with no moral compass; he'd proven that last night at the Lorelei. Thirteen told Lewis how Hermann Schwinn had pointed out the weaknesses in the harbor. He took another gulp of the hot coffee. "There's more. And it isn't good."

Lewis nodded, ready for it.

"The SS officer was a real Nazi heavyweight. He had orders directly from a kraut named Himmler and they also said something about somebody named Joseph Goebbels."

Lewis put down his coffee and leaned forward and Thirteen knew he'd been right to be worried. "What do you know about them?"

Thirteen had figured Lewis would ask, but he didn't have much of an answer. "Chancellor Hitler's close pals, is all I know."

Lewis made a sound of agreement. "Very close. Himmler is the man Herr Hitler relies on for his Aryan race policies, and Goebbels is the new minister of propaganda—brilliant at it, from all accounts."

Propaganda. Meaning information—and misinformation. That made sense of what he'd heard. "The ship officer told Schwinn that his bosses want to move forward with the plan for the studios. Bring the truth to Americans and Europe through the power of film, he said."

Lewis's brows came down. "He said that?"

And plenty more. "This was the time—and he said this exactly—'to get rid of the Jewish control over films.' He named Mayer and Thalberg. And the Warners. But I got the impression he meant any Jew." He swallowed. "And he said to put the plan into action."

Lewis looked like a man who'd been sucker punched. "So soon?"

Schwinn and Winterhalder had been giddy with the idea as they drove back to the city that evening. He had itched to ask them about it but couldn't without revealing he knew German as well as either of them. They hadn't translated all the officer said—meaning they didn't trust him.

Thirteen hoped he was wrong about how serious this was, but from the furrow on Lewis's brow, he wasn't. Chancellor Hitler was making a bold move, a dangerous move. But it just might work. "The *Obergruppenführer* handed off an envelope to Schwinn. I didn't get a look at it."

"Funds, maybe," Lewis said, "or perhaps instructions."

Thirteen shrugged. He'd badly wanted to see it but Schwinn had tucked it away like it was a gold watch. "Then they had an argument about Georg Gyssling."

At this, Lewis sharpened his gaze.

"Schwinn complained about him, said he wasn't doing his job keeping the studios in line. Doesn't like the guy." It was strange, how they spoke of the German vice-consul. The man was a Nazi, wasn't he? But they acted like he was the enemy.

Lewis stared into the distance, as he did when he was turning over the facts, examining and filing the information. Comparing stories and looking for links. Not for the first time, Thirteen wished Lewis would let him in on the whole operation.

Thirteen patted his pocket and found the crumpled remains of the pack of Lucky Strikes he'd told himself needed to last to the end of the week. There was one left and it was, what, Wednesday? He struck a match and lit it.

"I need to go to DC," Lewis said finally.

Thirteen coughed out a cloud of smoke. Had he heard right? "What?"

Lewis repeated himself.

It was like a general walking out on the morning of a battle. "You can't."

"We need help—you said it yourself. There's a congressman from New York, Dickstein. He's been to Germany and knows what's going on there. He came back and called on Congress to begin a formal investigation of Nazis in the United States."

"But?" He could tell there was a *but* coming.

"But he's Jewish." Lewis let out a frustrated breath. "Hoover buried it. Nobody wants to sound like they want another war with Germany, not even the Democrats. The issue at hand is the economy, the Depression, unemployment."

"So what can you do?"

"There are agencies in DC who do this kind of thing. Espionage. Surveillance. And we need money. To pay you and me and everybody else. Nothing comes cheap in this town."

"I thought the studios were financing you?"

"They said they would, but the only one who has come through has been RKO and not with what they'd promised."

That was just wrong. Lewis and his operatives were risking their lives and guys like Mayer and the Warners wouldn't cough up the dough? "Tell them what I told you. That should light a fire."

Lewis raised a brow at him. "You think they'll believe it?"

Lewis was right. Who would believe the chancellor of Germany was looking to take over the American moviemakers? Hollywood itself? From what Thirteen was starting to realize about Herr Hitler, he was more than anybody figured—bolder, smarter, and more brutal. And the men he attracted were the same. If they weren't stopped before they got momentum . . . it wouldn't be good.

They sat in silence for a few minutes. Lewis thinking. Thirteen going over the facts. The bum on the bench woke up and stretched, sat up, and looked around like he didn't know where he was.

"What I don't understand," Thirteen finally said, "is why the moguls—guys like Mayer and Thalberg—why they put up with any of it. Being kept out of the men's clubs, the neighborhoods that say no Jews allowed, the slander in the newspapers about them being Communists. They have the power in this city. They could shout from the rooftops about anti-Semitism, but they don't."

Lewis frowned before he spoke. "Consider it this way. Most of these men—Mayer, Warner, Zukor—they came from poor families, Jewish immigrants who knew what it was to be persecuted and killed because of their religion. They are only one generation past that kind of life. You don't leave that behind with knowing it could happen again."

"But with their power and money?" That was hard to believe.

"You'd think money would make them feel safe, but it does the opposite, doesn't it?" Lewis pointed to the bum, who was eyeing Thirteen's smoke. "That man isn't afraid anyone's going to steal his wallet. He doesn't have one. But when you have much, much can be taken away."

"So they won't stand up for their own people?" That seemed backward thinking.

"It would play directly into the stereotypes they want people to forget—complainers, exaggerators. And—" Lewis looked at him meaningfully—"that would hurt their bottom line."

"But good people—Christians, let's say—they gotta see what is happening and stand up against it." It was what the Bible said; he knew that much from what he'd taken in as a kid.

"You would think," Lewis said with a sigh. "But it is easier to turn a blind eye." He tipped his head to the crowd of men hoping for a day's work. "Especially when you have troubles of your own."

Thirteen thought Lewis was too forgiving. Turn the other cheek only went so far in his book. He got up, walked over to the bum on the bench, and gave him the half-smoked cigarette. The man thanked him like he'd handed him a life vest on a sinking ship. He returned to Lewis and the dog. "So when will you leave?"

Lewis tipped back the last of his coffee, grimaced, and crumpled the cup. "Today. The sooner I get to DC, the sooner we'll know how much help we have and get the funds to pay you and the others."

Thirteen didn't care about the money. He had enough to get by and anyway, this wasn't a job anymore. "What do you want me to do while you're gone?" Other than kowtow to Hermann Schwinn, put up with Winterhalder's lechery, and spend time with his new friends in the Klan.

"Find out what you can about Georg Gyssling," he said. "I can't get a bead on the man and he may have the answers we need."

Thirteen agreed with that.

Lewis looked at his watch. "When did you see Seventeen last?" he asked as he threw his crumpled cup in the trash. "He was scheduled to meet me last night and didn't show."

Thirteen thought about it. His late night had made him a little fuzzy around the edges. "Last I talked to him, he was going to try to get into that storage room in the basement of the Alt Heidelberg. See what they're hiding." He remembered Schwinn's comment about Seventeen with unease.

"See if you can track him down," Lewis said. "I'll be in touch when I get to DC." He turned to go, then turned back suddenly as if he'd forgotten something. "Be careful, Thirteen," he said, his face somber. "Things are beginning to get very dangerous."

CHAPTER 30

LIESL

I had lain awake long into the night, considering my position. Whatever was in the third file drawer must be important to Leon Lewis. I thought from all angles and had no answers when I finally fell into a fitful sleep. When the morning light came through my window, I woke with an idea.

I dressed and readied for the day quickly. Before I left to walk Tess to school, Mutti stopped me with a sharp frown. "Liesl, what is your brother mixed up in?"

I did not have an answer for her. I had been afraid to ask Fritz about it—afraid of what he might tell me. "I don't have time to talk about it, Mutti." True, but not the truth.

I fastened the swastika pin on my collar during the trolley ride, but when I arrived at the Alt Heidelberg, Thekla barely glanced at me and offered no greeting. The chill coming from her was as cold as a wind from the Bavarian Alps. What had become of the appreciative woman of last week?

She would be irate if my plan today worked, but it couldn't be helped.

My first task was to take dictation. Hermann had Paul Themlitz in his office and they were smiling like adolescents playing a prank. He leaned back in his chair and looked at the ceiling as I waited with my pencil poised on my steno pad.

"To Franklin D. Roosevelt, president of the United States," Hermann declared, glancing at Paul. He went on to dictate a rant against President Roosevelt's plans to help the country out of the Depression, including some veiled threats against his person and some not-so-veiled slurs against his heritage.

Paul added his two cents worth. "Make sure and say 'The Jew Deal'—that's *J-E-W*, Liesl—will bankrupt our country. And put in there that we're good Christian folk who vote."

Hermann chuckled and finished the letter with "a concerned Christian" instead of his own name. I nodded briskly, as if this were just another letter to the chamber of commerce, while my insides agitated like an automatic washer.

Could this be the proof of treason Leon Lewis needed?

"And, Liesl," Hermann said, "keep this between us." He meant no carbons, no copies on file, no record. Except of course for the shorthand in my stenography book, which I would send to Lewis—in fact, as soon as I was able.

I closed my steno pad as Paul excused himself to see to the bookstore. Before I could follow him out, I found Hermann blocking my way. I dodged, but he countered. He reached out to finger the button at my neck. "You needn't hurry so, Liesl." He slowly pulled, opening my blouse at the collar.

He smiled innocently.

"Pardon me, Mr. Schwinn." I veered around him and left the room with as much dignity as I could. Why did men insist on such silly games? Thekla looked up from her usual seat on the divan as I sat at my desk. Her gaze fell on my disheveled neckline and her mouth went hard. I did not care. She should direct her anger where it belonged—at her brazen husband.

Hermann Schwinn was becoming increasingly bold—not only in his advances toward me under his wife's nose—but in his campaign against the Jewish people of Los Angeles. I would need to be bold in return. I would put my plan into action that afternoon.

During the course of the morning, my strategy fell into place. Wilhelm Otto and Hans Winterhalder—who had a scratch on his cheek that looked suspiciously like it was from a fingernail—left together for a clandestine meeting downtown. Thekla made her ten o'clock visit to the lavatory to freshen her lipstick.

It was time.

I began by collecting the fountain pen from Hermann Schwinn's office. "I noticed you were in need of a refill," I said.

"You are the soul of efficiency, Liesl," he answered.

At my desk, I laid out my handkerchief and proceeded to take the pen apart and refill the barrel with an eyedropper. Thekla returned, breezing past me without a word, but I stopped her. "Thekla, I've finished with Hermann's fountain pen. Would you mind terribly returning it to him?"

She glared at me as if I'd asked her to scrub the floor with a toothbrush.

I willed my own hand not to shake as I held out the pen to her.

She snatched it from me and . . . the pen came apart in her hands. Navy ink spurted like blood, dark droplets spreading to spot her lemon silk blouse. She looked down in horror, fumbling with the two parts of the pen that I had failed to fully screw together. More ink smeared on her skirt.

"Oh, my—oh, my goodness." I took up my handkerchief, attempting to blot her blouse. "Please, let me—I'm so sorry—"

"*Dummkopf!*" Thekla bit out, pushing my hand away. She threw down the pen, snatched my handkerchief, and dabbed at her blouse herself. The stains only spread. "Hermann!"

Hermann appeared, exclaiming and agreeing she must change her clothes immediately. He ushered her out the door within minutes, muttering about Thekla learning to drive an auto.

"My Mutti swears that rubbing alcohol will take the stains right out,"

I called to Thekla as she left. She threw an angry look over her shoulder that failed to cause me any remorse.

I rushed to the window to see Hermann helping Thekla into the auto, her head swiveling like an angry hen. As soon as the green roadster pulled onto the road, I rushed to Hermann's office.

After another quick search for the key, I pulled a hairpin from my pocket. Fritz had been a notorious troublemaker on the MGM lot, and that included finding ways to get into places he shouldn't. I'd seen him do it and hoped it was as simple as it looked. I glanced at the clock on Hermann's desk. I'd have perhaps half an hour—maybe longer—for Hermann to bring Thekla home, wait for her to change her clothing, and return.

After a moment of tinkering, the mechanism clicked open.

I pulled out the drawer with trepidation. What would I find there about the Friends of New Germany?

The folders were labeled in German and tidily arranged.

I flipped through them. Leon Lewis was correct when he said that Germans kept excellent records. That was an advantage to my search but a disadvantage in that Thekla and Hermann would know if even one of these files went missing. Which meant I could not take them.

Anti-Jewish World League, Institute for Germans Abroad, Nordic Society, Peoples League for Nazism Abroad. I glanced briefly at each file. What was I looking for? I hoped I would know it when I saw it. And I did. A file in the back of the drawer, unlabeled and not in alphabetical order as the rest. It contained only two sheets of paper, both with Hermann Schwinn's bold handwriting—all in German.

The first, a list of locations: the San Diego armory, Los Angeles Power and Light, Boyle Heights, MGM, Warner Brothers. A chill prickled through me. The notes under each heading were nothing more than disjointed words and phrases: shotguns, water supply, poison, bombs. Nothing that made a great deal of sense, at least to me. But perhaps they would to Mr. Lewis or one of his other operatives.

The second sheet was another list. This one of names. Louis B. Mayer, Irving Thalberg, Al Jolson, Gary Perl—a who's who of Hollywood that took up half the page—and the last name on the list, underlined with a violent stroke of navy ink . . . Leon Lewis. The chill turned to a cold flood of dread. This, he must see. I pulled out the single sheet, folded it, and slipped it into my skirt pocket. Then, reconsidering, I took the list of locations as well. In for a penny, I told myself.

I checked the clock. Twenty minutes had passed.

I needed to get back to my desk. It would not do to be caught in Hermann's office again. I shut the drawer with a metallic clang. The mechanics were not as easy to lock as they were to unlock and after a few minutes of fumbling, I gave up. I'd have to hope Hermann would not notice.

I had just sat down at my desk when Hermann returned without Thekla. I asked after her with more apologetic words. He answered me shortly that she had remained at home; then he disappeared into his office.

The last hour of the day stretched like a rubber band, tense and ready to break. Hermann did not speak to me. The telephone did not ring again. I stayed at my desk, typing the minutes to the latest alliance meeting. I made three mistakes and had to start over. Every moment wondering if Hermann would notice the unlocked drawer, the missing papers.

If he did, what would I do? My only option would be to run. Of course the Friends of New Germany knew where I lived. They knew my children's names. Tess's school. Mutti. My fingers fumbled on the keys. I needed to talk to Mr. Lewis. He would know what to do.

Finally at three o'clock I gathered my things and left the office. "Goodbye, Mr. Schwinn," I called out. I wished only to get home; even a trolley full of strangers would be a great comfort.

My relief was short-lived, for Wilhelm Otto waited beside his auto. He was hatless, and the breeze ruffled his hair, making him look younger and less serious, but his jacket was on and I had no doubt the gun was beneath it.

"You need not drive me every day," I snapped and instantly regretted my words when his brows flicked up in surprise.

He opened the door for me, his face once again placid. "Keeps me out of trouble."

I had little choice but to slide into the seat and wait as he came around. I glanced sideways, wishing to know what he was thinking. Did he know of my ploy with Thekla? He was not an easy man to fool and would surely be suspicious. But his profile was like marble and I'd have better luck learning the thoughts of a statue.

We turned down Pico and he pulled a crumpled cigarette packet out of his pocket. Empty. He threw it down on the seat between us. When we came to my house, he put the auto into park but did not open his door.

Tess was not yet home from school. No sign of Mutti and Steffen.

He looked straight ahead and said in a deliberate way, "Mrs. Weiss, I'd advise you to be careful."

My pulse ratcheted. Was this about Thekla or did he know I had been looking in the files? "I don't remember asking your advice," I said as if I hadn't a care.

He shrugged. "Think of your kids, is all I'm saying." His cold eyes sliced sideways to me.

Alarm jolted me. Was Wilhelm Otto trying to scare me?

If so, it was working.

He let out a breath like he regretted the conversation, then went around the auto and opened my door. The thought of his touch repulsed me and I did not take his offered hand.

"Goodbye, Mr. Otto," I said coldly after I'd stepped out of the auto.

He grimaced. "Take care, Mrs. Weiss."

I watched him drive away with my blood boiling. Had that been a threat? To my children? My family? If Wilhelm Otto thought he could scare me, he was right. After what I'd seen in that file, what I was carrying in my pocket, I was terrified.

But it was anger that eclipsed my fear. How dare they? How dare Hermann and Thekla and Paul and Wilhelm Otto plan such terrible things—threaten women and children because of their own twisted hatreds? To think they had the right? It was monstrous. They were monstrous.

I would get these lists and the letter to Roosevelt to Leon Lewis—today. We would stop them. We must stop them.

CHAPTER 31

LIESL

I was on pins and needles as I saw to the children and did my Wednesday chores—mending socks and ironing the freshly washed pillowcases. Just a moment of privacy was all I needed to place a call to Mr. Lewis.

As it turned out, he called me.

Fritz was at the kitchen table playing Sorry! with Tess and Steffen. Mutti had left to catch the trolley to Culver City, where she had a monthly evening of sandwiches, pinochle, and gossip with the girls from MGM.

The telephone rang. For once, I didn't even think of Tomas as I answered. Lewis's voice was businesslike and hasty. "I am sorry to call you at home, Edelweiss."

"I'm glad you did," I whispered, pulling the telephone cord as far away from the kitchen as it reached. "I need to see you as soon as possible." I had perhaps a few minutes before Fritz would finish the game.

"I am calling to inform you that I will be out of touch. I'm leaving tonight for Washington, DC."

"Sorry!" Fritz crowed and Tess squealed her dismay.

Leaving? This couldn't wait until he returned. "I must give you something." My voice had risen in desperation and I leaned over to peek through the kitchen doorway. Fritz was about to win and I had little time left. "Something you must see."

The line crackled with static for a moment. "I have less than two hours before my train leaves. I can meet you now. Near the station."

Dismay crept through me. Fritz would be leaving for his shift soon. Tess had homework to do and Steffen . . . How could I leave? But Lewis must know of the danger—and see the letter to Roosevelt.

I had no choice. "Tell me where to meet you."

Twenty minutes later, Fritz left for his shift and I told the children to get their jackets on. The wind had come up and although it was still September, the nights were chilly. "What about dinner?" Tess said. This was unusual, and she was a child of routine.

I turned off the gas under the chicken and dumplings. "We'll have it tomorrow," I said. "Tonight we're going on an adventure."

Tess looked intrigued. Steffen unsure. I raided the tea tin, which had a total of one dollar and three dimes. It would have to do.

"Are we eating at a restaurant?" Tess said in the same way one would ask if we were taking flight in an airplane.

"I told you it was an adventure." I smoothed her hair and tweaked her sweater. "I'll need your help with Steffen."

We were just in time to catch the city bus on the corner of Pico and Memorial. The train station was less than a mile away, but not in the best of neighborhoods. We stepped off into a gathering dusk, close enough to the station to hear the squeal of train brakes.

"Take my hands, both of you," I instructed. The three of us crossed the street. On the corner, a group of men in ragged coats warmed their hands over a trash barrel fire. As we passed by, they tipped their hats and Tess sang out a polite hello. Steffen squeezed my hand and pressed closer to my side.

The station cafeteria was a decent establishment, and I was thankful that Mr. Lewis had chosen something clean and well-lit. Tess's eyes went wide as we entered. A long glass-and-chrome display case held an array of sandwiches, cold chicken, vegetable salads, and great slabs of cake and pie. "I'm hungry, Mommy," Tess whispered. Steffen nodded in agreement. A black menu board listed the prices of each offering. Most of the dinner selections were over fifty cents. Our meager budget would not go far here.

Leon Lewis was waiting at a table. He stood in surprise as I approached with the children, but recovered quickly. "Who do we have here?"

I made the introductions. He directed us to sit as Tess gawked at the display of food.

"Would you mind if I—?" I gestured to the counter, where a man waited to take orders.

"Please, allow me." He made to stand and reached for his wallet.

"No," I said firmly. I had insisted upon this meeting and brought my children along. It would not do to let him pay for our dinner, even if it would take every penny I had—less the fifteen cents I'd need to get us all home.

"What are we having?" Tess asked, her face hopeful.

"You'll see." I left them at the table. When I returned, Tess's mouth dropped open. Steffen smiled with delight.

"Ice cream for you both." I smiled, passing them each a tall glass of vanilla ice cream covered in chocolate sauce, whipped cream, and a cherry on top.

"For dinner?" Tess said in awe.

"Are you complaining?" I tucked my handkerchief under Steffen's chin. He had already started eating and I didn't hear another word from Tess. Ice cream for dinner. What was I thinking? That I needed to keep the children occupied while I gave life-and-death information to a spymaster.

I pulled the two sheets of paper from my pocket and smoothed them out on the table.

His eyes skimmed the bold handwriting. His brows rose. "I see."

"You see?" I felt a rising impatience with his calm. I tapped the papers. "Plans of attack, assassinations. Your name is on that list. We can have them arrested."

"Or . . ." He looked at me sadly. "Just scribblings on paper. No way to prove it is a plan or who is planning it."

"Do people have to die before anyone believes us?" My voice had risen and the children stopped eating ice cream to stare at me. I took a breath and pushed the steno pad toward him. "Hermann dictated this to me. That is treason, is it not?"

He looked it over, reading the shorthand easily. "Perhaps, if we can prove he sent it."

My hope deflated. "There's something else." I told him about the Silver Shirts membership file. My name and the children and Mutti listed on Fritz's application.

At that he frowned and met my eyes. "Reprisals."

"You mean—?" He couldn't mean that. "If Fritz . . . ?" If he changed his mind, wanted out of the Silver Shirts.

"It is how they ensure loyalty."

Reprisals. I thought of Wilhelm Otto. *Think of your kids, is all I'm saying.*

I asked, "And what am I to do—?" If something happened, if Thekla or Hermann discovered what I was doing.

Lewis pulled a pencil stub and a notepad from his pocket and scribbled something. "This is the number for the assistant district attorney, Mr. Torgeson."

"Is he one of us?" I didn't need to explain my meaning.

"No. I don't entirely trust him." He pushed the paper across the table. "But if you are in dire need." He left it at that. "And I'll get word to him about the Roosevelt letter. See if he can do something."

That was a small comfort. "But what am I to do while you are gone?"

"Keep doing the same," he answered, "and stay in the good graces of the Schwinns at all costs."

I had failed at that already.

"Another thing, Edelweiss—find anything you can about the German vice-consul, Georg Gyssling."

Georg Gyssling? The name rang a bell. Hadn't Stella said something about him?

Lewis tapped his finger on the table. "Listen for anything about *der Angriff* or the people on this list. I will come back quickly and with help." He stood. "Thank you, Edelweiss. Your work is invaluable. Please believe that."

"It's just that . . ." I was suddenly overcome by doubt. With all I'd brought him—what I'd risked to get it—I'd thought he would call in the cavalry and arrest Hermann and Thekla for treason. That this whole nightmare would be over. It did not look to be so. Leon Lewis was leaving and Thekla and Hermann suspected me. Was I doing anything right?

He sat down again across from me. "I understand, Mrs. Weiss," he said kindly. "I have felt the same. And I wonder, is it any use? Is what we are doing making a difference?"

He understood, but of what help was that when my family was in danger?

"I can only tell you what I believe, and in the words of a rabbi, translated and interpreted over centuries: If not me, who? If not now, when?"

He looked at me as if that should help.

If not me, who? If not now, when? Was that supposed to comfort me? And yet it was true. Who else would stop these people? No one but us.

Leon Lewis stood, tipped his hat to me and the children, and left me as unsure as ever. I helped Tess and Steffen clean their faces, forcing myself to smile in a reassuring way and ask them if the ice cream had been as delicious as it looked. As I gathered my handbag and gloves, a commotion broke out at the entrance. A woman—dark-skinned and with two little girls—stood just inside the door.

"Says right on the sign, lady." The man who had taken my order and winked at me while he'd put extra chocolate sauce on the ice cream was all scowls. "We don't serve Negroes and Mexicans here." He pointed to a hand-lettered sign in the corner of the window.

The girls stepped back at his harsh voice, leaning into their mother's legs. The mother wore a cotton dress, mended and too short in the hem. Her smooth-skinned face had a pinched look. I knew that look. It was not her own hunger that caused it but that of her children. "I have money." Her voice had a Southern twang. "We'll eat outside. Only we have to catch a train."

"Get out before I call the cops. This is a clean place, lady, you hear me?"

"Mommy?" Tess looked from me to the woman at the door. Steffen stared at the two children. It was a scene played out in restaurants and shops everywhere and hardly unusual. Had I not seen the same at Grundbacher's?

I had stayed silent that day and regretted it.

The little girls gazed at the fat sandwiches and slabs of cake, just out of their reach. Not because they hadn't the money, but because of the color of their skin. Leon's words echoed in my thoughts. *If not me, who? If not now, when?*

The woman turned, ushering her children back outside. I grabbed Tess and Steffen and ran out the door, catching her half a block away. "Ma'am. Can I do something to help?"

She looked at me with surprise and suspicion, and well she might. My golden hair, fair skin, and stylish dress were unlike her own.

"You want to help me?"

"If I can," I answered.

She pulled money from her handbag. I marched back into the cafeteria and ordered sandwiches, cartons of milk, and three large cookies from the scowling man. When I returned, Tess and the two girls were giggling together and Steffen was joining in.

"I'm sorry about that," I said, giving the mother the food and the change. She hadn't told me her name and I didn't ask.

"You don't have nothing to be sorry for," she said. "It's the way of the world."

It was the way of the world. But it should not be. As we said goodbye and she hurried toward the station, I hoped that someday the world would change.

CHAPTER 32

LIESL

Mutti met us at the door in her apron, a scrub brush in her hand. "Where have you been, for pete's sake?"

Tess and Steffen recounted in detail their adventure. The cafeteria, ice cream for dinner.

"Of all the cockamamie things," Mutti said as if I'd taken the children to the Cocoanut Grove for cocktails and dancing.

"To bed now. It's late," I told Tess and Steffen. I was weary to the bone.

"What about homework?" Tess asked.

I could not face the spelling list and mathematics tables. "Not tonight," I said. "I'll send a note to your teacher." Ice cream for dinner and no homework, what kind of mother was I becoming? One like my own, as I had declared I would not be?

I helped Steffen wash his sticky hands and brush his teeth, then spoke sharply to Tess more than once before she settled into bed. Ice cream was not conducive to good behavior at bedtime. I came back downstairs to find Mutti sitting at the kitchen table waiting for me. "What is it?" I asked. The pervasive smell of vinegar and scrubbing powder meant something was bothering her.

She did not answer but brought a book from her lap and set it between us. *Mein Kampf.*

I flushed with a shame I didn't merit but felt keenly nonetheless. How to answer her unspoken question? I could not tell her about Leon Lewis. Not with her tendency toward outspokenness. "Mutti, it's not—it's for work." It was the truth and yet not what she wished to hear.

"And Fritz?" she asked. "Is he part of this—this New Germany business?"

"I'm not sure." I refused to speak for Fritz when I was lying enough for myself.

The questions kept coming. "Is this why you aren't on speaking terms with Miriam?"

My reaction was an unbidden "No!" Then I reconsidered. It was the reason I could not apologize to her as I wished. "I mean, yes, in part." Mutti would do well as a sergeant. I needed to end this conversation before she managed to pry out secrets that she would not keep to herself.

"It's that man," she said grimly. "I was right about him, you know. He did work for the studios. The girls knew his name tonight and told me all about him."

A jolt of alarm went through me. "What did they say?"

"It was years ago, when Bette did makeup for Paramount. She remembered a Wilhelm Otto who used to drive for Mr. Zukor. He got a girl named Eva Taylor in trouble. You know what I mean."

I did know what she meant.

Mutti went on. "He left town. Bette said the girl had the baby. Doesn't know what happened to her after that but she didn't work at Paramount again."

"Was she sure it was him?" Wilhelm Otto was dangerous, but he didn't seem the type to run out on his responsibilities.

Mutti snorted. "For pity's sake, she described him right down to that scar on his lip. He's trouble, Liesl."

"It's just a ride home, Mutti," I assured her. "And I'm tired." I picked up the copy of *Mein Kampf* and tucked it under my arm. "Please don't worry," I said to her. "This isn't what you think."

She looked unconvinced, and I did not blame her. Yet I had far more to worry about than Mutti's prying and Wilhelm Otto's womanizing.

Mr. Lewis was gone, on a train across the country. I was alone and facing two more days of deception with Hermann and Thekla—who was clearly suspicious of me—before the weekend. If they discovered my deception . . . reprisals, he had said.

My family was in danger.

Somehow I must restore myself to Thekla's good graces and waylay Hermann's advances. And I must find what I could about Georg Gyssling and *der Angriff*. I would be counting the days until Leon Lewis's return and hoping he came back with help.

For if I did not stop the Friends of New Germany, who would? And if not soon, it might be too late.

I woke to a quiet house filled with moonlight.

I climbed out of bed and tiptoed past Tess and Steffen, touching each of their brows briefly, assuring myself of their safety. They slept peacefully, no doubt dreaming of ice cream dinners. I stopped in the small bedroom where Mutti snored. She meant well and one day I would tell her the truth. Downstairs, the kitchen smelled of vinegar. A single drop of water hung on the silver faucet, catching the gleam of moonlight like a diamond.

Fritz slept on the divan in the sitting room, as he often did when his attic room was stuffy or he couldn't be bothered to climb the ladder. In sleep he looked like the boy I'd spent my days with on the MGM lot. Quick and funny and always in trouble. I stood for a moment, remembering how fiercely I had loved him. I still did. How could I get through to him? Talk to him as we used to do, like brother and sister instead of adversaries? What would it take to bring him back from this brink of hatred?

I went back to my bed, thinking on what Mr. Lewis had said about fear . . . and love.

The next morning, I took a chance. Fritz was in the bathroom, shirtless and shaving, the door cracked open. I ducked in and shut the door behind me, locking it with a firm click.

"What are you doing?" Fritz plucked his shirt from where it hung on the hook and shrugged into it with an outraged look.

I sat down on the closed toilet. "I've seen your bare chest before." I'd changed his diapers as he well knew. "Tell me what happened to Yitzak." I didn't really want to hear the answer.

He turned back to the sink and picked up the straight razor. Fritz had the peach fuzz of a twelve-year-old boy and yet insisted upon shaving every day. "He got what he deserved."

How could he say that? Yes, they had their differences—mostly Fritz being angry because Yitzak cut the grass or cleaned out the gutters, making him look bad—but this was a man who was our neighbor for six years. "Did you do that to him?" Could he have?

Fritz drew the straight edge over his cheeks and down his throat, avoiding my gaze in the mirror. "The boys at the precinct." He rinsed the foam-coated razor in the sink with an angry flick of his wrist. "Liesl, he attacked women and children." He sounded like he was trying to convince himself, or was that just my own wishful thinking?

He pulled the plug and the water began its descent down the drain, leaving a film on the basin. "Whose side are you on, anyway?"

Yours, I wanted to say. My anger flared at him and then I remembered what Leon Lewis said about fear. What could Fritz possibly fear? And about love. But Fritz knew he was loved. Yet there was no harm in telling him so. It was, of course, the truth—even if I was so frustrated with him I wished to give him the spanking Mutti should have administered years ago.

"Fritz." I tried to see in this angry young man the sweet boy I had known, the one I remembered last night. "I know I don't say it often but . . . you know I love you. Don't you?"

He stopped, his eyes meeting mine in the mirror. "What?"

"I love you. You know that, *nicht wahr*?" I slipped into German. "And so does Mutti, even if she doesn't say it."

A flash of confusion, but also something else, went over his features in the cloudy mirror. "Sure, I know that."

I left him then, wondering if I'd made anything better. It felt awkward, talking about such feelings. We did not do that in our family . . . but perhaps we should.

CHAPTER 33

LIESL

Never had I longed so much for a Friday to be over.

The atmosphere in the Friends office since the ink incident was positively arctic. I'd apologized profusely to Thekla, but she was unforgiving. Now she stood over my desk with her hands on her hips, questioning me about the flyers I'd sent to members two days ago. "Gertrud informed me hers did not yet arrive in the mail." Her tone was icy. "You're quite sure you brought them to the post?"

"Perhaps they were delayed, Thekla."

She gave me a look that said she did not believe me.

Hermann became bolder still. He'd managed a pinch on my behind and a few suggestive comments, which were—in the entire scheme of what I was doing for Leon Lewis—small worries, but how I wished to slap his overly handsome face. Thankfully, he left with Wilhelm Otto to do whatever it was they did together and I was relieved of them both.

The task of replacing the papers in Hermann's office was a difficult one with Thekla watching me like a prison guard. But I knew her daily routine. When she went to freshen up at her usual time, she found the upstairs lavatory out of order. I had a precious few minutes while she went downstairs to the restaurant. I slipped quickly into Hermann's office and found—thankfully—the drawer was still unlocked. I smoothed the papers as best I could and slipped them back in place. I was back at my desk by the time she returned. "Liesl, call a plumber for the ladies' room," she said curtly.

"Of course, Thekla," I answered, my pulse still pounding, the wrench I'd used to shut off the water hidden deep in the bottom of my handbag.

At two o'clock, Paul Themlitz asked for my help in the bookstore. I escaped Thekla's cold presence to organize Paul's receipts and listen to his despicable chatter. "You know of course, Liesl," he said, "how they run the studios, promoting all sorts of filth."

I continued adding receipts and clamped my teeth together. The Aryan Bookstore, I discovered, was not a profitable business. In fact, it was running at a considerable loss.

"It's because they're weak and immoral. It is part of their nature." He smiled and looked for all the world like a cheerful frog from a children's story. "We must spread word of this great danger, as they are doing in the fatherland. The printed word." He gestured around his untidy bookstore. "But also radio and newspaper. Better yet—films!" He leaned forward and dropped his voice to a whisper. "Think of it! To wrest the studios from the control of the Jews and have at our fingertips the greatest propaganda machine the world has ever known."

I did not wish to consider it. Paul Themlitz in control of the film industry of Los Angeles, taking orders from Adolf Hitler and his propaganda minister in Berlin? A preposterous notion, and yet what if Lewis was correct? What if the leaders of the world were underestimating the German artist-turned-chancellor?

"But how could that be done?" I asked Paul. The studios were big business. The Friends of New Germany couldn't waltz in and take them over.

He smiled. "You must have faith, Liesl. We are working toward it as we speak." But how quickly, and in what way, he did not enlighten me.

When three o'clock finally came, I said goodbye and made myself walk sedately out the door, under the flag of the Third Reich, and into the September sunshine, hoping against hope that Wilhelm Otto would not be waiting for me.

My hope was in vain.

He leaned against his shiny blue car, smoking a cigarette. He tossed it away when he saw me and opened the passenger door. Could I not be rid of this man and the rest of the Nazis?

I settled in the comfortable seat and took in Wilhelm Otto's hard face, the coiled watchfulness and menace that lurked beneath his tailored suit. I considered what Mutti said about the girl at Paramount as he nosed the auto through the afternoon streets. I should not be surprised that this was a man who shirked his responsibilities. He was a Nazi, after all.

I remained silent, determined not to speak. Wilhelm Otto, though, seemed to be intent on making small talk. An unusual occurrence that made me suspicious after so many silent journeys.

"That girl of yours, Tess is it?" he asked suddenly. "How old is she?"

I was instantly uneasy. I wanted him to know nothing of my children and yet what reason did I have not to answer? "She's six."

"And your boy?"

"Steffen's four," I said, hoping my short answers and cold tone would deter him.

"You don't look old enough to have two children, Mrs. Weiss."

I was indeed old enough and some days felt far older. Was he getting at something? Another threat? I tried for a light response, such as Thekla might say. "Are you trying to flatter me, Mr. Otto?"

"Is it working?" He looked over and for a moment I could have sworn I saw a glimmer of humor around his eyes. Was Wilhelm Otto, Nazi watchdog, flirting with me? It could not be.

He parked in front of my home. Steffen lay in the front yard, watching the anthill he had taken an interest in for days. Tess sat beside him with Chester. Both jumped up and came running toward the car—Tess with Chester in her arms like a baby—before I could make my goodbyes.

"Hello, Mr. Otto," Tess said. "This is Chester." The kitten we took in six months ago had grown into a large and docile cat, more often lying on the furniture than deterring mice from our pantry. Tess took one of his white paws and held it out. "Pleased to meet you, Mr. Otto."

I watched and wondered how someone of Wilhelm Otto's serious nature would respond to this silliness.

He solemnly shook the offered paw. "Likewise."

Chester let out a chirrup and the children both broke into giggles.

Wilhelm Otto smiled.

I was utterly astonished. Not only that he *could* smile, but at the transformation it brought about. The scar over his lip vanished and a dimple—of all things—became quite apparent just off the left corner of his mouth. Even the mustache became less repulsive. Reluctantly I agreed with Thekla's opinion. He was, perhaps, a little handsome.

Chester struggled to get out of Tess's arms and jumped to the ground. He promptly lay down and rolled on the warm concrete sidewalk. Steffen looked up at Wilhelm. "I feed him," Steffen said. "It's my job. He likes cheese. And sausage. But not vegetables."

My astonishment doubled. It was the most I'd ever heard Steffen say to a stranger. He rarely spoke that many words in a row to me.

"That's why he's so fat," Tess told her brother in her bossy way. "You feed him too much."

Wilhelm crouched down and rubbed Chester's expansive white belly. The sun glinted on his chestnut hair and the cat purred like a motorboat. For that moment, I forgot who Wilhelm Otto was—and what he was.

He stood, and I snapped my attention back to reality. "Off you go now," I said to the children a little more sharply than I'd intended. "Change out of your school clothes and start your chores."

Tess let out a groan, her shoulders drooped, and she trudged toward the house as if she'd been assigned to ten years hard labor.

"Tess," I said sternly, "manners."

She did not even turn around. "Goodbye, Mr. Otto," she intoned in a voice so put-upon I fought a smile.

Steffen scooped Chester back in his arms. Wilhelm leaned down and touched his shoulder, then whispered in his ear. Steffen's mouth dropped open. "Really?"

Wilhelm Otto nodded.

Steffen squeezed Chester to him and ran after Tess.

"What was that about?" I asked with some trepidation. I did not like him whispering to my child.

The smile flickered once again over his stern features. "Nothing much." He watched the children go into the house, then leaned back on the hood as if he had nowhere to be on a Friday afternoon. "Must be nice." He tipped his head toward the house. "Having kids and all."

It was a strange sentiment and it made me wonder. I thought of the girl, Eva, and suddenly wished to provoke a response from this inscrutable man. "You could try it."

His reaction was almost imperceptible. A tightening around his mouth. Not exactly anger. Regret? He stuck his hands in his pockets. "Not every man's a family man, are they?"

No, not every man. Not him and not Tomas. Tomas said he wanted children, but in the end he ran away from his family. From the responsibility? Or from me? I might never know. "You're right, I suppose."

Wilhelm rounded the auto and folded himself into the driver's seat, then leaned over to speak to me through the open window. "By the way, Mrs. Weiss?" He motioned to the house where the children had disappeared. He once again betrayed that dimple, if only in a flash. "Chester? He's a she. And she's not fat; she's pregnant. You're going to have kittens in a week or so."

I shut my gaping mouth as the auto purred to life and pulled away from the curb. Kittens. The last thing I needed.

And Wilhelm Otto. The man was actually human—at least in that moment.

I walked slowly into the house. I did not wish to think of him as such—so much easier to consider him an automaton, a Hitlerite, a watchdog for Hermann Schwinn. And a threat. Not someone with feelings and a past. Regrets and hopes for the future. A soft spot for children and animals.

I wished I had not seen that side of him and tried to put it out of my mind.

CHAPTER 34

"Will Daddy ever come back?" Tess said in a whisper that wrenched my heart.

The excitement over Chester caused chaos, and by bath time, I was ready to wring Wilhelm Otto's neck. Finally Steffen settled into bed and closed his eyes, his arms around Chester, who purred by his side like she hadn't any idea of her recent transformation.

"Mommy?" Tess said when I didn't answer.

I sat on the bed beside her, *Alice's Adventures in Wonderland* open on my lap. Did she suspect her father would not return? Did she feel the same abandonment that I did? I would give anything to keep that darkness from her. But how could I? I considered my answer carefully. She would see through vague assurances and I would not lie to my children. "I don't know, sweetheart. But I know one thing. Daddy loved you."

"If he loved me, why did he leave?" Tess asked.

I had no answer to that. "I will never leave you," I said. "I promise."

Tess surprised me, as she often did, with an abrupt shift. "Why does God let people do bad things, Mutti? Like the mean man at the cafeteria?"

It was a night of hard questions, and a proper answer did not immediately come to me. I thought of the man in the cafeteria, refusing service to a woman with hungry children. Men who said they loved you and left. Men who wanted power and hated. Women like Gertrud and Thekla. Why did God allow it? "I think God allows people to choose. And some choose bad."

"But he could stop the bad, couldn't he?" Her little face was so serious, so intent on my answer, I felt a flutter of panic. What if I got this wrong? But the answer came to me after a moment. One that I thought correct. "He can do anything. And he does—sometimes. Maybe not how we would do so. And maybe we don't see it right away." Or even in our own lifetimes, I wanted to say. But that was too much for a child her age to understand. Too much for me to understand.

"And God can do something else," I told her, snuggling down close to her. I could tell Steffen was still awake, still listening, even as he pretended sleep. "He can make good come from bad. Like when he let his Son die on the cross, everybody thought he was dead and was sad, weren't they?"

"And then he was alive and everybody was happy," she finished.

"Yes, just like that."

Tess was not done with her questions. "What do you do when you do something bad and you wish you hadn't?"

An easier answer, one I was sure of. "We ask God to forgive us. And if we hurt someone, we ask them to forgive us also."

She fidgeted with the pink satin ribbon at the neck of her flannel nightgown, twisting it around her finger. "Hildy and Katya, they told me not to play with Frieda. That she had germs."

Here was the heart of the matter. I waited for her to go on.

Tess's face was the picture of misery. "Am I a bad person? Like that man?"

"No, honey." I pulled her into my arms. Tears streaked her cheeks. Guilt clawed at my chest. I should have stopped this from the beginning. I was afraid that Tess wouldn't have friends. That she would feel different, as I had. I blinked and swallowed. I settled her where I could look at her face. "You are a good person who made a mistake. You can tell Frieda you're sorry. And I think—I know—she'll forgive you." I hoped she would.

"Can I do it tomorrow? Will you come with me?"

Miriam. I owed her the same apology. One I could not give . . . yet. "Yes." I could at least help Tess make amends. "We'll do it together."

The next morning, I walked with Tess to the Stahrs' front door. Saturday, the Sabbath. Yitzak and Miriam would be leaving for the synagogue in a few hours, then have Yitzak's father over for lunch.

What would Miriam say? Would she let Tess make up with Frieda? I wouldn't blame her if she didn't. I could not explain about Fritz or why I worked with people who hated her.

Tess turned her face up to me, the worry lines between her blonde brows again. "What if she doesn't forgive me?" she whispered.

"She will, sweetheart." Forgiveness might come easily to Frieda, but I had little hope of it from Miriam.

We reached the door and Tess dropped my hand. Her shoulders rose and fell in a deep breath. She knocked. Footsteps sounded from inside, light and quick. Miriam opened the door. She was in her good dress, an apron tied over it, and shined brown lace-up shoes. Her face, so dear to me. I'd missed the smiles and laugh lines, the wrinkle on her brow as she thought over an idea. Her brown eyes were guarded as she looked from me to Tess.

"Mrs. Stahr." Tess's voice was small and uncertain. "May I talk to Frieda?"

Brave girl. Braver than her mother.

Miriam's jaw was set and I looked away, my heart squeezing with regret.

"Please?" Tess added in a whisper. Miriam's face softened. She stepped back and Frieda peeked around her mother, looking tentatively at Tess.

Tess swallowed but came out with it quickly. "I'm sorry, Frieda."

Frieda did not answer.

Tess's words shamed me. I should be saying them to Miriam. But our situation was complicated. She couldn't forgive me, and I had no right to ask it of her. Not yet.

Tess went on in a rush. "Frieda, I want to walk to school with you again. And sit with you at lunch and play at recess. And have you play at my house. And play at your house."

Frieda bit her lip and looked at her shoes.

"I don't want to be friends with Hildy and Katya. They're mean. I don't want to be mean." Tess stepped forward. "Frieda." She lowered her voice to a whisper. "Chester is going to have kittens."

Frieda's head jerked up and she looked in disbelief at Tess. I glanced at Miriam and her brows went up.

Tess nodded slowly. "He's a girl."

Then they were both giggling. Tess grabbed Frieda's hand and pulled her toward the steps. "Come see how fat he is." And just like that, they were gone to find the cat and I was left with a concerned Miriam.

"I don't want her hurt again, Liesl." Her tone was frigid.

I knew what she meant. She worried Tess would turn her back on Frieda when it came time to face the other girls at school. "She means it, Miriam." Tess might have made a mistake, but she knew better now. "I know—I know things aren't good between us," I said. An understatement. "But if we could . . . get along . . . and let them play again. It would mean so much to Tess. To both of them."

She regarded me with suspicion. She knew I loved Frieda, didn't she?

"She's still Jewish and you're still—" She shook her head. A Nazi, she was probably going to say. Or German. Perhaps it meant the same to her. "I thought you were different . . . better," she said.

Than Gertrud and the rest, she meant.

"But you are just as bad as them. Worse, because you pretended to be my friend."

I did not—could not—say a word in my defense.

"Don't let my little girl get hurt, Liesl." Miriam shut the door without another word.

I was at the kitchen table with the household accounts spread before me when Fritz came home from his night shift.

Tess, Frieda, and Steffen were making a bed for Chester out of an old crate, some scrap fabric, and a great deal of giggling. Mutti grumbled in the bathroom, where she was scrubbing the tile with an old toothbrush. Tess and Steffen ran to Fritz like he was returning from war, throwing their arms around his legs and begging him to play. Tess breathlessly giving him the news of Chester's impending motherhood, to which he reacted with the proper amount of congratulations to Chester.

I watched him with apprehension. Would Fritz be cruel to sweet Frieda, when we'd finally repaired their broken friendship? If he was, I would have choice words for my little brother.

But he smiled at her. "Now that we have three little goats, we can play Billy Goats Gruff." He let out a roar with his best troll imitation and held up his hands like claws. Frieda and Tess screamed and ran for the back door. Fritz scooped up Steffen and threw him over his shoulder.

He turned back to me, Steffen still squirming on his shoulder, and slapped a handful of dollar bills on the table beside me, a triumphant expression on his face.

"What's this?" I genuinely did not understand the money nor my brother's high spirits.

"My pay," he said as if I was an idiot. "You're the one who keeps telling me to help out."

I stared at him. "Who are you, and what have you done with my brother?"

He didn't even balk at my teasing. He went to the sitting room and deposited a giggling Steffen on the divan. "I mean it, Liesl." He came back to me, empty-handed and serious. "The auto, I guess maybe it wasn't the best idea. I'm sorry about that."

I took up the money and counted it. Twelve dollars. With what I'd gotten from Leon Lewis in my post office box yesterday, we could pay off the rest of the overdue bills and get Mutti's injections. We might even put some extra away. "What brought this on?" I really wanted to know.

"Figured it was time to, you know—" he shrugged—"be the man of the house."

I didn't know what to say. "Thank you. It will help a great deal."

He smiled and called out to the children, "Who's that trip-trapping over my bridge?" and started for the back door.

"Fritz?" I stopped him. This man was so like the brother I remembered, perhaps I could reach him. I lowered my voice. "Do you believe what they say about the Jews?"

His smile vanished. "Don't you?"

I didn't trust Fritz enough to tell him much. But could he at least begin to see? "Not all Jewish people are like Mayer and Gary Perl." I motioned toward the yard. "What about Frieda?"

He looked uncertain. "She's just a kid," he said. "It's not the same. Winterhalder says we're going to get back what we deserve. Respect. Honor. A good place for Tess and Steffen to grow up. You want that, don't you?"

He sounded like a Dictaphone recording stuck on a groove. Repeating what he heard a hundred times from men like Hans Winterhalder and Hermann Schwinn. Slogans and emotion, not thought or reason. As for respect, I had no respect for the likes of Hans Winterhalder. And honor was not something I saw at the Friends of New Germany. But Fritz had stepped up to help the family. And he didn't hesitate for a moment when he saw Frieda. Was his own good heart finally surfacing?

"Hey." He looked abashed and lowered his voice. "You didn't tell, did you?"

He meant Mutti and I wondered how he could defend the Silver Shirts and still not want Mutti to know. Didn't that say he wasn't completely in the grip of the National Socialists?

I shook my head. "No, but you should. She's worried about you."

"She's always worried." He dismissed my words. "And, Liesl . . ." He turned away to scoop up Steffen, who was trying to sneak by him. He threw him over his shoulder with a troll-like growl.

"Yes?" I put two dollars and some change in an envelope for the electrical.

He looked back at me and for a moment, I saw a flash of the boy I'd known. "I love you too."

CHAPTER 35

AGENT THIRTEEN

Thirteen went looking for Seventeen at the Disabled Veterans on Saturday morning. "Haven't seen him since Wednesday," one of the old-timers said. "Not like him to miss the Friday night poker game."

Thirteen wondered at that. Maybe the man decided that working for Leon Lewis wasn't for him, but his gut told him Seventeen wasn't the type to quit without a word. Thirteen decided he'd track him down later, after he did his business in Germantown.

Brody had gotten back to him with some rumors he'd heard about Tomas Weiss. With footwork and the right questions, he should be able to find answers. He drove the Cadillac back to Germantown and parked it on a side street, got out, and walked the rest of the way.

Why was he even doing this? It sure as shooting wasn't because he owed Liesl Weiss something. He was kicking himself about the chance he'd taken with the flyers, but cripes, it had felt good to dump them in the trash barrel behind the post office. Liesl Weiss paid the price with Thekla. But wasn't that his job, to create suspicion among the Friends— keep them from trusting each other and slow down their progress? He wasn't in Germantown because he felt guilty about the secretary. It was just that now he'd started, he had to follow the trail and find the answer.

Ming's Chinese Laundry was a smallish storefront with a hand-lettered sign that listed cheap prices for shirts, linens, and the like. He'd studied the report from Donna in archives and something didn't smell right. On May 3, Tomas Weiss and Mickey O'Neil walked their usual beat in Germantown, with Ming's the last stop of the day. On May 4, Weiss was reported missing by his wife. "I asked around," Brody had said. "I was told to get my nose out of it." He smiled. "So that was something to think about." They'd agreed Ming's was the place to start asking questions and here he was.

A set of bells on the door chimed as he entered and a man looked up from a ledger. When he saw Thirteen, he looked scared. "We closed," he said, then a string of Chinese words.

"You speak English?" Thirteen asked. He tried to look friendly. Smiled. Didn't work.

The man scurried out a door in the back, leaving him alone in the shop. He looked around. It was a nice operation. Big canvas carts filled with clean linens. Some baskets of neatly folded clothing. A rack of hanging shirts with receipts pinned to the collars. Smelled like soap and bleach. Nothing fishy.

Mr. Ming appeared through the door, this time with a kid—maybe eleven or twelve—and a woman that might be Mrs. Ming. "We closed," the boy said, his accent less pronounced than his father's. "Moving to San Francisco."

Hmm. Interesting. "I just want to know a few things." He reached for his wallet. Ming and the kid jumped, closing ranks in front of the mother like he was pulling a gun. "Hey, nothing to worry about." He held out his wallet, pulled out a five-dollar bill, and offered it up. Jumpy, weren't they?

Ming put out a cautious hand for the money.

"I want to know about Tomas Weiss," he said to the kid. "Police officer, used to work around here a couple years back."

At Weiss's name, Ming backed away from him and the money, shaking his head and saying some words in Chinese.

"We don't know him," the kid translated unnecessarily. He'd struck a nerve, all right. "Can't help you, mister."

They looked like a nice family. He'd try the honest approach—it was worth a shot. "Listen, I'm not police." He talked straight to Mr. Ming. "I'm not looking to get you in trouble. But the wife—Mrs. Weiss—she deserves to know what happened to her husband. I'll keep your name out of it best I can." He couldn't make any promises, but Brody would back him up.

The kid talked to his father. Then the whole family chattered for a while—Mr. and Mrs. Ming having some kind of disagreement. Finally the woman seemed to win out and said some words to the kid. He looked apprehensive, and she snapped at him.

"My mother says to tell you, Mrs. Weiss is nice lady. She came here sometimes. Mother feels bad about her mister."

"What happened to her mister?" He didn't like where this was heading.

The boy told him and it wasn't a pretty story.

"My mother says she sorry about it. Sorry to Mrs. Weiss."

He was too. More than he could say. In fact, his heart did a little dip, something he'd never felt before, when he thought about how he'd have to break it to her. But she deserved to know.

He thanked them and made the man take the five-dollar bill and another one. Then he gave the kid some instructions for when Brody got in touch to do what needed to be done.

As he left the laundry, he felt like he was dragging a fifty-pound weight behind him. This town had an underbelly that never failed to turn his stomach. He had his answer about Tomas Weiss, but he wished to heaven he didn't.

Sunday morning, Thirteen took the dog for a long walk in the hills.

He hadn't stepped foot in a church since the old man's funeral, unless the synagogue with Leon Lewis counted. But a couple times in the past years he'd felt something—a presence, he'd call it if he had to put a word to it. One time, when he'd been working in Monterey, he got it in his head to go to Las Vegas, heard it was a good time. He made a stop about a hundred miles inland at a national park to take a walk. Ended up spending the rest of the day in the woods. Never did get to Vegas. Those trees. The sun glinting through them. The silence and the presence of something bigger than his own understanding. He didn't know what to call it, but maybe it was what people called God.

The dog disappeared into a knot of juniper, running down a gopher or chipmunk. He kept walking. The trail through the San Gabriel Mountains wasn't like the woods up north. Scrub pine instead of cedars and the hot, dry smell of the desert instead of the cool, mossy air of the forest. But it was good to get away from the city. Gave him a chance to think. Maybe even feel that presence again. Pray, maybe. He hadn't prayed in a long time. When he was a kid, sure. Prayed his father wouldn't get angry, wouldn't come after his mom and him. Those prayers mostly went unanswered. During the war, his buddies prayed. Most of them were buried over there.

Made him question humanity. And question God, too. Why would a God who was supposed to be so good let all this bad happen? His sister and mother. The war. And now Nazis in Los Angeles.

And why did he feel like it was his duty to do something about all the bad in the world?

He could be taking it easy on a beach somewhere, maybe traveling the world. He had enough money to do whatever he wanted. Instead, he was yes-sirring to the likes of Hermann Schwinn and Hans Winterhalder. He climbed the last hill and looked over the valley. It stretched brown and green to the misty horizon. He took a moment to catch his breath.

Leon Lewis asked him a question once: *Would you rather put your faith in God or humanity?* It was a trick question, and he declined to answer. But that didn't mean he didn't think about it. If he had to choose between the two, he'd come down on the side of God. He'd seen too much evil in men to put his eggs in that basket.

So yeah, he was willing to try praying. For the kids in the Silver Shirts, for Lewis, and to keep his temper around Hermann Schwinn and that scumbag Winterhalder. And what was he going to do about Liesl Weiss?

He whistled and the dog came loping out of the brush. The sun was halfway up in the sky and he figured he better go. The problem of Seventeen had gone from an itch in the back of his mind to an all-out worry. He'd find his friend today or know the reason why.

And if the man upstairs wanted to give him a hand, he'd welcome the help.

Back at the Biltmore, Thirteen changed into his usual uniform of suit and white shirt. He considered his holster and revolver, then shrugged it on. Better safe than sorry. He drove back to Germantown. Nobody answered when he knocked on the door of Seventeen's bungalow. He took a walk around the back. An empty clothesline and some wilted geraniums, but no sign of the wife and kids. Thirteen got in the Cadillac and stared out the window. One more place to check.

He drove faster than he should and tried praying again. Why hadn't he checked on the man days ago? He'd been distracted by the mystery of Liesl Weiss. He'd never forgive himself if something happened to the agent he'd recruited.

He parked the automobile in front of Central Hospital. By then, he was pushing down panic. Inside the doors, nurses in white uniforms with white caps and clunky black shoes hurried down hallways that smelled of disinfectant and canned corn. He fidgeted while a nurse at the reception desk looked at the hospital records. She ran her finger slowly down a column of names, then looked up. "Yes, room 240. Second floor."

He took the stairs two at time. Please, he couldn't face a widow and three fatherless boys. Opened the door to room 240 with his heart in his throat. "Karl!" Thirteen's relief left him weak. The man they'd dubbed Seventeen looked bad—real bad. But he was alive.

"I was going to call you as soon as I got out of this joint." Karl Weber sat on the edge of the hospital bed. He had a black eye and a gauze bandage on one side of his face. A cast on his left arm was making it difficult to put on his jacket.

"What happened?" Thirteen's blood was still pumping at fighting level.

"Not sure," Karl answered, giving up the struggle and letting one arm hang loose while he used his good hand to push himself to standing. "One minute I was minding my own business; then a big guy was all over me with a tire iron."

Thirteen pushed him back down on the bed. "Sit. When? And where?"

"Thursday." Karl told him he'd been walking home from the Lorelei. He frowned at Thirteen. "It was Monroe. Called me a Jew lover and all that bunk."

"How did he figure it out?" If they knew about Karl, was his cover blown too? But if it was, why did they let him on the *Estes*?

"Tuesday," Karl said, shaking his head. "My own fault. I thought I had some time to take a look in the basement of the Alt Heidelberg." He frowned. "Liesl Weiss—she saw me. Must have told Monroe."

Thirteen frowned as he remembered the quiet conversation Liesl Weiss and Monroe had in the storage room that afternoon—how Monroe had left in a hurry. She must have suspected Karl and blown the whistle. She almost got the man killed. The thought stabbed him in the area of his rib cage. He'd hoped he was wrong about her but it looked like he wasn't.

Karl swallowed and tried to stand again. "That's not the worst of it. My boys—he cornered them on the way home from school the next day. Scared 'em pretty bad, called them traitors to their race. Told them what he'd do to them and to my wife."

Thirteen felt a helpless fury rise in him. He wanted more than anything to take it out on Monroe. What kind of coward threatened children?

Thirteen went with Karl in the elevator and down to the front desk. "I'll settle the bill," he said. "Do you have somewhere safe to go?"

Karl pulled his injured arm close to his body. "Wife has a sister up in Santa Barbara. She's there with the boys. I'll go for a while, but you have to get a message to Lewis for me."

"He's gone to DC for reinforcements."

Karl grunted. "We're going to need them."

Thirteen didn't like the sound of that.

Karl leaned closer and lowered his voice. "Before Liesl Weiss ratted on me, I got into that storage room in the basement." Karl's voice turned grim. "I found guns—rifles, maybe two dozen—a case of grenades, gasoline bombs, and a lot of ammo. Looks like army issue from the San Diego armory, just like we figured."

A cold knot tightened in Thirteen's gut.

"Look," Karl said. "From what you told me, they're going to do something big. Something that will cripple the studios so they can get their own people in—if what you heard on the *Estes* wasn't just blowing smoke."

The *Obergruppenführer* didn't strike Thirteen as a man of idle threats.

Karl kept on with a calm sort of logic. "If you were Herr Hitler, how would you take over the studios?"

That was easy. He'd do just what the SS officer on the *Estes* told Schwinn. "Get rid of the ones running the show." And that meant the bigwigs like the Warners and Goldwyn, but also the producers—Thalberg and Perl—and even the actors with power like Al Jolson and Eddie Cantor.

Karl nodded. "Then put in your own people."

Sure. Guys like Monroe and Schwinn would jump at the chance to be film stars and executives. "But aren't they worried about getting caught if they start killing bigwigs all over Los Angeles?"

"They'll sacrifice some of their own for the cause," Karl said. "Most likely those kids we saw out training in the hills. You know how it works—the kids will take the blame, go to prison or worse. The job will be done and the bosses in Berlin will move on with the next step of their plan."

"You think people here won't kick up a fuss?" But he already knew the answer.

Karl did too. "Plenty of people in LA want to see the moguls go down, especially after the pamphlets our friends have been putting out."

True. Some people—a lot, maybe—would be dancing in the streets to see the rich and famous get their comeuppance. "But how are they going to do it?"

Seventeen tipped his head. "That's what you need to figure out. And quick."

CHAPTER 36

When I walked into the Friends of New Germany office Monday morning, something was very wrong, indeed.

The day had started pleasantly. I walked Tess and Frieda to school. The morning held a crisp hint of autumn, with a promise of short-sleeve weather by midmorning. The girls skipped and hopped over the cracks on the sidewalk as we walked. It was good to see a smile on Frieda's face. When the schoolyard came into sight, Frieda's steps began to drag and her face clouded with anxiety. Hildy and Katya stood on the wide steps leading up to the doors.

Frieda stopped, her head dipped as she looked to the ground. I watched Tess. My daughter did not hesitate but grabbed Frieda's hand. Frieda's head came up. Tess tugged at her and they walked with determined steps, hands clasped, past Hildy's and Katya's surprised faces.

It should have made me hopeful, seeing the two girls—one German and one Jewish—walking hand in hand, but despair settled on me instead. How could children as young as Hildy Grundbacher already be poisoned by hate? Her mother and father had taught it to her and been taught the same by their own parents. Could she even be blamed for her bullying ways? And how was the cycle of hatred to be stopped?

When I entered the office, my questions were replaced by fear as

Thekla did not return my morning greeting. Her mouth was tight and her eyes as hard as a rattlesnake's ready to strike.

"Is something wrong?" I asked, glancing at Wilhelm Otto, who stood at his regular place near the window. Watching.

She did not answer but tapped her pink-polished fingernails on the desktop. "Hermann," she said in a sharp voice. "She is here."

In the next five minutes, my work of the past two weeks threatened to be undone.

Hermann announced the news in a cold voice. "Paul was arrested this morning when he arrived at the bookstore. He is charged with writing threatening letters to President Roosevelt."

Paul Themlitz? That wasn't right. I told Leon Lewis that it was Hermann Schwinn who wrote the letter.

"Writing that letter was foolish," Thekla snapped at Hermann. "I told you it would bring trouble. And now—there is only one person who could have reported you." She turned to me with an icy stare.

"No," I said automatically. "I did no such thing." My stomach dipped like I was looking down from a high precipice.

"Only the three of us knew of the letter," Hermann said coldly.

"But—"

"And let me remind you, Liesl, that you took an oath," Hermann said. "To the National Socialist Party. And those who betray—"

"I meant every word." I interrupted him with an indignant look. I knew the danger of my position. I was spying on Hermann and Thekla, who could well be operatives sent from a foreign government. Wilhelm Otto was a dangerous man with a gun at his side. I was fighting for my life and must be convincing. "I believe in what the Friends are trying to accomplish. Surely you know that. Why else would I come here every day for no pay?"

Hermann stared at me for a long moment. "If it wasn't you, then who was it?"

I felt a small breath of relief. Hermann looked to be swaying to my side. "I don't know—truly I don't. I'd like to know as much as you do. It's despicable to betray the Friends." I put all my angst for Frieda and Tess into my words.

Hermann's face relaxed slightly.

Thekla's frown twitched down. She was not convinced. "We cannot be too careful. Already we have found a traitor—someone we trusted— was working with the Jew lawyer."

"Who?" I did not have to pretend to be stunned.

"Karl Weber," Hermann said. He looked to Wilhelm Otto with an accusatory glare.

"Sorry, boss. Like I said, wouldn't have guessed Karl was a Jew lover."

My breath caught. Karl Weber was the other operative, not Travis Monroe. What had happened to Karl?

"He's been taken care of," Thekla said as if she read my mind.

A cold fear fingered up my spine. Taken care of. Reprisals. Neele and the boys—were they all right? I felt ill. I thought suddenly of Alice's upside-down story—Thekla as the merciless Queen of Hearts, ordering her soldiers to take off the heads of any who displeased her. But this was no children's story and Thekla far more dangerous, as was Hermann. I glanced quickly at Wilhelm Otto. Did he take care of Karl Weber? I remembered the menace of his threats to me. *Think of your kids, is all I'm saying.*

Tess and Steffen. And Mutti. If I was in danger, so were they.

The Friends office was as tense as a stretched rubber band for the rest of the morning.

I worried for Karl, for Neele and her boys. And for myself. I attempted to see to my duties but made three errors on one letter and needed to retype it. I took dictation from Hermann, fumbled my shorthand, and asked him to repeat himself twice. I wished desperately to telephone Mutti, ask if she'd heard anything about the Webers, but didn't want to be overheard.

Was what I was doing worth the risk to my family—my children? The list of people I'd seen in the unmarked file—Mayer, Gary Perl, Al

Jolson—I had no love for them. But it was not for them that I wished to stop the Friends of New Germany. It was for Miriam and Frieda, for Stella and Leon Lewis and the rest of the innocent people the Friends despised because of their heritage. To do what was right and just. To stop the teaching of hatred to our children.

At 10:22, the telephone rang. Thekla was down the hall freshening her makeup and, for the moment, not watching my every move. "Friends of New Germany."

"Liesl, put me through to Hermann." It was Paul Themlitz. I put the call through but kept the receiver at my ear, covering the mouthpiece with my hand.

"I've been released," Paul said when Hermann answered.

"What did you tell them?" Hermann snapped.

"Nothing, of course." Paul sounded irritated. "You owe me, Schwinn."

I heard the snap of heels outside the door and quickly put the receiver in the cradle as Thekla returned. Hermann came out and announced the good news about Paul.

"Paul would never betray the Friends." She looked at me as if to say I was not of the same good character. "But there is a traitor among us, and we will find out who it is."

I returned to my typing, thinking hard as I tapped at the keys. I would have to regain the trust of the Friends, not only for the sake of Leon Lewis's operation, but for my own family's safety. As I considered Paul Themlitz's words, I had an idea of how to do precisely that.

———————

This moment was undeniably one of dire need.

At 11:28, I gathered my handbag. "Thekla, I'm going to lunch." She answered with a glacial nod. What I needed to accomplish would take longer than my half-hour lunch break but adding to Thekla's displeasure could not be helped.

I waited for the trolley, watching the reflection of the Alt Heidelberg in the window across the street. No sign of Thekla following me. Yet. I stepped aboard the red line and made my way to the back of the trolley. At the first stop, I hopped off the back and trotted quickly around the corner, then walked three blocks to the blue line and got on the first bus heading downtown. I got off at the Biltmore Hotel.

I was dressed nicely enough in a gabardine suit and two-tone pumps. My hat was one of my newer ones, straw with a spray of silk lily of the valley at one side. I straightened my back—*Don't slouch like a ninny, Liesl,* Mutti's voice said in my head—and I walked with purpose through the marble and gold lobby as if I were a guest. On the back wall was a bank of telephones. My cotton gloves were damp as I lifted the receiver and asked for the number I'd memorized.

"Ted Torgeson," the extension was answered after the third ring with a brisk voice.

I let out a breath and composed my thoughts. I must get this correct.

"Hello?" The voice was impatient.

"My name is Edelweiss," I said. "I work with Leon Lewis."

He let out a long breath as if he wished I hadn't said that. "Go on."

"I need to see you." I could have told him my predicament over the telephone, but I felt exposed with the lobby of the hotel at my back and a fear that Thekla was lurking. And I needed to see him—to take his measure. *I don't entirely trust him,* Mr. Lewis had said.

"Meet me at the King Eddy."

The King Eddy speakeasy was the worst kept secret in Los Angeles and not somewhere a lady would go alone, but that wasn't what had me tied in knots as I walked out of the Biltmore and turned down Fifth. It was a ten-minute walk, which gave me enough time to second-guess and then third-guess my plan. Was this really the only way?

By the time I'd reached the crumbling King Edward Hotel, I'd run through every option I could think of and come back to this. I went around back and twisted the knob on a bell that must ring somewhere deep within the basement speakeasy. The door was opened by a pouchy-faced bouncer who didn't blink at a woman arriving alone. He didn't ask for a password, just ushered me down a dingy staircase. I straightened my spine and lifted my chin.

The speakeasy was dark and smelled of late nights and bad decisions. Cigarette smoke hung in a thick fog along the low ceiling and a sorry-looking three-piece band plucked out an off-key rendition of "Rhapsody in Blue." An assortment of lawyer types and studio people sat at the bar and a scattering of tables. Plenty of writers from MGM thought of the King Eddy as their second home, but none who would recognize me, I hoped.

A man of around thirty sat at the bar with an empty martini glass in his hand. He had blanched hair, pink skin, and pale-blue eyes. He straightened as I entered and raised a blond brow. "Edelweiss?"

I sat down on the stool beside him, my back to the rest of the room.

"Want one?" he asked, waving his empty glass.

"No thank you." I had ten minutes before Thekla would start looking for my return. "I'm under suspicion," I began without any preamble. "I need to get the Friends of New Germany to trust me."

"What do you expect me to do about it?" Torgeson said in an unhelpful way.

I told him what I needed and his part in my plan.

Ted Torgeson's eyes widened with surprise. "You'd do that?"

I didn't want to but it was my only chance. "If you can make it work."

He rubbed his whiskerless chin, eyeing me with perhaps a bit more respect. "It will have to be convincing. And people would know."

I had more to worry about than my reputation. "Can you do it?"

"Your boss is going to owe me one," he said.

Did no one in this town do what was right for its own sake? I met his pale gaze and put out my hand. Leon Lewis could manage the assistant district attorney when he got back from DC. I had more pressing concerns.

Ted Torgeson's grasp was weak and paper-dry. "Tomorrow," he said and signaled to the bartender for another martini. "Be ready."

CHAPTER 37

LIESL

"Did you hear about the Webers?" Mutti asked when I arrived home in the afternoon.

I looked up from Steffen's clinging embrace with a sickening lurch in my chest.

"Neele packed up and left," she said. "Took the boys and didn't tell anyone where she was going or why."

My mouth went dry. "What about Karl?" What could Thekla have meant by "taken care of"?

Mutti shrugged. "Nobody knows, but the lady who lives across from the Webers told Mrs. Mueller that she heard Karl was in bad trouble with the law or some such nonsense."

Worse than the law. In trouble with Hermann Schwinn and Wilhelm Otto. And poor Neele with three boys. Where was she and was she safe? Would the Friends of New Germany really hurt children? I thought of the woman at the Deutscher Tag. Yes, I believed they would.

The telephone rang the next day at two o'clock. I'd kept up a cheerful facade, pretending all was in order. Thekla had given me the tedious task of retyping the membership list in alphabetical order. With every name, anxiety tightened in my chest. More of my German neighbors acceding to the darkness of fear and hate. "Friends of New Germany," I said into the receiver.

It was Ted Torgeson's flat voice. "It's all set." I hung up without replying but my pulse matched the quick tempo of my typewriter keys and a flush of dread crept up my spine.

"Who was that?" Thekla asked. She was filing her nails and watching me type.

"A wrong connection." I checked off a name and hit the return lever as if I hadn't noticed her suspicion. How would Torgeson make it convincing?

One hour later, I gathered the outgoing mail and put on my gloves and hat. "I'll take these to the post office, Thekla," I said. But it wasn't to be that easy.

"I'll accompany you." She stood quickly. "Wilhelm can drive us."

My insides turned to curdled milk. Already the plan was going wrong.

Wilhelm opened the front door of the auto for Thekla, then settled me in the back seat.

The route to the post office was filled with Thekla's flirtatious remarks toward Wilhelm, for which I was grateful. At least her attention was not on my ever-increasing consternation as we drew closer to the post office and my setup with Ted Torgeson. My pulse quickened as Wilhelm pulled the auto to a stop.

I pushed open my door. "I'll just be a moment."

"I'll walk with you," Thekla said.

Why would it take two people to post the mail? But I did not argue with Thekla. Torgeson said he would make it look convincing—but would it be convincing enough for Thekla?

Wilhelm Otto's brow flickered, but he remained in the auto—a small mercy. I kept my eyes on the sidewalk as we walked in silence. A walkway and short set of stairs led to the doors. A uniformed police officer stood outside the door. As I approached, he stepped forward. "Liesl Weiss?"

I froze. This was it. I tipped my head as if in confusion. "Yes?"

He showed me a badge. "If you'll come with me, miss."

My gaze snapped to Thekla, then to the door, where a second officer appeared, as if I would try to escape. Even as I knew it was a sham, my mouth went dry. "Come with you?" My voice was higher than normal. "What is this regarding?"

Thekla drew back as if she didn't know me.

"Just some questions, ma'am." He took my arm above the elbow and motioned me toward a black Ford waiting at the curb. I had no need to feign fear, for it was real enough. My legs were rubber, my steps faltered. I hadn't imagined the men to look at me with such contempt nor their grip to be so firm.

Suddenly Wilhelm Otto bounded up the steps, his face determined. "What the—?" The officer dropped my arm and his hand went to the gun on his belt. My heart jumped to my throat. This was not what I planned. Wilhelm froze, raising both his hands, his palms out. "Take it easy. Just want to know what's going on, is all."

"Mrs. Weiss is under arrest," the officer said briskly.

"On what charges?" Wilhelm Otto asked, his jaw set and his voice hard.

"Treason." The officer gripped my arm and directed me to the waiting auto. "She'll be at the Hall of Justice."

"I'd like to speak to Mr. Torgeson, please." I attempted a polite tone as the taciturn officer walked me into the Hall of Justice.

"Noted," he answered abruptly as we stopped at the front desk. "Officer, bring Mrs. Weiss down to the women's prison. Book her."

Book me? This was supposed to be a sham arrest. And where was Ted Torgeson?

What followed was an efficient process that included taking my handbag, my hat, and my photograph. The young officer, his face crimson, checked my skirt pockets and found nothing. The clerk at the desk asked me standard questions of name, address, and birth date and typed my answers with quick fingers onto a file card. I found myself in a cell that contained a hard cot, a washstand, and a toilet—right out there in the open. "Anyone you'd like to call, Mrs. Weiss?" he asked.

Absolutely not. Mutti would have a conniption. Fritz—what would I say? I sat down on the cot as the door clanged shut. I'd be home soon enough if Mr. Torgeson kept his side of our bargain. But would he?

Thekla's reaction at the post office arrest was unsurprising. She hadn't raised a finger to help. Wilhelm had been ready to fight, but I was glad he didn't. A gunfight over a fake arrest would have been a disaster. Wilhelm and Thekla probably went straight back to the Friends office to tell Hermann. Hermann would worry, wondering if I would betray him about the letter. If I were unreliable—as both Thekla and Hermann seemed to think—I would crack, tell Torgeson about the letter to the president, and point fingers. Instead, I would prove to them that I believed in the cause. That I would not break my oath even if it meant going to jail for the Friends of New Germany.

A wall clock ticked over the door, the second hand sweeping in circles, counting off the minutes, then the hours. Impatience rose in me, then panic.

Would Ted Torgeson betray me? Leave me here in jail? I never should have trusted him.

I paced again. I railed at Torgeson and myself. I prayed. I worried over Tess and Steffen. When I didn't come home at my usual time, would they think I'd left them, as their father had done? What was Mutti thinking?

By now, word would be getting around Germantown. The neighbors would be talking. Someone would tell Mutti what had happened at the post office. Miriam would find out. The gossip would be spreading like wildfire. Arrested. Treason. A Nazi. Good for my work at the Friends of New Germany but shame for Mutti and a further confirmation to Miriam of my betrayal. It was part of the plan, but I didn't like it.

At 10:43 p.m., the door of my cell finally opened.

A fresh-faced cadet marched me to a windowless room at the end of the hall. Ted Torgeson sat at a table and motioned me to an empty chair. The assistant district attorney was dressed in evening wear far too expensive for a public servant. His pale face and ice-chip eyes held no remorse for making me wait half the night. Indignation swelled within me but I resisted the urge to tell Ted Torgeson exactly what I thought of him.

"Please, have a seat." He motioned to a chair across from him.

I did not sit. "We had a deal, Mr. Torgeson."

Torgeson leaned toward me. "I did my part—got you arrested on charges of treason and now released. You should be thanking me. It's not an easy trick."

"You could have done it faster," I said.

He raised a colorless brow. "I told you it had to be convincing. You're in the clear with the Friends of New Germany just like you wanted, lady. Show a little gratitude. And tell Lewis I helped you out."

"It's the least you could do," I said. This was the same man who wouldn't help Leon Lewis get the Friends of New Germany out of Los Angeles.

"Listen, Edelweiss," he said, using my code name like an insult. "It's not like I don't appreciate what Lewis is doing. But the Nazis just aren't a big concern."

I did not bother to hide my surprise—and my disagreement—from my expression.

He went on as if explaining to a child. "It's the Reds we need to keep an eye on, you understand? And those kraut friends of yours—sorry, the German Americans," he corrected, "they're doing us a favor, keeping the Commies in line."

"Communists and Jews are not the same," I interjected.

He shrugged. "Whatever you say. The point is, I have a lot on my plate. Not to mention the repeal and all the immigration problems in this godforsaken city. The Jews aren't my problem, if you get my meaning."

I got his meaning. We were on our own. Leon Lewis and his operatives. I must have looked as dejected as I felt. Torgeson pulled at his collar, adjusted his bow tie. "Listen, I'll throw you a bone, Edelweiss."

I was unsure of what he meant by that phrase, but it might be a good thing.

Ted Torgeson leaned forward and fixed me with a stare. "If you want to take down Hermann Schwinn and the krauts, Georg Gyssling is the man to talk to."

He had my attention. Mr. Lewis had told me to find out what I could about the German vice-consul. "Isn't he one of them?"

"He is." He shrugged his padded shoulders. "And he isn't."

"What does that mean?" I needed more than that cryptic statement.

A knock on the door made me jump. The young officer came in. "Paperwork is done."

Torgeson looked at his wristwatch as if he had a film premiere to attend. "It's been a pleasure, Mrs. Weiss. Don't forget to give my regards to Lewis, like we said."

I wanted to ask more about Georg Gyssling. What had he meant? How could I talk to the vice-consul? But Ted Torgeson straightened his evening jacket and was gone. I was suddenly and utterly weary. I followed the young cadet to the main desk, telling myself the worst was over.

I was wrong about that as well.

CHAPTER 38

LIESL

I'd kept myself in tight control with Torgeson but now my knees wobbled.

Wilhelm Otto stood next to the chest-high precinct desk in a black wool overcoat, his sharp fedora pulled low over his forehead, looking like one of those Chicago gangsters. Fritz, shorter by a head and dressed in his police uniform, stood beside him.

"Liesl, are you all right?" Fritz met me, his concern so genuine, a welling of emotion surprised me.

"Yes." I couldn't break down in front of Wilhelm Otto. "I just want to go home."

"Don't worry," Fritz assured me. "Mr. Otto will take you."

Of course they knew each other. The Silver Shirts, the Friends of New Germany. All Hitlerites. I wrapped my arms around my middle to stave off a shiver—from shock or the cold marble of the Hall of Justice, I did not know.

Wilhelm Otto's sharp gaze missed nothing. He shrugged out of his overcoat and draped it around my shoulders. It was heavy and the warm silk lining smelled of hair oil and tobacco. My eyes prickled in an alarming way. I was surely at the end of my rope if Fritz's sympathy and Wilhelm Otto's kindness threatened my composure.

231

Fritz motioned to the desk clerk. "Mr. Schwinn telephoned, and boy, is he hopping mad. Somebody's going to pay for putting you through this."

The plan seemed to have worked; that was a relief. "What did Mutti say?"

He made a gesture of dismissal. "I told her it was all a misunderstanding." He squeezed my hand. "I'm so proud of you, Sis."

My affection for Fritz vanished at his words. Proud that I had been accused of treason—of threatening the president of the United States? Who was this man who looked like my brother? When had he been replaced by this person gone so astray? I had regained the trust of the Schwinns, but had my scheme reinforced my brother's wrongheadedness?

Wilhelm Otto took my arm. "Let's get you home."

Those were, I believed, the best words I'd heard all day. And that I heard them from Wilhelm Otto was proof it had been an upside-down day.

The wind cut like a knife as we left the Hall of Justice. Wilhelm helped me into the auto and started the engine. The auto was a familiar comfort and I let out a long breath. Wilhelm Otto did not shift the gear and pull into the street. Instead, he lit a cigarette and took a puff, then turned to me.

"Can I ask you something, Mrs. Weiss?" His tone was serious.

"Yes," I answered but wished he wouldn't. My brain was sluggish. I wanted nothing more than my own bed, my children beside me, and sleep.

"Why'd you do it?" he said, watching me through the veil of smoke.

"Do what?" For a moment, I'd thought he meant sign on with Leon Lewis. I was tired and I needed to be careful. I reminded myself that this man was not a friend, he was an enemy.

"Stay quiet for Hermann Schwinn? It could have ended with you in federal prison."

This sounded like a trap, except that he really seemed sincere. I couldn't tell him the truth, so I would have to lie. "I believe in what he's doing, of course." I tried for a sharp and convincing tone. "Don't you?"

He didn't answer, just threw the barely smoked cigarette out the window and pulled out onto the street. He didn't speak again as we passed nightclubs spilling light and music into the night. Women in bright dresses and furs, men in sleek tuxedos. Soon we left downtown behind. On Pico, the houses of the practical Germantown residents were buttoned up tight. He pulled up outside my house where a single lamp glowed in the downstairs sitting room. Mutti, waiting for me. I did not leave the auto, nor did Wilhelm get out to open my door.

What would I tell her?

"Sometimes, it's best to say nothing," Wilhelm said.

I gave him a questioning look. Had he read my thoughts or had I spoken aloud?

He jerked his head toward the glow of the window. "I had a mother once." His lips flickered into an almost smile, as if he knew such a thought difficult to believe.

"Do you still?" I asked. Did she know what he had become? Was she proud of him?

His hint of a smile died. "Not anymore."

"I'm sorry." Even if he was a Nazi, I had a flash of sympathy. I would be lost without Mutti, even with her difficult ways. "What happened?" Suddenly I wanted very much to hear his answer.

"Influenza," he said simply.

So many had been lost in those days. I could easily have been without a mother myself. I looked at him, his face illuminated by the glow of the streetlamp. Still and impassive, staring straight ahead as if he were look-ing all the way to the ocean. I didn't make a move to go. The blanket of dark wrapped around us in an unexpected intimacy.

"I left home when I was fourteen. My dad and I—" he gave a little shake of his head—"one of us had to go and it wasn't going to be him. Left my sister there. She was just a little thing, seven years old. The old man, he took out his fists for Mom and me, but he didn't touch her." He glanced sideways at me. "She was a firecracker. Pretty, too, like your girl."

I remembered how he'd looked at Tess. My heart constricted and I saw a flash of that young man—hardly more than a child himself. A little girl who loved her big brother.

He turned to me then and the yellow light of the streetlamp lit his face for a moment, showing a different man than the one I thought I knew. "When I got back from the war, I went to get them. Figured I could give Lily and Ma a better life."

I hadn't believed I could feel sympathy for the man beside me. But I did. Whatever had happened after, he had been a boy once who had loved his mother and his sister.

"They'd both died from the epidemic. Just a month before I got back. The old man . . ." He shook his head. "He was too mean to die, I guess."

I didn't know what to say. "I'm sorry" seemed inadequate. We sat in silence, him staring out into the dark, me looking at his pensive profile and wondering which man was sitting next to me—the Nazi or the son who loved his mother.

Finally he pushed open his door and unfolded himself from the auto. He came around the silver grille slowly, as if he'd grown old telling his story. He helped me out and I stood for a moment, looking up into his gray eyes, dark under the shadow of his hat.

"Thank you for driving me home and . . ." I looked for the words. "The rest." Confiding in me. I slipped out of the overcoat and the cold sent a shiver through me. I returned his coat to his hands. "I'm sorry about your mother and sister, Wilhelm."

His shoulders lifted. "It was a long time ago. Doesn't keep me awake at night."

I thought that was perhaps untrue.

He looked sideways, toward Germantown and the Alt Heidelberg, perhaps. "The people you work for, Mrs. Weiss, they may seem like they are doing good, but they're dangerous." He waited for me to answer.

My throat went as dry as sand. I could not answer him.

"I just wanted you to know that." With that, he got in the auto and pulled away. I watched the rear lights disappear around the corner of Pico.

The people you work for. Did he mean Thekla and Hermann? He couldn't know about Leon Lewis, could he? His words could again be taken as a threat. Except this time, he hadn't seemed threatening. Was he warning me?

I walked to the house, my feet as heavy as lead, and opened the door.

Mutti stood in the sitting room, her hands on her hips. "Liesl Violet Bittner, just what is going on here?" she said in a tone I hadn't heard since I was seventeen and caught kissing Tomas on the front porch.

"Shhh." The last thing we needed was to wake the children. I shut the door behind me and locked it, wishing I could lock out Wilhelm Otto. The Hitlerites. And even Leon Lewis.

Mutti waited, foot tapping. Word had traveled and she wanted an explanation.

I couldn't give her one. I thought of Wilhem's mother and sister. How Mutti worried for me despite her bluster. How lost I'd be without her. I put my arms around her and pulled her into a tight hug. "I love you, Mutti."

Mutti was not one to hug—like Tess that way—and I couldn't remember when either of us had last spoken of love. She remained stiff and unyielding. I drew back and trudged, exhausted, up the stairs to my room.

Mutti was, mercifully, at a loss for words.

CHAPTER 39

AGENT THIRTEEN

It had been a no-good day.

Thirteen passed the keys to the Cadillac off to Tony without a word and stalked into the Biltmore. He wanted to hit someone, and that someone was Hermann Schwinn. Or maybe that half-baked assistant district attorney. How had Torgeson bungled it so badly? Thirteen picked up the dog at the front desk and glanced at his messages. He'd missed a call from Lewis, when he'd been trying to get in touch with the man since Saturday.

Didn't that just tie a bow on it?

Today had started out with him groveling to Schwinn and Monroe about Karl. He'd hated doing that but it couldn't be helped. They seemed to buy it, but Schwinn told him next time he introduced a friend, make sure he wasn't trying to jam them up.

Then the whole business with Liesl Weiss. He hadn't meant to get the secretary in hot water. When Lewis had given him information on the threatening letter to Roosevelt, he'd passed it on to the DA. Threats to the president weren't taken lightly and should have been used to build a case against Schwinn, but Torgeson made a mess of it. He'd grabbed Themlitz right off, then let the bookstore owner go when he didn't rat on Schwinn. Then Torgeson went and brought in Liesl Weiss. She should have blown the whistle on Schwinn, but she didn't. He hated to admit it, but he'd nurtured a hope that Liesl Weiss wasn't a true believer. Then Schwinn had called him tonight to pick her up at the station, and there was her brother.

He hadn't seen that coming and it hit him like a wrecking ball. Fritz Bittner, the Silver Shirt, and his sister, the Nazi secretary. It made sense.

He let himself into his room and threw down his hat. It wasn't the first time he'd been wrong about a woman. He poured himself a bourbon and considered the amber depths in his glass. Liesl Weiss was the kind of woman who made his collar feel too tight. That cool demeanor and serious nature got to him. Most women he knew were like Thekla, pulling that schoolgirl baloney. Not Liesl Weiss. When he was alone with her, his throat went dry and his mind went blank. Or worse, he started running off at the mouth like some schoolboy with a crush.

What an idiot. He sure as shooting couldn't fall for a Nazi.

"And she is a Nazi." He said it out loud, determined to extinguish the flicker of hope for good. It hurt more than he expected. Maybe there was something between her and Schwinn. She could be one of those women who went for a powerful man—didn't matter if that power was good or bad. And if he and Lewis failed, Hermann Schwinn would have power in Los Angeles. He'd run the studios and have an army of Silver Shirts at his back. Was that what Liesl Weiss was hoping for? What she and her brother were working for together?

The bourbon wasn't going to help his dark thoughts. He threw it down the drain and flopped on the divan. "And what am I supposed to do about the husband?" he asked the dog.

She thumped her tail and whined.

That rock had been sitting in his gut for three days. Liesl Weiss wouldn't thank him for telling her the truth about her missing husband. Not to mention he'd have some explaining to do about why he went poking around. But he had to tell her. Then he could forget about her. Keep his mind on his job for Lewis. Save those idiot boys from themselves.

What a mess this was turning into. "I should just forget her," he told the dog. She nuzzled his hand and he gave her a good scratch behind the ears. At least he'd found out about Liesl Weiss's loyalties before he'd come down with feelings for her. That had been lucky.

He picked up the telephone. "Jimmy, get me a long-distance operator." Several clicks later and he told the tinny voice the number he needed. The telephone was answered on the second ring. "Boss. Sorry to wake you."

"You didn't."

That wasn't good news. "What's happening?"

"Nothing at all." Lewis sounded fed up. Angry, even. He'd never heard the man anything other than calm. "They say I'm overreacting."

Thirteen understood all too well. When he'd first met Lewis, he thought the Jewish lawyer was a crackpot. Until he saw what was happening at the Alt Heidelberg, at the Klan headquarters and out in the Hollywood Hills. But with the way people were—what everybody held as truth about Jews—Lewis would be accused of exaggerating. Crying wolf, they'd say. Problem was, the wolf was truly at the door.

Lewis went on and Thirteen could tell he was pacing as far as the telephone cord would allow. "The partisan bickering in our nation's capital is all about the repeal of Prohibition, the economy, unemployment." Lewis sounded defeated. "And of course, the Communists, which doesn't help our cause any."

Thirteen could feel the frustration coming through the telephone wire. He'd bet his left pinkie that plenty of the senators in Washington thought Adolf Hitler was onto something. Guys like Mayer and Goldwyn hadn't made a lot of friends in politics—heck, Thirteen didn't have any love for the moguls—but a lot of innocent people were going to be hurt if the Nazis got a foothold in Los Angeles. And those boys in the Silver Shirts were going to be used to do it.

"We need evidence," Lewis went on. "Hard proof, is what one of them said to me, that the German government is involved. That they're financing the operation and initiating violence."

"They know the flaw in that plan, don't they?" Unless Thirteen and Lewis got lucky—really lucky—they wouldn't know about violence until it happened. That meant people had to be hurt before politicians in Washington would get off their fat fannies and do something. There was only one thing to do. "I'll get evidence," Thirteen said. Somehow. "I'll check out Gyssling, like you said. The money trail is our best bet."

"How will you manage it?"

"A friend owes me a favor." He'd call in the favor, then rely on some good old-fashioned luck or whatever people called it—the hand of God, maybe. "Listen," he said, "I have bad news, too. Seventeen got figured."

"What happened?" Lewis's voice went tense.

"Got beat up pretty bad. It was Monroe." He had to tell him the rest. "And listen, they know Karl was working for you."

Lewis was quiet for long enough that Thirteen took the phone away from his ear and looked at it, thinking maybe they'd lost the connection. Finally Lewis spoke. "That is unfortunate. But don't worry about me."

Don't worry? Schwinn and Winterhalder, they'd just as soon kill a Jew as sit next to one on the bus. And they wouldn't take kindly to one of them spying on their operation. "I don't like it." Then he told Lewis about Themlitz and how the Feds had botched it with the letter to Roosevelt. He didn't mention Liesl Weiss. Didn't know why— maybe he was afraid Lewis would hear something in his voice about the secretary.

"Hmm," Lewis said. "My other agent needs to be warned to take care." He paused as if making a decision. "I need you to do that for me."

"Sure thing, boss." At least Lewis was talking sense.

Lewis gave him a post office box number. "Send a letter to this box."

"Code name?" Thirteen said, writing down the number.

"Edelweiss."

His pencil stopped moving. That sounded like . . . "Wait, is this agent a—?"

"A woman. Yes," Lewis answered briskly. "I know what you're going to say, but it was necessary and—"

"Leon." Thirteen bit out the man's first name. "These people are dangerous."

"She knows that."

He clenched his jaw. A woman. He thought of the women he knew in the alliance, the Mothers of America. Wives of veterans at the Disabled American Veterans Association. Could be any of them. A sudden thought hit hard.

Liesl Weiss?

No. Not after that fiasco with Torgeson. Not with how cool she'd been, defending herself in front of Thekla. How she snitched on Karl. She was a real Nazi who believed in the cause. Her brother was in the Silver Shirts, for crying out loud. And besides, how could someone like Liesl Weiss meet up with a Jewish lawyer like Lewis? Didn't make sense. What did make sense was that she was a Nazi and he was grabbing at straws in hope that she wasn't.

He was an idiot.

"Take utmost care not to be found out, Thirteen. I'll be back in Los Angeles on Tuesday evening. We'll go from there."

Thirteen hung up the telephone and shrugged out of his coat. He wrenched off his tie, then fell onto the divan. He just wanted this day to be over. The dog rubbed her muzzle against his knee. "Come on, then." He moved his long legs to one side to make room. The mutt jumped up on the end of the divan, circled once, and settled down, resting her head on his ankles.

He closed his eyes. The silence of the room was broken by the muted hum of cars passing below his window and the tick of the clock on the wall. He opened his eyes.

Edelweiss. A woman. Maybe someone he knew.

He wasn't going to be able to sleep until he did something about her. He took a sheet of paper from the desk and began to write. He would tell Edelweiss to be careful, as Lewis had ordered. But he'd do more than that.

They needed to meet.

Lewis wouldn't like him taking things into his own hands, but by the time the spymaster got back to Los Angeles, it might be too late.

He sealed the envelope, put it on his desk to go out in the morning, and went to the window. He'd do something about Liesl Weiss, too. Something that would get her out of his head for good. It was time she knew the truth about her husband, whether she wanted to or not.

She'd hate him for being the bearer of bad news, but he didn't care. He really didn't.

CHAPTER 40

LIESL

I was welcomed back into the Friends of New Germany like the prodigal daughter.

Thekla, bright-eyed as a blue jay, flew at me as I entered the office. "Liesl!"

Hermann appeared from his office and took my hands in his. "My dear." He led me to my desk and pulled out my chair for me. "You were treated terribly. To arrest a woman—a widow—it's unconscionable."

"I must admit it shook me." I produced a faltering smile and took my hands back from his firm grip.

"Of course it did." Thekla guided me to sit as if I were an invalid. "You deserve a medal for what you've been through."

Hermann was in agreement. "They dropped the charges, of course?"

"Yes, but not until after they'd kept me in a cell . . ." I let my voice break. "I didn't tell them anything."

"We never should have doubted you, isn't that correct, Thekla?" He looked at her as if she were completely at fault. "You're a true believer in the cause."

A cold dread knotted my insides. Hermann's cause was not to America; it was to Adolf Hitler. "You both have been so good to me. Taking me in, giving me a real . . . purpose." I could hardly believe the words coming out of my mouth. But from the look on Hermann's and Thekla's faces, they did. "I could never betray you."

I'd done what was required to gain back Thekla's and Hermann's trust. I must make sure it was worth what my mother and neighbors would think of me. What all of Germantown was talking about. Liesl Weiss, arrested for treason. Liesl Weiss, a Nazi. All would be well when we stopped the Friends of New Germany, would it not? It had to be.

When I had a moment alone, I telephoned Stella. "Can you meet me for lunch?" We agreed on a place and I hung up before she could ask any questions.

The morning was taken up with a new task. "Isn't it wonderful?" Thekla said, giving me a file of notes. "It is a youth camp that we've just procured funds for," she explained. "We shall teach our boys and girls the spirit of New Germany."

I thumbed through the file. A letter to membership announcing a camp in two weeks at Hindenburg Park. Only real Germans. Uniforms and physical fitness. German songs and the history of the Aryan race.

"Your friend Gertrud is organizing the programming to be exactly like the wonderful camps they already have in Germany," Thekla gushed. "They have almost two million children participating, can you imagine?"

I could imagine, and it was horrifying. Hatred taught to millions of children in Germany, with Gertrud Grundbacher and the Friends doing the same here in Los Angeles.

"Won't Tess and—what is your boy's name? Steffen?—have a wonderful time at such a camp?" Thekla noticed my hesitance and assured me, "Of course the camp fees will be waived for you, Liesl, what with all you do here."

I gave her a grateful smile. "That is very kind. I'll get this typed immediately, Thekla."

———

I met Stella in the old vault on Lot One. The weather had turned and Culver City was like an oven, the heat lying heavily on the studios and soundstages. The old vault was a squat adobe building with thick walls and no windows that stayed blessedly cool.

Stella looked like a fashion model in checked black-and-white wool with a red silk blouse and matching red heels. She flopped down beside me on an old velvet couch—a leftover set piece that smelled of dust and grease makeup. "Long time no see, pal. You leave me here and don't even telephone me with a how's-your-love-life?"

She was right. I was a terrible friend. After I got the job with Leon Lewis, I'd written her a quick note of thanks, promising to fill her in soon. I hadn't. "I'm sorry, Stella. It's just—"

"I'm kidding, you dolt." Stella shoved me and smiled.

"So how is your love life?" I said, and I really wanted to know.

She sighed and waved a hand. "We don't have time to go into it. What's the story, kiddo?"

We both knew Stella had only twenty-eight minutes before Mrs. Adler would be watching for her. I pulled out the lunch I'd brought for her. Stella wouldn't have time to go to the commissary and she got terribly cranky when she was hungry.

"Ooh, liverwurst and pickles." She bit into one half of the sandwich, chewed and swallowed with an expression of delight. "So? Don't keep me in suspense."

I didn't beat around the bush. "What do you know about Georg Gyssling?"

Stella stopped midchew, her brows raised like two upside-down smiles. "Not a lot more than you," she said around the food in her mouth. "A thorn in Mayer's side and all that."

"Nothing else?"

"Well . . ." Stella grabbed the paper napkin I'd brought along and wiped her lips. "You know about the film your friend Gary Perl is working on?"

"No." I hadn't heard anything about Gary Perl since the day I slapped his face.

Stella put the sandwich down. "Oh, honey. You really have been out of the loop. It has the whole studio in a tizzy. Mr. Perl bought a new screenplay from Herman Mankiewicz—such a sweetheart."

Stella thought highly of Herman Mankiewicz and always volunteered to type his screenplays. He feuded with Thalberg, drank like a fish, and there were whispers of Communist sympathies. But most writers were strange in one way or another, and Mank's films always made money, so the higher-ups kept him on.

"Gyssling—you know how he has to put his stamp of approval on every film if they want to sell it to Germany—had a conniption when he saw the script. It's about a European dictator who hates Jews apparently. So Mayer shut it down just like that." Stella snapped her fingers. "Can't upset the German market, you know."

"But Gary Perl is still working on it?" That was bold—but I'd always known he was bold.

She took another bite and nodded, chewed, and swallowed. "Private funding. He's using the soundstages and production rooms when he can get away with it."

Georg Gyssling, a film about a dictator who hates Jews, and Gary Perl. How would it all fit in with Leon Lewis and the Nazis? I filed that away to think on.

Stella put down the sandwich and looked at me with concern. "What's going on, hon?"

I stood, walked past the racks of film canisters—old silents that they stored in the cool safety of the vault—and stopped at a broken-down projector in the back of the room. I spun the wheel and watched it creak to a stop. I couldn't tell Stella what I was doing. I had promised Mr. Lewis to keep his operation secret. Yet MGM was a hive of information. Reports circulated through every department, the messengers delivering news as they did letters and packages, the custodians passing along dirt, makeup assistants repeating overheard gossip. She had to know some-thing. "Anything else about Gyssling?"

Stella tipped her head at my avoidance tactic. "Just your typical," she said. "He's a charmer, a real social butterfly. Does his job for the boss in Berlin but it doesn't stop him from hobnobbing with the film stars and producers. Even Mayer and Jolson go to his parties."

"He invites Jews?" I asked. That was a surprise.

Her eyes narrowed. "Say, Liesl, what's all this about?"

"Can you do something for me, Stella?" I asked instead of answering, something I'd learned from Leon Lewis. "Keep your ears open about him. Let me know anything you hear."

"Sure, hon. But you gotta tell me what you're up to," she insisted.

"I can't. Not right now." I was sorry for that but it couldn't be helped.

Stella didn't press but I knew her. She would do as I asked because she was a loyal friend, but soon I'd have to tell her something.

"I'll ask around and telephone you tonight." She motioned to my untouched half of the sandwich. "Are you going to eat that?"

I was going to be terribly late getting back to the Alt Heidelberg, but I got off the trolley at the Germantown post office nonetheless.

Mr. Lewis had been gone for a week. I received my pay last week, but nothing more from him in the post office box I checked every day. I hoped for a note, a telegram. Anything that might give me direction.

As I hurried into the building where just two days earlier I was arrested, I noted the people around me. A shabbily dressed man loiter-ing inside the door. An older gentleman in a suit and a hurry. No one seemed to take any notice of me. I took the little key from my coin purse and opened my box.

An envelope. It was addressed in firm, neat print with my code name and box number. No return address. A flicker of hope. I tucked it into my handbag and looked around again. Nothing suspicious. Back on the trolley, I pulled the single sheet of paper from the envelope. It was not from Leon Lewis.

We must meet. Saturday. The plaza at noon. Make sure you aren't followed. It was signed with only the number thirteen and then, as if an afterthought, *a friend.*

My thoughts tumbled. Was this the other agent? But wouldn't Lewis have contacted me instead of telling another agent to do so? Not by telephone—not with the possibility of Fritz answering or overhearing. But by telegram or letter? Something seemed wrong. It could be a trap. Or it could be the help I needed. I had three days to decide.

Saturday. The plaza at noon. Make sure you aren't followed.

If I did meet this agent, how was I to know who I was looking for—who was a friend and who was an enemy?

I was on edge all afternoon at the Alt Heidelberg. I made several errors, one of them caught by Thekla, who was unusually understanding. "Go home early, my dear," she said. "You've had an ordeal."

I was glad to and left before Wilhelm Otto showed his face to drive me. That was a relief. After the other night, the thought of being alone with him was disconcerting.

The telephone rang that night after dinner as I helped Tess with her spelling words. Steffen was paging through the pictures in an old encyclopedia and Mutti was scrubbing the oven with a toothbrush and scouring powder.

"Hello?" I said, catching the telephone before the second ring.

It was Stella. "Just a moment," I said and raised my voice to Tess in the kitchen. "*S-a-i-d.*"

"But, Mommy," Tess argued, "that isn't right."

"It is. Write it out and go to the next word." I turned away from her and gave my attention to the telephone, stretching the cord as far as it would go into the hallway. The scratch of brush against enamel ceased.

Mutti was listening. After my incarceration, she'd been watching me with silent disapproval. She had no doubt heard the gossip in town. It was just a matter of time until she demanded an explanation.

Stella's voice crackled through the line. "What are you doing next Monday night?"

"The usual," I answered carefully. The Monday routine—finishing the baking with Mutti, wrapping the bread loaves for the week, homework, and bedtime. "Why?"

"You know that fella, Cecil, the assistant production manager on the second floor?"

Cecil Fisch. A decent man at MGM, one of the few. He'd always gotten a little flustered around Stella. He asked her out a time or two but she always declined. I suspected it was because he was Jewish and she didn't want her parents getting ideas.

"Well, I was picking his brain about Gyssling today and—he's really sweet when he gets all red in the face, you remember?—anyway, he said he got an invite to the party at Gyssling's big mansion up on Curson Avenue. It's Hindenburg's birthday or something like that. He asked if I'd be his date."

My heart sank to my knees as I hoped desperately this wasn't going where I suspected.

"He was pretty surprised I took him up on it, I'll tell you what. But I said I'd only go if he got a double for my friend."

No. This was not what I had asked her to do.

"Sooo . . ." She drew the word out in the silence. "He said he knows a guy and he's got it all set up. Got anything fancy to wear to a shindig like that?"

Stella finally took a breath, but I didn't know what to say. What to wear wasn't what was making my hand sweat and the receiver slip in my grasp.

Her enthusiasm came down the line crystal clear. "Cecil—we're on first names now—he says Gyssling puts on a real show—studio heads and film stars and all of it. If you want to know about him, go straight to horse's mouth, right?"

I did not wish to even consider her idea, but what if I could find something there? Information for Leon Lewis. Perhaps about *der Angriff.* But a date? My insides knotted. I was married. It had been two years since Tomas, yet I hoped . . . still, I hoped.

"Liesl?" Stella said. "You there?"

She knew about Tomas—at least most of it. Not about the money and the note. But she knew he'd left me.

"Listen, hon," she said quietly, understanding in her voice. "It's not a real date. Just going to a party. You're not marrying the guy."

She was right. It was too good a chance to pass up. An opportunity to bring Leon Lewis something valuable. I swallowed hard and straightened my shoulders. "That's terrific, Stella," I managed. "I can't wait."

CHAPTER 41

LIESL

Friday afternoon I found Wilhelm Otto waiting for me outside the Alt Heidelberg and for once I was grateful. The faster I could get away from the Friends of New Germany, the better. The week had seemed never-ending and tomorrow's meeting with Agent Thirteen was looming.

I slid into the front seat and Wilhelm pulled onto the street in silence, but something was amiss. His hands twitched on the steering wheel and his left knee jerked with a sporadic rhythm. He was nervous. We did not turn west on Pico but went east.

Alarm shot through me. "Where are we going?"

Wilhelm Otto did not answer. My pulse began to hammer in my throat. Did he know something? About Leon Lewis? Was I to have the same fate as Karl? I swallowed hard and my fingers tightened on my handbag. Would jumping out of a moving auto kill me?

"Mr. Otto—"

"I'll explain when we get there," he interrupted. His face was unreadable.

We passed over the railroad tracks and approached the Main Street Bridge that led to Lincoln Heights. He glanced sideways at me and looked—what?—apologetic? Was he already feeling guilty for whatever he was going to do to me?

He pulled over and put the auto in park. We were in front of the Lincoln Heights jail, a bluff of stairs rising to a block of dirty white concrete and five stories of blank windows.

Why were we here?

He switched off the motor and looked straight out the window, to the dirty Los Angeles River winding its way to the Pacific. "Knowing, Mrs. Weiss, is better than not knowing."

I looked at the jail, looming beside us. He couldn't mean . . . "Mr. Otto," I said with rising panic, "take me home."

"I can do that," he answered, his voice surprisingly gentle. "But is that really what you want? Or do you want to know about your husband?"

Wilhelm Otto knew where Tomas was. The answer was here.

I swallowed, my mouth as dry as the sandy riverbank. I could put an end to the questions I'd poured out in the dark of night—*Tomas, where are you? Why did you leave me?*—or I could go home and continue to hope.

I let out a long breath. I needed to know.

Wilhelm Otto opened my door for me and held out his hand. I took it, my legs like jelly. I refused to consider why he was doing this. Was it a ploy? A trap? If it was, I was walking straight into it. But I could do nothing else.

"I'll be with you the whole time," he said. How strange that I could be comforted by those words from a man I feared. But what I feared even more was what I would find behind those institutional doors.

Inside the jail, a high desk guarded a barred entrance. A printed sign read *All Visitors Must Sign at the Front Desk*. Wilhelm Otto spoke to a middle-aged guard with a long scar down one side of his face. He signed a clipboard, then pulled the gun from under his jacket and passed it to the guard before we were ushered down a hall. The guard stopped in front of a door.

"Fifteen minutes," he said.

I concentrated on my breathing, my heart beating heavy and hard in my chest.

It was a small room with one table. A man sat on one side dressed in a dull gray jumper. A man I knew. A man who had lied to me. The man's face registered surprise and then shame. He spoke to Wilhelm. "I didn't know you were bringing her."

Wilhelm's expression hardened. "She deserves to hear the truth from you."

Mickey O'Neil licked his lips and didn't meet my eyes. "He should have just let it lie."

I waited. My throat had closed with tension. My body was ice-cold. Wilhelm Otto stayed close, his eyes on me as if I was going to break into a million pieces.

I was not going to break. Not here. I sat down, kept my back straight. Waited for Mickey to look at me. I spoke clearly and with no tremor in my voice. "Where is my husband?"

He looked down at his hands and took his time answering. Finally he spoke. "It was just a regular stop at the laundry, picking up what was owed to us."

I wanted to ask questions—who? where?—but bit them back.

Mickey went on, "Weiss was never part of the racket. I usually picked up the cash when he was doing foot patrol. But this time he came in." Mickey's voice was defensive.

I was beginning to feel ill, my resolve seeping away as I listened. *No. I do not want to know.* Wilhelm's hand covered mine. *Knowing is better than not knowing.* I took a breath and looked Mickey full in the face. "What happened?"

"He should have just let it lie," Mickey said again, looking away. "I wasn't going to use the gun," he said. "I was just trying to scare him, is all."

A sudden weakness went through my limbs and I began to tremble.

"He jumped in. Got all over me, talking about turning me in. And then . . . I didn't mean to—" He swallowed and blinked.

"And then?" I needed to know the rest.

"And then we had a body, see?" He said it like it was something I could understand. "We had a body, and I didn't know what to do with it."

A body. Tomas's body. My hand clenched into a fist under Wilhelm Otto's warm palm. The body that had lain beside me at night in our bed. Held our children in his arms. Tomas's laughing eyes, his rough stubble, his knobby knees. All those small and infinitely important parts that made up my husband was not just a body.

Mickey was still talking. "Made Ming put it in one of those big carts of his. Took it out in the harbor—way out—and dumped it." He shrugged and looked away. "I liked the guy. Really, I did. He should have let it lie, like I told him."

Wilhelm Otto leaned forward, his shoulders tense as if he was trying hard not to reach over the table and grab Mickey by the throat.

"But you told me—" My voice broke. I couldn't say it. He'd told me Tomas had left me.

Mickey shook his head. "I had to tell you that story, or you'd never let up, you'd keep asking questions. I thought the money would help. Said I was sorry."

The note. *I'm sorry*. It had been Mickey, not Tomas. I swallowed, tried to breathe. Sorrow and grief and shame filled my chest, pushing out the air. All this time, I'd thought he'd left me. It had seemed so wrong, and yet I'd believed it. After the quarrels we'd had. His talk of adventure. Of leaving Los Angeles.

He would never come back to me. I could no longer hope.

Wilhelm touched my arm. "We're done here."

I was surprised I could stand. My legs followed my commands even as my body seemed somewhere separated from my mind. We left Mickey there. I wished never to see his face again. He'd denied my children their father and me the man I loved and dreamed of living my life with.

Maybe someday I could forgive him. But someday was not today.

Wilhelm spoke with the guard, retrieved his gun, and guided me out the door. Down the concrete steps. The sound of birds that I hadn't noticed when we'd entered the building. The smell of the river. Wilhelm started for the auto but I stopped.

"I need to—" I motioned to a small patch of grass. "Just a minute alone." I left him there and went to the edge of the river.

I stared at the trickle of water that wound through the rocks and dried grass of the riverbed, waiting for the rains of winter to fill it. I tried to put words to my feelings. They roiled within me like a whirlpool. Sorrow. Grief. Horror at the thought of what had happened to Tomas. Anger at the injustice.

My Tomas.

I would no longer hope each time the telephone rang. I would not despair every time I opened the door and it was not Tomas. I would not look at every man in a crowd, wishing and fearing I might see his face.

I would not see him again. Not in this life.

My knees quivered, my muscles weakened as a knife of grief sliced through my heart and into my soul.

Then something else. Memories flickering to life like a film reel. Tomas holding Tess for the first time, bright love lighting his eyes. Waking up to his warmth on a rainy winter morning just after we were married. The ridiculous jokes. The taste of Juicy Fruit on his lips. The smile that had melted my reserve. His soft heart, so like Steffen's. The arguments, when they were over—how he'd come to me, tell me he loved me, that he was sorry. And I would say the same and all would be well.

A rush of relief—unexpected but comforting. I had not driven him away. Not with my rules and regiments. Not with our quarrels. He had been a good man. How could I have thought otherwise? My doubts had eclipsed those beautiful memories like a black shadow. But now, with the doubt gone, the love I had known came back with clarity. Of course he did not leave me.

I had loved him. And he had loved me. He was gone.

The grief hit me so hard I couldn't breathe.

I closed my eyes. The pain like a knife blade. The sorrow and the anger right behind it. At Mickey. At myself for doubting Tomas's love. At God and this terrible world that could take a man with so much life in him. How long I stood, I did not know. The anger ebbed. The sorrow settled like a black shroud. The relief remained, a small kernel of comfort.

Dimly I remembered Wilhelm Otto, waiting for me.

I must go home. Somehow continue. Tell the children and Mutti. Fritz.

I walked back to the auto on legs like wood. Wilhelm helped me into my seat. He gave me his handkerchief and it was only then I realized I was weeping—when had I started weeping? But I could not stop. Tears wet my cheeks; my breath built up in my chest. Silent sobs shook me. I bent forward, the handkerchief over my eyes, my shoulders quaking.

Wilhelm Otto waited silently.

When my breathing settled and the tears slowed, I realized I was holding his hand. Clutching it like a life preserver. Had I reached out to him or had he offered comfort to me? I pulled my hand back, put it in my lap. I should be mortified by Wilhelm Otto witnessing my innermost pain, but I felt only a bone-deep sorrow and exhaustion.

We drove back to Germantown in silence. When he parked in front of my house, he finally spoke. "O'Neil confessed after Mr. Ming made his statement to the police. Turns out he was part of a protection ring they've been trying to crack down on. He's on his way to San Quentin. Brody, the detective on the case, will fix it for you with the Hall of Records."

I understood what he was saying. I would officially be a widow, with the widow's pension and the end to the whispers and gossip. There would be time to think on that. Not now.

He opened the door for me and I let him help me out. I needed to say something, and I didn't know what. Why had he done this? Out of kindness? It didn't fit with what I knew about Wilhelm Otto, but I was beginning to realize I didn't know as much as I thought.

"Thank you," I began, "for . . ." What? Finding the truth? Breaking my heart? Holding my hand?

He stood silently for a moment, then said only, "Don't mention it, Mrs. Weiss."

CHAPTER 42

LIESL

Tomas was dead. I had been a widow for almost two years and had not known it.

I did not tell Mutti—not yet. And I did not tell the children. I locked myself in the bathroom and washed my face. Took a few deep breaths.

Then I made a dinner of cabbage and wurst while Tess and Steffen played crazy eights. We took our usual Friday walk to the park and I pushed the children on the swing set. When eight o'clock came, I supervised toothbrushing, read a chapter of *Through the Looking-Glass*, and listened to Tess and Steffen say their prayers. Perhaps I had grown adept at deception. Or perhaps—more likely—I was numb, my mind still coming to grips with the truth.

There would be time to tell them. When I decided how best to do so.

I woke in the night to fresh grief. I stumbled downstairs where I would not disturb the children. I asked no questions of God this night. I had been given my answer—but was it the answer that I wished for? How was I to live without the hope I'd held for so long? I felt as if something precious had been taken from me, leaving a great gaping space where it had once been.

I wandered the house, tears coming again in the silence. Remembering. The evening Tomas returned from work and I told him I was pregnant

257

with Tess. How he'd picked me up and twirled me around the kitchen, then set me down with alarm. "Did I hurt the baby?" And we laughed. Tess's first word—*Dada*—right there beside the table. He'd been so proud I thought he would burst. The quiet moments on the divan, listening to the radio after the children were in bed, his head on my lap.

How I wished to tell Miriam. She would understand the profound relief that warred with my sorrow. A relief that seemed wrong. And she would have wise words on how to tell the children. But I could not.

I went back to bed and, surprisingly, to a deep sleep.

When I woke, I locked my grief away. Perhaps it was strange that I was able to put my thoughts of Tomas in a closed-up corner of my mind, but I could not do otherwise. Not now, with so much danger to myself and my family. I must be single-minded in meeting with Agent Thirteen.

I dressed as if I were going to the grocery—a pink blouse and sweater with a flowing skirt. I applied lipstick and a pat of powder. Thirteen could be anyone—someone from the studios, the alliance, even one of the veterans who came in and out of the basement of the Alt Heidelberg. How would I know him when I saw him? Or would he know me?

I took in my appearance in the mirror and reminded my reflection to take care. I'd risked too much to regain the Schwinns' trust. I could not lose it again.

Downstairs, Fritz was slumped at the kitchen table over a plate of untouched eggs and toast. Mutti was nowhere to be seen. I poured myself a cup of coffee from the percolator and sat down next to my brother. "What's wrong?"

He rubbed his hand over his face and didn't meet my eyes. "Nothing."

I knew better than that. I put down my cup, concern fluttering in my throat. "Tell me."

He looked up, an unsure furrow on his brow. "Do you think Vati would be proud of me?"

I paused and discarded my immediate response—a definite no. Vati would be ashamed of Fritz parroting the hatred of Winterhalder and Schwinn. But I could not say such a thing. "He would be proud of you for being on the police force. For taking care of your family."

"That's what I'm doing, don't you see?" Fritz sounded as if he were trying to convince himself. "Vati went to war in France, but this war— the one I'm fighting—is right here on American soil."

There was no war except for the one that Hermann Schwinn was starting. I spoke carefully. "Do you think Vati would agree with what Hans Winterhalder says? Vati had Jewish friends. He told us this was a country for everyone." Did Fritz believe what they were saying in the Silver Shirts, or was he starting to question?

He looked uncertain. "That was before. He wouldn't think that now, with Jews running the country, the studios treating people like they did Mutti and you."

"Fritz, I—"

"And don't start on all that 'love your neighbor' and 'Jesus said this' with me," he jumped in. "Jesus ran the money changers out of the Temple, didn't he? That's what Winterhalder says we are doing. God's work, Liesl."

I hadn't brought Jesus into the discussion. He did. Mutti's heavy steps sounded on the stairs.

"What is it, Fritz?" I asked quickly. Something was troubling him. "What is coming?"

He glanced up in surprise and I knew I'd hit upon it. "Don't you know?"

A shiver of dread chilled me. "Tell me—"

Mutti's strident voice broke in. "Why aren't you eating? Are you sick, Fritz?"

I groaned inwardly, the moment of confession broken as Fritz assured Mutti that he was well and began to eat.

"Somebody better tell me what's going on around here," Mutti demanded.

I raised my brows at Fritz. It was his place to tell Mutti about the Silver Shirts. As for my many secrets, I was not ready to confess. Not about Leon Lewis and the Friends. And not about Tomas.

"I'm going to be late for my shift." Fritz took a last bite and grabbed his hat. He left the house like the devil was after him.

How I wished later that I had made him tell me everything.

My apprehension increased with every block as I took the trolley downtown. At the Olvera stop, I stood, watching each passenger who disembarked. They all hurried to their destinations, giving me not a glance. I walked the three blocks toward the plaza past shops crammed with pottery, brightly colored fabrics, and Mexican scarves. A man with a donkey cart, a woman with a basket. No one glanced my way, but I did not let down my guard.

Across the street from the plaza, I stepped into a grocery store and peeked out the window. Mexicans waited in the square for work. Old men played chess. A mother with a baby carriage—and a man standing in the shadow of a palm tree. I moved closer, behind a stack of orange crates. My pulse rocketed as I recognized the hard lines of his face, the soldierly bearing.

Wilhelm Otto. What was he doing here?

He turned his head, appraising the noonday idlers on the benches. He was watching for someone. Me? Or Agent Thirteen? I waited. Was he following me as Thekla had done? Or was he following the other agent?

Wilhelm Otto. He was a contradiction. The man from yesterday who held my hand and offered comfort. And the man in the plaza, menacing and dangerous. How could he be both?

One thing I knew. I couldn't go to the plaza and meet anyone. Not without him seeing me. Whatever it was that Agent Thirteen needed to tell me, it would have to wait. I left the store, carefully going out the back door and out of sight of the plaza. How had Wilhelm Otto known of the meeting? Was the other agent in danger? I needed to get in contact with Lewis, warn him that we were being watched. But how?

I stepped onto the trolley, deposited my nickel, and sat down quickly. Leon Lewis would—I hoped—be on a train from Washington, DC, to Chicago, then on to Los Angeles. I would need to wait until he contacted me. But from what I'd learned from Fritz this morning, I knew one thing for sure.

We were running out of time.

CHAPTER 43

By the time Monday came, I regretted agreeing to Stella's plan with every ounce of my being.

The weather had turned overnight, with a lowering gray sky and the stillness of an approaching storm. The noxious fumes from the manufacturing district fouled the air with not the slightest breeze to sweep them out to sea. As I walked the girls to school, we covered our noses and blinked our stinging eyes.

The mood at the Friends of New Germany had turned just as oppressive. Instead of bustling activity, an odd stillness permeated the office. Hermann gave me no dictation and closeted himself with Hans Winterhalder and Paul Themlitz most of the day. Thekla spent the morning in the basement with Travis Monroe and the veterans and did not return to the office after lunch.

Was I imagining the secretive atmosphere?

At one thirty, a messenger arrived with an envelope for Hermann with the distinctive MGM seal stamped in the corner. I tipped him with the coins we kept for that purpose, then sat down at my desk. I undid the brass clasp and peeked inside the envelope. Two gate passes, dated for the next day and signed by none other than Gary Perl. Why would Thekla and Hermann be visiting MGM—and Gary Perl of all people? I refastened the clasp, put the envelope in Hermann's in-basket, and tucked the information away with the other disconnected pieces of this puzzle.

With no letters to type, I spent the rest of the afternoon in the Aryan Bookstore, recording and filing invoices for Paul Themlitz, wondering how much time we had before *der Angriff* and thinking about Tomas. Even Paul Themlitz was not his usual buoyant self, and when I informed him that the bookstore was thousands of dollars in the red, he hardly blinked.

Thankfully, I did not see Wilhelm Otto. I was unsure what I would say to him or even how to act. He was sympathetic and sometimes kind, but also a Nazi—and a threat to Leon Lewis's operation, as his presence at the plaza had proven.

Neither was I ready to face a blind date and a party at Georg Gyssling's mansion. After my telephone call with Stella, I had begged Mutti's help with an appropriate dress.

"What kind of party?" she asked, looking up from scrubbing the sink.

"Formal," I answered. "A gown." Not something we could afford on our budget.

Her eyes narrowed. "Is this about that man, Wilhelm Otto, who drives you home?"

"No, Mutti," I said. "It's a favor for Stella—you remember her, from MGM?"

"By Monday?" She shook her head. "Not possible." But I could already see her planning.

"Thank you, Mutti." I kissed her cheek. I'd tell her everything when it was safe to do so.

She shrugged me away. "None of that nonsense."

When I got home—thankfully without encountering Wilhelm Otto—I found Gina from Custodial waiting on my porch with a box the size of a kitchen table. "I wish I could stay to see it on, sweetheart,"

Gina said, depositing the box in my arms. "Bette sends her love and the rest of what you need right here." She gave me a small makeup case and a kiss to my cheek, then roared away in her Ford truck.

I opened the box and even Mutti was speechless.

The gown was, in a word, divine. It was of a heavy satin damask the shimmering silver-blue of the Pacific. The halter neckline plunged in a shameless way, the back cut so low it was hardly decent. Then there was the narrow skirt with a knee-height slit and dyed-to-match silk sandals with glittering buckle trim. The ensemble must have cost more than I made in a month.

"Where did Gina get it?" I asked Mutti.

Mutti evaded the question. "Better if you don't know."

I readied myself for the party with the contents of Bette's makeup kit. I tweezed my brows and filled them in with a pencil a shade darker than my hair. A soft-gray shadow on my lids that brought out the blue of my eyes. I hadn't used mascara in ages but applied the wetted powder with a tiny brush to each lash and made myself not blink until it was dry. With a coating of deep-red lipstick, I was ready.

I went downstairs to give Mutti final instructions. "Eight o'clock bedtime and not a minute later," I told her as Tess burst through the back door.

"Mr. Stahr says Chester is going to have his kit—" Her mouth dropped open. "You look like a princess."

Steffen pushed in behind her, his eyes wide and startled, as if he didn't know me. I crouched down, the slim skirt constricting me. "Be good for Mutti tonight. You can visit Chester at the Stahrs' after dinner, but home by bedtime." If Chester was really having her kittens, Mutti would have her hands full getting them in bed on time.

Tess was already scheming. "Mommy, can I sleep at Frieda's tonight? Mrs. Stahr says—"

I cut her off before she got started. "Absolutely not. It's a school night."

She countered, "We don't have school tomorrow."

I'd forgotten. I'd received a note from the principal last week, telling parents that the school would undergo an earthquake inspection on Tuesday. I wavered but then decided. "You can go over to check on Chester. Home in bed by nine at the very latest." Mutti frowned and I gave her a warning look. "I mean it."

I draped myself with the filmy wrap that matched the dress and was waiting at the door when a long black Bentley pulled up to the curb. The wind cut through the thin fabric of my ensemble, the sudden chill reminding me of the dangers of Nazis and vice-consuls and the Friends of New Germany. A uniformed man with a dour expression got out and came around the auto.

"A driver?" I asked Stella as he opened the door to the back seat.

"My father insisted," she answered. "Said it wasn't right for me to drive myself to a date."

I darted a look toward Miriam's. The curtains twitched and I suddenly wished with all my heart to be in her kitchen, talking of the children and new recipes. Instead . . . the dress, a limousine and driver, and apprehension souring my stomach. I remembered with a jolt that I had not gone through my goodbye ritual with Steffen. The auto was already pulling away from the house. I'd be home in a few hours, I told myself. Steffen would be fine.

"You look a treat," Stella said as I arranged myself on the leather bench seat.

"Not too shabby yourself," I retorted. In truth, Stella looked stunning. She was dressed in a black sleeveless sheath, her bobbed hair a gleaming dark cap. A single strand of perfectly matched pearls set off collarbones any woman would envy.

"Cecil and his pal are meeting us at the Biltmore."

I gave her a look. "Cecil must be trying to impress you."

"He said his friend will drive us to the party so we won't have Fred hanging about." She rolled her eyes at the man sitting stiffly in front of us and whispered, "He's a terrible tattler to Daddy."

I wasn't worried about her father or Fred. I was worried about what I'd do when I gained entrance to Georg Gyssling's mansion.

I'd spent some time at the Central Library periodical room on Saturday after my failed encounter with Agent Thirteen. Alma Whitaker, the columnist for the *Times*, was a great admirer of the vice-consul. According to Alma, Herr Gyssling was a consummate host, an avid gardener, and apparently the best bridge player in the city. Of Mrs. Gyssling, she wrote very little. Ingrid Gyssling—a medical doctor—was rarely seen and the duties of the vice-consul's wife were left to the house-keeper, Christine Boone. The Gysslings had a precocious daughter and a son who had been born with a physical handicap and was institutional-ized. Precious little to go on.

Stella checked her reflection in her compact mirror, then snapped it shut. "So you want to know about your date?"

I did not wish to think on my date at all. "I'd rather hear what's going on at MGM," I said. Specifically anything to do with Georg Gyssling, but I didn't say as such. I owed Stella an explanation that I was not ready to give.

She filled me in on the gossip as the driver expertly brought us down-town. Mrs. Adler, the girls in the typing pool. The envelope sent around for a flower donation for David Selznick's father, who'd passed away the day before and his funeral was tomorrow. "I didn't have the heart to tell them that Jews don't send flowers when somebody dies," she said. "It's the thought that counts, right?"

I hadn't known that myself.

She took up her black-beaded handbag as the auto slowed. "Here we are."

The triple towers of the Biltmore came into view, flanked by palm trees and opposite the lush greenery of Pershing Square. It wasn't yet dark, but lights glinted like diamonds from the arched windows. Men in evening wear escorted women from shining autos to the door of the hotel.

When Stella's driver helped us both out of the back seat, heads turned.

Stella slipped her arm through mine as we walked toward the waiting doormen. I considered how we appeared. Stella, raven-haired and olive-complected in a slim column of black silk. Me, fair, blonde, and shapely in a dress the color of the twilight sky. Both looking carefree and ready for a night on the town. How deceiving appearances could be. I did have cares and far too many. Suddenly the idea of a date waiting inside for me was unsettling. What would I say to a stranger?

We walked through the lobby and into the Emerald Room, crowded with a five-piece orchestra and white-linen tables. Stella pointed her chin toward the back of the restaurant. "They got us a table." She pulled me along behind her with an enthusiasm that made me wonder if she was more interested in Cecil than she let on.

I veered around white-coated waiters and a couple with entwined hands making their way to the dance floor as the orchestra struck up a lively tune. Stella came to a stop at a table in the corner and two men stood politely.

My heart dropped to my satin sandals.

One of the handsome men was Cecil Fisch, smiling in a ridiculously smitten manner at Stella. The other—my date—was Wilhelm Otto.

CHAPTER 44

"M-mr. Otto—" I stuttered.

"Mrs. Weiss." I hadn't thought Wilhelm Otto capable of showing surprise. It was quick, but I saw it. Surprise and something else I could not name.

Stella saw my consternation and stepped in smoothly. "Goody, you already know each other. That makes this so much nicer."

Cecil pulled out a chair for Stella. Wilhelm Otto did the same for me. I sat down, smoothing my gown while my mind registered the implications. Wilhelm Otto, friendly with Cecil Fisch, a Jewish producer from MGM?

Both men were dressed in evening wear. Cecil, in a formal black tailcoat and black trousers with a satin stripe. Wilhelm Otto, more up-to-date in a deep-burgundy dinner jacket with satin lapels, a white tie, and trim black trousers.

His unruffled demeanor firmly back in place, he sat down beside me. I imagined he was wondering a few things about me, as I was of him. Not the least being my friendship with Stella. I hadn't seen him since the afternoon at the jail with Mickey, except for when I'd observed him at the plaza. Neither encounter was something I wished to think on just now.

"Can I get you something?" He motioned to a white-coated waiter hovering nearby.

Apparently Prohibition had already been repealed at the Biltmore. I didn't drink often, but perhaps something to steady my nerves. I looked to Stella, who had been watching me while flirting outrageously with Cecil.

"Bubbly," she announced with confidence. "But just one each. We need to get to the party, right, gentlemen?"

Stella carried the conversation while we waited for our drinks, which arrived in delicate coupes. Cecil toasted to the evening and we all raised our glasses. The effervescence tickled my nose as I took my first sip.

Wilhelm turned his attention to me. I was certain he would ask a question I didn't want to answer, so I plunged ahead first. "Tell me, Mr. Otto, how do you know Cecil?"

An innocuous question, if he were not a Nazi. If the man across the table was not Jewish. If his daytime activities did not consist of hateful propaganda toward people like Cecil.

"We go way back," he said with a nonchalant smile. "You and Stella worked together?"

I smiled sweetly. "We did. At MGM." If Wilhelm Otto could act like nothing was amiss, so could I.

Cecil and Stella talked shop. The new soundstage and if Irving Thalberg really was ready to come back to the office. Wilhelm and I watched the dancers in silence and sipped our champagne. Was it coincidence that put Wilhelm and me at the same party with Georg Gyssling? Coincidences could not be trusted. And neither could Wilhelm Otto.

Mercifully, the band finished its song and Stella put down her empty glass. "Let's go, kids."

Wilhelm Otto put my wrap over my shoulders and guided me through the crowded room, his hand warm and firm at my waist. It could have been the champagne responsible for the unbalanced feeling as we walked to the shiny sedan parked neatly on the street, but I knew it was the man beside me.

I slid into the familiar polished wood and leather interior. Stella kept up a steady chatter as we left downtown, and by the time we climbed the hill to the vice-consul's estate, I had given myself a stern talking-to. I must still find out what I could about Gyssling and *der Angriff*, even with Wilhelm Otto at my elbow. I must not think of Tomas, even with the man who had seen my grief beside me.

We drove up the long driveway and Stella let out a whistle of appreciation. The home of the German vice-consul was indeed a Los Angeles Neuschwanstein, as they said in the papers. The imposing entrance was a wide staircase flanked by marble columns. Mullioned windows scattered fragments of light on a meticulously cut lawn guarded by a regiment of junipers. Wilhelm came around to open my door and Cecil did the same for Stella as a valet in a black uniform hopped in the driver's seat.

Wilhelm Otto offered me his arm. His expression was what I'd come to know—that of an emotionless mechanism. The flash of humor and the kindness he'd shown Tess and Steffen, the subtle flirting in the afternoon sun, the confidences in the dark of night—that seemed a different man. And the man who had brought me to the jail and silently held my hand as I'd wept for Tomas? He was nowhere to be seen.

We walked up the sidewalk behind Stella and Cecil. Two flags graced each side of the doorway—the American Stars and Stripes and the Nazi swastika. I was entering enemy territory. Wilhelm Otto glanced at my hand, where my fingers were tightly clenched on his sleeve. I loosened my hold, made myself breathe.

The double doors opened, spilling out warm light and laughter, music, and the clink of glasses. To my surprise, standing in the doorway was not the butler—as the elegance of the house suggested—but Georg Gyssling himself.

"Cecil! You've finally accepted my invitation." The German vice-consul looked to be in his midthirties, with dark hair and a pencil mustache such as one would see on a leading man, instead of the toothbrush style favored by his country's leader and the man beside me. His voice was a warm, modulated tone with an accent, and a welcoming smile lit his face. He shook Cecil's hand, but his eyes were on Stella. "And you've brought a beautiful companion."

Cecil made the introduction. "Miss Stella Levine."

Gyssling bowed smartly over Stella's hand like a Prussian soldier. "Please allow me to steal at least one dance."

Stella tipped her head and smiled brilliantly. "I'm counting on it."

Cecil continued with introductions and Herr Gyssling reluctantly took his eyes from Stella to turn to me. "Welcome, Mrs. Weiss," he said, then shook Otto's hand. "Good to meet you, Mr. Otto."

Wilhelm took my wrap and handed it to a waiting maid dressed in a pristine blue-and-white uniform. We moved into the music- and laughter-filled ballroom. Stella raised a perfect dark brow at the larger-than-life portrait of Adolf Hitler staring down at us from the mahogany-paneled wall. "Charming man," she murmured in my ear. Whether that remark was meant for Herr Hitler or Herr Gyssling, I did not know.

I tucked a hand through the crook of Stella's elbow. "Perhaps we should freshen up?" We made our excuses to the men and the pretty maid pointed the way down a narrow corridor papered in dark-green silk. I found the door that led to the powder room and pushed Stella inside. I shut the door behind us and leaned against it with a long exhale. "You didn't tell me my date was Wilhelm Otto."

She looked at me with suspicion. "What's with you two, anyway?"

"Nothing," I lied. "But I need your help."

Ten minutes later, we left the powder room. Stella had agreed to my plan, but not without some promises.

The ballroom was spacious, rising two stories with a winding staircase that led to an upstairs mezzanine from which more guests looked down on the orchestra and the dancers. I looked for Wilhelm Otto and saw him not far away, speaking to Cecil, a glass of champagne in his hand. He looked like a complete stranger. It was not just the smile on his face and the quick laugh at something Cecil said—that was shocking, of course. But the relaxed way he stood, one hand in his trouser pocket, casual and easy. Utterly unlike the man who lurked at the Alt Heidelberg.

He turned and saw me watching him. He straightened and the smile vanished. I was saved from this increasingly awkward moment by none other than Herr Gyssling.

"My dear," he said, "let me introduce you and Mr. Otto to my friends."

We were welcomed into a cluster of guests. Georg Gyssling introduced us around the group, ending with Christine Boone. "Tissy is a wonderful hostess," he said with an indulgent smile at the thin woman in a fluttering dress of pink silk. Tissy put a possessive hand on Gyssling's arm as the vice-consul launched into a story of his stint on the Olympic bobsledding team at Lake Placid the previous winter. "I'd never seen a bobsled before in my life, I tell you," he laughed, his grasp of English grammar impeccable. "They put me on as brakeman and I was the worst you could imagine."

A robust man with a sparkling diamond tiepin said in a droll way, "If I remember correctly, Germany came in seventh in that event."

"Yes! Last place and they owe it all to me." Gyssling laughed at himself as did everyone else.

He certainly was charming. There was no talk of Jews or Herr Hitler or the fatherland. I glanced at the flat stare of the führer in the portrait above us.

"You know," said a woman's voice, close to my ear, "he's not at all on board with that business in Germany." I turned to find Alma Whitaker in a fluffy confection of organdy and feathers.

She introduced herself. I did the same and watched her brow flicker as she tried to place my name on her list of Los Angeles socialites.

"You were saying," I prompted her. "About the vice-consul and the Nazis?"

She obliged me by answering. "It's just that Georg really isn't a Nazi, per se. There are plenty of Jews in this room and they're all his friends."

A high-ranking German and a friend to Jews? No wonder Hermann Schwinn despised the man. "I thought perhaps we would be fortunate enough to meet Ingrid," I said as if I didn't know the first thing about Georg Gyssling's absent wife.

"Oh no." Alma's lips compressed. "Poor Georg. And the son," she whispered. "That's why he can't be sent back to Germany, you know. The new regime doesn't welcome his kind."

Wilhelm Otto approached through the crowd as Alma's attention wandered, realizing I was not someone famous to mention in her column. She took the opportunity to make her goodbye and floated off in a drift of feathers.

Wilhelm Otto held out his hand as the orchestra started a Strauss waltz. Did the man never speak when a look would do? I considered his outstretched hand with trepidation, remembering weeping in his auto, that same hand clutched in mine. In that moment, I had felt safe with him. Now I did not know what to feel. Was the person before me a different man? Or the same?

CHAPTER 45

LIESL

I reluctantly put my hand in Wilhelm Otto's and we joined the whirl of dancers.

I misstepped and almost stumbled. He steadied me and I looked up into his flint-gray eyes with an apology. "It's been some time since I've waltzed."

His dimple flashed, the scar disappeared, and for a moment he was handsome and familiar again. "Just follow me."

It wasn't hard, as he was an excellent dancer. As we moved together, I glanced at his honed features, the straight lines of brow and cheek. Like Georg Gyssling, he was a contradiction. The flashes of kindness. The brutality of the Friends of New Germany. His friendship with Cecil. It didn't make sense—*he* didn't make sense. And that was beginning to nag at me.

The music ended and we stood together for a moment, our bodies aligned. My cheeks were heated and probably quite pink. I searched my mind for something to say. Wilhelm Otto did not seem to have the same compulsion. He stood silently, looking down on me with an expression I could not fathom.

Stella appeared out of the crowd. "Can I steal your date?" she asked me with a flirtatious look at the man beside me. "I can't find Cecil and I need a break from Herr Gyssling."

Wilhelm Otto raised his brows to me in question.

This was what Stella and I had planned. "Of course," I answered, my mouth drying. As the music began again, he and Stella stepped away. With her dark beauty and his perfect profile, anyone would say they made a lovely couple.

If one didn't know she was Jewish and he, a Nazi.

As soon as they were out of sight, I made my way to the edge of the ballroom and considered my next move. I had perhaps two songs before Wilhelm would look for me.

I gathered my courage and moved down the dim green hallway.

As the strains of the orchestra receded, I came upon a line of paneled mahogany doors and peeked in each one. A sitting room. A broom closet. What looked like a children's playroom. My pulse beat in my ears as I moved further into the dark. At the end of the hallway, a narrow stairway. What seemed to be a library just past the stairway emitted a muffled giggle and then a man's low voice. I went up the stairs as quietly as my heels would allow.

At the top of the stairs, a hallway with three doors. The first two doors were open, the third shut. I peeked in the open doors. Bedrooms. I silently turned the crystal knob on the third door. Unlocked. The room was dark, with a heavily draped window. In the murky darkness I made out a desk, the bulk of a typewriter. An office. If I were to find anything of import, it would be here.

The orchestra swung from the waltz to a foxtrot. I imagined Wilhelm quick-stepping with Stella. At least I hoped that was what he was doing.

I pulled the door shut behind me and opened the floor-to-ceiling velvet panels to let in a shaft of silver moonlight. The desk was a decorative affair with three drawers. I carefully slid the first drawer open. Neat lines of ink pens and sharpened pencils. Paper clips and rubber bands. The second drawer: a few sheets of stationery. I quietly eased open the last and largest drawer.

Household accounts, neatly filed. Electrical, the telephone line, the gas company. Invoices from a cleaning service showed that Tissy might be a wonderful hostess, but she didn't do much in the way of house-keeping. Nothing whatsoever on the Silver Shirts, the Friends, or *der Angriff*. A silent frustration rose within me. Would I end this evening knowing nothing more than when I began?

I thumbed through the rest of the files and froze. Was that the tread of footsteps in the hall? I straightened. The crystal knob, glinting in the light of the moon, slowly turned. I looked desperately around the room. Nowhere to hide. No time to do so.

With a quiet click, the door opened just wide enough for a dark figure to slip through, his back to the room. My pulse pounded in my ears and I held my breath. I knew that form, the height, the assured movements. What was Wilhelm Otto doing in Georg Gyssling's office? And what would he do when he saw me?

He closed the door and locked the knob before he turned to the room. His head snapped up. He stared at me for the space of a heartbeat. "Mrs. Weiss, what are you—?"

"I could ask you the same," I interjected before he could finish.

He narrowed his eyes. "I asked first."

I floundered. "Looking for the powder room." Ridiculous, I realized, but all I could think of.

"I don't believe you."

It was an inane conversation, cut short as the crystal doorknob rattled so suddenly and violently we both jumped.

Our eyes met. Neither of us should be here. In an instant he was across the room, his hand snagged my arm, and he pulled me behind the velvet window coverings. Not the best hiding spot, but perhaps in the dark effective enough.

Or perhaps whoever was at the door did not possess a key.

A vain hope. The slide of metal into the lock. The snap of a bolt. The turn of the knob.

Wilhelm Otto's arms went around my middle, pulling me as close as an embrace. We both held our breath. The swish of the door and a single footstep into the room. No lights switched on. I was intensely aware of Wilhelm close to me, his held breath. My pounding heart. The faint scent of his cigarettes.

The cigarettes.

The idea flashed so suddenly—like a camera bulb in a dark room—that I bit back a gasp of surprise. Wilhelm Otto tossing a half-smoked cigarette out the auto window. The discarded cigarettes in the ashtray in front of Leon Lewis at the Blue Owl.

The startling notion took hold. Half-smoked cigarettes. The nagging contradictions in his nature, the flashes of kindness. The flyers that never reached their destination after he delivered them to the post. And tonight, a friendship with Cecil and his purpose at Georg Gyssling's home.

Whoever was in the room with us was still there. Waiting. Watching. Perhaps knowing we were there behind the curtain, deciding what to do. I stayed completely still but raised my eyes to Wilhelm Otto's face, illuminated in the moonlight. He was watching me. The contradictions aligned to a sensible order.

Think of your kids. He had not been threatening me. He was warning me.

The day at the plaza. He had not been following me. He was waiting for me.

And at the jail. Holding my hand as I wept. The real Wilhelm Otto.

The door closed softly. Steps receded in the hall. Wilhelm let out a breath and his arms relaxed his hold but neither he nor I moved. His breath warmed my temple.

I looked up, met his gaze again, my mind reordering to this new perspective. He was a contradiction and a question mark, an actor worthy of a contract at MGM. But he was not a Nazi. He was an agent for Leon Lewis. How had I not seen it before?

I looked him in the eye with confidence. "Agent Thirteen, I presume." It was not a question, for I had no doubt.

His head reared back. His hands dropped to his sides and his eyes went wide with surprise. "What the—?"

I felt a moment's triumph. Wilhelm Otto was entirely dumbfounded.

CHAPTER 46

WILHELM

Liesl Weiss was Edelweiss.

He was an idiot not to have figured it.

All the clues had been right in front of his nose. But that cool demeanor, her perfect Aryan looks—not to mention the arrest at the post office and her Silver Shirt brother. He'd swallowed it hook, line, and sinker.

When he opened the office door and saw her there—an arrow of moonlight turning her hair to silver—he'd gone a little weak in the knees. Then the rattle of the door and every instinct was to protect her, even if she was a Nazi.

But she wasn't. She was Edelweiss.

Later, after they got out of this mess, he'd give Leon Lewis a piece of his mind. What was the man thinking? Liesl Weiss had children and a mother who depended on her. She shouldn't be taking chances. But there would be time to rant at Lewis later. "We need to go," he said. Before whoever had followed them upstairs came back with reinforcements.

"We need to find something on *der Angriff*," she countered. "There's nothing in the desk but household accounts."

He joined her in searching the room, still kicking himself for missing something so obvious. He'd been fooled by her pretty face—more than pretty, he admitted, glancing at her. *Exquisite* would be the word. The no-nonsense secretarial outfits she wore to the Friends downplayed her looks. It was smart—her not wanting attention from Schwinn and Winterhalder. But in that dress, with the color bringing out her alabaster skin and those vivid blue eyes, plenty more than pretty. And a good spy, he had to admit, as he checked the bookshelves behind the desk. She'd spouted those slogans like she really believed them.

He pushed the memory of her crying in his auto firmly to the back of his mind. Nothing to do with this moment and he didn't need the distraction.

"Anything?" she asked, looking through a credenza on the other side of the window.

"No." Just the usual leather-bound classics. Some German tomes, a set of encyclopedias that looked like they'd never been cracked open. He moved quickly to the obligatory portrait of Adolf Hitler with his maniacal eyes and ridiculous mustache. He tested the frame. It came easily away from the wall, swinging on a hinge. Behind it, a recessed wall safe.

He stepped back. "You know how to crack a safe?" He wouldn't be surprised if she took a doctor's stethoscope from some secret pocket in that dress.

She shook her head.

"Let's go, then." Someone at this party was suspicious. They needed to get out of this room—out of this house—before whoever it was talked to Gyssling. The man was no idiot. He would put things together and neither of them could afford to have their story questioned and reported back to the Friends.

"Wait." She scooped a crumpled black carbon from the trash basket, holding it out to the light. "I can't read it but maybe it's something." She carefully folded it and handed the square to him. "Put it in your pocket. Careful—don't get ink on your hands."

He tucked the thin sheet of inky paper in his jacket pocket. She was a better spy than he was.

He opened the door slowly and checked the hallway. Empty. They left the office and his arm went around her waist. "In case anyone's watching." He hurried her to the back stairs and started to the ground floor at a quick clip.

"Slow down," Liesl whispered. She was right. They didn't want to attract attention. He was rattled—she'd rattled him. He needed to pull himself together.

He slowed, and they stepped into the ballroom. Wilhelm looked for the blonde maid to get Liesl's wrap. Too late. Georg Gyssling shouldered his way through the crowd to intercept. "I'm afraid I can't allow you to leave," Gyssling said with a direct look that was not that of a host to his guest, but that of an adversary.

Wilhelm's grip on Liesl tightened.

"—until I've danced with Mrs. Weiss," Gyssling finished.

The back of Wilhelm's neck prickled. Liesl tensed beneath his hand, but she put on that cool smile that fooled him so well. He hoped it would work with Gyssling.

"Of course," she said as if she'd like nothing better.

Wilhelm figured she could take up acting when she was done with Lewis. He forced himself to loosen his grip on her and managed a nod.

Georg Gyssling led her to the dance floor. Wilhelm stood with his hands clenched. He knew from the kraut's hard eyes, the man had more on his mind than a dance.

———————

LIESL

As Herr Gyssling led me to the dance floor, the strains of the violin began a familiar tune. "You know the ländler, do you not?"

"Of course." It had been years, but no self-respecting German did not know the traditional dance. We lined up with the other couples as the music began, his hand holding mine. My mind was still reeling with the idea of Wilhelm Otto as part of Leon Lewis's operation. He had been so convincing. The moments that his facade cracked—that had been the real man.

I had a great deal to talk about with Wilhelm Otto, but first I must get through this dance.

"I'm glad we're getting an opportunity to speak, Liesl," Herr Gyssling said as I followed his steps of the opening promenade. "May I call you Liesl?"

My mouth suddenly went dry. Georg Gyssling's tone was not that of a polite dance partner. Had he already been informed that Wilhelm and I had been in his office? Or perhaps it was he who had opened the door and stood in the dark. The tempo changed and I remembered only just in time to do the short step-kick—difficult in my narrow dress—and then Herr Gyssling was twirling me under his arm.

We crossed arms and joined hands to promenade again. "Liesl," he said, his voice low and controlled. "I am disappointed that you and Mr. Otto felt the need to snoop in my office."

I faltered a step as panic flashed through me. I could not help but twist my head to find Wilhelm Otto's face in the crowd. He was watching and looked worried.

"Nein—" Herr Gyssling's grip tightened. He smiled but the good humor did not reach the ice in his gaze. "Act naturally, Liesl." He relaxed his hands and went on to the next step of the dance but his words chilled my blood. "You were doing your job. We all have our responsibilities, something I understand more than most."

We stopped, placing our palms together and stepping toward each other, then away. I fumbled but he guided me to the next set of steps. "I wish you to take a message for your superior."

My superior? Did he mean Hermann Schwinn or Leon Lewis? I chose to stay silent while my pulse beat at a quicker tempo than the orchestra. We crossed arms and stepped together, moving around the perimeter of the dance floor. He released one of my hands and twirled me under his arm three times. When we faced each other again, he continued. "I, too, have people who bring me information." Gyssling's pleasant demeanor was gone. "And what I hear is unacceptable." His grip on my palm tightened convulsively and I could see he was very serious indeed.

I'd worked out the steps to the dance but was stumbling to keep up with the conversation.

"Do tell Herr Schwinn that this absurd plan must be abandoned." Gyssling's accent became more pronounced but his voice remained low. "Tell him that he is to leave studio business with the consulship. I have the matter in hand with Mayer and I refuse—" He took a breath through his nose and let it out slowly as if containing his temper. "I refuse to allow his interference. His blatant attempt to gain the attention of Berlin and usurp me will not be tolerated." Herr Gyssling turned his back abruptly to me.

My hand went on his shoulder—the tension in it an indicator of Herr Gyssling's anger—and we circled the floor for the last time. The clicking of his heels in rhythm to the music rang out like rifle shots. My mind spun with the implications of his statement. What was the absurd plan? Most importantly, when?

I could ask him, but that would not do. Our host believed I was here at the behest of Hermann Schwinn and that I knew precisely what he was talking about.

We faced each other once again. The music came to an end and he bowed politely. *"Verstehen Sie mich, Liesl?"*

No, I did not understand. I did the required curtsy. "I shall pass along your message, Herr Gyssling."

I did not say to whom.

———

WILHELM

Wilhelm watched Liesl and Gyssling dance with a growing sense of dread.

Something was wrong. Whatever Gyssling was saying between steps that looked as complicated as a troop maneuver, it wasn't polite chitchat. Wilhelm forced himself to remain calm, get his head screwed on right. Think about Gyssling and Lewis and that they hadn't found anything here that they didn't already know. Except about each other.

That was something, at least.

The dance finally ended, and Liesl curtsied to Gyssling but something about her movements—the line of her shoulders as she walked back toward him with Georg Gyssling right behind her—didn't look right.

Gyssling jerked his chin at Wilhelm, all sign of the amiable host gone. "I am sorry you must leave." It didn't sound like an apology; it sounded like an order.

Wilhelm glanced at Liesl. She was pale but composed.

The vice-consul lifted his hand in a salute. "Heil Hitler, Mr. Otto."

Wilhelm could not bring himself to return the salute. Interesting, how Gyssling seemed to be both honoring and mocking the man whose portrait looked down upon them.

The blonde maid was already offering Liesl her wrap. Stella appeared, looking curious. "Cecil can find you a taxi," Wilhelm said as a goodbye and steered Liesl out the door, where the valet had his auto waiting. Herr Gyssling was efficient at removing unwanted guests.

He helped her into the car, wondering what he'd say when they were alone and away from listening ears and watching eyes. He'd figured she thought him a complete dolt, the way he was tongue-tied when he drove her home from the Alt Heidelberg. The truth was, all those times he never trusted himself to speak. And with good reason. Whenever he opened his mouth around her, he ended up saying things he'd never intended.

Now they had plenty to talk about. How she'd come to work for Lewis. What she knew that he didn't know. And what Gyssling said while they danced. They had a lot to work out, but he needed time to think it through before they did.

She turned to him, opened her mouth. "What did you—?"

"Not while I'm driving," he cut her off. He hadn't meant to sound harsh, but she addled him in ways he couldn't explain. "Let's get somewhere we can talk."

"Where are we going?" She pulled her wrap closer around her. It was hardly a warm thing, just a piece of silk, really. Another reason to have this conversation elsewhere.

He turned the auto toward the Biltmore. "My place. I don't want to talk about Lewis or Gyssling until we get somewhere safe."

She was silent as if in assent but then turned in her seat to look at him. "Then tell me about Tomas."

He knew what she meant. She wanted to know why he did it. Why he'd tracked down her husband when he thought she was working for the Friends. He looked at the speedometer and realized he was going too fast. He let up on the gas. Loosened his death grip on the steering wheel. "Let's not do this right now."

"I need to know."

He glanced sideways at her. She needed to trust him, was what she was saying. That made sense and he didn't blame her. He'd played his part almost as well as she'd played hers. "I don't know," he said and was surprised to hear a defensive note in his voice. "I just . . . wanted to figure out the story. Make sure you were who you said you were." He couldn't tell her the rest. That he thought about her every evening after he dropped her off at the little house on Pico. That she made him nervous like a kid with a crush on his teacher.

"But I wasn't," she said. "And neither were you."

He let out a resigned breath. "It didn't seem right, a guy leaving a woman like you." He stopped, like he wished he hadn't said that, then rushed on. "And when I found out . . . what I found out . . . Nobody should have to live with that. Wondering what happened." He cleared his throat. "He was a good man, standing up for what was right. You deserved to know that." He pulled the auto to the front of the hotel with relief. Maybe now she'd trust him.

He helped her out of the Cadillac and tossed the keys to Tony. It was time to think about *der Angriff*. Figure out when and where and who. Since he stepped into Georg Gyssling's mansion, he'd had the uncanny feeling that somewhere there was a bomb counting down to detonation. And if they didn't figure it out soon, something was going to blow.

CHAPTER 47

LIESL

Wilhelm said hello to the clerk and picked up a key before I realized it—Wilhelm Otto lived at the Biltmore Hotel. The front desk clerk did not raise an eyebrow at me. I supposed at the Biltmore, it wasn't unusual for unmarried couples to go to a room together.

Wilhelm had not answered about Tomas to my satisfaction, and I didn't entirely trust him. Yet we needed a place to talk and it must be private. Any one of the guests in this grand lobby could be part of the alliance or the Friends. And so I was going to a hotel room with a man I despised up until one hour ago. Not only despised but feared. And now he was my ally. Like Alice tumbling down the rabbit hole, I did not know what would come next.

Wilhelm thanked the front desk clerk by name and then let out a low whistle. A sleek dog padded from behind the desk and followed us to the elevator.

A dog. In a hotel.

The elevator operator, a young boy in a perfectly pressed uniform, said, "Mr. Wilhelm," with a smile. After he punched the button, the boy knelt and the dog went to him easily. "Good girl." The elevator creaked to a halt and the door opened.

"Night, Joe," Wilhelm said. He unlocked a door at the end of the hall and ushered me into a room that was the definition of modern luxury. A spacious sitting room with comfortable armchairs of black leather, a glass coffee table, and white divan. Windows open to the night air and framed in billowing white organdy gave a view of the lights of downtown and further on the twinkle of the harbor. A tiny kitchenette. A bedroom with a bed the size of a ship. Meticulously clean, every surface polished and gleaming.

"Have a seat," he said. "I'll just be a minute."

In the kitchenette, Wilhelm opened a can and dumped what looked like beef stew on a gold-rimmed dinner plate. I sat on the divan and glanced at a stack of books on the end table. Well-read, the covers scuffed and worn. Longfellow, Frost. *Mein Kampf.* A shelf next to the mirror held a single faded photograph. A lovely woman, a little girl in a lace dress and a boy of about twelve with an anxious expression. Wilhelm with his mother and sister?

Wilhelm set the plate on the floor. The dog ate with dainty bites and I wondered suddenly if Chester had had her kittens tonight as the children had hoped. The clock on the wall showed the time to be 11:23. All would be safely in bed, the house quiet and peaceful. I wished I were there instead of here.

Wilhelm took off his maroon jacket and threw it over the back of the chair. He was not wearing his gun holster. He undid the bow tie at his neck with a jerk. "Can't stand these things," he said as an explanation.

He poured two glasses of what looked like brandy, handed me one, and sat down across from me. I took a sip and the golden liquid burned a warm trail down my throat.

He eyed me. "You set up the post office arrest?"

I nodded. "Thekla was suspicious."

He looked chagrined and I supposed he had something to do with that. He took a gulp of the brandy. "What was all that with Gyssling, when you were dancing?"

First I needed to know more about him. "How did you get in with Lewis?" I asked.

He looked at me for a long, unblinking moment. "In a roundabout way."

"Start at the beginning." I wanted to know his whole story. Take his measure.

He took a sip of his drink and started again. "Grew up in Pennsylvania. After the war, after my mom and sister—" he waved a hand toward the photo on the mantel—"I came to California. Got a job as a driver. Tried my hand at acting."

"You were in films?" That surprised me. I never imagined Wilhelm as a film star.

"Didn't take to it," he said. "Then I got hired by the Pinkertons."

A detective. That explained some things. *Knowing is better than not knowing, Mrs. Weiss.*

He took another long sip. "I didn't mind it when I was tracking down criminals, doing some work for the Feds. That kind of thing." Wilhelm frowned. He opened the lacquered case on the table. A single cigarette was inside. He shut the top without removing it. Pulled at the top button of his dress shirt until he got it undone.

I waited for him to cease fidgeting.

"I guess I was good at my job. They put me to work against the unions. Sent me up to Monterey in '28."

I remembered from the papers, a couple years after Tomas and I married. The strike by cannery workers turned violent. "And?"

"I looked at myself and didn't like what I saw. I walked out."

I weighed his words. They rang true. But nothing about Leon Lewis yet. "Then what?"

He leaned forward. "Look, this would go a lot faster if you just trusted me."

I wanted to trust him, but I needed to be sure. "Then what?"

He stood, walked restlessly to the kitchen, and refilled his glass. Sat down again. "I went down to Mexico for a while but couldn't sit on a beach all day. When I heard about the veterans up here, the way they were being treated, I came back to LA, thinking I might do some good. That's when I met Lewis."

The dog finished her dinner and padded over. She seemed to sense his distress and laid her head on his leg. He ran a hand over her ears.

"Why did you agree to work with him?"

He stared into his drink for a long moment. "I don't like bullies," he said simply. "Guys like Schwinn and Winterhalder. Give them a little power and they use it. And Adolf Hitler?" He looked up then and his face was grim. "He's the biggest bully of them all." He rubbed the back of his neck. "And so I got in with them. It wasn't so hard, with my background and—" he shrugged—"a certain demeanor."

"You were convincing," I said. He had been. Terrifying, in fact. Leon Lewis had once told me he was a good judge of character. I was beginning to believe he was correct in Wilhelm Otto's case.

A ghost of a smile flashed across his face. "Your turn," he said. "Why are you doing this with a family—kids and all? You gotta know it's dangerous."

I felt shame of my own then. Wilhelm might be the hero type, wanting to protect the world from bullies, but I wasn't. I didn't want to save Jews—at least not when I agreed to work with Lewis. I had my own prejudices and to be honest, I wasn't much better than Thekla or Gertrud. He deserved to know the truth.

"I needed the money." I watched his expression alter to surprise. "At first," I tacked on. "I lost my position at MGM. I had the children, Mutti. Fritz . . ." I hesitated.

"Fritz," Wilhelm said. We needed to talk about him, his tone implied.

I went on with my confession. "But then, after the Deutscher Tag, when I saw what they did . . ." A shudder of remembrance. "I read the books that Themlitz gave me, the pamphlets. And you know about the flyers."

"You knew you couldn't stand by."

I nodded. A moment of silence stretched as an unspoken affinity took root. We had more to discuss—Fritz, Tomas. But for now, we could work together to find out what was coming.

Wilhelm leaned forward. "What did Gyssling say?"

I told him about Gyssling's message to Hermann Schwinn. "He thought Schwinn sent us," I finished.

He let out a breath. "So he doesn't know about Leon."

"I don't think so." I wasn't sure of much when it came to Georg Gyssling. "He knows something is coming and he doesn't like it."

Wilhelm rubbed the back of his neck. "But what?"

I had no answer. "Let me see the carbon." Perhaps that would shed some light.

He pulled it from his pocket and smoothed it out on the glass table-top. The black-on-black ink was hard to read. I angled it to catch the light and then . . . "I don't believe it."

"What?" Wilhelm put his head close to mine, squinting at the carbon.

"It's a letter to Leon Lewis."

I read through it quickly, then once again slowly. Wilhelm did the same. The letter was short and to the point. Anonymous. Dated the day before yesterday, the inside address that of Lewis's office on Seventh Street. It was a warning that certain fascist organizations—unrelated to the German consulship—were planning an attack on the Jews of Los Angeles.

"It has to be *der Angriff*." It was really happening.

"But nothing specific." Wilhelm's jaw was tense and I mirrored his frustration.

"Except this part: He says the Schwinns' immigration papers are—" I checked his exact wording—"'not in order.' Why would he say that?"

Wilhelm rubbed his jaw. "Maybe he's giving Lewis something to work with, a way to get at the Schwinns, but we don't have time to tie them up with red tape at the State Department."

"And Lewis isn't here to do it." The letter was no doubt sitting in Leon Lewis's post office box, the copy filed in the safe in Gyssling's office. An attack on the Jews of Los Angeles. *Der Angriff*. When would it be? And where? "Could we bluff? Go to Schwinn and tell him what the vice-consul said? Perhaps Schwinn would call it off?" Whatever *it* was.

Wilhelm deliberated, then shook his head. "Too risky for us. And I have the feeling Schwinn won't have a qualm about going against Gyssling's advice."

We were at another dead end.

Georg Gyssling was a Nazi, and he wasn't. He did his job for the German film board, but he wasn't an ally with the Friends of New Germany. Had he known we were operatives for Leon Lewis—instead of sent by Hermann Schwinn—he might have given us more information at the party. Then again, he might not. I wished for Lewis's strategic mind that seemed always a step ahead and to know inherently who could and who could not be trusted.

I ran my hand over the dog's soft ears, looking for some kind of comfort. "Do you know when Lewis will be back?"

"Tomorrow evening. The 5:30 train from Chicago." Wilhelm paced back, took the drink from my hand, and downed the rest of it. "What about Fritz?" he asked as he set the glass on the table.

I wasn't sure what to say. Fritz's loyalty to the Silver Shirts and what they stood for—and who they stood against—had infected him like a virus. But sometimes . . . I saw a glimmer of the brother I knew.

Wilhelm frowned at my silence. "Any chance we can get him to talk to us, tell us what he knows?"

"I—" My throat closed up. I shook my head. He couldn't be trusted. I felt the sudden weariness of a long night.

Wilhelm shrugged back into his jacket and handed me my wrap. "It's late, and there's nothing we can do tonight. And you're tired."

I was not surprised by Wilhelm Otto's observant nature, as I had seen much of it at the Friends. We would wait until Lewis returned tomorrow. Hopefully he would know what to do. And we would have time to do it.

Fifteen minutes later we reached the streets of Germantown. My eyes were heavy as the warmth of the auto and the movement lulled me.

The auto jerked as Wilhelm suddenly braked. "What's that?" Wilhelm pushed on the accelerator and the auto surged forward, faster than should be driven on a residential street. I leaned forward, looking up Pico. A red-and-yellow glow, a billow of gray smoke in the dark night sky.

"It's—a fire." Alarm rushed through me. What house? It was impossible to tell.

We came to the corner of Vermont and I could see clearly. It wasn't my home with fire leaping from the front window, licking the rooftop. It was Miriam and Yitzak Stahr's.

Miriam. Frieda. *No, dear Lord.*

We screeched to a halt as Mutti stumbled out of our front door, her face stricken. She ran toward the Stahrs' as if to go in the front door and into the inferno.

I was out of the auto in a flash, running after her, my heels sinking into the grass and slowing me. "Mutti, don't!" I grabbed her by the arm.

"I must—the children!" she choked out.

Did she mean Frieda? "Yitzak will get Frieda. You can't—"

"Tess and Steffen!" The names came out as a wail. "They begged me—the kittens—" She clawed at me and struggled toward the burning house. "Oh, my Lord, what have I done?"

CHAPTER 48

LIESL

It took me less than a second to understand, but it seemed the longest moment of my life.

Mutti had defied my instructions. Again. Tess had begged to stay at the Stahrs' and Mutti relented.

Tess and Steffen were inside the burning house.

Wilhelm yelled something to me but I didn't hear. "Tess!" I ran to the front door, where flames licked out the broken window and up the frame. The fire crackled and roared. The acrid smoke burned my throat but I didn't stop. I pounded on the door. "Steffen!"

Wilhelm grabbed me and pulled me back from the heat. "Liesl, the back!" he shouted. We ran around the house to find Yitzak and Miriam, both coughing, each carrying a child. Mutti fell to her knees as Yitzak, racked with coughing, put Tess on the grass.

"Where is Steffen?" My voice was high and hysterical to my ears and Yitzak was already turning, stumbling back toward the house, where smoke poured out the door.

Miriam collapsed to the ground, wheezing for breath. Frieda lay unmoving in front of her bent body. Halfway to the house, Yitzak stumbled, felled by a fit of coughing.

I ran past Yitzak but Wilhelm grabbed my arm, stopping me with a viselike grip. "Stay." He pushed me back. He removed his jacket, bunched it in his hand. The roar of the flames increased, licking the top of the roof. "Where?" Wilhelm demanded of Yitzak, who was pushing himself to standing.

He pointed toward the front of the house. "Front. Down . . . stairs."

Wilhelm put the jacket over his nose and mouth and disappeared into the smoke.

I waited. My breath did not come. My heart did not beat. Steffen. I had not kissed him goodbye. *Please, God, let him be alive.* My legs weakened like melting wax.

Tess struggled upright, crying and coughing, reaching for me. I knelt at her side, put my arms around her, and pulled her close. The pain in my chest built like a dam holding back a flood. Still, my breath did not come. My heart did not beat.

As if a long way off, I heard Mutti. Crying. Praying. Saying Steffen's name over and over. Or was that my voice repeating it like a prayer? Miriam and Yitzak bent over Frieda, who lay silent. Was she dead? I could not bear the thought.

I watched the door.

How long had Wilhelm been inside? Seconds? Minutes? Behind me, I heard Miriam start to sob, call Frieda's name. The pain in my chest swelled to unbearable.

Please, God, not Steffen. Not my sweet boy, who loved Chester and all creatures. Not Frieda, that gentle girl. I squeezed Tess close to me and prayed. Soundlessly, wordlessly.

Suddenly Wilhelm's tall form came out of the smoke. A small body in his arms. He stumbled, breathing in choked wheezes. He went to his knees, cradling Steffen and carefully laying him on the grass beside me.

Steffen's eyes were closed, a gash of blood on his arm. He was so still.

Wilhelm leaned over him, his face streaked with soot and a singed stripe along his left arm. He put his ear to Steffen's chest. "He's breathing," he rasped.

I could hardly feel relief. Not with Steffen so still and pale.

Wilhelm looked to where Frieda lay on the grass, Miriam kneeling beside her, weeping. "We need to get them to the hospital. Now." He scooped up Steffen. "My auto, let's go," he said to Yitzak with a jerk of his head toward Frieda.

Mutti wrapped her arms around her chest like she was holding herself together.

"Stay here," I ordered her. "I'll telephone as soon as we—" I picked up Tess and didn't finish the thought but ran after Wilhelm, who was striding across the grass with Steffen in his arms. Yitzak, carrying the still-silent Frieda, Miriam following behind.

Wilhelm drove to the hospital like a maniac.

Miriam held Frieda in her lap in the rear seat with Yitzak, who was alternately cursing and praying. Tess whimpered beside me. "It's my fault. Chester was . . . and Oma said . . ."

"Shhh. We'll talk later," I managed. Steffen's chest rose weakly and his hands were cold. I checked Tess as best I could. Her hair was singed on one side and an angry red burn covered her arm. Her bare feet, tucked up on the bench, were bleeding. Time enough for blame and explanations after the children were seen to. The doctors would know what to do. They must.

I tried to pray but my thoughts were scattered and my mind a dark void of fear. I should never have left them. I should have been there. This would not have happened.

Wilhelm veered around corners, using the automobile horn to clear the way past late-night drivers. And finally—finally—he jerked the auto to a halt in front of the hospital. He jumped out and ran to open the rear door for Yitzak, then for me. He took Steffen from my lap. I slid out, then scooped up Tess. Then all was running nurses and shouted orders. "Children's ward, get a gurney! Two!" Another nurse asked their names and jotted down words on a clipboard.

In moments, we stood watching white-uniformed orderlies roll

Steffen and Frieda away. A nurse—a stout older woman with the bearing of a field marshal—took Tess by the hand. "Stay here," she said, her orders taking in Miriam and Yitzak, me and Wilhelm. "A doctor will be out to speak to you soon."

We stood silently in the sterile waiting room, empty but for one old man asleep in a chair, Miriam in pajamas, Yitzak in dungarees and a white undershirt, Wilhelm and I in evening dress—all of us covered in soot and reeking of smoke. My insides were a sick whirl. Steffen—would he awaken? Tess. Frieda. I turned to Miriam. "What happened? How did the fire—?"

"It wasn't a fire," Yitzak snapped. He turned on me. "I heard an auto in the street. I didn't see it but there was yelling and—" his hands clenched into fists—"they said . . . 'Dirty Jews.' Then a crash, the front window. And a bang like a bomb . . . or a gun."

Wilhelm asked quickly, "Who?"

"Who do you think?" Yitzak said, his anger flaring.

I jerked my gaze to Wilhelm. Nazis. Silver Shirts. But why the Stahrs? Why Tess and Frieda and—? The room tilted and my knees didn't seem to work. Wilhelm stepped forward, his hand on my elbow. "Sit," he said, tipping his head to a row of chairs.

I shook my head and forced my legs to straighten. No. I would not fall apart. Not with Steffen barely alive, with Tess hurt and Frieda—oh, little Frieda. This was no random attack, and it had something—somehow— to do with the Friends of New Germany and Leon Lewis.

Somehow it was my fault.

———

"Mr. and Mrs. Weiss, Mr. and Mrs. Stahr?" A doctor in a white coat stood in the hallway. I jerked toward the voice. Yitzak and Miriam staggered to their feet. No one corrected the doctor's assumption about Wilhelm.

The doctor began to speak, but it was as if in a foreign tongue. I watched his broad face, his sympathetic brown eyes. Was it bad news? I blinked and tried to concentrate through the fog of my fear and guilt.

Wilhelm stood beside me, his glance alternating between the doctor's face and mine. His hands at his sides like a soldier's. Miriam clutched at Yitzak's arm.

"—was seriously injured." He checked the clipboard he held. "Flash burns on her legs and what looks like a concussion."

Frieda. He was talking about Frieda.

"She has regained consciousness and we've given her something for the pain."

"What does that mean?" Yitzak demanded.

"Can we see her?" Miriam's voice was softer but no less urgent.

The doctor answered Yitzak's question first. "She may have some scarring, but it will be minimal. As for the concussion, we'll know more as time goes on." He looked then to Miriam. "She's sleeping. But you may see her in a few minutes. The nurse will take you."

I looked at Miriam and Yitzak. Their faces reflected my own feelings. Worry. Confusion. A modicum of relief.

He turned to Wilhelm and me. "Mr. and Mrs. Weiss," he said, and he hesitated just a fraction. Enough that I knew. Bad news—worse than Frieda. "Your daughter is doing well. She has a few small burns, some wheezing due to the smoke. She'll be fine. You can see her soon."

He paused.

Tess. My relief for her was immediate. But now he glanced away from me. Steffen. My breath stopped and I swayed. Wilhelm stepped closer and took my arm while I steadied myself. Readied for what was to come.

"Your son is in critical condition." The brown eyes met mine. "He remains unconscious. We're giving him oxygen. He may have had some time of oxygen deprivation, enough to affect him in a permanent way—"

I must have made some sort of noise, for Miriam came to me then, hand around my waist. The rest I heard in disjointed words: "Respiratory. Seizure. Wait. Hope."

I swallowed hard. Steffen. Despair and regret rising in a tide. Me, clutching for a lifeline of hope, choking on a wordless prayer.

Then we were following a nurse down a bright hallway. The scent of antiseptic, the taste of bitter chemicals in the back of my throat. She ushered us into a dim room with two identical beds, a chair beside each. In the further bed, Frieda. Her face was washed of the blood and a bandage covered one temple. One arm was wrapped and placed outside the white sheet.

On the other bed, closest to me, lay Steffen. His breath rasped weakly through an oxygen mask. Panic rose in my throat as I knelt down beside him. "Can he hear me?"

The nurse had dark hair and a thin, apologetic face. "It doesn't hurt to speak to him," she said. "And you can hold his hand, if you like."

She left us with a few small squeaks of rubber soles on linoleum. I reached out to Steffen, lifting his small hand. It was warm, and that was a surprising reassurance. "*Liebling*, I'm sorry," I whispered. For what, I did not know. This was no random occurrence. Whatever I was doing—with Leon Lewis or the Friends of New Germany—had caused this terrible thing.

Miriam murmured to Frieda and I heard her small voice answer. *Thank you, Lord.* For Frieda. *Please, let Steffen wake up.* As if he knew my legs were about to give way, Wilhelm pushed the chair closer and guided me to sit. I prayed for I didn't know how long. Dimly I was aware of Yitzak, pacing and muttering. The quiet presence of Wilhelm.

A muffled voice, anguished and familiar, broke through my thoughts. In the hall and coming closer. A nurse's commanding response and then—

Fritz staggered in the door, a hand supporting him on the frame. A nurse followed him, protesting, but he ignored her. He let out a low moan, stumbled to the bed, sinking to his knees and pressing his face into the white cotton sheet over Steffen's legs. His silver shirt was rumpled and he smelled of gasoline and alcohol. "I'm sorry, Steffen. I—I'm so sorry."

I looked at him blankly. What did he mean? Was he drunk?

Fritz swallowed a sob and looked to me. "Tess? Where is she? Is she—? I didn't know they were there. I swear—I tried to stop him—"

I stared at Fritz and felt suddenly as if I might be sick. "What?" I asked, pulling him up and away from the bed. "What did you do?"

He dropped his head in his hands. "I tried to stop them. I didn't think . . ." He choked on the words.

My heart twisted in my chest; my mind rejected the idea. My own brother—who played crazy eights with Steffen, loved Tess—had he . . . ? I couldn't bring myself to ask.

Yitzak was quicker to understand. "You—" He grabbed Fritz by the front of his shirt and shook him like a rag doll. Fritz wilted as if his bones had turned to rubber. "My little girl." Yitzak, his cheeks wet with tears, pushed Fritz up against the wall. Fritz didn't even try to defend himself.

"I swear, Yitzak. I didn't do it—I didn't know—"

Wilhelm was there between them, blocking Yitzak's punch with his upraised arm. "Not here, not with the kids," he said. He pushed Yitzak back. Grabbed Fritz by the collar and gave him a long look. Fritz let out a sob and dropped his chin.

Wilhelm hauled him to the door. Yitzak followed but Wilhelm stopped him with a hand on his chest. "You can have at him, Stahr," he said. "But not until I'm done with him."

I stared as Wilhelm wrestled my brother out of the room. My brother? The boy I'd raised and loved was gone and in his place a stranger I did not recognize. One who would commit atrocities such as this. I failed my family, my children. I somehow failed Fritz.

I sank down beside my silent little boy.

Would I lose my Steffen as I lost Tomas? Would God allow this evil to take away my little boy? *Please, I beg you, Lord. Not Steffen, too.*

CHAPTER 49

WILHELM

Blocking that punch had hurt like the dickens.

He didn't blame Yitzak Stahr. He could see the desperation in the man's eyes. He'd known that pain, the helplessness when Lily died. That's what kids did to you.

What he'd like to do was punch Fritz himself, but that wouldn't get them anywhere.

He'd thought he wouldn't find the boy. He'd been blinded with smoke and he held his breath as long as he could, his lungs screaming for air. The smoke—when he took a shallow breath—seared his throat, but something pushed him on those last few steps. Steffen. He was just a kid and kids shouldn't die. When they did, your heart died with them. And then you lived the rest of your life with a big hole in your chest. He was proof of that.

His chest still burned with the smoke but with something else, too. Anger. Desperation.

How much worse it must be for Liesl. Both of her children. And her a good mother.

He'd wanted more than anything to comfort Liesl as she watched the nurses take the boy and girl down the hall, but he didn't have that right. What he could do was find out what happened and make whoever did it pay.

He'd been trying to work it out, between what he saw at the house and what Stahr said. An explosion. Fire. Slurs against the Jews. The acrid smell—he could still taste it in the back of his throat. Gasoline. But why this family? They were Jewish—he'd figured that much out. And they lived next door to Liesl Weiss, who worked for the Friends of New Germany and for Leon Lewis. How did that fit together?

Fritz was going to come clean if he had to beat it out of him.

Wilhelm half carried Fritz down the hall and pushed him into a small waiting room. He threw Fritz on a bench. He had a sick feeling in his gut. He shut the door, leaned on it, his back to the room. Took a breath to steady himself.

Stupid kid. Stupid, stupid kid.

He turned around. Fritz hadn't moved except to put his head in his hands. He felt a sharp pang of recognition. Himself, not so long ago. After Monterey. It took years for him to see what he'd become, to decide to do better. He didn't have years. How was he going to get through to this broken boy?

"Tell me what happened." Listening, he'd found, was a good start.

Fritz rocked back and forth over his knees. "I didn't mean to hurt them—not Tess or Steffen. God knows I wouldn't hurt them."

Wilhelm's temperature went up a notch. Fritz just didn't get it. "But you meant to hurt somebody." The Stahrs. That little girl, Frieda, who lay pale and small in the next bed. Didn't he care about her? He forced himself to stop. He couldn't unring the bell and recriminations weren't going to help.

Fritz shook his head. "No, honest. I didn't mean to hurt anybody."

"Tell me. Now." Wilhelm dragged a chair over and sat down across from Fritz.

Fritz squeezed his eyes closed. "We were just fooling around, you gotta believe me." He talked quickly, as if to get it out. "Winterhalder, he called us in after my shift . . ."

Wilhelm leaned forward. "Who?"

"Me and Monroe and some others. He said to go have some fun—before things started up for real. He gave Monroe some things . . . grenades and a gasoline bomb." He bent over, his head almost to his knees. "I thought we were going to just—"

"Just what?" And what did he mean by "before things started up for real"? Fritz needed to slow down. Make sense.

"The Stahrs' house was my idea," he said miserably. "I was just going to throw one in their yard," he said. "Mess up some grass, you know, Yitzak and his perfect lawn. But Monroe was drunk and he threw a grenade through the window, then the gas bomb. And it just went up." He rubbed his hands over his face. "I wanted to help them, but the guy driving took off. I came back as soon as I could, but . . ." He shook his head.

But the damage was done and the children were hurt. Wilhelm clenched his jaw. Was this really about a neighbor's lawn?

Fritz looked up then and his face hardened, the tears gone. "If he'd stayed with his own people, in his own neighborhood, I wouldn't have . . . Tess and Steff wouldn't be—"

"Fritz!" He said the name like a gunshot. The kid was seriously trying to push the blame for this? "You don't buy that garbage. Not really."

Fritz swallowed and flicked a glance at him, confused. "But you . . . you said it."

Wilhelm had played his part well, maybe too well. The boys in the Silver Shirts looked up to him, believed he was as much of a Nazi as Winterhalder or Schwinn. Was he responsible, in part, for what they'd become? A good question. He'd think on it, but not right now.

Right now, he had to get through to this kid.

He'd been like Fritz once. So sure he was doing right, until he realized one day that he was the guy on the wrong side—the bad guy. When he'd finally realized it, he'd been about to hit a woman in the head with a billy club. He'd looked at her and asked himself what he had become. He didn't like the answer. That's when he'd walked away from his job, his so-called friends, Monterey.

He paced across the room, to the window overlooking the parklike grounds behind the hospital. The moonlight turned the pathways to silver and shadowed the tall palms and stubby eucalyptus trees.

Could he tell Fritz the truth?

He weighed the risk of coming clean. The kid might go straight to Winterhalder and rat him out. Or he might see sense and switch sides. He'd seen Liesl look at her brother like she didn't know him—like she'd lost him. He wanted more than anything to bring this kid back. For Liesl . . . and for himself.

He turned away from the moonlit view to the sanitized room, the white walls and gray linoleum floor and hard-backed bench. Fritz sat with his head almost on his knees, his hands covering his face. The kid had been lied to. Taken in by men with an agenda. Used. He'd been looking for something to believe in and landed in the wrong camp. It wasn't too late for Fritz. Wilhelm had to believe that. He made his decision.

He sat down across from Fritz again. "Tell me about your father."

Fritz looked up sharply. "What about him?"

"Was he a good man?" Liesl hadn't said much, but the man died for his country.

"I hardly knew him," Fritz said with a bitter edge to his voice. "He left me and Mutti and Liesl. Is that a good man?"

Wilhelm had a glimpse of how deep the hurt ran in this kid. "Sometimes men have to make choices. Hard choices," Wilhelm said. "You think your father would want this for you? You think he'd be proud of this?" He gestured to the uniform, the swastika armband.

Fritz looked defiant. "I don't know. Maybe." Then he hung his head and looked away. "Maybe not." He let out a long breath. "He's not here to tell me. But why are you all over me like this? You're part of the Friends. You and Liesl—"

Wilhelm held up a hand to stop him. "No," he said. "We're not."

Fritz's head whipped upward. "But you—"

"Your sister and I are part of something else."

Fritz stared at him with no comprehension.

"We work for a man who is trying to stop them." He waved his hand. "Stop the alliance and the Friends of New Germany. The Nazis. They are poison, Fritz. The Nazis, the KKK, the Silver Shirts. And we are doing everything we can to get them out of Los Angeles, out of the whole country."

Fritz blinked at him, realization slowly dawning.

Wilhelm waited and watched as the whole thing came together for Fritz.

Fritz's voice rose. "You mean you and . . . and Liesl?" He half rose on the bench.

Wilhelm stuck a hand out and not-so-gently pushed him back down on the bench. Maybe this was a mistake. "Fritz, listen," he said, reining in his ire with difficulty. "These men aren't trying to save America. They're not even Americans. They're traitors. With those flyers and riling up kids like you to do their dirty work—"

"I'm not a kid," he flared.

Wilhelm was getting hot under the collar. "If you're a man, start acting like one. Don't swallow what you're fed by stooges like Monroe and Winterhalder. Wake up, look around." He pointed at the door toward where Tess and Frieda lay injured. Wilhelm stopped and made himself breathe. Calm down. Let the kid catch up. "Is this who you are? The kind of man you want to be?" *The kind of man who hurt kids?* But he didn't say that. He didn't have to.

"I want to be a brave man, like my father."

"Bravery doesn't always mean guns and grenades and slogans."

Fritz blinked. "So all this time. You weren't really my friend."

Wilhelm felt the kid's pain of his betrayal. "Fritz, look at me."

Fritz didn't meet his eyes.

"Who's a real friend? Somebody who goes along with what's wrong? Or somebody who wants better for you—and tells you so?"

Fritz rubbed his face. Stood and walked across the room.

Wilhelm could tell the kid was trying to figure things out. *Please, Fritz, figure it out.*

His shoulders slumped and Wilhelm saw he'd hit a roadblock. "Liesl. And Mutti. They'll never forgive me."

"They will." He hoped he was right. It probably depended a lot on whether Steffen pulled through. But he had to get this kid firmly on their side.

Fritz turned back to him. "I need to see Steffen and Tess. Talk to Liesl—"

Wilhelm stopped him with one hand on his chest. "Tell me what you know first."

"What I know about what?" Fritz asked, but he knew what Wilhelm wanted.

Wilhelm could feel the guilt and regret coming off Fritz like a bad smell. This was it, Wilhelm thought. The moment Fritz had to decide. If he came clean, there was a chance for him. *Come on, Fritz. Tell me what you know. Big guy, if you're up there, give this kid a push in the right direction.* Praying was coming more easily to him these days and he hoped the man upstairs was listening.

"*Der Angriff,*" Wilhelm said. "I know it's coming. And I'm asking you to help me stop it. You have to decide, Fritz. Whose side are you going to be on?"

CHAPTER 50

LIESL

Moments after Wilhelm took Fritz away, Mutti burst into the hospital room, Mr. Dog clutched in her hands.

"Liesl, *was ist*—?" Her voice as loud as if she were shouting up the stairs at home. She saw Steffen. Her eyes filled and she sank to her knees beside his bed. *"Es tut mir Leid. Mein Liebling, es tut mir Leid."*

I knew she was sorry, but if she had learned to say no—not only to Tess but to Fritz—we would not be here tonight. I told her succinctly what the doctor said about Steffen and Tess. She covered her face with her handkerchief and wept. I was too wrapped in worry to be angry at her, but neither could I muster any words of comfort. Mutti managed to speak to Miriam. "Frieda? Is she—?"

"We must wait," Miriam said.

Frieda had awoken for a few minutes. She cried, asked what happened, where she was. The nurse came, checked on her bandages, and gave her a shot of pain medication. "She'll sleep," she said to Miriam and Yitzak. "You should, too. Go home and come back in the morning." Miriam wouldn't hear of it. She put her hand on her belly and I knew she was thinking of the child she carried, wondering if Frieda would meet her new brother or sister.

"Tess is in the children's ward, sleeping," I told Mutti, trying to make my voice kind even as my anger at her swelled.

Tess had sobbed, telling me over and over she was sorry. "Steffen wanted to sleep beside Chester, Mommy. I made Oma say yes." It was not her fault that her grandmother could not follow simple instructions. If Steffen did not recover, Tess would blame herself. What would that do to her already-hurting heart?

Mutti looked regretfully at Yitzak, slumped at the foot of Frieda's bed. "The fire department put out the fire. But the house . . ." She shook her head and her voice broke. "I'm so sorry."

"Are you?" Yitzak snapped, looking at me as if it were my fault. And perhaps it was. I hadn't seen the danger, hadn't stopped Fritz somehow. I had watched him turn to hatred and violence and done nothing. Now he was lost to us.

Mutti's brows drew down at Yitzak's anger, and her mouth opened to speak. Then she stepped toward the door and sputtered, "What on earth?"

Fritz stood in the doorway in his stained shirt, with rumpled hair, a tear-blotched face. "Mutti," he choked out.

Yitzak bolted from his chair and all was confusion. Fritz raised his hands to ward off the blow. Wilhelm stepped in front of Fritz, catching Yitzak before he got a hit in. "Yitzak, stop—" Miriam pulled at her husband. Wilhelm growled at Yitzak, one arm protecting Fritz, the other hand closed around Yitzak's shirtfront.

"Was ist—?" Mutti bellowed, slapping at Wilhelm's shoulder as if he were the one at fault.

"Stop. This. Instant!" A voice like a commanding general's rang out and every one of us froze. The steely-eyed nurse stood in the doorway, her face like thunder. "I demand you leave this room if you cannot let the patients rest."

"I'm sorry," I said, glaring at the men. I wasn't leaving Steffen's side for any reason.

"There will be no more warnings," she said firmly and marched away with a rubber-soled squeak.

Yitzak stepped back. Fritz slumped against the wall but Wilhelm did not relax his guard.

Mutti turned to me with a loud whisper and a glare toward Wilhelm. "Liesl, why in the name of heaven is this man—?"

Wilhelm interrupted her. "You need to tone it down, ma'am." Then to me, "Liesl, we need to listen to Fritz."

Mutti looked flabbergasted. Fritz looked anywhere but at me and his mouth was clamped in that stubborn way of his. He had recovered from his earlier guilt and he looked . . . unsure.

"I'm not leaving him," I said, putting my hand on Steffen's bed. "So whatever Fritz has to say, he says right here." I had a sudden and unwelcome thought. I looked at Fritz and then back to Wilhelm. Something had passed between them. I pulled in a sharp breath. He couldn't have. "You didn't tell him?" *Please say you did not.*

Wilhelm looked resolute. "I had to."

Fritz would betray us. He would go to the Silver Shirts, to Winterhalder. I thought of Karl. Of Thekla's ice-cold stare and the pistol in Hermann's drawer. "What were you thinking?" My voice came out high and shrill.

Wilhelm's answer was quick and sure. "That he deserved a second chance."

Yitzak and Miriam watched us silently. Mutti opened her mouth. I raised my hand to stop her words. We did not need her outrage at this moment. Wilhelm wanted to give Fritz a second chance after what he'd done? Who made him judge and jury?

Wilhelm rubbed a hand over his face. "He knows about *der Angriff.*"

Alarm jolted through me. *Der Angriff.* What was at the top of my mind just hours ago had ceased to matter as I'd sat beside Steffen's bed. Held Tess's hand. Comforted Miriam as her own child whimpered in pain.

Now it returned to me. An attack on the Jews of Los Angeles. The terrible list of violent acts I'd found in Hermann Schwinn's files. No longer threats, but real and right in my own backyard. I turned to Fritz, wishing I could slap some sense into his head. "When is it?"

Fritz clamped his mouth shut.

Wilhelm answered. "Tomorrow, so we have some time to figure it out."

"No." Fritz's voice was a croak. He swallowed and shook his head. "I meant—I said tomorrow, but—" He looked at the clock on the wall, its tick suddenly as loud as gunfire. Three sixteen in the morning. "But I—I meant *this* tomorrow," he stuttered. "Today."

Today. Panic crept up my chest. "Tell us, Fritz. What is it?"

Fritz hung his head.

I stepped toward him. "How many men? Where?"

He shook his head. "They don't tell us much. Probably so we can't back out—or squeal." He looked shamefaced. "We're meeting at ten o'clock at the training ground. That's all I know. I heard something about the Wilshire Boulevard Temple. They said we're just going to scare them. A show of force." He turned to Wilhelm. "Honest, nobody's gonna get hurt."

Today. The Wilshire Boulevard Temple. That was why the mood of the Friends of New Germany was tense and expectant—had that been just yesterday? *Der Angriff* was today.

"You really believe that, Fritz?" Wilhelm said. "That's why Winterhalder and Monroe have gas bombs and guns, just to scare them?"

"That's what they said. I wouldn't shoot anybody—you've got to believe that."

Mutti jerked her gaze to Fritz. "Do you mean you've been in that terrible group of boys?"

"Mutti." I stopped her. "Not now."

Miriam made a sound. I expected outrage, but what I saw when I looked at her was something else. Knowledge, a secret. She glared at Yitzak. "Tell them," Miriam said to her husband.

"Tell us what?" Wilhelm demanded.

"No," Yitzak said with a furious look at Miriam.

"We're on the same team, Stahr," Wilhelm ground out. He glanced at me. He was going to tell them all of it but it couldn't be helped. "Liesl and I are working with a man who is trying to stop the Friends—the Nazis—from getting a hold on the city."

"What?" Mutti squawked and she jerked her gaze to me. "That's what you've been up to?"

Miriam's brow furrowed, her voice quiet but questioning. "You've been working against the Nazis, not for them?"

"I wanted to tell you," I answered Miriam. I wanted to tell her all of it, how I was sorry and I hadn't understood. How I was doing this for her. "I promise I will." *But not now.*

Wilhelm kept on at Yitzak. "Stahr? Tell us what you know."

Yitzak clenched his jaw and let out a huff of air from his nose. "It's the Selznick funeral."

I remembered now. Stella had talked about it. My gaze met Wilhelm's. Of course. Jewish studio heads, producers, and actors would pay their respects to the beloved father of David Selznick, a producer at MGM and Louis B. Mayer's son-in-law.

Yitzak continued. "And the Silver Shirts aren't going to be the only ones at the temple."

"How do you mean?" Wilhelm pushed.

Yitzak grimaced. "The Brotherhood," he finally came out with. "They'll be there for protection. I got a telephone call yesterday telling me to show up."

That didn't make sense. "How did they know about the attack?" Wilhelm and I didn't know and we worked with the Nazis. And why did Wilhelm look as if he wanted to punch someone?

Yitzak pressed his lips together.

"Let me guess," Wilhelm said with great control. "An anonymous tip."

The look on Yitzak's face answered his question.

Wilhelm's jaw went tight. "Winterhalder. I'd bet my hat on it." He stepped toward Yitzak and the anger coming off him made Yitzak shrink backward. "Are they armed—the Brotherhood? Tell me the truth or so help me."

Yitzak jerked a quick nod.

Wilhelm put his hand to his forehead as if he was suddenly exhausted.

"What is it?" I was slower to catch on than him.

He explained. "Winterhalder. He's setting them up for a shoot-out. That way, he can kill Jews and claim self-defense or some claptrap. Plenty of people, including the newspapers, will buy it." He paced to the door, turned back. "And plenty of people are going to die. Studio people, just like the Schwinns have been threatening. We have to stop them."

"Can't you tell the police?" Miriam asked me. "This thing that is happening, they can stop it, can't they?"

If only it were that simple.

"The police?" Yitzak spit out. "They're in on it."

"Maybe," Wilhelm confirmed. "At least some of them. And we don't know who else is involved."

Yitzak growled some words I knew Miriam didn't like him to use and they were aimed in Fritz's direction.

Miriam was still thinking. "What about this man you work for? Can't he do something?"

I shook my head. "I can't get in touch with him. He's on a train from Washington, DC."

Mutti was catching up. "So you must warn these people at the temple?"

Yes, we must. If they would believe us. And through the sleepless fog of my worried brain, something else was nagging at me. Something didn't fit.

I went to Steffen, sat down beside his small form on the bed. Gently I pushed the blond hair from his forehead. I had seen the hatred that came from the Friends of New Germany, heard the rhetoric and what they were capable of—what they wanted for their ultimate goal. To drive Jewish people from Los Angeles. Winterhalder wouldn't hesitate to use those guns. Especially on the kind of Jews who were going to be at that funeral. Studio heads, producers, and actors—the very people they vowed to eradicate in their pamphlets. Everyone on the list I'd seen in the file.

And yet, what Fritz told us did not fit entirely with Georg Gyssling's warning. What seemed like days ago, when we'd danced the ländler together. The absurd plan he spoke of. *Leave studio business with the consulship. I have the matter in hand with Mayer.* Something didn't sit right. "Is that all?" I asked Fritz. "You don't know anything more?"

Fritz shook his head. "That's all I know, I swear."

CHAPTER 51

LIESL

Wilhelm stepped close to me. "I have an idea. We need to go."

I could not leave Steffen, not even to save the lives of the people in the temple. And if we stopped it—or even if we didn't—what would happen then? The Friends of New Germany would know our deception. Mutti and the children—hadn't I put them in enough danger? And yet how could I desert Leon Lewis with so much at stake?

Wilhelm turned to Yitzak and Fritz. "And I'll need both of you."

What was he thinking? Fritz was a Nazi and Yitzak, a member of the Jewish Brotherhood. Surely they could not work together.

Wilhelm saw my disagreement. "We need all the help we can get."

Not me. I shook my head and looked at Steffen. "I can't leave him."

Mutti came to me. "I'll be here. I won't leave his side. Or Tess." I knew she would not and yet . . . was it not right for me to be with my children—but also right for me to stop what Winterhalder and the Silver Shirts had planned against innocent people?

I looked to Miriam. Her hand was over her burgeoning middle. Her child, her home had been attacked because of this hatred for her people. How could I stand by? To do nothing, to remain silent, was to let evil win. That was surely the case at this moment. If I did not do what I could to stop them, I was as guilty as the day I did not speak in the grocery against Gertrud—more so, because in this case people would die.

Wilhelm watched me from the door. He understood the danger as much as I, and he needed my help, or he would not ask. I pushed the blond hair from Steffen's forehead and traced a heart on his smooth skin. Closed my eyes. Kissed his soft cheek. "Mutti, if he wakes . . ." My voice faltered. "Tell him . . ." I could not finish. *Tell him I'll always come back.*

"Liesl," she whispered. I turned to her. She did not want me to go—I could see it in her face. But instead of the chastisement I thought coming, she put her arms around me and squeezed. It was an awkward embrace with my arms pinned to my sides. She let go, turning away quickly with an abrupt sniff. "Don't do anything stupid."

I knew what she was trying to say. "I love you, too, Mutti."

Then I went to Miriam. "I'm sorry, Miriam." They were the simplest of words, and I had far more to say to her, but this was the most important. Hot tears pricked the backs of my eyes and I drew a shaky breath. "I'm sorry I was like them—Gertrud and the rest."

That was the truth of it. I'd been so caught up in my own sorrows and worries, I'd been blind to what was happening in Germantown. To Miriam and Yitzak and Frieda and what they faced every day. For years I had remained silent, not just that day at Grundbacher's.

She took my hands in hers. "You aren't like them."

But I had been. When I met Leon Lewis, I hadn't believed—hadn't wanted to believe—what was happening to the Jews in Germany was even true. I refused to see what was happening in my own neighborhood. I told myself it was not my problem. It wasn't up to me to stand up for those people . . . Miriam and Frieda. Yitzak. Stella.

But they were not *those people*. They were *my* people. My friends.

"Can we—do you think—can you forgive me for that day?" And for all the times I remained silent in the face of prejudice.

She sniffled and nodded. It was a start. We drew apart, wiping tears from our eyes.

Miriam glanced toward Wilhelm. "And when you come back, you need to tell me all about that man," she whispered.

I had much to tell her. About Tomas and Leon Lewis. But Wilhelm? I didn't know where to begin or what to say about him.

Wilhelm walked with me to the children's ward and I was glad for his silence. I did not know his plan, but I knew who we were facing and they were dangerous. To us and to all those we loved. I had no business being a part of it, and yet I had no other choice.

Tess lay in the large room with a dozen beds, half of them occupied. She was awake, staring at the ceiling with tears making trickling paths from the corners of her eyes to the pillow. A fist clamped around my heart. I sat down carefully on the edge of her bed.

She did not look at me. "Is Steffen . . . is he going to die?"

"No," I said fiercely. "No," more softly. I took her small hand in mine. "He's going to be well." I had to believe it.

"What about . . . ?" She blinked hard and another tear escaped. "Ch-Chester?"

My throat went tight, as I considered the inferno of the Stahrs' house. "I don't know, sweetheart."

A small sob came from Tess. Steffen—when he woke—would also grieve the loss of his beloved pet. I could do nothing about that sorrow. "I have to go for a little while, my sweet girl, but I want you to know something."

She looked at me then, and I saw all the regret and shame she was holding inside.

"This was not your fault, Tess." Her face crumpled and her body quaked in a sob. She clutched at my hand. I slipped from the bed to my knees. "It was not your fault." It was the fault of hateful men, of ingrained prejudice. But I would not talk of that now. I kissed her tear-wet face. My sweet girl. Would she forgive herself?

She took a great breath as if she had been underwater. I hoped she believed me and I prayed her brother would wake up. Recover. For his sake and for hers. I bowed my head over our clasped hands, praying for my children. For Fritz. For what we would face going out of this room.

When I came to myself after minutes, it was to see her sleeping peacefully, just as I had watched her do so many dark nights. I turned to find Wilhelm close by, looking down at Tess.

"How do you do it?" he asked, his face hard to read in the dim light.

"Do what?"

He swallowed. "Live with the fear that they might die?"

I did not know how to answer him. I didn't know how to explain to a man who I suspected had closed himself off after his sister and mother died. A man who believed he was not cut out for family. And yet everything I'd seen told me he was a protector, a guardian—a good man. But a man who was afraid to risk his heart again.

"I don't know," I answered truthfully. "You just do."

We drove to Germantown in silence—me in the front seat beside Wilhelm, Fritz and Yitzak in the back. The sky was yet dark and yellow streetlights cast a sickly glow over the streets. Fritz did not speak, and for that I was grateful. My anger at him simmered still, and as the Stahrs' home came into view, it flamed back to full force.

The front window glinted in shards on the burnt grass, paint peeled in great strips from the singed door. Yitzak did not say a word but I could feel the fury coming from him white-hot.

Wilhelm pulled up to the curb and turned to me. "Get what you need quick," he said. "We don't have much time."

I gathered all Wilhelm had instructed. A dress for me—the yellow one with the buttons down the front—as well as underthings, a hairbrush and pins, and some cosmetics. From Fritz's attic room, I took his police uniform and hat.

Half an hour later, Wilhelm brought Fritz, Yitzak, and me through the back door of the Biltmore and up narrow stairs to his room. Yitzak's eyes darted from the fashionable furniture to the view like he was walking into a trap.

I washed up in a room with a bathtub the size of a small swimming pool and white towels as soft and thick as clouds. The yellow dress made the most of my figure and had a neckline just barely above indecent. I'd worn it just once to the Alt Heidelberg and after the ogling Winterhalder had given me, I'd never worn it again. I patted on powder, applied my rose lipstick, and left the bathroom much improved in appearance if not disposition, my thoughts never far from Steffen, Tess, and Frieda.

The scent of coffee greeted me, as well as a platter of toast and jam, bacon, and scrambled eggs. Fritz helped himself and Yitzak took my place in the bathroom.

Wilhelm poured me a cup of coffee and laid out his plan.

"That's it?" I said. I might as well have stayed at the hospital with Steffen and Tess.

"It's not completely fleshed out," he countered with a defensive edge.

"It is not a plan." I stood and walked to the window, looking out over Pershing Square. The rising sun threw a murky light over the paths and hedges. "It's a vague idea." With several gaping holes and a hearty dose of uncertainty.

"You got a better one?" he snapped. "Listen, Lewis is always two steps ahead of the Nazis. So I'm trying to think like him—figure what he'd do."

My voice rose in response. "And you think he'd lure Winterhalder here to get information? And then what? Stop twenty men from attacking the synagogue in—" I looked at the clock—"less than three hours, with Fritz, who I don't trust, and Yitzak, who's in the Brotherhood?"

Wilhelm looked like he was clenching his teeth and I felt some remorse at my tone. He was right; we needed to think like Lewis. But I wasn't Lewis, and neither was he.

"Why can't we just go to the temple, warn the people as they show up to go home?" It seemed simple enough.

"Will they believe us?" Wilhelm asked. "They might listen if it was

Lewis, but with the Brotherhood there for protection, I think they'll carry on with the funeral. We can't take the chance."

He had a point. Lewis himself had difficulty convincing the studio heads they were in danger. But what else could we do?

"And then what?" Wilhelm went on as if I were the adversary. "Our cover story is blown. Winterhalder and Schwinn are still out there. Lewis is back to square one."

"So what will this plan accomplish?" I asked, feeling like I had to defend myself.

"What we need is to stop the men who are going to the temple and also get proof that the Friends of New Germany are behind them." He sat down heavily in the chair I'd just left.

He was right. But how could it possibly work? "So we get Winterhalder here. What makes you think he'll talk to you? You just said he doesn't trust you after Karl."

"But he trusts you," Wilhelm said. "And in that dress, he won't be thinking straight."

I looked down at the dress and understood. Winterhalder did have a weakness for women. But would he really tell me the who and where of the attack? Even if he did, there was still a major flaw in the plan. "How do we get hard evidence? It's not like we have a recording device like a—" I stopped as a ridiculous idea struck me.

"What?" Wilhelm sharpened his gaze.

I shook my head. It was unlikely to work.

He leaned forward. "Whatever it is, it's better than nothing."

I told him. Fritz stopped midchew.

"It might work," Wilhelm said, considering. "If you know how to set it up."

Of course I did. I'd graduated top of my class from Dickinson Secretarial. I looked at the clock. "I'll telephone Stella."

I placed the call to Stella's house, half-hoping she'd tell me no. I wasn't sure who answered, one of the maids or possibly her mother. Whoever it was sounded put out to be called at 5:32 in the morning, but she got Stella for me.

"Are you in jail?" she asked when she heard my voice. She sounded chipper, which was a relief. Her evening with Cecil had to have been better than mine with Wilhelm.

I ignored her question and told her quickly what I needed. "Can you manage it?" I asked. Stella would have to be told the whole story and that would put her in danger. But I hadn't any choice in the matter now.

There was a long pause. She could get fired for what I asked, perhaps even arrested. "Sure, hon," she said as if she got this kind of call all the time. "It'll take me a bit. Where are you?"

CHAPTER 52

Stella showed up at 7:35 with a black suitcase and a questioning expression.

Despite the early hour, she looked impeccable in an apple-green day dress with a cashmere beret—as if she were going to a ladies' luncheon, not stealing a Dictaphone machine from MGM and hauling it up the back stairs of the Biltmore.

"Well?" she said when I answered her knock on the door. "Are you going to let me in? This thing is heavy."

I stepped back and ushered her inside.

Stella took in Wilhelm, cleaned up and changed into one of his ubiquitous dark suits. "If it isn't Mr. Personality." She turned to Yitzak. "And who's this tall drink of water?" He'd cleaned up and dressed in one of Wilhelm's suits. A bit slack in the shoulders and the cuffs were an inch too short, but he looked decent. Fritz stood beside Yitzak in his trousers and undershirt, his mouth hanging open as he took in Stella from her bobbed hair to her Cuban heels.

"Yitzak, Fritz, this is Stella Levine."

She said hello and turned to me. "Gonna finally give me the scoop?"

Wilhelm took the Dictaphone and set it on the table. "Later," he said, looking at the clock.

321

He was right. It was close to eight o'clock and we had much to do. I looked at her expectant face. "I promise," I told her as I snapped open the metal clips on the case. The Dictaphone was smaller than the ones I'd worked with and I said as much to Stella.

"I had to get this one," she explained. "The others were too heavy to move on my own."

Wilhelm paced from one end of the room to the other. "Will it work?"

"Yes," I said. It had to.

"Make the call." He nodded to me.

My pulse quickened. I wiped damp palms down the front of my dress and picked up the telephone. "Los Angeles 1423." My eyes locked with Wilhelm's flint-gray gaze. This part was crucial. A groggy Hans Winterhalder answered. I let out a relieved breath. "Hans, it's Liesl," I said with more familiarity than I'd ever used with the man. "I need your help. Could you meet me?"

He sputtered a question and I answered quickly, "Not over the telephone." I told him where I'd meet him, then made my voice pleading and soft. "Please, Hans, don't tell Hermann or Thekla. I just want to see you, alone." I hung up before he asked any more questions.

"I'd believe you," Wilhelm said but he didn't look pleased with my performance.

Wilhelm told Fritz to watch the Alt Heidelberg. "You sure you don't need me here?" Fritz asked, buttoning up the shirt of his police uniform.

I wasn't sure I wanted him out of my sight but Wilhelm was intent on trusting him. "Keep a lookout for Hermann and Thekla or Themlitz. We need to watch them."

I turned to Stella. Her arms were crossed and she had a look on her face that said she'd waited long enough. "Spill the beans, Liesl. What's going on?"

I told her the bare bones about Leon Lewis and his spy operation and the Friends of New Germany. I'd never seen my friend speechless before, but it was a relief. We didn't have time for questions and answers. But I did have to warn her. "It's dangerous, Stella. If you want, you can leave now and stay out of it."

She stared at me for a moment, then shook her head. "I'm sticking with you, sister. Tell me what to do."

At 8:20, I sat at a table in the Emerald Room of the Biltmore Hotel, waiting for Hans Winterhalder.

I wasn't happy with the arrangement. The breakfast rush at the Emerald Room might just drown out whatever Hans Winterhalder confessed to me. If he confessed to anything. And I still wasn't sure the Dictaphone would work. "We should have set up the meeting in the hotel room," I said to Wilhelm, who was pacing and watching the window. It would have been quieter and made a better recording.

"And leave you alone with that dog, Winterhalder?" he answered back with a frown. "Don't let your guard down even here. You don't know this guy like I do."

He'd gotten me settled at a table in the corner and motioned over a plain-faced girl in a slim black skirt and white blouse. "Lita," he said as she arrived, her cheeks pink and her eyes all over him, "we need a telephone, please."

She looked at him like she'd do a backflip if he asked it of her.

"How are we going to hide it?" Wilhelm asked when she brought a telephone set to the table and plugged it into the wall.

I hadn't figured that out. It made better sense to have the Dictaphone right here, but we'd discarded that idea. Too cumbersome, and the humming noise it made would be a dead giveaway. So Stella was in Wilhelm's room, ready to switch on the Dictaphone as soon as I telephoned. In theory, she'd hold the Dictaphone mouthpiece to the telephone on her end, and anything Hans Winterhalder said would be recorded on the wax cylinder as evidence.

In theory. The problem being, we needed the telephone receiver as close to Winterhalder as we could get it but without him catching on.

Lita remained next to Wilhelm, listening. "Wait, I have an idea." She disappeared and came back a moment later pushing a serving cart covered in a white linen cloth. She positioned it between the table and the wall and set the telephone on the shelf below the silver coffee service, then arranged the white linen to cover it. "Will that work?"

It was close to Winterhalder's chair and it was hidden. The best we could hope for.

"Thanks, Lita." Wilhelm bestowed his infrequent smile on the girl and she fairly floated back to her duties. He glanced at his wristwatch. "I'll be at the table in the back in case anything goes south."

I picked up the receiver. "Room 642, please." I was connected and Stella answered in the middle of the first ring.

"Room service."

"Is it set?"

"Sure thing," she said. "Ready to roll. Make sure to talk as loud as you can. And hey," she added, "there's a dog up here and it's making sounds at Yitzak. Ask Mr. Nazi if his dog bites Jews."

I glanced at Wilhelm. He'd heard her strident voice coming through the receiver.

"She doesn't bite anybody."

Stella didn't sound convinced. "What's her name, in case I need to tell her what's what?"

Wilhelm Otto looked away and for all the world seemed embarrassed.

"She has a name, doesn't she?" Stella pressed. "You don't have a dog in your hotel room and not have a name for it."

Wilhelm let out a quick breath. "Lady. Her name is Lady."

Lady. It was a sweet name and didn't fit with Wilhelm Otto's stern ways. We could hear Stella's guffaw as I arranged the receiver on the cart, the mouthpiece angled toward the chair where Hans Winterhalder would sit, and positioned the cloth to hide it. Wilhelm pointed to the table in the back of the room again. "If you need me."

I wondered how I'd ever thought him inexpressive. I could see from the small changes in his mouth and eyes far more than I wished. He was worried. And more even than that, Wilhelm was afraid. Not for himself, but for me. I felt a shiver of apprehension. If something went wrong—if Winterhalder didn't believe my story. Or if he didn't come alone . . . I needed to be ready for anything.

"I'll be fine," I said.

He lingered as if he wanted to say something more or perhaps make some kind of gesture. What? Shake my hand and wish me luck? But he just dipped his head and turned away.

I opened my handbag and took out my compact. Smoothed my hair in the tiny mirror and reapplied my lipstick. My thoughts went to Steffen. To Tess and Frieda. I snapped the compact closed and prayed. For the children. For whatever was to happen in the next few minutes.

Hans Winterhalder arrived in a fog of aftershave so thick I could taste it.

I breathed carefully and prepared myself. I'd never wanted to be an actress, but I'd seen enough actors work through scenes to know how it was done. "Hans," I said, letting relief color his name, "I'm so glad you're here."

"You know I'd do anything for you, Liesl." He sat down across the table from me and close to the telephone receiver. So far, so good.

I risked a glance to the back of the room. Wilhelm was staring at Hans. The clock on the wall opposite our table said 8:42. The wax cylinder on the Dictaphone would record for just under fifteen minutes.

I had no time to waste.

I swallowed and ran my tongue over my dry mouth. Gave him an uncertain smile. "Hans, I'm worried. About what's going on today."

His expression turned from expectant to unsure. "You know about today?"

"My brother is involved, and I'm just—" I put my hand to my mouth and blinked. I didn't have to pretend, thinking of what Fritz might have gotten himself into—and what heartbreak it had already caused.

Winterhalder reached across the table and grasped my hand. His was warm and moist. "Don't you fret your pretty head, Liesl. It's going to all go off without a hitch."

"Oh, Hans, do you know what he's doing—if he'll be safe?" I was improvising, much like following a dance for which I did not know the steps. I made myself meet his gaze.

"Do I know?" He lifted his chin with self-importance. "Liesl, I'm pulling off the whole operation. It was all my idea to start with."

I widened my eyes and looked impressed.

He didn't need any more of an encouragement. "As soon as old Selznick kicked the bucket, I said to Hermann, this is our chance to take out a pack of Jews at once. They're gathered like rats—won't even know what hit them. And after we're done with the Wilshire Boulevard Temple, and what Hermann and Thekla are doing at MGM, we'll be able to take over the studios. All of Los Angeles will thank us, Liesl."

I hid my surprise with effort. *What Hermann and Thekla are doing at MGM.* What did he mean by that? A cold apprehension filled my chest.

Winterhalder was just warming up. "Monroe's got a load of guns and ammo, backup from the Klan, our best boys picked out. You should be proud Fritz is part of it." Winterhalder's fingers groped up my wrist. "It's going to be a beautiful thing, Liesl." He brought my hand to his lips, his attention on my cleavage as he kissed my knuckles. He was stirred up and every word, every touch, increased my alarm.

I checked the clock. Nine minutes left of the recording. Perhaps I should have been more subtle, but I hadn't the time for subtlety. "What are Hermann and Thekla going to do at MGM?" I prompted, breathless with a mounting revulsion.

He began to administer kisses to my fingers. "Show them they can't make a laughingstock of the fatherland." He let go of my hand to form his own into the semblance of a gun, point it at me, and pull the trigger.

Fear shot through me. Kill someone at MGM? But who? And where? We needed to know more. "How—how are they—?" I didn't even know how to ask.

Winterhalder came closer. "We have people helping us. A spy at MGM—we got one real close to Perl—told us exactly where to be." Winterhalder leaned so close I could feel his hot breath. "I can't tell you how long I've waited for this moment, Liesl," he whispered, his eyes gleaming as they moved over my body. "I have some time. Let's get a room upstairs, some privacy."

"I—Hans." I choked and panic rose in me. I scrambled for a way— some way—to find out more without arousing suspicion.

My face must have shown something less than the ardor he was imagining, for his own passion abruptly cooled. "Hey." He straightened. "What's with you?"

Hans Winterhalder might be a womanizer, but he wasn't stupid. My mouth dried. "I just—" I swallowed. "I'm worried about you, Hans. And Thekla and Hermann." I was babbling. "My brother . . ." I searched for words and found none.

Winterhalder's face hardened. One hand closed over my wrist, circling it like a handcuff, hard and punishing. He looked around the room suspiciously. "What's with all the questions, Liesl?" His voice was cold steel.

We'd run out of time. I tried to formulate an answer but my mind was blank. I glanced to the back of the room for Wilhelm. He wasn't there. Winterhalder's grip tightened, pain shooting up my arm. He wrenched me close, his face hard and unyielding. "You got some kind of racket going on?"

CHAPTER 53

WILHELM

The plan was going south quicker than a Jack Dempsey knockout.

It took every ounce of control Wilhelm possessed not to clock Hans Winterhalder right there in the Emerald Room. Even from twenty feet away he could tell what was going on in the Nazi's dirty mind.

He hadn't liked the plan from the start. Liesl, on her own with that dog. The man was a degenerate and dangerous. It didn't matter that they were in public. Wilhelm had seen proof of that at the Lorelei. But if they were going to have a chance of stopping what was coming, they needed to get Winterhalder to talk.

But the way he was manhandling Liesl got Wilhelm's blood boiling.

That, and Wilhelm's left hand was starting to hurt like the dickens. The hard-boiled nurse had been the one to notice his hand after he'd had his heart-to-heart with Fritz. He didn't remember what had happened to it—something when he was carrying the boy out of the burning house. "Second-degree burn," she said and, with a surprisingly gentle touch, cleaned and bandaged him from his palm to above his wrist. Problem was, that was his shooting hand. He'd have to make do with his right hand like everybody else if need be. He'd switched his holster to the other side, but the gun felt wrong under his left arm and made him uneasy.

He watched Winterhalder from behind this morning's newspaper. That barracuda smile, looking Liesl over like she was his next meal. Didn't the mug have any decency at eight thirty in the morning? Wilhelm clenched his teeth and made himself stay in his chair.

From what he could see, Liesl was holding her own. She actually looked like she enjoyed his pawing and was listening to him like he was the latest and greatest. He knew she could act—hadn't she convinced him she was lock, stock, and barrel with the Friends of New Germany?

Winterhalder was flapping his gums, hopefully telling her everything they needed. Then Winterhalder started kissing her hands, just about made him sick. Under the table, Wilhelm's knee started that jiggle he always got when he was nervous.

Wilhelm tensed. Something was going on. Winterhalder's face was hard, his hand around Liesl's wrist. She looked scared.

That's when he knew the jig was up.

He put down the newspaper and ducked out the side door of the restaurant, down a hallway, and into reception. "Jimmy, I need your help."

Jimmy was all ears. Wilhelm whispered what he needed as quickly as he could. By the time he got back into the restaurant, Winterhalder and Liesl were standing—he had a grip on her arm and she looked frightened. His blood was burning through his veins and he wanted nothing more than to clock the man.

"Otto," Winterhalder said with surprise as he approached. "What are you doing here?"

"Saving your bacon," he said. "The Feds are here and they're looking for you."

Winterhalder dropped Liesl's arm. "What? How did they—?" He narrowed his eyes at Liesl.

"My guess is Schwinn." Wilhelm was glad he'd planted that distrust for Schwinn over the past few weeks. Came in handy.

Winterhalder sputtered. "He wants to take all the credit for today. I knew he'd turn on me."

Wilhelm looked over his shoulder. Jimmy was right on time.

"Sir, are you Mr. Winterhalder?" Jimmy asked in a whisper. "There are some men in the lobby who would like to talk to you." Jimmy looked appropriately nervous. "They say they're federal agents." If Wilhelm had his way, he'd put the kid up for one of those new acting awards they were giving out.

"How do I get out of here?" Winterhalder looked desperately around the restaurant.

Wilhelm took his arm and pulled him away from Liesl. "There's a secret door in the coatroom. Then you gotta get out of town. I'll take you to the station, you jump a train."

"I can't leave. I have—"

"Rather go to prison?" Wilhelm said. "I think they'll arrange it for you."

Winterhalder turned back. "Come with me, Liesl."

His suspicion of Liesl had disappeared fast.

"Oh, Hans," Liesl said. Wilhelm had to hand it to her; she looked distraught. "I have children to think of."

As if Winterhalder didn't. But the man didn't seem to give a flying monkey about them or his wife. Winterhalder started with some baloney about sending for her, that they could be together. Wilhelm had enough of the bad melodrama. "Come on." He gave Winterhalder's arm a jerk. He'd be hard put not to give this mug a knuckle sandwich on the way to the station.

CHAPTER 54

LIESL

"Are there really men in the lobby?" I asked the hotel clerk when Wilhelm and Winterhalder were gone.

He shook his head.

I wished there were. We needed help. This was worse than we thought, much worse. My mind was reeling with Hans Winterhalder's revelation. *What Hermann and Thekla are doing at MGM.* What did that mean? I was afraid I knew.

Der Angriff was more than the attack at the Wilshire Boulevard Temple.

I uncovered the telephone and picked up the receiver. "He's gone. Did it work?"

A moment of silence, then a click and Stella's voice as serious as the grave. "Get your fanny up here, Liesl."

I raced up five flights of stairs. Yitzak jerked open the door at my knock.

I was breathing hard. "Did you hear it? Did it—?"

Stella held up a hand to silence me. She wore the Dictaphone headset over her ears, her face a study in concentration. An interminable minute passed.

She slipped the headset off and nodded. "Faint, but you can hear it."

I was full of questions that needed answers. "Stella, what is going on at MGM? What was he talking about with Gary Perl?" But even as I asked, I remembered Herman Mankiewicz's film.

"*The Mad Dog of Europe*," she said, confirming my thoughts.

"What's that?" Yitzak said.

"It's a film about a housepainter named Mitler who goes on to be a dictator in Transylvania. Hates Jews, wants to take over the world." Stella rolled her eyes. "Sound familiar?"

Yitzak looked appropriately confused.

I tried to work it out. "Gyssling shut it down and so did Mayer, right? But Gary Perl decided to do it on his own." Gyssling. What had he said last night? He had things in hand with Mayer. Was he referring to *The Mad Dog of Europe*?

Stella kept on. "He's finishing up the filming soon, trying to get it released in some theaters. But it isn't likely, with Mayer against it."

"Are they filming today?" Something clicked through the fog of my sleepless night, the worry for Steffen, and the rush of danger in meeting with Winterhalder. The envelope from MGM. Two studio gate passes with Gary Perl's signature on them. *A spy . . . we got one real close to Perl . . . They can't make a laughingstock of the fatherland.*

Stella nodded. "I think so."

They were going to try to stop *The Mad Dog of Europe*. We hadn't much time. And yet, what could we do? And what about the Wilshire Boulevard Temple attack?

I felt like I'd downed several cups of Mutti's strong coffee. Winterhalder, MGM, the Selznick funeral—all of it whirling in my thoughts. What were we going to do? The dog—Lady—let out a whine. Two seconds later, there was a knock on the door.

Yitzak opened the door to Wilhelm, looking grim-faced, and Fritz. Wilhelm asked quickly, "Did it work?"

"What did you do with Winterhalder?" I asked instead of answering him.

"He's on a train to San Antonio," Wilhelm said. "That should get him out of our hair for a while."

One Nazi gone. That was something, at least.

I ushered them both inside. "Did you see anything? The Schwinns?" I asked Fritz.

"I sat outside the Alt Heidelberg. No sign of the Schwinns or the roadster. Themlitz closed up the bookstore and took the trolley toward downtown. I followed as far as I could, then figured I better get back here."

"You did right," Wilhelm said.

Wilhelm looked at Stella, who was resetting the Dictaphone. She offered him an earpiece. "You're going to want to hear this."

He put one earpiece close to his ear. I leaned over and listened in the other. As Winterhalder's comments became more suggestive, I could feel the anger coming from Wilhelm like a heat wave. At the mention of MGM, he met my gaze with alarm. When the reel went to scratchy silence, Wilhelm threw down the headset and paced to the window. Then back.

Stella told him about *The Mad Dog of Europe*. I told them both about the gate passes.

"Thekla and Hermann have some kind of plan to stop the filming," I said. "But what?"

Wilhelm turned on Fritz. "What do you know about this? And tell us the truth, Fritz."

Fritz's reaction was legitimate surprise. "I swear I don't know."

Wilhelm paced away again, then back. He pushed a hand through his hair, his expression dark. "We need to get to the synagogue and stop the Silver Shirts," he said. "And to MGM for whatever Thekla and Hermann are planning."

"What time is the funeral?" I asked Stella.

"Eleven," she said.

I looked at the clock. Nine twenty-five. We knew now what *der*

Angriff was. Monroe and the Klan attacking the Selznick funeral. The Jewish Brotherhood armed and waiting. A setup for violence. And a second attack—Hermann and Thekla on their way to MGM to somehow stop Gary Perl and *The Mad Dog of Europe.*

It was impossible.

Wilhelm checked his wristwatch and straightened. "We've got to split up."

I wished for nothing more than to go back to Steffen's bedside. Hold Tess's hand. Be with my children. Shrink my world back down to the tiny sphere it was months ago. Not the responsibility of strangers' lives on my hands. And yet I could not turn away from this. *If not me, who?*

I considered the people in the room: Wilhelm and Fritz, Yitzak, Stella, and myself. Split up. Yes, but then what? I paced to the window with the beginning—just a flicker—of a plan. "Stella, you and I will go to MGM." I turned to Wilhelm. "You and Fritz and Yitzak go to the synagogue."

"No, I'm going to the studio," Fritz said to me. Why must he always disagree? "I know the lot and the people. We don't even know where they're filming."

"He's right," Stella said, surprising me. "It's too much area to search. And I don't know what these two jokers—the Schwinns—even look like."

"But that leaves Wilhelm and Yitzak—"

"Hey, I'm not going to—" Yitzak interrupted.

Wilhelm cut him off. "Stahr and I can manage the synagogue. Fritz, do you have a gun?"

Fritz shook his head. Wilhelm strode to the small kitchen. He pulled out a drawer and came back with a revolver.

"No." There was no way I was allowing Fritz to carry a weapon. I stepped in front of him. "Give it to me."

Wilhelm looked at me in surprise. "You know how to use it?"

"Yes." I did target practice at the Western set, shooting bottles off the fence when I was fourteen. It would come back to me. I checked the cylinder—loaded—then stowed the gun in my handbag. Wilhelm didn't argue, and I liked him all the more because of it. I corrected myself quickly. I did not like Wilhelm. I respected him. He was sensible and smart and trusted by Leon Lewis. That was all.

"We need to make sure Lewis gets this tonight, as soon as he arrives," I said, snapping the Dictaphone case shut. I didn't know what would happen to us and we needed this evidence in the spymaster's hands. "But it will mean making a stop before we go to Culver City."

I hoped I was right about who could help us get the Dictaphone to Lewis.

Before we left, I had one more telephone call to make. "Central Hospital," I said into the receiver. I recognized the voice of the nurse who answered—not the sympathetic young girl but the matron with the military stare. I dared to hope for a miracle.

"No change, Mrs. Weiss," she said, and my hope wilted. "Tess is sleeping peacefully. Your little boy has not yet awakened." She paused as if checking her clipboard. "Frieda Stahr woke up and ate some breakfast. She is doing as well as can be expected." She spoke as if reporting on the weather. I asked to speak to Mutti. She sounded tired when she got on the line. "I need some help at MGM," I said. To her credit, she didn't demand much of an explanation.

"I'll tell the girls to meet you in the commissary."

I replaced the receiver and relayed the news of the children to Yitzak, who paced the room. The dog watched him from her place on the divan.

"Wait a minute," Stella said, concern in her voice. "What happened to the kids?"

With as little emotion as possible, I told Stella everything that happened after the evening at Gyssling's. She had tears in her eyes by the time I'd finished.

"Oh, Liesl, honey." She reached over and clasped my hand. "I'm so sorry." She turned to Yitzak and said the same to him. "I hope these Nazi scum get what's coming to them."

Wilhelm pulled me aside as we headed for the door. "Hurry," he said. As if I didn't know that time was running out. "And be careful."

I snapped, suddenly angry. "You're the one who told Fritz. That wasn't careful."

"Trust him." Wilhelm's voice was gentle. "He's a good kid."

I did not know if I believed that anymore. But I wanted to.

———————

Stella's auto was a cherry-red convertible coupe with a white leather interior, and she drove it like she'd had lessons from a blind man.

"Could we get anything more noticeable?" I said, holding on to the door as she jerked the wheel just before we hit the curb.

"Beggars can't be choosers, kiddo," she snapped. "I didn't know I'd be the getaway driver."

"I could have taken my—" Fritz began.

I cut him off. "That piece of junk wouldn't make it to Culver City."

My mind was spinning with what we were heading toward. Stella said the filming of *The Mad Dog of Europe* was hush-hush, but nothing was a secret at MGM. There was always someone who knew. We just had to find that someone. Then stop Hermann and Thekla and—if possible—get them arrested, all the while keeping my cover story as a Nazi.

Our chances of success were as likely as flying to the moon in Stella's red coupe.

But first, we made a stop at the Stevenson Agency.

Stella jolted to a halt outside the door and I jumped out with the Dictaphone. The same sentry in shirtsleeves stood guard, and he recognized me. I leveled my gaze at him. I had no time for this nonsense. He stepped aside.

Mrs. Porter did not smile when she saw me and I did not blame her. "I'm here for Leon Lewis." She raised her brows and I knew my instinct had been correct. "Get this to him as soon as he arrives on the five thirty train tonight." I put it on the floor next to her desk. "Make sure the wax cylinder—"

"—stays cool, yes, I know."

I was back in the front seat of the auto within three minutes and Stella lurched back on the road. "Don't you say a word about lady drivers," Stella warned Fritz, eyeing him in the rearview mirror.

He did not. In fact, Fritz looked miserable. And so he should.

"Liesl, I—" His words cut out with a strangled choke.

"I don't want to hear it." I would not feel sympathy for him. He didn't deserve it. He did not get to ask forgiveness after what he did.

Fritz leaned up on the seat, close to me, and I could see the gleam of tears in his eyes. "You've got to believe me—"

"Believe what? That you didn't mean to hurt Steffen and Tess? But what about Frieda?" I looked at Stella. "How about Stella? She's Jewish. What would your Silver Shirts think of that?" My voice had gone up and I realized just how angry I was—furious, in fact. I blinked back tears. How could Fritz have gone so wrong? "Vati would be ashamed of you." It was the worst thing I could think of to say and it hit its mark.

Stella glanced sideways with a disapproving frown.

"What?" She couldn't think that I was being too hard on him. He'd almost killed my children and Frieda. There was a chance Steffen wouldn't make it. And the hateful things he'd said—about her and Miriam and Yitzak.

"Maybe just listen to him. Let him tell his side."

I took a breath. If she, of all people, was willing to hear him out, I supposed I could. I turned sideways in my seat so I could meet his eyes. "So? Tell me."

He looked like he didn't know what to say. "It's just . . ." He ran a hand over his short-cut hair. "I don't know. It was Vati—he died for his country, to prove he was a good American. And look what it did to us. We were thrown out of our home. We lived on the street, Liesl. People called us huns and treated us like dirt because we were German."

I thought perhaps he didn't remember those days, but I'd been wrong.

"I think of that and then how Mutti worked so hard—and for what? To make guys like Goldwyn and Mayer richer than the president? Just to put a roof over our heads."

These were excuses, not reasons, and he could tell he wasn't convincing me.

"The thing was, when I got on the force, I felt like . . . like I belonged somewhere. Finally. You know how it was. We didn't have friends growing up. Not really. Hynes took an interest in me, invited me to this group. It was . . . good, to be part of something."

I could understand his need for friends. I'd felt that myself. "But, Fritz, the way they talk. What they believe. How could you?" My voice had gone accusatory again.

"Liesl," Stella warned. She jerked the auto onto Culver Boulevard and looked back in the mirror at Fritz. "You're looking for a place to belong, right? And they give it to you. And something to believe in—a better America and all that. It's understandable."

Fritz looked at her like she'd grown a third eye. "It is?"

"Understandable but still terrible," she amended.

He swallowed, his Adam's apple bobbing hard in his throat. "I was just so angry. All the time. At the world, at Tomas."

Tomas. I needed to tell him about Tomas. But now—so close to the studio and not knowing what we would face—was not the time.

Fritz's voice got accusatory then. "He didn't just leave you, Liesl. He left me, too. He'd been like a brother—and then he was gone. And you and Mutti, you treated me like a kid, like I couldn't be the man of the house."

"You acted like one," I couldn't help but mutter. Stella shot me another look.

Fritz let out a long breath. "I tried. I did. But you—you were always perfect, doing everything for Mutti and me. I couldn't measure up."

That stopped me. Was that really what he'd thought, that he had to measure up to me? I was far from perfect.

I took a breath, trying to reconcile to his words. His accusations. Perhaps it was partly my fault. "But, Fritz, they talk about killing Jews. Exterminating." I didn't want to use the word in front of Stella, but she didn't flinch.

"I don't want to kill anybody. I just—" He hung his head. "After what happened at Deutscher Tag, it got everybody fired up. I really believed it was the Jewish Brotherhood, like they said. But since then . . ." He rubbed his eyes and I realized he was fighting tears. "Something Wilhelm said got me thinking—I didn't really want to be this kind of person. This man. I've known that for a while. I just didn't know how to get out."

Maybe Stella was right. It was understandable but still terrible.

"But what about the Stahrs?" I asked him. "They are our friends, and what you did—"

"I didn't do it. Monroe did," he said stubbornly.

I wasn't buying that for a second. He might not have burned down the house, but he was partly responsible.

He saw the disbelief on my face and his hardened again. "But I was mad at them. Yitzak was always so ready to show me up. And then Tess, she told me Frieda wouldn't play with her anymore. And Miriam stopped talking to you after what good friends you had been—even I could see how much that hurt you."

My heart sank. *Oh, Fritz, how did you get it so wrong?* It had been my fault that Miriam and I weren't friends, that Tess and Frieda stopped playing together. The white marble pillars of Metro-Goldwyn-Mayer were before us and I didn't have time to explain it all to Fritz. We had a job to do. People's lives were at risk and I had to know if Fritz was with me or against me.

"Fritz," I asked, "can I trust you now? Because I really need to know."

CHAPTER 55

LIESL

"You can trust me, Liesl," he said, his anguished blue eyes meeting mine. "Honest."

I'd have to take him at his word because I needed his help. More than that, I needed a plan. I tried to think logically. Cleverly, like Thekla. One step ahead, like Leon Lewis.

If the Schwinns succeeded in whatever they were planning—and if the Silver Shirts massacred the Jewish studio heads at the Wilshire Boulevard Temple—every studio in Culver City and Hollywood would be affected. There would be opportunity for Nazis to take key positions in the studios and indoctrinate National Socialism across America through films and newsreels. A great step forward for the Nazis . . . and a disaster for the Jewish people of America.

Adolf Hitler was either a fool or a genius, and I feared he was not a fool.

Just weeks ago, I would not have believed the ideology of the National Socialists could gain ground here, in Los Angeles. But Lewis was right. People were looking for a scapegoat and the Jewish people were an easy target. The Nazis could make strides here just as they had in Germany. And what would happen to people like Leon Lewis and Stella and Miriam? Would we exclude Jews from schools, take their jobs, their businesses and property? Make them second-class citizens? Put them in camps?

It was up to us to stop it. Me, Stella, and Fritz. Wilhelm and Yitzak. We could not fail.

Stella pulled up to the tall white pillars that marched on either side of the Culver Boulevard entrance. "I don't have an auto pass," she said, glaring at the closed gate.

Gus shuffled out of the guard's hut with a smile. "Miss Liesl and young Fritz." Gus would let us in on foot, but autos were strictly limited. Too many in the crowded studio streets created chaos.

"Park here." As I grabbed my handbag, the weight of the gun inside reminded me of the seriousness of our mission. I didn't feel the sleepless night nor the fact I'd had nothing to eat since yesterday. My blood was pumping and my senses were on alert as if I were entering a battle. I jumped out of the auto as Stella parked crookedly on the street and we ran to the gate.

Gus opened the walk-through gate and I thanked him. "To the commissary," I told Fritz. "The girls will know where Perl is shooting the scene." At least, I hoped they would.

We hurried past Administration, then Costuming and Property. We passed the ten-foot schedule board outside the casting office. The studio was in full production, but no *Mad Dog of Europe* listed with the other films. I hadn't expected it to be that easy.

Stella bent down to rub her foot. "Why did I wear these shoes?"

We ran down Culver, passed the Lagoon, and cut around the powerhouse, where electrical lines crackled overhead. The commissary was between meals, and we found the girls sitting together at an empty table, drinking coffee and sharing a slice of Lottie's famous cheesecake.

Lottie took one look at me, Stella, and Fritz and put down her fork. "What's going on?"

"No time to explain." I bent over, my hands on my knees, and tried to catch my breath. "I'm looking for Gary Perl. He's in trouble." No need to watch my words with the girls. If one of them was the traitor at MGM, I'd eat Lottie's dirty apron.

"Oh!" Lottie straightened as if someone poked her. "I heard about Mr. Perl's film."

"So did I," Bette said. "Mayer is fit to be tied. Did you know Gary Perl bought the script from Mank for over—?"

"Bette," I interrupted. "We don't have much time. Where are they filming?"

Bette looked put out. She wrinkled her nose. "I'm not sure. But it's happening today."

"They waited until Louis B. was off the lot," Gina put in. "You heard about poor David O.'s father, didn't you?"

Lottie nodded sadly. "He was such a nice man, and to go like he did, so sudden—"

"Lottie," I cut in. "It's important."

"Oh." She recollected herself. "Well, let me see." She pursed her mouth. "Mr. Perl put out a call for extras—there's supposed to be hundreds of people. Some kind of crowd scene."

A shiver of cold went over my arms. Hundreds of people.

Gina jumped in. "It's somewhere on the east side. Property had a big truckload go that way. And I heard they used every gun in stock."

A truckload of guns. Of course they would be fake—or at least fire blanks—but the back of my neck prickled with alarm.

"It has to be one of the bigger soundstages," Lottie added. "Maybe—"

"Stage Fifteen," Fritz cut in.

He was right. Gary Perl would use the newest and largest of the soundstages for his clandestine film while Mayer and Thalberg weren't looking. Stage Fifteen was on the other side of the lot, through a labyrinth of narrow streets. It would take twenty minutes to get there on foot, even if we ran the whole way and if Stella wasn't wearing three-inch heels.

Gina picked up on our thoughts and handed me a set of keys. "Take the truck."

I gave her a quick hug, then said goodbye to Lottie and Bette.

"Give our love to your mother," they called out, waving as if we were going off to a school dance. It was better that they didn't know the truth of it.

"Let me drive," Fritz said as we piled into Gina's custodian truck outside the commissary. Stella didn't disagree.

My stomach lurched as we careened down Quality Street and through an alley that cut around the water tank. Fritz laid on the horn as a flock of chorus girls in boas and sparkles flitted in front of us. "Move your tail feathers, ladies!" Stella yelled out the window. We passed the actors' bungalows at a breakneck speed as I considered what we knew. Hundreds of extras. Thekla and Hermann Schwinn with a pass from Perl's office. Guns from Property.

We came out in the middle of a shoot on Western Street. Fritz accelerated past the saddle shop and a setup of cameras, barely missing a rolling boom cart and leaving men in our wake with raised fists.

"What's our plan?" Stella said as the soaring roof of Stage Fifteen came into sight.

"To warn Gary Perl if he'll listen to us," I answered. I thought of the gun in Hermann Schwinn's office. "And make sure no one dies." Also get Hermann and Thekla arrested and root out the spy at MGM. If we could manage all that without the Friends of New Germany finding out I worked for Leon Lewis, it would be a miracle.

Fritz parked on Seventh Street, and we ran for the stage entrance. A guard stood at the door, checking passes.

"*Mad Dog of Europe*?" I tried to come up with a story to get us in without a pass, but the guard took one look at Fritz in his uniform and stepped aside. I supposed having a police escort was of some use.

We entered the cavernous Stage Fifteen. It was over three hundred feet long and at least a hundred feet wide, constructed of steel and concrete, windowless so the light could be controlled. Scaffolding held racks of spotlights and camera gear, audio cables and reflector shields. The hum of voices bounced and echoed from the forty-foot ceiling.

My sight had yet to adjust to the gloom when Fritz grabbed my arm. "Liesl." Something about the way he said my name struck a chord of apprehension.

As my gaze swept the interior of the barnlike structure, I understood the anxiety in his voice. The set on the opposite side of the building could have been taken directly from a Germantown restaurant. Tables covered in checked red cloths, a polka band with a tuba and accordion, a bar lined with beer barrels and steins. A red, black, and white swastika flag hung in a spotlight.

But it wasn't the Nazi flag that made my breath stop in my throat. It was the hundreds of extras between where we stood at the door and the make-believe beer hall at the other end. Not men and women dressed in street clothes as in a typical crowd scene. These extras were all men, all dressed exactly alike in black trousers, silver shirts, and armbands with the bloodred swastika.

The vast room was packed with Nazis, and every last one of them carried a gun.

CHAPTER 56

WILHELM

Wilhelm slid into the driver's seat of the Cadillac. He didn't like leaving Liesl on her own—not without knowing what she'd be facing at MGM. But she was tough, he had to admit. And from what he'd seen of her tall friend, she wasn't one to cross either.

Then there was Fritz. He believed in the kid. But did the kid believe in himself? The Nazis—Monroe and the Silver Shirts—they'd given Fritz something to fight for, but it was the wrong thing. Would he figure out that Liesl needed him to fight for what was right?

He started the auto and pulled onto Grand. The Wilshire Boulevard Temple was a ten-minute drive—if he ignored the posted speed limits and traffic officers—but he had a stop to make first.

"Where are you going?" Stahr said as he turned onto Figueroa.

"To cut off the reinforcements," he answered. If he could catch them in time. "Tell me what we're looking at when we get there," he said. He needed to be prepared for anything, and a Jewish funeral wasn't something he had experience with.

"There will be a large crowd," Yitzak said. "Studio people, their wives, children. Probably hundreds."

Wilhelm swerved to avoid a milk truck puttering along at a snail's pace. "And the Brotherhood?" He'd underestimated Winterhalder and that burned him up. "How many will be there?"

Yitzak shook his head. "I don't know. Ten at least. We were told to bring what we could find for weapons."

Wilhelm clenched his teeth so hard they ached. Frustration and something like desperation rose in his chest. This wasn't Monterey. That time, it was him and five other Pinkerton agents on security duty for strikebreakers. The newspapers blamed it on the workers. Said they'd gotten out of hand.

That wasn't what happened. Not by a long shot.

He and his men were armed with guns and billy clubs. The strikers pulled out lead pipes and baseball bats. He knew the situation was going south, but he didn't know how to take down the tensions. He'd always been better with actions than words. Somebody fired a shot, a woman went down, and all hell broke loose. An agent named Fred—a kid who lived with his mother—took a hard hit to the back of his head. They dragged him to the auto, but it was too late. He died on the way to the hospital. The woman died in the street.

And for what? So that the canneries could keep paying their workers starvation wages while thugs like him got good money to keep the status quo. He'd walked away from Pinkerton that same day. But Fred and the woman stayed with him.

He wouldn't let it happen again. He wouldn't let another person die on his watch. Not an innocent person, not a guilty one. Not a Jew and not a Nazi. And if he could help it, he needed to keep his cover with the krauts. It would be a cute trick if he could pull it off. And he had to pull it off, because he had an uneasy feeling that this wasn't the final battle, but the beginning of a war.

He parked the Cadillac a block away from Klan headquarters. "Stay here," he said. Klansmen had an uncanny knack for recognizing a Jew. He found five men throwing baseball bats and tire irons into the trunk of a dusty Ford.

"Otto!" one of the men said with surprise. Wilhelm recognized him from his initiation. "Didn't know you were in on this."

"Perry," Wilhelm said with authority. He'd given some thought to his story and hoped it would work. "Change of plans. I was sent to warn you."

"What d'you mean? Who sent you?" Perry asked. The other men stopped loading the truck and drifted toward Perry. One carried an army-issue rifle.

Wilhelm's burned hand itched to check the gun under his arm, just to know it was there. He didn't. "Winterhalder sent me," he said. "Got wind there was going to be an ambush. The Feds."

The other men looked at each other and Wilhelm saw some doubt but also relief. They were a middle-aged bunch, most with soft bellies and pressed white shirts. Married, he guessed. "You can go ahead with it if you want." He shrugged. "But you're the ones who have to explain to the wife why you're in jail."

That hit home. "Come on, Perry," one of the older men said. "Delores will strangle me if I'm put in the pokey again."

Ten minutes later, Wilhelm was back in the Cadillac with Stahr, tapping the steering wheel impatiently and watching the door of Klan headquarters. Finally he saw Perry and the others go across the street into a tavern. They'd bought his story.

He started the Cadillac and headed toward Wilshire. They still had Monroe and his recruits to stop and it was already almost eleven o'clock. Before he'd left the Biltmore, he'd made a telephone call to the one man he thought he could trust to help them. He hoped he wasn't wrong.

They made it to the temple at 11:06 according to his wristwatch. He'd been banking on Monroe showing up after the funeral got started and it looked like he'd been right. The streets around the fortress of polished stone were lined with autos. Some Packards and Fords, but more gleaming Bentleys and a couple limousines. Wilhelm drove slowly around the block.

"What are we looking for?" Yitzak asked.

"Anything unusual." He parked a couple blocks from the entrance and they stepped out of the auto. "Keep your eyes open," he said to Yitzak. He touched the revolver in the holster under his jacket and hoped he wouldn't have to use it.

"The Brotherhood will be inside the front doors. Standing guard," Yitzak said as they moved quickly and quietly up the street.

"How long?" What did it take for Jews to speak of the dead?

"Twenty minutes or maybe an hour," Yitzak answered. "Hard to say."

The last time he'd been here was when he'd signed on with Lewis. Then he'd figured the Nazis as disorganized blowhards. He'd been wrong. Today, he hoped the Star of David over the door wouldn't be a witness to bloodshed—either Gentile or Jew.

He thought maybe he had it figured, the question that had hounded him since Monterey, the one about why God allowed evil like Winterhalder and the Nazis. Why he didn't stop them. He guessed that God did stop them—but not with fire and brimstone or smiting like Wilhelm would have done. No, he used people—good people like Leon Lewis, not-so-good people like himself. Gave them what they needed to work with and let them at it. Wilhelm would sure prefer the fire and brimstone, but maybe that's why God was God . . . and he wasn't.

He wondered if Liesl and Fritz made it to MGM and what they found. If they were in danger. He could do nothing for them. He had to focus on his task—stop Monroe and whoever was with him. Try not to show his hand to the Nazis. Whatever God had in store for him—and for Liesl and Fritz—he prayed they'd all make it out alive.

They skirted the wide stone stairs that led to the imposing doors. "We need to get you inside to talk to the Brotherhood, but not through there. Keep it quiet. Don't start a panic."

He wasn't sure about the Brotherhood, if they could be trusted. Better if they stopped the two groups from catching sight of each other. He'd rather be a messenger boy than some kind of swashbuckling hero. Leave the dramatics to somebody else.

Yitzak motioned to the side of the building. "Over here, maybe."

They moved around the temple to the south side, where a rose-shaped window of stained glass reflected the sun. His pulse settled into the calm he knew from the war, how he'd learned to survive when a split second could mean the difference between life and death, not only for himself but for others. He heard something—a rustling in the hedge bordering the stone walls. He motioned for Yitzak to stop and pulled the revolver from the holster. The gun felt awkward in his right hand. He sidled close to the hedge and peeked around, his pulse hammering.

He let out a breath. A kid—no, two kids.

They were dressed in neat suits, with the funny caps on their heads. Probably were supposed to be inside with their parents but snuck out of the service, like he used to do as a kid.

The bigger one caught sight of him—and the gun in his hand—and froze.

Wilhelm lowered the gun. "Kid," he said in a whisper, "how'd you get out here?" The kid looked wary. "Don't worry; we won't tell your folks."

The kids relaxed a little. The older one pointed to a pair of pillars and a narrow door behind.

"You go," Wilhelm said to Yitzak. "I'll stay out here, watch for Monroe and the Silver Shirts. You work on calming down the Brotherhood. Keep everybody inside until I give you the all clear. You understand?"

Yitzak nodded and disappeared through the hedge.

Wilhelm let out his breath and hoped the man could do the job. He looked around for the kids. They were gone. An engine rattled, the sound bouncing off the hard stone. The squeak of brakes in need of an oiling. He leaned around the corner. A Packard sedan, desert-dusty, came to a screeching halt at the foot of the stone steps. He caught the flash of Nazi armbands in the back seat.

His pulse surged and his mind cleared of all but what lay before him. He needed some luck, and he needed it now. Luck or the grace of God or whatever people chose to call it. He tucked the revolver out of sight, straightened his jacket, and stepped around the corner.

CHAPTER 57

LIESL

What was real, and what was the facade of Hollywood?

At least two hundred men in iron-gray shirts, gleaming black boots, and Nazi armbands stood at attention. They were extras, hired to lend authenticity to the scene. Sent by Central Casting, dressed in costumes furnished by Wardrobe, with guns provided by Property.

But what if they weren't?

Any of them could be real Nazis—Friends of New Germany or Silver Shirts. Anyone could be part of Hermann and Thekla's plan to put an end to Gary Perl and *The Mad Dog of Europe*.

We had to warn Gary Perl. Stop the film and get him to safety. How was it that I—the Heartbreak Hun as he had called me that day so long ago—must be the one to save Gary Perl? A question I had no time to ponder.

"Fritz," I said. "Stella and I will find Perl. You look for Hermann and Thekla. Stop them—whatever it takes."

All else inside Stage Fifteen was a typical film set. Barrel lights on the periphery and spotlights hanging from scaffolding lit up the set as bright as day. Electrical cords snaked along the floor to the main fuse box near the door. Assistants waited with clapper boards and reflecting umbrellas while dressers put last-minute touches on hair and adjusted hems. An air of organized chaos amplified by the sheer number of bodies throwing the floor.

"There he is." Stella, taller than the rest of the crowd, pointed to a boom cart near the center of the shoot and a hundred feet from where we stood. Gary Perl sat high on the cart, a megaphone in one hand. He bellowed an instruction to a group of actors standing at a podium in front of the Nazi flag. They wore somber business suits and homburgs, except one who stood apart, wearing a military dress uniform. He had dark side-parted hair and a toothbrush mustache. I grabbed Stella's arm. "Is that—?"

Stella nodded. "Cecil."

"I thought he was a producer?"

"He's always wanted to act." She pulled me forward into the throng. "Maybe he couldn't resist the irony of a Jew playing Hitler."

"Places!" Gary Perl shouted, his voice amplified and tinny. The Nazi soldiers closed ranks. A solid wall of men between Gary Perl and us.

"People, let's remember what we're doing," an assistant bellowed at the extras through his own megaphone. "Soldiers, silence. When Herr Mitler says the line, you point your rifles at the men up here." He pointed to the line of actors who looked like bankers. "And hold that pose. Everybody else, out of the shot!"

Stella pushed through a rank of soldiers like a steamship. I followed in her wake.

"Lights!" Gary Perl's voice came through the megaphone, distorted and metallic. The lights on the scaffolding snapped on, blinding white. The set bulbs, perched on stands ringing the podium, flared to life. "Where are my storm troopers?" Perl demanded. "Get them front and center and ready to fire. Remember, do not shoot until Herr Mitler has fired his pistol into the air."

I raised myself onto my tiptoes to see the set, blinking in the bright glare.

Ten Nazis stepped forward. They were all clean-cut Aryan types, almost identical in their uniforms and military hats. "Make it look good, boys," the assistant director added. "Even with blanks we need to see kickback."

That was when I saw him—Hermann Schwinn—among the storm troopers positioned in front of the podium. He had a rifle in his hands and I wouldn't bet Cecil's life that it was a prop. The man I knew from the Friends of New Germany wouldn't take well to a Jewish man blaspheming the chancellor of Germany. Cecil was in as much danger as Gary Perl.

"Wait!" I stopped Stella, looked desperately over the heads of the extras for Fritz. Where had he gone? Why wasn't he here when we needed his help? A tremor of unease flickered through me. He'd said I could trust him. "Stella." I pointed to the set. "Get to Cecil. One of those storm troopers is Schwinn, but don't let on you know. Not yet." I didn't want Hermann to know we were here until we found Thekla. Hermann was determined and brutal, but Thekla was clever. She would have a backup plan and I wanted both of them caught red-handed.

Stella veered toward the set.

I wove through the usual assortment of script holders, assistants, and assistants to the assistants, trying to hold down my panic. "I need to talk to Mr. Perl. Immediately," I demanded when a bottle blonde with black lashes and crimson lips stepped in front of me.

"Mr. Perl cannot be disturbed," she said in a crisp way. I recalled her then. Gary Perl's secretary, the one who had tried to stop me the day I slapped him. A bodyguard with shoulders like a prizefighter and an expression to match stepped up to block me.

"Mr. Perl!" I shouted toward the boom cart. The buzz of the lights and the shuffling of two hundred booted feet drowned out my voice. I looked desperately toward the set. I saw Stella, still twenty feet from the podium. As if in slow motion, I watched her heel snag on an electrical cord and she fell. She scrambled to her knees, wrenched off her shoes, stumbled in her stockings toward Cecil.

My eyes went to Hermann. He had his rifle at the ready but was not watching Cecil or Perl. His gaze was focused upward—at the catwalk above me. I looked up and saw movement. Someone was up there.

Then, through the glare of lights, I made out a form. Thekla.

Her hair was covered with a dark cap and she wore trousers and a work shirt, but I recognized those sharp features. I caught the glint of gunmetal. The silver pistol she held was not a prop. She crouched in the shadows of the scaffolding, directly over Gary Perl with a clear line of sight. Unless she was a terrible shot, she wouldn't miss.

I had little hope Thekla was a terrible shot.

"He's in danger—" I began to tell the assistant, to insist that I get to Gary Perl. But she was already looking at Thekla . . . and not with an expression of surprise.

I understood then. She was the spy—the one funneling studio information to the Friends and the passes Hermann and Thekla had needed to get on the set. Perhaps she had even given them Leon Lewis's name. Her hard eyes met mine. The muscleman stepped closer. I slipped my hand into my handbag and felt for the gun.

"Quiet on the set!" the aide said through his megaphone.

As if it were playing out on a screen, I saw the Schwinns' brilliant plan: Adolf Mitler fires into the air; on that cue the storm troopers fire at the men in suits. Hermann—with a real gun and ammunition—shoots Cecil, and Thekla takes her shot at Gary Perl from the rafters. He and Cecil, dead. Perhaps others. Hermann and Thekla get away in the ensuing panic.

I must stop the scene from rolling. I pulled the revolver from my handbag. A quick look up in the rafters. Thekla pointing the pistol directly at Perl. I raised my revolver and put my finger on the trigger.

"Cameras rolling," Perl said in the now-silent room. "Action!"

"*Mad Dog of Europe*, scene four, take one." The scene clapper came down with a snap and three things occurred in such quick succession as to be almost simultaneous.

I fired my gun into the air.

I heard the report of Thekla's pistol from the rafters.

And the entire soundstage went utterly dark.

Then all was disorder and chaos. A man's voice cried out. Panic as two hundred people reacted to the darkness. The rumble of feet, a crash as equipment was overturned. I stood entirely still, a rush of air as bodies passed by me, exclamations and cries. Had I stopped Thekla or had her bullet found its mark?

It was no more than thirty seconds before the electrical came to life with a click and buzz. A flood of light seared my eyes. I blinked to clear my sight. The assistants and aides, the grip boys, and the camera operators were gone, stumbling toward the periphery of the set. I stood alone, the gun still in my hand.

Gary Perl lay before me, a blossom of crimson on his shirtfront.

The blonde secretary screamed.

I looked up at the catwalk. Thekla Schwinn had vanished.

CHAPTER 58

WILHELM

The men—boys, really—who tumbled out of the dusty Packard were all familiar faces. Maybe it was an answer to his prayer or maybe dumb luck. He'd take it and be thankful.

Lenny, the redhead. Then the brothers, Kurt and Kyle. Eldrich, pushing his glasses up his nose. Wilhelm took account of their weapons. Lenny held a rifle, the brothers with pistols on their belts. Eldrich had that shiny Colt revolver. The driver stepped out—Travis Monroe with a sawed-off shotgun. Wilhelm wasn't so thankful to see him.

He schooled his expression. As far as they knew, he was on their side.

The thing was, he really *was* on these kids' side. They were pawns in this chess game that Monroe and Winterhalder—Adolf Hitler, even—were playing. These boys didn't know any better, and they deserved a chance to change their minds before they did something stupid.

Wilhelm rounded the corner and moved up the steps to stand in front of the tall triple doors. He learned in the war to capture the high ground, even if it wasn't all that high. Lenny looked up, and relief showed on his face. That told Wilhelm a lot.

"Who's in command, son?" He was afraid he already knew.

"I am." Monroe pushed Lenny out of his way and advanced up

355

three steps. The boys stayed back, looking uncertain. They didn't trust Monroe, and Wilhelm could use that.

Monroe's face was all suspicion and zeal. "I wasn't told you were in on this, Otto."

Maybe he could bluff, like he had with the Klan. "Winterhalder sent me to warn you," Wilhelm said. "The Feds are on their way. Mission aborted." He made his tone cooperative, not commanding. Men like Monroe didn't like taking orders. "We need to get out of here before they show up. Meet back up in the hills and regroup."

The boys in his line of vision visibly relaxed; the two brothers turned back to the truck. They didn't want to be here.

"Hang on." Monroe put out a hand to stop the retreat. He moved up one more step toward Wilhelm, looking up with narrowed eyes. "I saw Winterhalder last night. He didn't say abort."

"Just got word from Perry and his men at Klan headquarters," Wilhelm tried. He had a sinking feeling his ruse wasn't going over with Monroe.

"We're here to teach these people a lesson," Monroe said. He motioned the boys forward. "And we'll do our part without Perry if we need to."

The boys took a few steps. Stopped. Looked to Wilhelm for permission.

"He's not your commander," Monroe barked. "I am."

Wilhelm stayed at the top of the steps, guarding the doors behind him. Had Yitzak found a way to warn them? Would anyone believe him? Or would the Jewish Brotherhood come out ready to fight and he'd have a massacre on his hands?

He remembered how it was in the war. How at first it hadn't seemed real. Not in basic training, not even on the ship over to the front. Then the first battle. It had been a small skirmish, a few shots fired. Instead of panic and fear, he'd felt nothing but calm focus. When he thought it over later, that had scared him more than anything else.

That same dead calm was on him now. He considered the faces in front of him. If someone had talked to him before Monterey—if somebody would have given him a way to back down and still save face—would he have listened? He hoped so. Talking wasn't his strong suit. He'd always been better with action. But this time, he'd have to find the words to turn these kids around.

He abandoned reasoning with Monroe and spoke directly to Lenny. "You don't want to do this." He looked to Eldrich and the brothers, Kyle and Kurt. "None of you do."

They glanced at each other with guilty expressions.

"This isn't your—" Monroe sputtered.

He ignored Monroe, cutting off his bluster. "There are women and children in there. Old people. Did they tell you you'd be shooting at kids?" He lowered his voice, tried not to make it an accusation, but a real question they needed to think on. "Is this the kind of men you want to be?"

Monroe opened his mouth to protest, but Kurt beat him to it. "We're doing it for our country."

Figured. Spouting what they'd been taught. It was time to tell them the hard truth.

"Listen, Kurt, Kyle." His gaze took in each young man. "Winterhalder and Schwinn are bought and paid for by the German government. They're sending you on a suicide mission for their own ends. Do you know who's inside there?" He nodded to the big doors.

"Jews?" It was Eldrich who answered, but uncertainly.

"Sure," he agreed. "And the Jewish Brotherhood. Armed and ready to shoot."

Lenny jerked his gaze up to the doors. Kurt and Kyle each took a step backward.

Eldrich shook his head. "He told us—"

"Told you it was just going to be a show of force, right?" Wilhelm said. "Shoot up the synagogue. A little scare for the Wilshire Boulevard Jews? Nobody gets hurt."

He had them listening, at least. Problem was, he was going to have to lay his cards on the table. When he did, it would be impossible to keep spying for Lewis. But it couldn't be helped if he wanted to save these kids. "Winterhalder tipped off the Brotherhood and set up a gunfight. Nothing gets people riled like martyrs. And guess who they are looking at to die for the cause?"

The boys looked at each other. Monroe didn't move. This was news to him and he was figuring what to do. It was taking time in that slow brain of his.

Wilhelm tried to figure what else to say. What could change their minds? These boys had told him their stories over doughnuts and sandwiches; he knew what made them join up and maybe what would make them think again. "Lenny." He started with the kid who seemed to be one they looked to. "What will your mother and sister do? You're the only one bringing in a paycheck for your family." Lenny looked at the rifle in his hands with a frown.

"Eldrich, you want to go to college, right?" The kid had told him that. "Think about your future. You go in here—" he jerked his head back to the doors—"you won't have one." Monroe was coming up the stairs toward him. Wilhelm started to talk fast. "Kurt, Kyle. This isn't what you signed on for—"

"No more talking." Monroe barged toward him. "We're going to shoot some Jews."

Just like in the war, time seemed to slow. He saw Lenny falter, looking uncertain. Kurt and Kyle stepping forward as ordered. Eldrich stockstill, watching and thinking. Wilhelm wasn't going to pull his gun on Monroe and make these boys choose between the two of them. That was too risky. No, there was another way.

He clenched his jaw, lowered his shoulders, and charged at Monroe. The man had fifty pounds on him, but Wilhelm had the element of surprise and simple gravity. He hit him hard and together they plunged down the stairs. Carried by Monroe's weight, they hit the pavement like a train wreck.

He heard the shotgun go off, felt a burn in his shoulder. Monroe's heavy body jolted and rolled under his. A grunt of pain that wasn't his own voice.

Wilhelm assessed the damage. He hurt all over, mostly his right side, but he was still alive and kicking. He shook off the pain and scrambled to his feet. Monroe groaned but didn't get up.

The synagogue doors opened with a shrill squeal. A half-dozen men stood framed in the arched doorway, the dim sanctuary behind them. He tried to focus his blurred vision. At least two had guns; the others held clubs. Their expressions were grim and the way they stood at the door meant business.

He tried to think. He needed to get between his boys and the Brotherhood. "Don't move," he told Lenny and others. "Don't do anything."

His body wasn't moving as fast as it should. He stumbled up the stairs, kept his hands where the men could see them. He had a sudden memory of the front. The huns on one side, his band of wet-behind-the-ears soldiers on the other. No-man's-land in between.

Where was Yitzak?

He made it to the top of the stairs. Yitzak appeared at the door. "Stahr," Wilhelm said, his voice sounding not at all like it should. "Tell them not to shoot," he said. "It's over. Just a—"

"Papa!" A high voice came from Otto's left. The little boys from before. Where had they come from?

He heard the unmistakable cock of a shotgun behind him. He whirled around. Monroe was up, his weapon and his attention trained on the men in the doorway. Movement in the corner of Wilhelm's eye. One of the boys, running headlong into the no-man's-land between the Jewish Brotherhood and the Silver Shirts.

Monroe took aim.

The men in the doorway jostled. Yitzak shouted. Couldn't they see the gun? Wilhelm swayed, his reflexes slowed by the tumble down the stairs. He tracked the little boy's speed in what seemed like slow motion. Monroe was going to shoot at the men and that boy was going to die. He pulled his gun from the holster, his right hand awkward and pain ricocheting through his shoulder. He saw his weapon come up but knew he was moving too slow.

The crack of a shot. Wilhelm's heart dropped. He was too late.

The boy didn't fall. He reached a man in the doorway and threw his arms around his legs.

It was Monroe who went to his knees, the shotgun clattering on stone. Wilhelm snapped his gaze to the foot of the stairs. Eldrich lowered his revolver, his hands shaking and his face as pale as death. "He was . . ." He stopped. Swallowed. Looked at the gun in his hands as if it had life of its own. "The kid . . ."

Wilhelm felt a rush of relief so strong his knees almost buckled.

Police sirens split the silence.

"Lenny, Eldrich," he shouted. "Get out of here, quick." Suddenly it all came together. How it might just work for him and the boys.

Monroe groaned and clawed up the stairs, reaching for his dropped rifle. The man did not give up. Wilhelm took a few steps down, kicked the rifle clear. The boys stood there like idiots. "Go, all of you!"

They jumped as if coming out of a trance and ran for the Packard. If the kids had any sense, they wouldn't breathe a word of this to anyone. If they were smart, they would wash their hands of the Silver Shirts altogether. The Packard started and roared away.

Wilhelm turned to the men in the doorway who were bunching up and looking apprehensively toward the oncoming sirens and Yitzak. "All of you, out the back way with Yitzak."

"They didn't do anything," Yitzak said, looking at his comrades.

"You think the police are going to care?" Wilhelm motioned to their weapons. "They see you with guns and clubs, you're going to get arrested if you don't get shot first."

Yitzak jerked his head at Monroe. "What about him?"

Wilhelm looked at Monroe, cursing a blue streak and holding his hands over a bleeding wound on his thigh. "I'll take care of him."

CHAPTER 59

LIESL

Thekla hadn't missed her shot.

What about Hermann? I turned to the men at the podium. All standing, blinking in surprise and confusion. All except Cecil. He and Stella lay on the floor in a tangle of arms and long legs. Had Hermann gotten off a shot in the chaos? They rolled over, scrambled to their feet, both unhurt. I let out a relieved breath.

Gary Perl twitched, then groaned.

"Get a doctor!" I told the stocky guardian who had blocked my path and was now cowering behind the boom cart. The secretary had disappeared and not to get help for Gary Perl, I knew. One of the extras in a Nazi uniform sprinted toward us. "I'm a doctor," he said. He knelt down next to Perl and began to bark instructions at the onlookers.

Stella ran to me in her stocking feet. "Is he dead?"

The doctor looked up at her. "He needs to get to a hospital immediately. Who has a fast car?"

I looked to Stella. "Go."

I needed to find Fritz. Chase down Thekla and Hermann. I started for the door. They could have gone anywhere—on the lot or out the east gate. A guard stepped in front of me—the one who had let us in the soundstage door. He had a gun and it was pointed at me.

"Drop the weapon, ma'am."

I looked dumbly at the gun still in my hand as understanding dawned.

"Drop it." Now his voice was higher, nervous. His hand trembled as he aimed his weapon at me.

My thoughts, like an adding machine, suddenly calculated what had just happened. I was a disgruntled secretary fired from MGM. A known anti-Semite. Two hundred people had seen me standing over Gary Perl with a smoking gun. I slowly set the gun on the floor and raised my empty hands.

If I didn't find Thekla Schwinn and prove she was the one who shot Gary Perl—I would go to jail. In fact, I was going to jail right now.

"I've got it from here, Louis." Fritz came out of the dark recesses of the soundstage into the circle of light. The look on his face was cold. Fritz walked closer, kicked my gun to the side while the other guard kept his pointed at me. Fritz roughly pulled my hands together. My heart began to pound in earnest. The cold metal of handcuffs circled my wrists. "You are under arrest for attempted murder," Fritz said. "You better hope the Jew lives."

This was the Fritz from before—the Jew hater, the Silver Shirt, the Nazi. The brother I did not know and had hoped was gone forever. I should never have trusted him.

Fritz marched me out of the studio and into the hot glare of the sun. The handcuffs bit into my wrists and his grip cut into my arm. Had Fritz pulled the electrical switch and thrown the studio into darkness? Was he part of Thekla's plan all along?

A patrol auto pulled up and disgorged three uniformed officers. Fritz said a few short words about Captain Hynes and the Germantown station. "I'll take her in. You start with the statements," he said to the other officers.

He shoved me into the rear seat of the auto and got behind the steering wheel. We drove through the north gate. He lifted a hand in salute to the guard on duty. He drove to the first corner and pulled over. He turned around. My breath stopped. Was this my brother or a Nazi?

"Maybe I should have taken up acting instead of police work." He grinned. "The look on your face, Lies!"

I didn't know whether to hug him or smack him. I let out a pent-up breath. And a laugh. And a sob. "I—I'm sorry—Fritz . . ."

He stopped me. "Don't be sorry. I've been a real blockhead." He unlocked my handcuffs and started the auto again, pulling onto Culver Boulevard. "We need to get you someplace safe."

I scrambled into the front seat. Straightened my dress. Considered what we were facing. Thekla and Hermann could be anywhere by now. And it wouldn't take long for someone to figure out I was not on my way to the Germantown police station.

"A hotel, maybe?" he said. "Or we could drive to—"

"Take me to the hospital." I knew where I had to be.

"They'll find you there," Fritz objected. "They think you—"

"I know what they think." If I was going to go to jail for killing Gary Perl, I would spend my last free hours with my children. "Tess and Steffen first."

Fritz didn't argue.

We parked at the hospital and entered through the back door. What would I find here? I prayed for a miracle as we slipped into the dim room. Miriam slept in a chair beside Frieda. Mutti was gone. The gray-haired nurse stood over a cot set up between Frieda's and Steffen's beds. I peered over her shoulder to see a sleeping Tess and gave the nurse a questioning look.

"Your daughter," the nurse whispered in answer, "was quite determined to be beside her brother and her friend." She frowned. "She's very persuasive and it might do them all good. She's just fallen asleep, so do not disturb her."

I bent over Steffen, who looked just as he had when I left. Small and pale and silent. I glanced up at the nurse, hoping against hope.

"No change," she said gently. "I'm sorry."

She left in silence, passing Fritz, who guarded the half-open door as if a squadron of officers was coming for me.

I was suddenly overwhelmed with weariness. Gary Perl was shot, perhaps dead. Thekla and Hermann had escaped. I knew nothing of what happened at the temple, if Wilhelm had been able to stop the massacre. Would Hermann and Thekla and the rest of the Nazis get away with murder? Was Leon Lewis's spy operation exposed? Would I lose my little boy?

I had done all I could do—all I knew to do. It did not seem fair. I'd tried my best, done my duty, and all had gone wrong. I had nothing left to give.

I slipped off my shoes and gingerly lay down beside Steffen in the bed. Close to my sweet boy, with Tess's soft snore lulling me, I closed my eyes and slept.

CHAPTER 60

WILHELM

The Silver Shirts and the Jewish Brotherhood were gone by the time two police automobiles pulled up to the synagogue. Wilhelm sat on the top step keeping an eye on Monroe and holding a handkerchief over his own bleeding shoulder. Just a graze, but it hurt like the dickens and worse, it was his right arm. He'd better not have to shoot anybody anytime soon.

Monroe went from bluster to whimpers, his face screwed up as he stanched the wound on his thigh with both hands. Wilhelm didn't have an iota of sympathy for the man.

A crowd gathered behind him at the doors of the synagogue. Men dressed in fancy suits and women in black hats and veils. Plenty of witnesses, that was good. Now if he could get the rest of it to come together.

Brody trotted up the stairs, fast for a man his age. "Stay back, folks. Nothing to worry about." To Wilhelm, he said, "On your feet."

Wilhelm followed his order and put his hands together for Brody to put on the cuffs.

"I'll take this big guy," Brody told the two officers who followed him up the stairs. He nodded to Monroe. "You get that one to the station and probably a doctor." Monroe struggled and cursed while the two officers grappled him into the auto.

Brody made a show of putting Wilhelm in the back seat of his auto, then went around to the driver's seat and started the engine. "Where to?" he asked.

Wilhelm directed him to where the Cadillac was parked two blocks away. When they got there, Brody unlocked the cuffs. "Going to tell me what happened there?"

"Gotta get somewhere," William said.

"You need to get to the hospital." Brody frowned at his arm.

Wilhelm ducked out of the auto. The bleeding had stopped and he figured he could manage to drive. "Keep Monroe out of sight at the station. I don't want him talking until we figure out what to do with him. Plenty of your men are on his side of the fence."

"Don't I know it." Brody's bushy brows came together. "I've got a nice private cell for him in the basement."

It took Wilhelm far too long to get to Culver City, driving with his bandaged left hand. By the time he did, it was one o'clock. The MGM entrance was lined with police autos and uniformed patrol. Whatever happened with the Schwinns, he'd missed it.

He got out and tried to look like he knew what he was doing. He flashed the gun under his jacket to the first uniform he came upon. "Hynes sent me. What happened?"

The officer nodded. "Lady shot some bigwig on one of the sets."

A lady? Thekla Schwinn? "Get her name?"

The officer shrugged. "Some secretary. Had a beef with him, they say."

He didn't react but his mind was clicking. Didn't like the sound of that. "Who got shot?"

"A director somebody. He's gonna live." He didn't seem to care one way or another. "Just taking statements. Pretty cut-and-dried. Everybody saw it."

"Where's the secretary?" He wanted to shake the answers out of the complacent cop but he held his temper.

"On her way to the Germantown station."

What happened to Liesl? And what about Thekla and Hermann Schwinn? Anxiety drummed through him.

The officer kept on. "Sheesh. Never can tell. Pretty girl like that but—" he twirled his finger around his ear—"cuckoo."

He needed to find Fritz and Liesl, get caught up. Problem was he couldn't think where they would go. Not the station, at least he hoped not.

"Sir?" the officer said, looking concerned at the blood on his shirt. "You need to get to the hospital."

The hospital. Of course. "Yes, I do."

By the time Wilhelm made it to the hospital, he was feeling light-headed.

A nurse took one look at him, ignored his protests, and ordered him to a triage room. He wasn't about to sit around waiting for a doctor when he didn't know what had happened to Liesl, but when he tried to stand up, the room spun around him and the nurse gave him what for and a glass of orange juice.

A pouchy-faced doctor came in and cleaned the wound. "Just a graze, but you'll need to keep it clean and watch for infection."

As if he didn't already know that. He'd been in the war, for pete's sake. "Can I go?"

"If you must." The doctor put the instruments on the metal tray. "You're the second gunshot wound we've had today and a better patient than the other guy."

That got his attention. "Who else?"

The doctor rubbed his hound-dog cheek. "An executive of some sort from MGM. Everyone in the hospital is atwitter."

"He got shot? Did he—? Is he—?" Wilhelm stood, swayed a little, and grabbed his jacket. "Where is he?"

"Steady there, man." The doc gave him an assessing look. "He is alive, if that's what you are asking. In a private room on the second floor. He's not allowed visitors, so—"

Wilhelm was already out the door and looking for the stairs.

He found Gary Perl's hospital room easy enough. Just followed the sound of raised voices and the reek of expensive cigars. When he walked in, he thought maybe he really had passed out and this was some kind of fever dream.

Gary Perl—he presumed, since he'd never met the guy—lay propped up in the bed, smoking a cigar and having a heated argument with Fritz. What was Fritz doing here without Liesl? Then he did a double take. He wasn't imagining things. Liesl's mother was giving Louis B. Mayer a scolding to beat the band.

"I knew you when you were starting out, Louis." Her voice was like nails on a chalkboard. "Don't tell me you can't do anything—"

"Excuse me?" Wilhelm cut in. He wasn't normally disrespectful to older ladies, but he didn't have time for this. "Mrs. Bittner, do you—?"

"And you!" She turned on him next and he wished he'd kept quiet. "Ever since you showed up, my daughter—"

"Where's Liesl?" He tried Fritz.

"Sleeping," Fritz said unhelpfully.

"She shot me," Perl said with a distinct whine in his voice. "And I want her arrested."

Wilhelm had an almost-overwhelming urge to slap the man.

"She's had it in for me since she worked for MGM and everybody knows it."

Mrs. Bittner turned her ire on the man in the bed. "She did not shoot you, young man. And if you say that one more time, I'll put that cigar where—"

"A-*hem*!" Silence descended as a steely-eyed nurse marched into the room, plucked the cigar from Gary Perl's mouth, and pointed it at the door. "Out. All of you."

They complied, filing into the hallway in a silence that didn't last long. Mrs. Bittner started in again on Mayer. "Louis, I—"

"Nell," Mayer interrupted her, "I'm not going to drop the charges just because you used to work for me. She's got to answer for what she did."

"She did no—"

"Mutti." Fritz put a hand on her. "You've said your piece. The children need you."

That seemed to take the wind out of her sails and she gave Mayer one last glare, then one for Wilhelm, and turned with a huff to walk away. He could see where Liesl got her gumption. He met Fritz's gaze. Whatever happened with Liesl, they needed to get it cleared up. He turned to Mayer. "Can we talk somewhere private?"

Mayer didn't look like he wanted to talk at all, but he brought them out the side door of the hospital where a black limousine was parked in a doctors-only parking space. The driver opened the door. The back seat was the size of a train car, with two leather benches facing each other and plenty of legroom. They all took a seat and Mayer opened a polished silver humidor, selected a cigar without offering one to either of them, and began to speak. "Now, let me tell you—"

"With all due respect, sir," Wilhelm interrupted. "I want Fritz to tell me what happened at the studio." Sure, Mayer was used to running the show but Wilhelm didn't have time for posturing.

Fritz told him a story that had his mouth gaping like a landed fish. "Wait," he couldn't help but interject. "Why did you knock out the electrical?" It seemed like a dumb thing to do, seeing that there were guns involved.

"I figured it would stop everybody. And we didn't know how many of the Nazis were real and who were extras." He shook his head and looked contrite. "But it didn't work that way."

"So Thekla got away and nobody saw her shoot Perl." It wasn't really a question.

"That's what he says," Mayer jumped in with impatience. "But Perl doesn't agree."

"That's what happened," Fritz said firmly. "I took Liesl into custody."

That was smart. He was glad the uniform had come in handy.

"She wanted to come here, to be with Steffen and Tess," Fritz finished. "But it won't be long before Hynes and the rest start looking for her."

"As it should be," Mayer said, puffing at the cigar as he held a flame to the end. "Let the police sort it out. If she's innocent, then she has nothing to worry about."

Wilhelm didn't believe that, and Mayer should know better. What he wouldn't give for Lewis's gift of diplomacy. Instead, he'd have to work this out his own way. "Mr. Mayer." He pinned the executive with his flat stare. "I believe you were at the Selznick funeral today?"

Mayer stared back. "Yes, and I heard about the brouhaha that went on, if that's what you're getting at." He breathed out a thick veil of smoke.

Wilhelm's neck got hot at that. He leaned forward. "Let me tell you what that *brouhaha* was, Louis." He said it with the ice in his voice that never failed to get people's attention. It worked this time, too.

He told Louis B. Mayer very clearly about the guns and grenades, the Klan and the Silver Shirts. The Hollywood mogul went pale and didn't notice the cigar dropping ash on his trousers. As Wilhelm went on with the details of Travis Monroe and the little boy who almost got shot, the president of MGM looked like he might be sick.

"That was what Leon Lewis's agents stopped, Mr. Mayer," he concluded. He pulled his jacket open to show the blood still staining his shirt, the bandage visible under the torn fabric. "Edelweiss and her brother saved Perl's life and the lives of who knows how many others at your studio today. Yitzak Stahr and I saved your sorry backside and dozens of men, women, and children in the Wilshire Boulevard Temple."

Mayer choked a little, tapped the dripping ash into a compartment on the door beside him. "I see your point, Mr.—" He frowned. "I didn't get your name."

"You don't need my name." He kept on with the cold demeanor that worked well to convince people he was a Nazi. "You need to tell Mr. Gary 'Crybaby' Perl to drop the charges against Liesl Weiss. And then you're going to pony up the funds you promised Leon Lewis so he can stop these Nazis, who, by the way, are not going to give up until they kill every Jew in this city."

Louis B. Mayer stared at him, maybe finally comprehending the danger that these men posed not only to the studios, but to America.

Wilhelm glanced at Fritz, who was watching with undisguised admiration.

Mayer recovered himself, harrumphed, and hesitated. Finally he held out his hand. "You have a deal."

CHAPTER 61

LIESL

Through the fog of a bone-weary sleep, I felt a featherlight touch on my cheek.

"Mommy."

I was home and it was time to get up. Breakfast, then dishes and get Tess to school. Laundry day. Or was it Saturday and cleaning? The soft warmth of the little boy beside me lured me back to sleep. A little more time.

"Mommy?" Steffen's voice.

Something about his voice was wrong—raspy, as if his throat was dry. The hand touched my cheek again, my hair. I pulled myself from the cocoon of sleep. A sterile room and dim lights. The hospital, the fire. I jerked up and focused. Steffen's sleepy eyes were open. My hope bloomed. I touched his face, unable to speak. My tumble of thoughts—MGM, Gary Perl, the Schwinns—none of it mattered. Steffen was awake.

Thank you, Lord.

He was so pale, his eyes unfocused. Worry jolted through me. "How do you feel?"

"Thirsty," he whispered.

Mutti was by my side in an instant, her voice loud and insistent. "Get the nurse—the doctor!"

Miriam awoke from her vigil beside Frieda. Tess stirred in her cot.

I took Steffen's hand, his small warm fingers curling into mine, bringing me a surge of comfort.

Within minutes the nurse and doctor were there. Steffen drank a small cup of water and said he was hungry. "A positive sign," the doctor said. He put the stethoscope to his lungs. "As good as can be expected," he added. "He'll need watching. And a few more days here, but I'm hopeful there are no internal injuries."

I kissed Steffen's hand. Reached out for Tess with my other and held them both to my heart. *Thank you, thank you, thank you.* My children were both with me, both alive. And nothing else mattered.

An hour later, Steffen was once again asleep when Wilhelm Otto and Fritz appeared.

Wilhelm carried a wooden crate in his arms and hesitated at the door. Fritz went directly to Steffen and knelt beside his bed. "Is he . . . ?" he asked me with a hitch in his voice, staring at Steffen's still face. I told Fritz what the doctor said. "It will take time, but he's going to be well."

Fritz sagged in relief, pressing his face to the bed beside Steffen. A sob jerked through his body. I reached for his hand and held it. I felt no anger for him. Just a heavy sadness that he had gone so far astray. I needed time, too—to forgive what had been done. I looked around the room. Miriam. Mutti and Fritz. Our families. Our friendships. All had been damaged by hate and prejudice. But now, I hoped, we could begin to heal.

Wilhelm hovered outside the circle of family. He swallowed hard as if something had been lodged in his throat. The crate shifted in Wilhelm's arms and emitted a soft mew.

Steffen's eyes fluttered. Tess sat up straight and pinned her gaze on the crate.

"What on earth?" Mutti exclaimed.

The mew came again. Steffen's eyes popped open. "Chester?" he whispered, hope in his voice.

Wilhelm came close to the bed and tilted the crate so both children could see inside.

Chester. On a folded blanket and looking quite put out. Two tiny kittens with tightly closed eyes sleeping in the curl of her body.

Fritz spoke. "We found her under the rhododendron in the back."

"How did she . . . ?" The fire had been so intense. She couldn't have survived it.

Wilhelm ran his finger over her ears. "I figure maybe she got out the window before the fire," he said. "Sometimes animals have a sixth sense."

Chester lifted her head to peer out of the crate, saw Steffen, and gave a loud chirrup. Steffen's face lit up. Frieda and Tess giggled.

Wilhelm smiled.

The militant nurse returned. "There are altogether too many people—" She caught sight of the crate and Chester. Her eyes went wide. "Of all the—" She pointed to the door with a fierce look. "Out. All of you. Until morning. And the cat. Let these poor children rest."

We left the hospital to find the stars twinkling in a clear night sky, the haze of the day swept away by a fresh wind from the Pacific. Fritz's rattletrap truck was parked next to Wilhelm's shiny Cadillac and an old but well-cared-for Model T.

Yitzak's father opened the door of the Model T for Miriam. He would take her to his home in Boyle Heights, where Yitzak waited. Miriam gave me a tired smile. We had much to talk about. The baby. Where they would live. Leon Lewis and Wilhelm Otto. Our friendship would need nurturing and honesty to heal. She put her arms around me. I hugged her back and it felt natural and right to do so.

The Model T rumbled into the night. I turned to Wilhelm and let out a long breath and said what I'd been thinking since the nurse ejected us from the hospital room. "We can't go home, can we?"

He shook his head.

The children would be safe under the eagle eye of the hospital staff, and the Stahrs had nothing to fear in Boyle Heights. But the Friends of

New Germany knew where I lived. Hermann and Thekla were out there somewhere. And they were still dangerous.

Wilhelm put the crate with Chester and the kittens in the back of Fritz's truck. "You know where to go," he said to Fritz. "Tell Jimmy I sent you. He's got a room ready."

Mutti started to bluster, but Fritz bundled her into the truck. "I'll explain on the way, Mutti."

Then it was just Wilhelm and me in the Cadillac. His face was drawn, his movements jerky as he started the auto and drove toward downtown. He looked like he needed to sleep for three days.

"Thank you," I said. "For Chester."

I had more to thank him for. Saving Steffen, what he'd done for Fritz. I had an idea of what had happened at the synagogue and that he had fixed things somehow with Gary Perl and Louis B. Mayer so I wasn't spending the night in jail.

"They're good kids," he answered, not looking at me as he turned onto Broadway. "I'm glad—" He stopped and cleared his throat. "I'm glad they're going to be okay."

Silence again.

I had questions. Where was Leon Lewis? Did he get the Dictaphone recording? When would it be safe to go back to our home? What had happened to Stella? Those could wait for tomorrow.

One question could not wait. This man was not who he had been pretending to be. He said he wasn't a family man—he told me that from the start. But he was lying—to me or to himself. Everything I learned about him, about the real Wilhelm Otto, did not fit with the story Mutti had told me about the girl from Paramount. I didn't know how to ask him, so I just came out with it. "Tell me about Eva Taylor and her baby."

His hand tightened on the steering wheel and his shoulders lowered. "Sounds like you already know the gist of it." He stared through the window.

"Tell me what really happened."

He glanced over, surprised. Let out a long breath. He rubbed a hand over his face. "There isn't much to it. I was a driver for Paramount. Eva was coming up as a star—but she was a handful."

A handful. I'd known plenty of women like that at MGM. Young starlets who thought the world was their oyster.

"Got herself in trouble."

He didn't have to spell it out. The question was, with whom?

He looked over, saw the question on my face. "No, it wasn't mine. The father, he was married." He watched to see if I believed him. "He wanted her to get rid of the baby. Paramount put the pressure on, like they do."

I knew what that meant, too. The studios were notorious for pushing contracted actresses to have abortions. They didn't like their investments to be tied up for nine months.

"I convinced her to have the baby. She wanted to get married, but I knew it wouldn't work."

"Because you're not a family man?" I asked him, even though everything I'd seen said he would be a good father.

"That's right," he said, his voice a little harsh. "And because a kid deserves parents who love each other." He slowed down for the turn onto Olive Street, the steering wheel slipping awkwardly under the grip of his bandaged hand. "Eva put it around that the baby—Josie, that's her name—was mine. By then I was out of town, working for the Pinkertons. I didn't care what she said as long as she took good care of the kid. I made sure she did."

That story sounded like the man I knew. "So do you really think you're not a family man?"

He looked over at me with an expression that bordered on angry. But I wasn't afraid of Wilhelm Otto any longer. I knew what kept this man at a distance, what closed his heart from any kind of love. It was fear.

How do you do it? he'd asked me at Tess's bedside. *Live with the fear that they might die?* Wilhelm Otto was afraid to lose someone he loved, like he had his little sister and mother. I could understand it more than he knew. To love meant to take a great risk. A great and terrible risk.

But it was worth it.

Of course I could not tell him that. Wilhelm would have to figure that out himself.

He pulled up in front of the Biltmore. The lights spilled from the sparkling windows and glowed over the palmettos and orange trees. He didn't get out of the car but pulled a crumpled packet from his pocket and tapped out the last cigarette. He put it between his lips and fumbled with his useless left hand to open the lighter.

I plucked the lighter from his hand, flicked it on, and held it for him as he leaned forward with his cigarette. He took a puff and leaned back in his seat. "What are you going to tell the kids? About your husband?" he asked abruptly. "Tess needs to know."

His question to me was just as difficult as mine had been to him. He'd been honest and deserved the same in return. I thought of my little girl, who loved her father and struggled in her own way. The temper and willfulness. "I'll tell her the truth. That her father was a good man and he died. That he loved her."

He looked at me in that sidelong way. "I think maybe she knows that already."

Wilhelm knew more about kids than he liked to pretend. I looked at the man I'd thought menacing and dangerous. "You know, you really would make a good family man."

The silence stretched long. Then he finally met my gaze, his eyes no longer hard as flint but softer, considering. "Maybe I would," he answered. "Maybe I'll give it a shot someday."

CHAPTER 62

Two days after *der Angriff*, the telephone rang.

"Who is calling at this hour?" Mutti shouted from the bedroom of our suite at the Biltmore.

I sat up on the divan, still disconcerted at waking in a hotel room. I looked at the clock on the wall. Five twenty-seven. The shrill ring came again.

I reached for the receiver before Mutti's complaints woke the whole floor. "Hello?"

"I'm sorry to wake you, Edelweiss," Leon Lewis apologized and asked me to meet him.

I dressed quickly in a short-sleeved blouse and button-up skirt, washed my face, and ran a comb over my hair. Ten minutes later, I walked through the Biltmore's deserted lobby. I crossed Olive Street, not an auto in sight this early, and followed the brick-paved path into the green shade of Pershing Square.

The wind was October cool and raised a shiver on my arms. I followed the path lined with banana trees and benches to where Lewis waited in a shady arbor just before the central plaza. Wilhelm stood nearby, his back to a thick clump of bamboo, Lady obediently at his feet. He wore trousers and a button-up work jacket instead of his dark suit, his chestnut hair mussed by the breeze. The only sound was the trickle of the central fountain and the song of larks in the shrubs.

Lewis got to his feet and removed his hat. "Edelweiss, I believe I owe you a great debt."

I opened my mouth to disagree. I had failed him. Yes, we had stopped *der Angriff*, but the Schwinns were at large. The Friends of New Germany, the Silver Shirts, and the Klan were all still a threat to Los Angeles. His spy operation was in shambles. Leon Lewis owed me no thanks.

He raised a hand to halt my protest. "I've come with a request." He motioned to the bench.

I glanced at Wilhelm, but his face was unreadable. I sat down with a sense of unease. My children were in the hospital. I was without a home for fear of Hermann and Thekla Schwinn's reprisals. I looked at Lewis's kind face and had an unwelcome premonition.

In Leon Lewis fashion, he approached the matter in a roundabout way. "I have decided not to give the Dictaphone recording to the authorities."

"What—why?" After what I'd done to obtain it? "What about Winterhalder?" I wanted that man in jail, where I would never see him again.

An elderly woman dressed in flowing trousers and a bulky sweater appeared on the path, a paper bag in her hand. She passed by us and settled on the bench beside the fountain, where she was immediately surrounded by squawking birds.

"It's not enough," Lewis went on quietly. "The best we could do would be a charge of conspiracy. And that is if the evidence is not conveniently lost and if the judge is not bribed. Many of those in the justice system have sympathies."

Sympathies to the Klan and the Nazis, he meant. My heart sank. Had all I'd done been for nothing?

Lewis went on in a softer tone. "In addition, a trial would put you in a difficult situation."

"She's already in a difficult situation," Wilhelm countered.

Lewis meant I would have to testify. His operation would be public knowledge and we would all be in danger. I rubbed my hands over my chilled arms, wrapped them around my body for warmth.

Wilhelm shrugged off his jacket and put it around my shoulders. The bandage was still on his left hand and his movements hinted that the gunshot wound to his shoulder was giving him pain.

"You mean the Schwinns, of course." Lewis shifted on the bench, looking toward the fountain. Seagulls and pigeons screeched and cooed, hopping on the woman's shoulders and vying for the seeds. Satisfied that we were not being overheard, he continued. "I received word from colleagues in Chicago that the Schwinns arrived by train yesterday and continued on to New York. The American consulate will be waiting for them. It seems their passports are not in order." He looked pleased with himself.

"Gyssling's tip-off?" Wilhelm asked.

Lewis nodded. "If we are fortunate, the Schwinns will be sent back to Berlin."

"So it is safe for us to go home?" I asked, my hope rising. Even with Wilhelm paying the bill at the Biltmore—which felt wrong—I wished to be in my own home. Living with Mutti in a hotel room was no picnic, no matter the luxury. Fritz had given up and moved across the hall to Wilhelm's room after the first night.

Lewis considered. "Gary Perl and Louis Mayer know of your work for me, but I trust they will keep it to themselves. The Schwinns no doubt suspect you but are across the country and not a current threat."

"What about the secretary?" I asked. She was the MGM spy and saw me try to stop Thekla. I didn't even know her name.

Lewis glanced at Wilhelm and I realized they knew something I didn't.

"I tracked her down," Wilhelm said. "Turns out she was one of Winterhalder's floozies." He gave me an apologetic look. "I gave her some things to think about. Like jail. She decided on a long visit to her mother in Florida."

I felt a little bit sorry for the woman, even after what she'd done. I hoped she'd take the second chance she'd been given.

"As far as anyone else knows," Lewis finished, "you are in good standing with the Friends of New Germany, perhaps even a hero if we play our cards right."

Lewis was right in what he said. Word had gotten out that I'd shot Gary Perl, but it might be assumed by those with allegiance to the Nazis that I was a hero—a part of Hermann and Thekla's plan. I knew what Leon Lewis was going to ask me next. Something I did not wish to consider.

"Edelweiss," he said, looking at me with that earnest way of his, "we need a body of evidence. Enough to bring them all to trial for treason and sedition. And for that, I need your help."

I had been right. He wished me to continue as a spy. And my answer was no. Absolutely no. But something, perhaps Leon Lewis's earnest gaze or Wilhelm's eyes on me, kept me silent.

Lewis stood. "Go home. Take some time to decide." He took a step down the path, then turned back. "But remember this, Edelweiss. The threat of Adolf Hitler is not going away. In fact, I believe we will see the influence of the Nazis grow in our country and in the world. With the right strategy and good operatives, we can stop them from gaining ground in our own small corner." He tipped his hat in goodbye. "I'll be in touch."

Wilhelm sat down beside me. Lady put her muzzle on my knee. The only sound was the occasional grumble of an automobile on Olive Street and the complaints of the birds fighting over the last of the scattered seed.

"What do you think I should do?" I asked Wilhelm. He knew the danger involved in working for Lewis and he knew my situation.

Wilhelm frowned at the path where Leon Lewis had disappeared.

Dappled sunshine found its way through the fronds and leaves. Light and dark in a constantly shifting pattern. Finally he spoke. "Liesl, you've done plenty. You have to think about the kids. Nobody would blame you if you wanted out. Not Lewis—" he met my eyes—"and not me."

He hadn't answered my question. "You're going to stay on with Lewis, then?" Of course he would. He'd keep at it, saving those boys from their own mistakes like he had with Fritz.

He lifted his wide shoulders. "I have less to lose."

"Do you?" I wasn't sure I believed that. I thought maybe this man wasn't the loner he pretended to be.

But he was right. I had a family. One that depended on me. Was it right for me to put them and myself at risk? "You think I should say no to Lewis, then?"

Again, he paused for a long moment as if gathering the right words. "I'm not telling you one way or the other. Can't." He sighed. "It's your call. But either way—" He stopped abruptly and looked away.

"Either way what?" I asked, my heart suddenly tripping.

A flicker of sunlight caught the slate gray of his eyes and turned them to silver. "Either way, I'll still be around."

My cheeks warmed. Wilhelm took a sudden interest in Lady, who was happy to have her ears scratched. I looked down at my shoes and told myself not to be ridiculous. But it was good to know he would be there if I needed him.

He made to stand, but I stopped him with a hand on his arm. "Wilhelm?" I had one more question. "Do you think he's right about the Nazis?" I asked quietly just in case anyone was listening. "About Adolf Hitler? Do you think this is just the beginning?"

Wilhelm's expression was serious; his voice held a regretful certainty. "Leon Lewis calls it like he sees it . . . and I've never known the man to be wrong."

CHAPTER 63

WILHELM

Wilhelm sat in the Cadillac outside the bungalow in Santa Monica. This time he was going in. He'd called ahead and so he couldn't back out. It was a nice day for it, sunny and cool. Nice with the windows down and the breeze coming in. Then why were his palms sweating and his hatband damp?

He tapped his left hand on the steering wheel and told himself to get out of the car. The burn itched like the dickens. His wound from Travis Monroe's bullet was sore but healing up good. Small price to pay for getting those kids out of the Silver Shirts.

With Fritz's help, he'd met up with Lenny and the boys at a little hole-in-the-wall restaurant he knew in Long Beach. He filled them up on spaghetti and meatballs and told them the truth about the Silver Shirts. By the end of the evening, they were quitting the Nazis. He made them promise to keep in touch—gave out his telephone number and told them to call anytime. He hoped they would.

The good news was that blockhead, Monroe, wouldn't be showing his ugly mug in Los Angeles again. After Brody took him in, he did some checking and found out Travis Monroe was wanted in his home state on a pile of charges, including counterfeiting and assaulting a federal officer. A US marshal showed up to escort him to Mississippi, where he'd sweat out a decade in a jail cell. Sometimes people got what they deserved.

Wilhelm got out of the auto and crossed the street to a little house with a nice-size yard surrounded by brown picket fencing. Smoke came out of the chimney and disappeared in the sea breeze. He let himself in the gate and went up the concrete sidewalk to the front door. His heart was doing dumb things in his chest.

What did he have to be nervous about? She was just a kid. She didn't bite.

He tried to bend his mouth up into a smile, the kind he'd give to Steffen or Tess. He'd spent some time with them and he'd gotten used to kids a little. That's when he figured he could do the same with Josie. He knocked on the door.

The door opened as if someone had been waiting. Eva's mother was a short, stout woman with a no-nonsense way about her. She was pushing fifty, he'd guess, but energetic as a ten-year-old. "Wilhelm," she said with a smile. She pronounced it in the American way, which he appreciated. "Come in."

Eva was waiting in a flowery sitting room, Josie beside her. The little girl was a pretty thing. She would be—Eva was easy on the eyes. She had something of her grandma in her too, he saw it right off. After they did the introductions, it wasn't hard at all. Nothing like he'd feared. They ate some cookies and Josie showed him her room. "I'm five now," she told him, jumping on her bed and bouncing up and down. He figured she wasn't supposed to do that but he didn't say so.

They played a game of Sorry!, which Eva won, and it was time for him to go. "I have something for Josie," he said to Mrs. Taylor. "What we talked about."

She looked at him with concern. "Are you sure?"

He was. He went to the Cadillac, where Lady slept, curled up in the back seat. "Come on, girl." From the trunk he took her leash and collar, a bowl and some dog food he'd picked up at the grocery.

It was love at first sight for Josie. "Can I really keep her?" she asked her mother, her arms already wrapped around the dog's neck and Lady licking her face like a long-lost friend.

Eva looked at Wilhelm. "You'll miss her."

He shrugged, his throat strangely tight until he swallowed down whatever it was blocking his voice. "I'll be back to check on her." He crouched down to run a hand over Lady's ears. "How about next Saturday? We'll take her out for a run in the park."

Josie agreed with a gap-toothed smile that grabbed him and didn't let go. Mrs. Taylor took him aside and thanked him sincerely for the monthly check, which made him embarrassed. "It's not all that much." He shrugged and looked away.

"It makes a big difference," she insisted. "And you didn't have to do it." She knew Josie wasn't his kid, but that didn't matter.

Eva walked him to his auto and wasn't in any hurry to say goodbye. She leaned on the hood, looking good in a skirt and blouse with flat shoes.

"She's a good kid," he said. "You're a good mother."

She met his gaze. "You'd be a good father."

He looked away. Second time in a week he'd heard that, so maybe it was true. He could see himself falling in love with the kid—heck, he was already there. But not with Eva.

Eva took his silence as an answer. "There's never going to be an us, is there?"

He put his hands in his pockets. Uncomfortable but the thing needed to be said. "Not like you mean," he said. "But there could be something. Friends. Check in on Josie and watch out for her." He could teach her to ride a bike. And when she was older, how to drive and maybe to shoot. Girls should know things like that.

"That would be nice." Eva gave him a sad smile.

Would it be nice? He hoped so.

There might be times when she'd be hurt. Or get sick, like Lily.

He looked at the little girl, chasing the dog around the yard and laughing. Thought about Liesl and how she loved her kids. The courage she had. Could he do that? Was it worth the heartache that he was letting himself in for?

He figured yes, it was worth the risk.

LIESL

"Why did Daddy have to die?" Tess asked in a small voice.

We stood together at the grave. Steffen and Tess in their best clothes. Mutti with a spray of canary-yellow lilies. Fritz with his hands in his pockets. I'd spent the two weeks after *der Angriff* with my children, gathering the courage to tell them of their father. To tell Mutti and Fritz and to go to the Hall of Records and do what was needed.

Rosedale Cemetery was a green oasis off Washington Boulevard. Close-clipped grass and marble statuary guarded by rhododendrons and cedar, with the scent of eucalyptus and pine on the breeze. A good place to rest beside his grandmother and his parents. Just a headstone since there were no remains of my husband to bury. A solid marker carved with the words *Tomas Weiss, faithful husband and father.*

"I don't know, sweetheart," I answered honestly. "But he loved you. He loved all of us." Our lives had been a mixture of struggles and joy but Tomas had loved me through the quarrels and our differences. I knew that now. I had not been abandoned. Not by Tomas and not by God.

Leon Lewis asked that first day in his office if I was a woman of faith. I had not been able to answer, my doubts crowding out what I knew of God's love. But now I could answer with certainty. Yes, I was a woman of faith. Faith in God. And faith in people. Even those not like myself. Leon Lewis and Stella and Miriam. Wilhelm Otto.

Tomas had been taken from me, and that was a great evil. But had God used that evil for good, like I had told Tess he could? Had he brought me to Leon Lewis for a purpose—to oppose the growing hatred coming from Adolf Hitler? To do something only I could do? These were questions with no answers. At least none I would know in this life.

"Your daddy was a good man," Mutti said to Tess and Steffen. "A hero like your grandpa. Don't ever forget that."

I reached into my pocket and took out a piece of Juicy Fruit gum, the scent bringing Tomas back to me in a flash of longing. I set it on the curve of the cool stone. "Goodbye, my love." I turned to the children. Tess, her eyes glassy with tears and struggling not to cry. Steffen, solemn and silent. Mutti and Fritz somber. We all mourned Tomas, all loved him, and the closure of today's ceremony was both an agony and a relief. I walked out of the cemetery, a child on each side. My doubts put to rest.

"At least he left you with a pension," Mutti said gruffly. "You don't have to work now that Fritz is helping out like he should."

Fritz stuck his hands in his trouser pockets and kicked a stone on the sidewalk. Mutti had been hard on him the past two weeks, but he didn't make excuses. He'd explained away the incident at the MGM studio to Captain Hynes and somehow come out the hero, with a promotion to officer and a raise. With that and the small widow's pension, we could cover our expenses. I could stay at home with the children. Take care of my family, keep to my own problems, and let others worry about the evil in the world.

I had done enough, was that not so?

Steffen dropped my hand and ran ahead on the sidewalk, spotting a brown lizard sunning himself on the warm concrete. He crouched down to observe it and my heart filled with gratitude for my sweet boy. He tired easily, and the doctor said we'd have to be careful when the winter colds came, but he was going to be well.

Stella telephoned every day. After she rushed Gary Perl to the hospital, she went back to MGM to find Cecil and tell Battle-Axe Adler she quit. "I got it in before she fired me," Stella crowed with triumph. She stopped by the hospital with an armful of balloons and stuffed toys for Tess and Steffen. Five days later, she went to Las Vegas with Cecil and they got married. "It's the newest thing." She told me the good news over the telephone. "They have a twenty-four-hour license bureau right there in the train depot." Her parents had a conniption until they found out Cecil was Jewish. "Now they're starting in about grandchildren," she complained. "I'll let them dream their dreams."

Fritz bent to watch the lizard with Steffen, then hefted him on his shoulders for a piggyback ride that had them both laughing and Tess running after, begging for her turn. The wind picked up, brushing the grass and rustling the fallen leaves along the sidewalk. We turned down Vermont and reached the outer streets of Germantown. A tidy part of the city. Calla lilies in the flower beds, tuberoses in the window boxes. Clean clothes billowed on backyard clotheslines. Orderly and neat, but was it really as wholesome as I had once believed?

We passed Grundbacher's, Johan polishing the display window. A sign on the door read *No Jews*. I turned my head so as not to see his friendly wave in my direction. Scholz's Soda Shop was bright and cheerful, but I knew that just inside the door was a sign reading *Whites Only*. Ming's Laundry was shut up tight with a *For Lease* sign in the window.

As we neared our house, the sound of hammers rang out, and workmen's voices floated on the wind. Karl Weber had started rebuilding the house next door. It would be bigger, with the luxury of two full bathrooms, but Miriam and Yitzak would not be returning to Germantown.

A week ago, I took the trolley to Boyle Heights with Tess and spent an afternoon with Miriam and Frieda. My friend had been welcoming, and we talked of many things. Tomas and Leon Lewis. Yitzak and what had happened at the synagogue. "I don't feel safe in Germantown." She put a hand protectively on her burgeoning waist. "I want my children to be safe."

I didn't blame her, but oh, how I would miss her. As Tess would miss Frieda.

I asked her what I should do about Leon Lewis. She looked at the girls, playing together. "I can't tell you what to do, Liesl," she answered carefully. "But I can tell you it's getting worse. The way people look at us, how we aren't allowed in some of the stores. Most landlords outside Boyle Heights won't even rent to us." Her eyes flashed with an anger I shared. "And what they say is happening in Germany, Liesl. What if it happens here?" She was angry—but she was also frightened.

Perhaps that was when I made my decision.

Adolf Hitler and his religion of anti-Semitism was not a Jewish problem. It was my problem. And if good people did nothing, the evil around us would continue to grow and flourish.

Yes, I must take care of my family. That was my duty. But taking care did not only mean putting food on the table and a roof over our heads; it meant standing up for what was right. As Vati and Tomas had done. It meant going to war against the hate and prejudice behind the tidy houses and neatly kept yards of Germantown.

My responsibility was not only to those I considered my friends— Miriam and Stella and Leon Lewis. It was to the Mrs. Adlers and Gary Perls who were not my friends. And to strangers, like the mother and her hungry children at the train station.

No, I could not stay silent.

"Fritz," Mutti barked as we reached the walkway to our home. "Get over there and help Karl, for pity's sake."

"Yes, Mutti," Fritz said. He had pitched in from the start, clearing the burned debris and helping rebuild, refusing any payment. His penance, he called it. He was not the brother I remembered. He was a man, one with regrets, who was trying to do better. And I loved him all the more for it.

Tess and Steffen ran up the walk and into the house, calling for Chester and the kittens. "Change out of your good clothes, children. It's time for chores." As I stood outside my home for a moment, Leon Lewis's words echoed in the strike of hammer on wood, in the whisper of the wind. *If not me, who? If not now, when?*

I'd done plenty, as Wilhelm said. But not enough.

CHAPTER 64

LIESL

Wilhelm Otto knocked on the door at precisely seven o'clock.

I considered my reflection in the chifforobe mirror. Golden hair smoothed into waves, rose-tinted lips, blue eyes with just a touch of mascara. The dress I'd chosen for the evening was a square-necked blue chiffon with a belted waist and a hemline that fell just below my knees. Pretty but not showy. The perfect Aryan woman.

For the final touch, I fixed the swastika lapel pin just over my heart. I glanced at my wedding photo, now in its proper place beside my bed. It no longer brought me sadness but comfort. Tomas would be proud of me, as I was proud of him.

I descended the stairs as Mutti opened the door. Wilhelm stood on the other side with a bouquet of daisies and without his caterpillar mustache.

"It's about time you shaved that monstrosity off," Mutti said as a greeting.

"Mrs. Bittner, these are for you." He gave the flowers to Mutti. "Thought you'd like them."

Mutti's cheeks went pink. "What a bunch of poppycock," she said with a snort, "buying flowers when they grow right outside the door."

I descended the last step as Mutti harrumphed off to the kitchen for a pitcher of water. "She likes you," I said to Wilhelm.

His gaze swept from my hair to my suede ankle straps. I'd learned to read his subtle expressions. The glance away that said he was pleased. The flicker of his lips that passed for a smile. This expression looked like admiration and I felt my cheeks warm.

"Mr. Otto!" Tess came thundering in from the back door. "Come see the kittens."

She pulled Wilhelm by the hand to the back porch, where Chester purred proudly in her crate with her roly-poly offspring. Wilhelm crouched down to scratch Chester between her ears. "What did you name these little monsters?"

"This one is Tweedledee—" Tess touched one fuzzy head—"and this one is Tweedledum," she said. Her face screwed up in confusion. "Or maybe the other way around."

Wilhelm laughed, a sound I'd heard on occasion but still surprised me.

"They're getting fat," Steffen added. "Chester is a good mommy."

"She is." Wilhelm glanced up to meet my gaze. The absence of the hideous mustache made it difficult for me to stop looking at him. The scar, although more apparent, was no longer menacing. In fact, his smile made my stomach do a little somersault.

He stood. "You ready for this?"

I was ready.

Wilhelm shook Steffen's hand.

"Goodbye, Mr. Otto," Tess called, a kitten tucked under her chin.

I kissed Steffen and Tess goodbye. Steffen's hug lingered but with affection instead of desperation. "No fuss about the dishes, Tess," I said with a meaningful look at Mutti, who ignored me.

The October evening was cool and the breeze held a hint of burning leaves. The first twinkle of stars showed in the periwinkle sky. Wilhelm opened the door of the Cadillac and helped me inside. I couldn't help but glance again at his upper lip. "You look good without it," I said as he slid into the driver's seat.

"I can grow it back if I need it again." He started the auto and drove slowly past the new construction of what I would always consider the Stahrs' house. He raised a hand to Karl and Fritz, who were putting in the front door.

"Are you the one who talked to Fritz about the hospital bill?" I asked. Fritz had sold the old Ford and used the money to pay our hospital costs and Frieda's. It meant a lot to me and to Yitzak.

Wilhelm shrugged. "Might have brought it up."

We drove in silence along the familiar streets. Now the silence was not one of unease but of determination with an undercurrent of anticipation. We passed the Alt Heidelberg. Below the sign for the Aryan Bookstore was a hand-lettered notice: *Opening Soon Under New Management.*

"Do you think they suspect us?"

A brief flash of concern tightened the corners of his eyes. He knew who I meant. The Friends of New Germany and the Silver Shirts, the Klan. But he shook his head. "Fritz did good with that."

Fritz was turning out to be a good operative. He'd circulated the rumor that what he and I did at the MGM studios was part of Hermann and Thekla's plan all along. When Gary Perl declined to press charges, Assistant District Attorney Ted Torgeson announced there was not enough evidence to prosecute, and my name was cleared. In the clandestine gatherings of the Silver Shirts and Ku Klux Klan, Fritz and I were hailed as heroes for the cause. Some even whispered that Liesl Weiss and Fritz Bittner had well-placed friends in the fatherland.

Wilhelm was less secure. Yes, he was arrested in front of a hundred Jewish mourners for a failed attempt to attack the Wilshire Boulevard Temple, but there were questions about what really happened. Tonight's plan would fortify his position.

"What's the word from Stella?" Wilhelm asked, turning off Alverado and leaving the Alt Heidelberg behind.

"They've stopped production on *The Mad Dog of Europe*," I said. Stella kept up on the gossip through Cecil and reported it to me. Herman Mankiewicz's warning of what was to come from Adolf Hitler was consigned to the trash bin at MGM. "Perl said it wasn't worth the risk."

Wilhelm patted his pockets for his pack of cigarettes. "A gunshot wound can do a number on a person's convictions."

It hadn't done so for Wilhelm, but I didn't mention that. When he didn't find his cigarettes, he settled for tapping his fingers on the steering wheel. He was more nervous about tonight than he let on.

At the corner of Hoover and Washington, a man in a tattered overcoat warmed his hands over a fire barrel. Wilhelm stopped at the curb. The bum opened the back door and slid into the seat behind me. Wilhelm pulled back out on the street.

"Edelweiss," the man said. "Thirteen. Thank you for meeting with me."

"Evening, boss," Wilhelm said.

I turned in my seat to face Leon Lewis.

He wasted no time. "You know what to do tonight." He leaned forward. "Test the waters. Find out who is rising to the top and who knows what about the Schwinns. Make sure they trust you."

I glanced at Wilhelm. Just as we'd already planned.

Lewis leveled his gaze at me. "Edelweiss, there's something else."

My attention sharpened. I knew that tone of voice.

"There's a new Nazi in town," Lewis said. "His name is Franz Ferenz."

I waited for more. There was always more with him.

"He's Austrian and from all accounts has close contacts within *der Führer's* inner circle. Not a man to trifle with, but we need to get closer to him."

"Any ideas on how to do that?" Wilhelm glanced at Lewis in the rearview mirror.

The spymaster cleared his throat, his serious gaze not wavering from my own. "I hear he's in need of a secretary."

Three blocks later, Wilhelm pulled the Cadillac over and left Leon Lewis on the curb.

We parked in front of the Lorelei Inn, a half-timbered chalet on

Washington Boulevard. Crimson geraniums spilled from window boxes under sparkling leaded windows. As Wilhelm opened the fortresslike door and ushered me inside, his hand brushed mine in a brief touch of encouragement. I straightened my spine and lifted my chin, reminding myself I was a good German—and a good American. I would do my duty as both.

An elegant man in a linden-green jacket appeared immediately. "Mr. Otto," he said in a Berlin accent, "your table is ready."

Of course it was. Wilhelm had planned every detail of this evening.

A blonde-braided waitress with pink cheeks and a smitten glance at Wilhelm guided us through the dimly lit dining room, heavy with dark wood and russet leather. Mounted stag heads and a toothy wild boar watched us with glassy eyes.

"Liesl, and my goodness, Wilhelm Otto!" Gertrud Grundbacher's surprise made her voice ring through the muted dining room. She took in the sight of Wilhelm and me together.

"Gertrud." I inclined my head. "What a lovely surprise." It was no surprise. The Grundbachers dined at the Lorelei every Saturday night without fail, and the waitress had led us directly past their table.

Johan stood to shake Wilhelm's hand. "Please have a seat," Johan said, motioning to two empty chairs at the table set with rose-patterned china and pewter drinking cups.

I glanced at Wilhelm. "Just for a moment," I said. "We don't want to interrupt your dinner." Wilhelm pulled out a chair for me and settled in his own, close enough that his leg brushed against the skirt of my dress.

"I haven't seen you in an age, not since—" Gertrud lowered her voice and looked at me with admiration. "Liesl, you were so brave."

"A credit to our race," Johan added with an appreciative nod. He poured amber liquid into one of the pewter cups and offered it to Wilhelm.

I looked at my hands in a show of modesty and to hide any flicker of dislike. "I did what any good German would do, really."

"You must tell me simply everything," Gertrud said. "When we can speak privately."

Of course I would tell her everything. Everything I wanted her to believe.

"It's a shame about Hermann and Thekla." I probed the extent of the Grundbachers' knowledge. "Have you heard from them at all? I just thought, since you were good friends—"

"Oh," Gertrud complied readily, "Paul said they were in New York, although I haven't spoken to her personally. I'm sure she's quite busy."

Wilhelm nudged my leg under the table. I did not look at him.

"Paul Themlitz?" I asked, my gaze taking in both Gertrud and Johan. "How is he?"

Johan snorted. "He's in hot water. Max Socha—the alliance president, you know—figured out that Paul was skimming funds. Paul skipped town before they could arrest him for embezzlement." He looked to Wilhelm. "What a *Dummkopf, nicht so*? Of course he didn't have any money. He gave away books for free."

Wilhelm raised his glass in tacit agreement.

"Such a sweet man and so devoted to the cause," I said with regret. More good news for Leon Lewis. For the immediate future, the leaders of the Friends were otherwise engaged.

"But—" Gertrud looked like she had a secret she was bursting to share—"Johan got a letter from Hans Winterhalder just this afternoon, didn't you, dear?"

My relief vanished. I had hoped to never hear the name Hans Winterhalder again.

Wilhelm's leg began a nervous jiggling beneath the table.

Johan frowned. "He's lying low, but he'll be back when the whole business about the synagogue settles down. Keeping up the good fight, right, Otto?"

Wilhelm nodded and gave that cold look he did so well. "Let me know when you need me."

The pink-cheeked waitress reappeared with perfect timing. "Your table, sir?"

Wilhelm stood, but I had one more task to complete. "Oh, Gertrud," I said as an afterthought. "Do let me know if you hear of anyone looking for a secretary. I am in dire need of work." I looked down as if ashamed of my need for income. "I'm sure you understand."

Gertrud perked up. "I think I may have just the thing for you," she said with enthusiasm. "Franz Ferenz—such a wonderful man—he came to the grocery and said our wurst was the best he'd had since he left Salzburg."

I looked mildly interested.

Gertrud continued. "He's writing a book about *der Führer* and needs a typist. I'll be sure to give him your name when I see him again."

"I'd appreciate it, Gertrud." I tucked my hand into the crook of Wilhelm's arm and gave her my best smile. "I do so look forward to continuing the work I started with the Friends." Wilhelm and I followed the waitress to a table in the center of the room, one where we could see and be seen. The perfect German couple. A credit to the fatherland.

"Thanks, Greta, you did good," Wilhelm said as the waitress presented us with leather-bound menus. She gave him a little bow before she left us. The candlelight cast a warm glow over the table, lighting his gray eyes as they rested on me.

My pulse quickened under his silent observation but not from the fear I once felt. Wilhelm, I realized, could say more in silence than most men in an evening of conversation. What he was saying in this moment made my heart dip and my cheeks warm.

His gaze did not waver. "You know, you really should be in pictures. I almost believed you myself."

"It was only the truth," I answered. Wilhelm and I would indeed continue the work we'd started with the Friends. Leon Lewis's work. To stop the Grundbachers and Hans Winterhalders and all who believed as they did.

A war had begun and was already raging. Leon Lewis could not fight it alone. He needed me and he needed Wilhelm.

If not us, who? If not now, when?

It must be us. And it must be now.

I would fight this war.

I would not be silent.

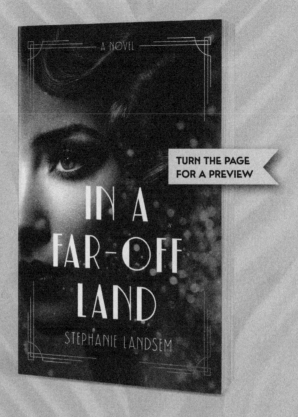

A NOVEL

IN A FAR-OFF LAND

STEPHANIE LANDSEM

TURN THE PAGE
FOR A PREVIEW

Step back in time to 1930s Hollywood in
a story about the price of fame, the truth
sacrificed on its altar, and the love that
brings a prodigal daughter home.

CHAPTER 1

Los Angeles, California
1931
MINA

Roy Lester's mansion was as ritzy a place as I'd ever seen. I had to pinch myself to make sure I was really there—me, Minerva Sinclaire—at one of the most glamorous parties in Hollywood. This was the moment I'd been waiting for. The part of the story right before the happy ending.

At least that's what I thought at the time.

When the towering mahogany doors swung open, it was like stepping into *The Hollywood Revue*. The high-ceilinged great room sparkled, lit by a chandelier as bright as any studio set. Women in jewel-toned silk took their places with men in midnight-blue evening jackets, all in glorious Technicolor. In the center of the room, a grand piano provided the score, accompanied by the swell of conversation and the clink of ice against glasses. Toward the back of the room, a champagne cork popped, and a woman shrieked a laugh. I half expected to see a cameraman on a moving platform or hear a director with a megaphone call, "Cut!"

Max joined me at the top of three marble steps that led down into the room filled with music and color. "Mark my words, Mina. This is a mistake."

"Don't start."

Max had been grousing since he picked me up at my boardinghouse an hour ago. "You're still my agent," I'd told him on the telephone, "and a girl can't show up at the door alone." With how things were between us, I couldn't tell him the truth that I needed him beside me. The thing that had happened between us over a month ago—what I called the New Year's Day Incident—had been a mistake and best forgotten. If only Max were more forgetful. But if Max wanted his 20 percent of the contract I was signing tomorrow, he'd help me out tonight.

Earlier, he'd helped me into his lemon-yellow LaSalle roadster like we were on our way to San Quentin instead of the gladdest party in Los Angeles. He drove into the hills like a madman—as if driving faster could get the party over with. He twitched a cigarette in one hand as we chased the half moon, headlights dancing ahead of us, the roadster spitting gravel behind. When we pulled through the gated entrance to Roy Lester's place, it was too unbelievable. Like one of those English estates had dropped out of the sky and onto the brown foothills of the Santa Monica mountains.

Max threw the stub of his smoke out the window and shifted to low gear on the smooth, winding driveway. He stopped sulking long enough to tell me about the place. "Twenty bedrooms, a theater that seats thirty, and a walk-in fur vault. There's a formal English rose garden and greenhouses, and behind there—" he motioned past an unnaturally perfect lake lit by an illuminated fountain—"is a maze you could get lost in for days."

We sped past sculpted box hedges, giant rabbits, and teapots casting moon shadows on a vast manicured lawn. Sodium lights blazed over two red-clay tennis courts.

"Your friend Roy has a cellar filled with real whisky and gin—the good stuff from Scotland and England. And champagne imported from

France. He's got a switch upstairs that locks it up tight if the Feds come calling." Max snorted. "As if the law would raid Roy Lester's little haven. They're paid off too well for that."

Max's glum take was starting to rub me the wrong way. "Since when is bankroll and booze a problem for you?" In the four months I'd known Max, he'd never taken offense at other people's cash—or turned down their liquor.

I watched his profile as he maneuvered the roadster around the circular driveway and came to a rolling stop. His scowl really did mar that handsome face. His hair was neatly combed back and his black fedora set at an angle. A dark lock curled over his forehead, giving him a touch of boyish charm, which he used plenty well. He had a jaw worthy of any leading man and a nose with a hint of a crook, as if he'd broken it years ago. His amber eyes, with lashes that would make Greta Garbo jealous, were guarded as he turned to me. "I don't like Roy Lester."

Max played his cards close, and usually I let him keep his secrets, but this time I pushed. "Then how do you know so much about him?" I waved a hand. "And about his place?"

"I just do." The roadster sputtered and went silent. "Be careful with these people, you got me?"

I got him, all right. What was good for the gander and all that applesauce. But my time was running out. I'd learned plenty in the ten months I'd been in Hollywood—to dance, to act, to pretend I fit in. I'd even learned to drink bootlegged whisky—not legally, of course, but nobody cared about that. And I'd learned to take my breaks where I found them—with or without Max's blessing.

Now, faced with a roomful of Hollywood's elite, I wasn't so nervy. My knees wobbled and my palms went damp. A Chinese butler in an embroidered silk robe and satin-tasseled hat greeted us with, "Good evening." I'd heard Oriental butlers were all the rage, but I'd never actually seen one.

I slipped off my fox wrap as if it were a full-length mink. Act like you belong, that's what everybody else is doing. I took a deep breath and passed the fur to Max. Acting had got me this far, and it would have to take me the rest of the way.

"I'm not the coat-check girl," Max muttered, but he took my fur just the same.

"Be careful—it's rented," I whispered.

Max took off his crisp fedora and leaned closer. "At least promise me you'll follow the rules."

That was rich, and I wasn't so nervous that I couldn't fire back at him. "Maybe you should try following them yourself, Max."

At least he had the grace to flush. He turned away, giving his fedora and my fox to the celestial butler, whose expression didn't flicker a jot.

With or without Max's help, this night was going my way. Granted, my plan since I left Odessa hadn't come off without a hitch. I'd stepped off the bus at Central Station as green and innocent as a South Dakota spring. Well, I wasn't green anymore, and I sure as sugar wasn't innocent. But I was at the end of my rope.

A NOTE FROM THE AUTHOR

"Where do you get your book ideas?"

It's a question I'm often asked, and the answer is different for every novel. Ideas come from many sources: my research, my own life experiences, and what's going on in the world.

Code Name Edelweiss came from all those places.

When I was doing my final research for my previous novel, *In a Far-Off Land*, I came upon an article about the rise of fascism in 1930s Los Angeles. Intrigued, I followed that white rabbit down the hole and found something interesting—the story of Leon Lewis and his spy network. That's when the idea for a new book was sparked.

Some of you may know how I love my German heritage. My father came from a strong German community in Pennsylvania. He was 100 percent German and 100 percent American. So American that he lied about his age and signed up to fight in WWII, although the war ended before he completed basic training. I was raised to respect the German ideals of duty to family and country. I studied the German language and traveled extensively in Germany and Austria as a teenager and in my twenties. I learned there about Hitler's rise to power, wept at the remains of the Dachau concentration camp, and walked on Unter Den Linden Strasse, where Hitler's troops marched to war. I asked myself, *How could good people allow such evil?* That question has always haunted me.

Then there was what was happening in our own time in the United States. The years between 2016 and 2020 were ones of increasing division in our country. Families split along political lines. Our partisan government bickered instead of leading. The media lost credibility. Starting in 2020, a global pandemic created fear, peaceful protests turned violent, and mob mentality destroyed cities. Every part of our society struggled with isolation, distrust, and division. I began to see more clearly what might have happened during the privations of the Great Depression, the tragedy of the Dust Bowl, and the heightened racial tensions of the 1930s.

How did good people allow the evil of the Nazis to flourish? Why did they follow—or at least not speak out against—Hitler and his party? I believe, as Leon Lewis said, it had to do with fear. We've seen an increase in that kind of fear in our own lives in the past few years. Fear has changed the landscape of our country and in some cases of our own families. I hope within the pages of *Code Name Edelweiss*, readers will be heartened to move past the fear with courage and love. Love for our families and friends—but more importantly for those who are different from us, those who disagree with us, even those who may be considered our enemies. For if not us, who? And if not now, when?

HISTORICAL NOTE

I'm often asked what is real and what is fiction in my novels. For *Code Name Edelweiss*, the answer might be surprising: the story is based largely on real events and real people.

Leon Lewis was a man we should all be thankful for. He really did have Christian agents of German heritage who infiltrated the German American organizations of Los Angeles to gather information about the Nazis and the takeover of the studio system. Through his efforts, the Nazi influence in Los Angeles was dramatically curtailed in the years leading up to World War II.

The actual work of Leon Lewis and his operatives covered over a decade and was primarily a legal battle that included a great deal of paperwork, documentation, meetings, and hearings—not the stuff fast-paced novels are made of! For that reason, I chose to write about the beginning of Lewis's crusade, when he did indeed have only a few operatives and was desperately attempting to get authorities to recognize the threat of a man named Adolf Hitler.

Leon Lewis had female operatives to whom he gave code names. Grace Comfort, Agent G2, and her daughter Sylvia, Agent S3, worked in much the same way that my fictional heroine does—pretending to be sympathetic to the Nazi cause and doing volunteer office work for the Friends of New Germany. His female agents attended social events and fascist women's groups, while secretly reporting their activities and smuggling documents to Lewis. The post office scene in which Liesl is arrested was inspired by the sham arrest Sylvia Comfort devised to solidify her position of trust within the Nazi organization.

Georg Gyssling was a real thorn in the side of the studio moguls during the 1930s. Hermann Schwinn was the leader of the Friends of New Germany and a member of the Nazi Party, although he didn't marry his wife, Thekla, until 1939. Other historical but fictionalized characters are Captain Hynes of the LAPD, Paul Themlitz, Hans Winterhalder, and Franz Ferenz. Oh, and also Hermann Schwinn's dog, Lump.

The Friends of New Germany, the Aryan Bookstore, and the other anti-Semitic organizations of Los Angeles were unfortunately quite real. Fascism grew at a phenomenal rate in the early 1930s all over the country, supported by Nazis overseas and homegrown organizations such as the KKK. There is plenty of evidence that these fascist organizations plotted many of the events that I've included in my novel. Schwinn and Winterhalder had connections to the San Diego armory and access to weapons. They had plans for attacks on the studios and a list of assassination targets that included studio heads and prominent Jewish actors. Thanks to Leon Lewis and his operatives, none of the violent events got beyond the planning stages.

Another truth-is-better-than-fiction part of *Code Name Edelweiss* is the script of *The Mad Dog of Europe* by Herman Mankiewicz. "Mank," as he was known in Hollywood, was a brilliant if difficult Jewish screenplay writer for MGM who—like Leon Lewis—saw the dangers of Adolf Hitler long before others. In 1933, he wrote *The Mad Dog of Europe*, a scathing attempt to wake up the American public to the dangers of what was happening in Europe. Unsurprisingly, he found no one willing to finance and produce the film. The film industry closed ranks on Mank, ensuring that even if he did get the film produced, no theaters would agree to show it. He eventually gave up the fight.

My aim in *Code Name Edelweiss* and in all my fiction is not to document a historical event but to write a compelling story about how a character reacts to this event, how it affects her life, and how she is changed by what she encounters. One of my favorite quotes about fiction is this: A story doesn't have to be true to tell the truth. This is what I hope you gain from Liesl and Wilhelm's story: the truth about courage, conviction, and love that both encompasses and transcends the historical record.

DISCUSSION QUESTIONS

1. Liesl believes her husband—who she thought was happy and loved her—has left her and their children. This makes her question everything in her life that she thought was true. Has anything like this happened to you, where an event shattered your trust in yourself and what you believed?

2. Liesl says early in the story, "If what was happening in Germany was true—and I wasn't certain it was—of course I felt terrible for those people. The Jews." Who are "those people" in your life? People you may have sympathy for but who are not "your" people and therefore not your problem? Has God ever called you to stand up for someone you think of as not your own, "other," or "them"? How did you respond?

3. Liesl wonders, "How could children as young as Hildy Grundbacher already be poisoned by hate? Her mother and father had taught it to her and been taught the same by their own parents." Are there biases or preconceptions you maybe have toward others because of the way you were raised? What are some ways parents can try to break the cycle of passing along inappropriate prejudices to their children?

4. Wilhelm observes that people are mostly concerned with their own problems and often don't see the injustices happening around them—or don't know what to do about them. How can we discern when God is calling us to step outside our own lives and address larger problems in the world with our specific gifts?

5. "All that is needed for evil to flourish is for good men to do nothing" is an oft-quoted statement. We frequently equate it with the evils of Hitler and the horrors of WWII, but it can also be applied to our everyday life. Where in our day-to-day do we see this played out? What part can we play in either letting evil flourish or standing against it?

6. Have you experienced a deep and meaningful friendship such as Liesl and Miriam had, someone with whom you can share your innermost fears and joys? Do your best friends tend to be like you or very different from you?

7. Liesl must answer Tess's question about the nature of evil and why God allows it. How would you answer a child's question of why God allows people to do bad things? Would your answer to an adult be different or the same?

8. In considering why God allows evil, Wilhelm decides that God does stop evil, "but not with fire and brimstone or smiting like Wilhelm would have done. No, he used people—good people like Leon Lewis, not-so-good people like himself. Gave them what they needed to work with and let them at it. Wilhelm would sure prefer the fire and brimstone, but maybe that's why God was God . . . and he wasn't." How does Wilhelm's conclusion reflect his own troubled childhood and experience of God? When have you wished God would do things your way instead of his? How do you manage to trust in God's plan instead of your own?

9. Liesl confides to Miriam that she is afraid she doesn't pray correctly, and her friend tells her there is no wrong way to pray. Do you agree? Why do we sometimes feel that our prayers might not be "correct"?

10. We often hear the admonition "Those who refuse to learn from history are doomed to repeat it." In 1933, the world had no idea of the extent of Hitler's brutality or the world war that was to come in which at least six million Jewish people were murdered, as well as the mentally and physically disabled, Catholics, and others who stood against the Nazis. What can we learn of human nature from this horrific war? Do you think this kind of war can happen again?

ACKNOWLEDGMENTS

I have many people to thank for their invaluable help in getting a book from an idea in my head to a copy in your hand. First and foremost, I thank the Holy Spirit for inspiration and guidance as I navigate the balance of my two greatest blessings, family and writing. I pray for continued guidance in both.

My next thanks, as always, is to my family: my husband, Bruce, and my adult children, who cheer me on, as well as my mom, sisters, and brother, and my dad, whom I miss every day. Thank you for showing me how a family loves, forgives, and prays for one another.

I'm grateful for the invaluable advice and support of my agent, Chris Park, and the amazing team at Tyndale House Publishers. Thank you, Karen Watson, Jan Stob, and Kathy Olson, for believing in this book and making it the best it could be. More thanks to the marketing staff and art department that gets my books into readers' hands. And to Jim Fellows, without whose technical expertise I would flounder in the world of websites and analytics. My thanks, also, to Becky Robinson of Weaving Influence for her marketing advice and the surprise blessing of a new friend.

My critique partners are the best! As always, thanks to Regina Jennings for walking through the process of this unwieldy story with me. I owe much to Ian Acheson for his advice and encouragement and LeAnne

Hardy for her helpful critique and continued prayers. And to Rebecca Kanner for her unique Jewish perspective and relevant suggestions.

Thanks to my friends, who are ever supportive and keep me from hermiting alone in my office for days on end: Sue and Joanie, Wendy, Becky, Molly D. and Molly L., Heather, Deb, Teresa, Michele, and of course Jeanne, who is a great supporter of my books and so many other authors.

I wish to thank Steven J. Ross, dean's professor of history and director of the Casden Institute for the Study of the Jewish Role in American Life. His brilliant book, *Hitler in Los Angeles: How Jews Foiled Nazi Plots Against Hollywood and America*, reads like a Clancy spy novel. It represents years of hard work and meticulous research. If you're intrigued by the history of fascism in Los Angeles, please buy and read Steven Ross's book.

Thanks also goes to California State University Northridge's digital collection, "In Our Own Backyard," and related archives. Although I was not able to visit personally during 2020, the primary documents relating to Nazi propaganda and Leon Lewis were available online and contributed immensely to my understanding of the very real threat posed by the Hitler cells in Southern California.

As always, thank you to my readers. I couldn't do this without your very real support and continued encouragement. Keep reading and keep sharing good books with your friends! And last, a special thanks to Joey, who warned me repeatedly that my search history on fascist organizations would get me on an FBI watch list. So far, I haven't gotten the knock on the door.

ABOUT THE AUTHOR

Stephanie Landsem writes historical fiction for women, about women. She's traveled the world in real life and traveled through time in her research and imagination. As she's learned about women of the past, she's come to realize that these long-ago women were very much like us. They loved, dreamed, and made mistakes. They struggled, failed, and triumphed. She writes to honor their lives and to bring today's women hope and encouragement.

Stephanie makes her home in Minnesota with her husband, two cats and a dog, and frequent visits from her four adult children. Along with reading, writing, and research, she dreams about her next travel adventure—whether it be in person or on the page.

TYNDALE HOUSE PUBLISHERS IS CRAZY4FICTION!

Fiction that entertains and inspires

Get to know us! Become a member of the Crazy4Fiction community. Whether you read our blog, like us on Facebook, follow us on Twitter, or receive our e-newsletter, you're sure to get the latest news on the best in Christian fiction. You might even win something along the way!

JOIN IN THE FUN TODAY.

 crazy4fiction.com

 Crazy4Fiction

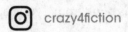 crazy4fiction

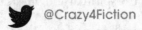 @Crazy4Fiction

CP0021

By purchasing this book from Tyndale, you have
helped us meet the spiritual and physical needs of
people all around the world.